THE PRESIDENT'S LAST L

Andrey Kurkov was born in St Petersburg and
now lives in Kiev. Having graduated from the
Kiev Foreign Language Institute, he worked for
some time as a journalist, did his military service
as a prison warder at Odessa, then became a film
cameraman, writer of screenplays and author of
critically acclaimed and popular novels including
Death and the Penguin.

ALSO BY ANDREY KURKOV

ANDREY KURKOV

The President's Last Love

VINTAGE BOOKS

London

Published by Vintage 2008

2 4 6 8 10 9 7 5 3 1

First published with the title *Posledniaïa Lioubov Prezidenta* in 2004
First published in Great Britain by Harvill Secker in 2007

Vintage
Random House, 20 Vauxhall Bridge Road,
London SW1V 2SA

www.vintage-books.co.uk

Addresses for companies within The Random House Group Limited
can be found at: www.randomhouse.co.uk/offices.htm

The Random House Group Limited Reg. No. 954009

A CIP catalogue record for this book
is available from the British Library

ISBN 9780099485049

The Random House Group Limited supports The Forest
Stewardship Council (FSC), the leading international forest
certification organisation. All our titles that are printed on
Greenpeace approved FSC certified paper carry the FSC logo.
Our paper procurement policy can be found at:
www.rbooks.co.uk/environment

Printed in the UK by CPI Bookmarque, Croydon, CR0 4TD

CHARACTERS IN THE STORY

Women in the life of Sergey Pavlovich Bunin

Zhanna	his first girlfriend
Nadya	an early girlfriend (from artificial limb workshop)
Svetka	his first wife
Mira	his second wife in a marriage of convenience
Larisa Vadimovna	Mira's mother
Vera (Verachka)	a colleague/girlfriend in the early '90s
Nila	his personal assistant
Svetlana	his third wife
Valya	Svetlana's twin sister who marries Sergey Pavlovich's twin brother Dima
Zhanna	a prostitute who becomes Svetlana's friend
Liza	Dima and Valya's daughter
Mila	an interpreter for Swiss police in Zurich

Mayya Vladimirovna
Voytsekhovskaya   a widow

Friends

David Isaakovich   a hermit, Mira's father, estranged
                       husband of Mira's mother

Father Basil   a man of God

Lieutenant Husseinov   District Militia Officer

Captain Murko   a policeman, witness at his third
                       wedding

Colleagues

Zhora   his boss early on in his career

Lvovich   his aide

Colonel Potapenko   Army Officer

General Sveltov   Head of Security

General Filip   Head of Internal Affairs

Acquaintances

Dr Knutish   a specialist in male fertility

Dr Resonenko   a heart specialist

Kazimir   an oligarch

Major Melnichenko   figure from Ukraine's recent history
                       who hid a tape recorder in a chair in
                       the President's office

1

Kiev, 1975

The scent of acacia and blossoming chestnut are in the air as I, aged fourteen, return home on foot from the city centre after a few drinks. Tupoleva Street is deserted; on my left, the aircraft factory, and on my right, behind a tall fence, the glow of hothouses denying cucumbers and tomatoes their sleep. Out of the darkness I hear footsteps coming towards me. I quicken my pace to join in step with the other walker, then I see a boy of my own age approaching on the other side of the road.

'From where to where?' I call.

'Blücher–Svyatoshino!'

'Saksagansky to Tupoleva!' I respond.

'All the best.'

'You, too.'

The effect of the port wine inside me seems to fade with his footsteps and I resume my normal pace. On the right, our local cross between park and garden, and beyond, rows of Khrushchev-era five-storey blocks. Block 18B, fourth floor, is where I live. I have a key, but see from the courtyard that our kitchen light is on. Mother has waited up.

For ten minutes there'll be hell to pay, after which peace. Then Monday.

2

The freckles appeared suddenly, a month after my operation. First on my chest then shoulders, then forearms, turning my whole body reddish-brown, spreading down the backs of hands to my fingertips. The dermatologist was at a loss. Nothing like shingles, he said, more likely genetic.

'Do freckles run in the family?' he asked.

'Strokes, heart attacks, breast cancer, yes. Identical twins, TB, no. Freckles, no idea.'

All the same, I reached for two dusty old leather portfolios of family photographs sitting on the lumber shelf. Of all the black-and-white faces not one with freckles. Just a jolt to the memory of cousins, uncles and aunts not seen in ages.

The professor of oncology pooh-poohed any notion of cancer of the skin.

'Cancer is a localised phenomenon, but you're covered from head to toe. Nothing to worry about. The climate's changing, as you see. Global warming . . . Could be a dozen causes, but your skin's healthy. What's this scar? Heart operation?'

My weak spot, that scar. Contemplating it in the mirror, I saw that the line of scar was the epicentre of my freckles, and the scar itself had become an extended freckle, strange as that sounds, a freckle being a point and as such incapable of extension.

3

It was early morning when I came round after the operation. My bed was by a large window of the two-room luxury suite looking east. Opening my eyes, I immediately screwed them shut. I heard birds singing. Not birds of today, but like those from the past; they sang differently then – with more ardour. The difference in sound is like comparing the quality of an old, scratched, tea- or beer-stained 78 against a CD – the 78 is muddy but more authentic. In the past even birdsong was more authentic. Now I just didn't believe them. Any more than I believed the television news which said that my visit to Malaysia had been postponed until June because I had a cold.

'The birds aren't singing properly,' I informed the duty aide sitting by the door.

He reached for the telephone beside him, then, with an apprehensive glance in my direction, left the room. Five minutes later I could make out faint sounds beneath my window. My aide returned to ask if I could bear with him a little longer.

The noise ceased then suddenly, birds were singing, well this time: full of joy and optimism.

It was not of great importance, but I asked what had brought about the improvement. 'Three feeders full of vitamins under your window,' said the aide.

In 1965 there had been another east-facing window, and me, a four-year-old lad, waking, screwing my eyes shut in just the same way, birds singing just as happily. Now, at fifty-three, I had undergone major repair by the best of surgeons. I had a guard on my door and my doctors were monitoring my condition. Meanwhile, my assistants would be profiting from my absence; placing their friends in the path of government funding. But I pushed that from my mind and tried to recall how birds sounded in 1965, and compared them with the ones I heard now. My chest was constricted as if in a vice. The wound had to knit, otherwise I was done for.

4

Kiev, March 2015

'Well, how are we?' asks the principal surgeon, bending over me, breast pocket of his gleaming white coat surprisingly embroidered with a blue trident.

He is no more than fifty, but his thick swept-back grey hair confers a certain patriarchal grandeur.

'Have one,' he says, offering a Ferrero Rocher.

'What for?' I ask, rather taken aback.

'Everyone on this floor gets one on my round,' he says, taking a step back. Then, by way of proof, he pulls a handful of chocolates from his coat pocket. 'They're included in the fee . . . Or maybe you would rather have a Ukrainian sweet?'

'No,' I say, calm again. 'Give it here.'

'You can receive visitors, beginning this evening, if you want to. But no more than two hours a day.'

'Isn't that a bit soon?' I ask hopefully.

'To be honest, yes, but your Head of Administration is on my case.'

'All right,' I say, 'I'll receive.' And turning to my aide, 'Who's waiting – got a list?'

He nods.

5

Kiev, May 1977

The big surprise on my sixteenth birthday was Zhanna's gift of a blackhead remover; part of a manicure set her father had brought back from Syria. There had been two such instruments: one for big blackheads – as on her forehead – and one for small – as on my nose. The instructions were in Arabic, so she had had to rely on the pictures for clues to operation.

While everyone was drinking my health, I was shut in the bathroom experimenting with my birthday present. I returned to the table, nose redder than a beetroot, but cheerful and warmly inclined towards Zhanna.

Once my parents left for the cinema, we switched off the light and put on a tape for a ladies' excuse-me. Zhanna chose me, romance blossomed. She lost her blackheads, I my adolescence.

6

First visitor was the Deputy Prime Minister with responsibility for humanitarian matters. Two leather armchairs had been brought in, my smart bed cranked to put me half sitting and a tabletop attached for the reception of a glass of tea and pen and paper. Meanwhile, I glanced down the list, crossing off three would-be discussers of the steel industry as I went. Nikolai Lvovich, Head of Administration, was at the bottom, but above him was a woman's name unknown to me.

The Deputy Prime Minister was an agreeable fellow, an idealist in politics, a pragmatist in his personal life.

'Mr President,' he began, 'catastrophe looms.'

'A spiritual catastrophe?' I interrupted, trying to divert his obviously prepared speech into a possible conversation.

'Pardon? Oh yes, quite. As you know, our twenty-fifth anniversary of independence very nearly coincides with the centenary of the October Revolution. I'm afraid, however, our population shows little in the way of patriotism and there's no sign of national resurgence. The jubilee of our independence needs to be marked by some ideologically positive, grandiose act, if we're not to be overwhelmed by the centenary of the revolution celebrations. I've brought some suggestions.' He produced a fat file.

'Leave it with me.'

'A brief word of explanation, if I may . . .'

'Very brief.'

'I've spoken to the Church and they're agreeable. A solemn oath of loyalty to Ukraine sworn on the Bible is what we should have, followed by the presentation of national identity cards to those come of age. With due solemnity. Priests in command – special prayer for the occasion, et cetera. All in Ukrainian.'

'Talked it through with all the Churches, have you?'

'With Philaret the Archbishop, yes.'

'And what about the Crimean Tatars? Catholics? Moscow Patriarchate Greek Orthodox?'

'Well, I was thinking, it might be an appropriate time to make the Kiev Patriarchate the state Church.'

'Still barking up that tree? Look, first bring all the Orthodox Churches together, and then we'll talk.'

'Can't be done.' The Deputy Prime Minister's eyes grew round.

'Find a way,' I advised, signalling my aide to see him out.

'Remind me later about those two jubilees,' I added.

7

Moscow, January 2013

Ukrainian delegates to the Fourth Centenary of the Romanov Dynasty Celebrations travelled in two express trains, the front train in the livery of the Ukrainian colours, the second in those of the Russian Federation. The trial run, viewed from a helicopter, had been delightful, so much did they resemble two elongated flags flying, three hundred metres apart, for twenty kilometres. Though it did occur to me that it would have been even more effective to have them running side by side, obviating any charge of disrespect for the Russian Federation. But enemies exist to provoke.

The official Ukrainian delegation included only the ultra-robust, and this following night training sessions at Koncha-Zaspa throughout December, within a cordon of military beyond the view of the press. Even so, with water 1° Celsius and a chill factor of -10°, not everyone made it, the third session resulting in the hospitalisation and subsequent retirement of the State Secretary for Health. (Noting which, I resolved to make it obligatory for all holding high office to qualify in winter swimming – an excellent way of weeding out ambitious deadbeats!) The others made a better job of their Young Walrus course. I myself had been a walrus of standing long before gravitating to the lofty heights of senior government. Had I done the choosing, it would have been a delegation composed exclusively of members of the Amateur Winter Swimming Association, except for their still being, as in Soviet days, not only intelligent, but imbued with a hatred of politics and politicians. Something I understood even better now.

After a pompous reception at Moscow's Kiev Station, an aide whispered that our journey had not been without incident: a *New Word of Kiev* journalist having bribed himself onto the footplate of the Russian Federation flag train, got everyone drunk, and tailgated us dangerously, sounding the klaxon. A situation the evening press took as a metaphor for the state of Russo-Ukrainian relations, stressing how Ukraine, by virtue of its economic and geographical position, blocked Russia's road to the European Union. Fortunately, at least one paper carried the Ukrainian Ambassador's brief but effective response: 'Albania is quite happy to remain outside the Union even though it's in the middle of it!' Overdoing it a bit, I thought, leafing through the press before an open fire at our Barvikha guest residence. Still, nothing beats the good one-liner! More and you lose your audience! Good man! I must reward him.

'Bring me a whisky,' I called to my aide.

'Your ceremonial attire has arrived,' he volunteered, rising from his chair.

'Bring that too then.'

The brown Brazilian-leather holdall containing it was clearly intended as a gift.

I could imagine tomorrow's headlines in the nationalist papers back home. The Romanovs had oppressed Ukraine and forbidden its language, true, but they had been building an empire, and empires weren't built on one nation alone. Empires required enslaving others, integrating them and their territories into your own, so to speak.

The whisky was Balquhidder, a single malt, forty years oak-cask-matured, according to the label.

Another label, this time on a bundle of firewood in the hearth, proclaimed it to be 'Russian birch. Made in Finland'.

I told my aide to enquire with the Minister for Forestry whether we, too, were supplying 'Russian birch' to Russia. If so, for how much, and if not, why not?

The ceremonial attire amounted to swimming trunks in Ukrainian colours, a towelling bathrobe in Ukrainian colours with blue breast-pocket trident, and a big shaggy towel.

8

Kiev, March 2015

The woman last but one on my list came in accompanied by Nikolai Lvovich. She looked about forty.

can I do for you?' I enquired wearily.

I,' said Nikolai Lvovich deferentially, 'introduce Mayya
ïrovna Voytsekhovskaya.'

'Pleased to meet you. How can I help?'

'I won't trouble you this soon . . .' she said.

'How do you mean?'

'I'll explain tomorrow or the day after, if you'll allow me.
Goodbye.'

With that and a pleasant smile she made for the door, pausing to
turn and nod in farewell. Nikolai Lvovich followed her out.

'Find out who she is and what she wants,' I instructed my aide.

9

Moscow, January 2013

On Sparrow Hills, a vast open-air swimming pool, replica of the one
now beneath the Cathedral of Christ the Saviour. And Moscow,
since dawn, a fairy-tale kingdom in dazzling white.

By order of Mayor Luzhkov Jr, private road traffic had been
stopped before 10 a.m., while fifty giant helicopters made aerial
tours of the enormous city. From a thousand metres up, the great
city looked unusually fine, the pristine covering of snow giving
streets and avenues the appearance of canals frozen for the winter.
From that height you could not help falling in love with Moscow.

Beside the pool were temporary wooden changing rooms in the
shape of mini peasant huts, each displaying a national flag on the
door for the convenience of delegates.

Changing into ceremonial trunks, donning bathrobe and pulling on plimsolls, I felt suddenly small, feeble, insignificant and at something of a loss – clearly the result of the flight over Moscow. The Federation's political psychologists had judged everything perfectly, including the effect of that aerial view. And there was I about to step out onto a strip of red carpet across the snow to a frozen swimming pool made into an inviting, smooth-edged, fir-and-pine-branch-adorned ice hole. So much for the bird's-eye view! Down here, at the ice hole, Russia was a very different place: primeval, bleak, cold, triumphantly obtrusive. A knock preceded my trusty aide, whose name I neither knew nor wanted to know. Difficulties with his predecessor had convinced me that it was best to keep aides at a distance, and ignorance as to name, home, etc. facilitated this. The nameless neither petition nor pester.

Walking the red carpet, crunching the snow beneath, I relished the cold penetrating my bathrobe. On an identical strip of carpet to my right, robed in the Union Jack, the youthful Conservative Prime Minister of Great Britain. Mincing his way forward on my left, a much aged Kim Jong-Il.

Looking around for Putin and seeing only a blur of faces and camera lenses, I spotted at last a veritable peasant-hut pavilion under the Federation flag.

The searing chill of water was exhilarating. This massive ice hole was reserved for heads of state, the rest being catered for some way off, though near enough for their floating trays of champagne and nibbles to be clearly seen.

But for us, no floating trays, and for me, without a large shot of good Ukrainian vodka to protect against the cold proved something of a setback. Still, experience of office had taught me to subjugate my own desires – I would have loved to raise pensions or wages, or pay miners what they were owed, make all of us happy and prosperous . . . But then, dear old Nikolai Lvovich or someone like him would appear and put an oar in: 'Wealthy country, less wealthy government. Less wealthy government, less wealthy President, fewer fine cars, less well-appointed presidential flight – loss, in short, of world respect.'

No sooner were Heads of State in the water than the doors of the pavilion changing room swung open, and to the strains of the national anthem, onto his strip of red carpet stepped the President of the Russian Federation, short, gaunt and little changed. He had been voted back into power the year before after four years in the wilderness. Ukraine had honoured him by presenting him with a kilometre of Crimean coast to build a summer villa. That was the only way to free the area of a gangster-run Centre for Crimean Conservation, which the local Simferopol authorities had been unable to deal with. Indeed, no sooner did Federation specialists arrive to take possession, than all the members of the said 'Centre' disappeared without trace.

Putin swam first to the new President of the United States, from there he would move to the President of Kazakhstan before striking out in my direction.

10

Kiev, March 2015, Tuesday, 2.45 a.m.
'Wake up!' cried Nikolai Lvovich, shaking me out of sleep like a piglet from a sack. 'Urgent news.'

'What?' He had had time to shave, so it couldn't be war.

'The Governor of Odessa must be sacked immediately. He's been discussing the Moldova–Ukraine border with the Moldovans. Yesterday, in Kishinyov, he promised them three kilometres of motorway.'

'In exchange for what?'

'Not clear as yet.'

'How do you know all this? Have we people in Moldova?'

'Our friends have.'

'We have got friends somewhere then?'

'This is serious, Mr President. I've prepared a decree. It's just a question of signing it.'

'Who are we replacing him with?'

'Brudin.'

'Weren't you at school together?'

'Yes, and that's why I recommend him. I need to know someone twenty years at least before I do that. I don't pick men off the street.'

'No, that's risky. Right. Leave me the decree. I'll look at it in the morning.'

My aide was asleep on his chair, as he had been throughout our conversation. I felt like shouting at him, and would have done if I'd known his name.

Unable to get back to sleep, I kept wondering who this Mayya Vladimirovna might be, if not some dangerous piece of intrigue on the part of Nikolai Lvovich. Mayya . . . May . . . Seeing it was now March, she was on the early side . . .

11

Kiev, July 1983, Friday

We were not alone in Syrets at the Dubki restaurant; four wedding breakfasts were in progress – three shotgun and one quiet and sedate: groom fiftyish, bride thirtyish, and eight guests only talking quietly around a square table. It looks just like an old friends' reunion, but for a red-faced man in striped three-piece suit and loosely knotted silvery tie who from time to time proposes, in the traditional manner, that the happy couple kiss. Ours being of the shotgun variety had only relatives present. So what? In a day or two I'll celebrate properly with my friends and without my wife.

The midsummer heat is melting the asphalt and the stink of it invades the restaurant. Vodka, held to the nose, neutralises the smell in a way that champagne did not.

Sawing my beef cutlet and pork fried in bread cubes with a blunt knife, I wonder if the stink of asphalt might not be a premonition – a metaphor of family life.

I look at my watch, a gift from my father-in-law a day or so before. It's stopped but I don't feel like winding it up to tick away the minutes of my new, trammelled existence!

One day I'll get a divorce, pay alimony, and give the watch back to my sometime in-laws. Meanwhile, our wedding breakfast is all forced jollity one minute and sage Jewish melancholy the next.

12

Kiev, March 2015

'Who is that woman?' I ask Nikolai Lvovich, downing spoonful after spoonful of semolina and crushed strawberry.

'The surgeon said I should wait a couple more days before I tell you.'

'Up to some intrigue, are we?'

'Really, Mr President!' he protests, shaking his head so violently he upsets his parting.

'Anyone ever tell you how like the young Beria you look?'

'Funny mood you're in today. As to Beria, you never actually saw him. As to the "young", it's me who's the elder.'

'I don't have to have seen him to know who's like him. The resemblance is symbolic, not exact.'

Moon face all smiles, I can see he's seething inwardly, eyes cold with fury.

'If you only knew the amount of dross I shovel on your behalf, you wouldn't have let a little decree defining the threshold of liability for financial damage done to the state go three months unsigned!'

'I sign nothing while under the influence of anaesthetic. And this "little" decree of yours will free a good dozen crooks!'

'One former president, two prime ministers and a few small fry. All right, don't sign – it will be you who gets banged up later on.'

'For what?'

I glance over at the phone table, by the door, where my poor, pale aide is sitting pretending to read a book. I wish I could see the cover.

'Incurring a loss to the state of three billion euros plus.'

'That much?' I demand, jerking the tabletop out of its grooves and sending my semolina dish to shatter on the floor.

'If you haven't, you will, or others will for you, leaving you to carry the can. So up the threshold of liability to ten billion. Costs nothing to do that. The law's upheld, and no one goes to prison.'

'Get stuffed!' I roar, causing my aide to jump up and drop his book which is, I see, the commendable *Dead Souls*.

As Nikolai Lvovich flies from the room like a loosened cork, my surgeon arrives, accompanied by a cleaner with besom and dust pan.

'Too early to be dealing with matters of state,' he says gently, switching his gaze to the book, which is quickly retrieved and tucked away by the aide.

13

Svyatoshino, Kiev, 31 December 1977
It's 11 p.m. We've a bottle of bubbly muscat at street temperature in a plastic bag, and me, Igor Melnik and Yura Kaplun are out of luck. We planned to see the New Year in at Svetka's, because her parents were going to friends, but disaster struck when Svetka's mum found a stash of money which hubby had not put into the family kitty, along with a packet of condoms. She let fly and hubby punched her in the eye. When peace was restored, her black eye meant celebrating New Year at home and they packed Svetka off to her cousins.

We had not prepared a plan B. Now, in -10° C, we wander the deserted streets from one public soda machine to another, but the cups have already been stolen by others. Behind every window the warm light of celebration. The Soviet grown-ups are drinking, the Soviet children are laughing and we have nowhere to go. No one to snuggle up to and no stove to gather round.

From the open window of a ground-floor window I catch the sound of the midnight chimes. The wretched owner turns the volume up and tears of bitterness gather in my eyes.

So into the nearest entrance hall we go to lean against the warm radiators. Yura opens the champagne, and we pass the bottle around like a Red Indian pipe of peace. It isn't easy drinking it from the bottle. The bubbles get up our noses and make us sneeze.

'Not to worry, there'll soon be other drunken folk about to keep us company,' Igor Melnik observes reassuringly.

14

Moscow, January 2013

Unable to hold out for the entire ceremony, the US President and British PM leave the ice hole to be received by aides bearing warm towelling bathrobes and young ladies in uniform Federation swim-suits and national headdress serving vodka, of which they each take a glass, before proceeding to the inflated hangar provided for the warmth-loving, and a table spread with traditional Russian fare.

The rest of us stay in the water, awaiting a word with President Putin. And wait we have to, which I, loving cold as I do, find easy, except for a need constantly to plunge deep to counter the surging warmth in my veins.

Our talk, when it finally starts, begins as usual with an expression of our mutual grudges, stock problems, easily deferred to the distant future, but regularly raised in default of anything else: our debt for gas, Sevastopol, relations with Turkey, and Ukrainian battalions in Federation service.

'Having made parliamentary elections proportionally representational, why forbid them in Sevastopol?' he enquires with customary indifference.

'Because, as you well know, parliamentary elections are contested by parties representing different financial interests, whereas those in the Crimea represent different ethnic groups. Proportional representation would give victory to the Russian Party of the Crimea, with 20 per cent to the Tatar Party of the Crimea, and the Ukrainian Party of the Crimea disenfranchised altogether. What would the twits of my Supreme Council be telling me then?'

'Maybe it's time you mentioned the little matter of their illegal foreign bank accounts. You do know, don't you, where your budget goes? If not, I've forty dossiers on your Supreme Council that will tell you. Should I send you copies?'

'No.'

'Ease your grip on the centre, and the periphery goes to pot. Seal frontiers, shut off valves, that's my advice.'

'That Operation Other Hands proposal of yours,' I say, switching to a subject congenial to him.

'Up for it are you?'

'As good as. Once we've picked who to sort out yours for you.'

'No need. I can tell you today who on your side our Security trusts. The thing for you to decide is just how far we go.'

I nod.

He looks at his watch, then passes me at the channel leading to the other pools of the complex.

'Now Turkmen Pasha,' he says, thinking aloud, eyes on the haze, out of which floats a table bearing tall glasses, champagne and caviar pancakes. Mid-pool, it hoves to, and above, in laser hologram, the Russian Royal Family appear, so realistically as to send a cold shiver up my spine. And as, for one brief moment, I dwell under the eye of the Tsar, enjoyment of a winter swim turns to cringing servility.

Suddenly the Tsarevich gestures, embracing all in the pool, his smiling eyes bright with joy and curiosity. 'See Moscow from the air this morning?' asks the President, still, surprisingly, at my side.

'All wonderful white avenues! Second St P., eh?' with which the President of the Russian Federation bobs slowly away in the direction of the Moldovan President.

While I, as if at the touch of some loyalty switch in my genetic memory, stare on at the Royals.

'To R-u-s-s-i-a!' thunders a much amplified male voice. 'To Russia, the Mother of Russian cities and Russian lands!' I swim for the nearest tall glass.

15

Kiev, March 2015
'Found out who she is?'

The aide shakes his head, looking guilty.

'Why not?'

'Those who will talk to me know nothing and the folk in your office sent me packing.' He sounds hurt.

'Not to worry: play your cards right and one day you'll be able to send them packing.'

His expression changes to one of gratitude and hope.

'Do you like Gogol?'

'No, but it's one of my daughter's set books and she doesn't have time to read it.'

'Why not?'

'She runs the young lawyers' group. At the moment she's in court every day, listening to cases.'

'How old?'

'Thirteen.'

'Bad number,' I murmur to myself, realising immediately that I am about to lose track of the conversation. 'But it's a good age, a golden one!'

16

Kiev, September 1983, Saturday

Beyond a filthy window the patter of rain on foliage. In the corridor not a sound. Under a cold radiator a saucer of milk and a lean ginger kitten asleep. A portly nurse in grubby white smock pauses to stroke it in passing.

'Poor little thing,' she says with feeling, ignoring me.

Screams, muffled by intervening doors and partitions, of

someone in labour. Svetka perhaps. I listen, but can't tell. A scream is not a voice.

Silence.

The kitten wakes and laps the milk.

A woman doctor, hurrying down the corridor, passes through a white door. With nothing to indicate what lies beyond it. Nothing. Just a woman giving birth.

Another scream. This time different.

'Excuse me, how long does labour last?' I ask the portly nurse as she passes with mop and a bucket bearing a number roughly daubed in red paint.

'Till baby comes,' she says, without stopping.

'Then I'll just have to wait,' I sigh, realising that I have not remembered to bring even so much as a quarter-litre of Crimean port to celebrate. 1.30 a.m. says my father-in-law's gift in white metal with chrome bracelet.

I notice the doctor approaching down the corridor; her gaze rests on me.

'Your baby was stillborn,' she announces, in a tone implying that I was somehow to blame.

'Boy or girl?' I ask, at a loss.

'Boy. We're keeping your wife in for three days until her stitches heal. You can go.'

21

17

Kiev, May 2015

General Svetlov could have been Defence Minister, if I had ignored Nikolai Lvovich, who thought him not tall enough. For Defence Minister you need an impressive figure – *figure* being the operative word, rather than personality. General Svetlov is an impressive personality and devoted to me.

He enters my office and stands waiting for me to indicate that he can sit down.

'Have a seat, Valeri. Tea, coffee?'

He shakes his head, opens a leather folder and looks up at me.

'I've brought their list for Operation Other Hands. Mainly from Moscow, but a few from Krasnoyarsk, Kronstadt and St P. – seventy-two altogether. For them I can vouch. There'll be no qualms of conscience there.

'And their list of ours?'

'Dated. Only forty of the fifty-three are available. Of those I'd answer with my life for twenty-eight. They're proven. As for the rest . . .' he shrugs. 'Best not to say.'

'Good. Leave the twenty-eight, add thirty or so of your own, and assemble them all at the Pushcha-Voditsa sanatorium. For 11 a.m., and our ears only. I'll be there. This is between ourselves.'

He nods.

Half an hour later, feeling like a bit of exercise, I go over to the mirror and do a bit of arm swinging in front of the mirror. But put off by my freckle-covered face I leave my office and walk the corridor. At the end of the corridor, just short of the security barrier at the head of the stairs, a chippy in overalls is busy unscrewing a plate inscribed

APPEALS REGISTRY
GREIS NADEZHDA PAVLOVNA

'What's happening here?' I ask.

Not having heard my approach, the chippy takes fright.

'Don't know. The boss told me to take this sign down.'

'The boss being?'

'Nikolai Lvovich.'

'Who's now where?'

'Busy in his office.'

'I'll tell him you're here,' squeaks his secretary, getting to her feet as I stomp into his office on the second floor.

'Don't bother!'

His two visitors I recognise as Deputies, though I can't say of which faction.

'Out!' I order, which, despite their corpulence, they do with silent ease.

'Everything's as it should be,' Nikolai Lvovich says quietly. 'No incidents to report. You'll have my sitrep within the hour.'

'Who are you putting in the Appeals Registry?'

'Been complaining, has she, the bitch?' A snarl replaces the nervous smile. 'And I promised her an equally good room plus TV and microwave . . .!'

'Leave Nadezhda Pavlovna out of it. She hasn't complained. Just explain what's happening to that office.'

He drew breath. 'Quiet conversation with you is impossible,

Mr President! It'll take a couple of hours to explain everything clearly.'

'Right. So put off your meeting with the Israeli Ambassador till tomorrow. I'll expect you in half an hour. With the sitrep.'

As I turn away, I note with satisfaction how very pale and agitated he has become. I wish he was like that more often.

18

Kiev, September 1983, Sunday, early hours

Rain on leaves, rain everywhere, underfoot and as far as the eye can see. Autumn – outside and in. The father with no child plods home, weary, uncaring, and as if in sympathy with the downpour, tearful.

Tupoleva Street is in darkness but for the watery yellow of street lamps and car headlamps and the luminescent glow of the vegetable factory hothouses. Outside the factory gate someone is sitting on a fallen lamp post. It's a young girl, and she is sobbing.

'Feeling bad?' I enquire, leaning over the drooping sunflower of a face.

'Awful. I've been sacked.'

'Why?'

'Not letting the boss get his leg over.'

'Good for you!' I say trying to cheer her up.

Peroxide blonde, make-up running, eighteenish, she is a picture of genuine misery.

'I feel awful too. My son's been born dead. My wife's in maternity for the next three days.'

'How heavy was he?'

I shrug. 'I don't think they weigh dead babies, but we'll need to think of a name to remember him by.'

'Did you see him?'

'No.'

'I'll come home with you, if you like.'

'We live with my mother.'

'Come to my hostel then. It's no distance, but you'll have to climb in. Our bitch of a warden has only to see a man, and she rings the militia.'

'All right.'

I have a number of reasons for not wanting to go home.

19

Kiev, Pushcha-Voditsa, May 2015

General Svetlov has a liking for civvies, possessing a suit by Voronin Jr, non-crease grey that in poor light glitters. A general who dresses like that can be trusted completely. He's obviously not dreaming of supreme command, nor driven by megalomania.

Standing with Svetlov at the sanatorium gates are Muntyan, the Director, and various of his staff, and behind them, shining in the sun, is the bald head of Colonel Potapenko, my man from Security, another enthusiast for civvies.

Our three Mercedes sweep noiselessly in and the gates swing shut. I am in the middle car. The first is empty, the third carries my aide.

'All assembled,' reports Svetlov, greeting me outside the main block, 'and waiting in the concert hall.'

'Switch them to the hunting lodge thirty minutes from now.'

'Let's say fifteen. Just in case.'

I nod.

'Any problems here?' I ask Muntyan.

'As always, but I don't complain.'

'Which is why you've been here ten years. Any coffee?'

Two minutes later we are in the sanatorium bar, being served espresso by a teenage waiter with visibly shaking hands.

'Whose boy's that?'

'His mother is the linen mistress. The dynastic's more trustworthy in our line of work.'

'In ours too. At least so the majority think. Expecting anyone from Bank Street?

'Nikolai Lvovich is still here. No one else expected. It's a working day after all.'

'Nikolai Lvovich here?' I see red.

'He arrived last night. He has someone with him. They're breakfasting in their room at the moment. His driver's come. So he'll be off shortly.'

'Who's with him?' I ask, thinking Mayya Voytsekhovkaya, of whom I still know very little.

'Young, gypsyish . . .' Muntyan is wriggling. He obviously knows everything. 'It's Inna Zhanina, the singer, if you must know . . .'

I can't hide my disgust and Muntyan is genuinely surprised.

'But she's very nice . . . You should get yourself a wife –'

'How dare you!' I shout, leaping out of the leather chair, fists clenched.

'Forgive me, forgive me, Mr President.' Muntyan is shaking. 'I'm afraid I'm overtired and anyway that is what Nikolai Lvovich said.'

'He's an idiot!'

'Yes, you're right. He is.'

The clean, open faces of the young men assembled to hear me are encouraging. Our source of strength is here, not in the employment agencies.

'Good day!' I begin, gesturing that there should be no response. 'You have been selected by General Svetlov for a vital state assignment. We and the Russian Federation have agreed a joint operation, code name "Other Hands". That, I think, says it all. You will do in Russia what Kiev and Chernigov Operation "Cobra" do regularly in the Crimea and Dnepropetrovsk respectively, while Russia returns the favour here. Only this operation is on the highest possible level. You go first to Moscow and from there out to the regions. Moscow will brief you concerning the regional officials involved in criminal activities. You, without informing local Internal Affairs or Special Forces, are to arrest them in the small hours and fly them straight back to Kiev for detention in Ukraine. A Russian group will be doing the same with our scum. Is that clear?'

The men nod. I sense they approve. They are keen to do battle with criminality in the top echelons of power. They would like to be doing it here and on a permanent basis, but that isn't on. Here, as in Russia, only other hands could undertake such radical operations. But God willing, we'll keep going.

'General Svetlov will be in charge of our side of the operation, and he will brief you further. Good luck.'

Returning to the main building by way of the lake (complete with a swan), I find myself wondering uneasily if the Russians were not planning to use our chaps simply to overthrow local leaders disloyal to Moscow. I will only be using the Russians for the type of assignment we have agreed on, high time though it is to sort out Nikolai Lvovich . . .

As I get into my Mercedes, I ask Muntyan if he is still here.

'He shot off the moment he saw you . . .'

20

Kiev, 8 May 2015, Friday

Nikolai Lvovich looks in, but being occupied with the Chairman of the State Holidays Commission, People's Deputy Karmazov, I tell him to come back in half an hour. Karmazov, seated on the legendary Melnichenko ottoman, has a crew cut that suits him, and the physique of a boxer, although by qualification he's a veterinary surgeon, and a good man, having, by the age of thirty-five, built up a network of clinics.

'This country's suffering terrible losses. It's time to cut down the number of national holidays,' he says. 'Just count them,' he adds, gesturing at the wall calendar, a present from the Judaica Institute. 'From 25th April on, the economy is in a state of collapse. So far there have been three requests from the Bundestag for the abolition of Victory Day. An archaic celebration if ever there was one – the victorious Soviet Union doesn't even exist any more. VE Day, which was a working day everywhere else, was scrapped in Europe a year ago. Come new victories, we'll pick a new day to celebrate. But we're a peaceful country. We don't war with anyone.'

I nod. 'I agree as you know. Stick it on the agenda, and my

representative will add my voice in Parliament. OK?'

Veterinary surgeon Karmazov is happy. He's been applying to see me for three months. Had I known his attitude, I would have seen him earlier, but I was afraid he would request new holidays.

'Get Nikolai Lvovich,' I tell my aide.

'He's not here.'

'Well, go and find him. Say I'm waiting.'

Nikolai Lvovich comes in, frowning and sullen.

'What were you and Karmazov discussing?'

'No business of yours. Victory Day.'

'And?' he asks, clearly suspicious.

'We're going to do away with it in order to bring the May output up to the level of April and June. Now, sit down.'

He sits down on the spot vacated by Karmazov.

'What do you want to hear?'

'First: why the Appeals Registry is standing empty; and second: who the woman you brought to me in hospital is.'

'Which is all one question.' He is not keen to talk, but now there is no going back. 'The woman is Mayya Vladimirovna Voytsekhovskaya.'

'So I've heard.'

'Three months ago she lost her husband. His private helicopter crashed. She was very much in love with him.'

'Do I have to listen to a Bollywood film plot?'

'If you haven't the time . . .' He makes to stand up.

'Sit down and get on with it.'

'In February, when you were in your coma and the stability of the country was at stake, an urgent decision had to be taken . . . Every effort had been made to save her husband's life, but the brain damage was too great. The possibility of using his heart for transplant was something she totally opposed. She swore never to be separated from it, and even arranged with some institute to keep it alive at a cost of $100,000 a year. For the sake of that heart, serious concessions were called for.'

I put a hand to my chest. I feel hot.

'In the end it meant signing a contract. You shall hear all the terms when you're completely recovered, but one of them confers the right to be in the proximity of her late husband's heart – at all times. Which is why the office you mentioned has been vacated. There'll be no nameplate for the time being. She doesn't know if she wants to be there or not.'

Locking my fingers together, I sit back and think.

'D'you think my freckles are getting worse?' I ask.

'No,' he says, examining my face.

'Was no other heart available?'

'This one was right next door in the operating theatre; any other would have involved a wait. Not one of society's better members, the donor, but Mayya Vladimirovna is bound to silence.'

'Where does she sleep?'

For just a moment he is taken aback.

'Desatinaya Street. In what was the old servants' rest room in the next apartment. Other side of your bedroom wall. Outside access. No need to worry. No one sees or knows anything about her. Well, practically.'

'Nikolai Lvovich, what *have* you done?'

'Saved your life and saved the state. The latter being what's important. You know precisely who would instantly cash in on your illness or death, declaring another war on corruption in high places, supplanting us in the process.'

'Us?'

'Our stratum and what it stands for.'

'Our stratum?' This usage of the term is new to me.

'Yes. Our society is as stratified as *gâteau napoléon* has layers. One layer of poor and any number of rich layers, interlaid with semirich, all believing wealth to be made not by economics but by politics.'

'Cut the lecture! What else is this woman promised?'

'For your heart's sake, Mr President, let's, as they say in *The Thousand and One Nights*, leave that for another time.'

21

Café Bûcheron, Paris, October 2006

'I want to marry,' she said, contemplating her glass of Beaujolais Nouveau.

'As sooner or later all women do,' I conceded, lighting a Gauloise from the waiter's match. 'More for stability than happiness.'

'In Brussels you said you'd give up smoking, said we'd meet every ten days at least. True, you didn't say you'd marry me, but it's been three years since your wife died. Surely your daughter needs a mother. Bring her back from America. Let me be her mother.'

Our every meeting began with an exchange of shots and grievances, and today was no exception. Veronika was beautiful, but losing her youth and demanding more of life and those around her in consequence. Vladimir Street was where she lived but not where we ever met. Kiev being out, a ticket to Paris was the answer.

One for me, and one on the next flight for her. At Charles de Gaulle I met her with flowers, conducting her to the Sheraton to luxuriate for an hour or two in the bath, after which aroma massage and champagne, letting her, twice a month, play grande dame and social lioness, at least in private.

'Why don't you say something?' she asked, sipping her wine and replacing the glass on the bar.

'This,' I said with a laugh, 'is a wine the poor make an occasion of. A young wine, which, remember, cannot, by definition, be fine.'

'Remembering your every gem would make me a mine of banalities.'

'Well, bear in mind, or rather, don't forget that you are a beautiful young woman wanting to marry.'

For just a moment she melted, but quickly recovering and narrowing her green eyes, she let me have it.

'And you are a technocrat, devoid of feelings and technically deficient! Even in love. Bashing on, never mind where!'

'No, I come here – dreaming of seeing you, doing my utmost to see you, neglecting my country to see you!'

'Don't give me that! You're not in front of your electorate now. Come to think of it, you're not anywhere. Not even here with me!'

'Wrong. I am,' I said, consulting my expensive watch. 'And you've another twenty minutes' bellyaching till we dine.'

Consulting her equally expensive watch, a thirty-fifth birthday present from me, Veronika nodded.

'I've not been unfaithful, but I do want to marry,' she said, no longer aggressive, 'And a month from now I shall, if you don't object.'

'The lucky man being?'

'Akhimov . . .'

'Father or son?'

'The son. Do you have to make a joke of it?'

'Dad's the richer, but the boy's got money too. And what's Dad's will come to him, barring hostilities on the petrol-pump front . . . So go ahead. I've no right to stop you.'

Her eyes brimmed with tears.

'But this isn't goodbye, is it? How about dinner?'

'No, it's not, we've two more days together. I've no right to walk out on you. Marriage is one thing, love another. Now and then they go together.'

Two little tears did now actually roll down her cheeks. Now she would have to adjust her make-up.

'It'll mean living with him,' I said thoughtfully. 'Not just meeting in Paris or Amsterdam. Not just strolling along the Thames Embankment.'

'I know,' she said, getting to her feet, smoothing her divided miniskirt. 'I won't be a minute.' And taking her vanity bag, she went to adjust her make-up.

It occurred to me that her prepared and rehearsed monologue had turned suddenly into a genuine *cri de coeur*. Something she had not expected herself and she had lost control. Now nothing but the powder-room mirror could help restore her powers. Those powers that reside in the face, in the warpainting of brows, cheeks and eyelashes, and the combination of firm voice and steady gaze. Being beautiful is hard work. Not just being it but living it. I didn't envy her. It was a road that all too often ended in sudden loneliness.

22

'See he doesn't drink the seawater!' says Mother, waving a hand at my brother Dima who is knee-deep in it, eagerly scanning the distant coastline and horizons. It's his first time by the sea, and his first outing in five years from the mental hospital, where he has been the quietest of patients.

'I'm going for some ices,' calls Mother. 'What sort for you?'

'Chestnut.'

'I'll get chestnut for him too, since you're twins.'

I watch her go, a solitary figure splashing through the shallows. It's a beautiful picture, one that will remain in my memory forever.

It has not long stopped raining, and holidaymakers are slowly returning to the beach. Dry sand is what they want to lie on. Dry or wet doesn't matter to us. We have come to show Dima the sea, and he gazes open-mouthed, unable to see enough of it.

He is wearing blue swimming trunks with white stripes. The cheapest going, but it is all the same to him. What matters to us is that he should appear fit and normal.

'What's over there?' he asks, turning to me and pointing to the distant horizon. 'Ships?'

'Odessa. Ships. Other countries.'

'Sergey,' he says, looking earnestly at me, 'I'm not ill. I just have no interest in living.'

He speaks slowly, and it occurs to me, as I look at him, gaunt, puffy-eyed, scarred nose, that no one but Mother could see him as my twin. The scar is the result of battling to protect a lorry of hospital supplies from idiot local looters. An act that made one doubt if Dima was ill at all, and wonder if it wasn't the doctor-in-charge who was sick in the head. Though maybe there had been nothing else for it but to summon help from the patients, when the looters surrounded the lorry and started dragging the driver from his cab.

A strange business, resulting in a citation from the doctor-in-charge, which Dima brought with him to look at last thing at night, and got Mother or me to read out loud to him.

> Awarded to Bunin, Dmitry Pavlovich, for bravery
> and disregard of self shown protecting the property
> of Nursing Home No. 3, Glukhovka, Chernigov Region.

'Your father had a medal like that,' Mother said the first evening she read the citation. 'A silver one. For bravery. You're just like him.'

23

Kiev, September 1983, Sunday, early hours
'What's your parents' telephone number?' demands the hostel warden.

The ceiling light has no shade. In one of the two beds, a fat woman of about thirty is sleeping, oblivious to everything. On the other, sitting in only a skirt, arms crossed over her flat chest, the girl I came in with. Who was supposed to have comforted whom I don't know, but fifteen minutes earlier, I gave her a leg-up to a rather high ground-floor window, then climbed in after her. She immediately took off her jacket and sweater, and saying she was cold, slipped next door for a bottle of Madeira from a friend's bedside locker. No sooner was she back than the bitch of a warden switched on the light, and that was that.

'I don't know *who* he is!' Flat Chest keeps insisting.

'Three days on the trot now, things have gone missing!' announces the warden – a sideboard of a woman who stands blocking the door. 'So, telephone number! Let them come and pay your fine, or I'll call the police.'

'Call them then.' I am past caring. It's a night of lost causes. I can't have anything else to lose.

But it seems I am wrong.

The warden shouts down the corridor and some half-drunk man-about-the-house appears to stand over me while she phones.

'Entry effected how – via the window?' asks the sleepy desk sergeant at District Militia Shcherbakov Street.

'Yes.'

'Intending to steal?'

'No.'

'Want a smack in the gob?'

'I was invited in by a girl.'

'She says she never saw you before!'

'We met, she took me back there with her.'

'A likely tale!'

I shrug. He consults his watch. It's 2.30 a.m. My mother comes in.

'What's he done?' she demands, eyes brimming with tears, then, turning to me, 'Parasite! Layabout! Guttersnipe! What is it now? You're the bane of my life!'

'Calm yourself, Citizen,' says the sergeant, clearly unimpressed. 'Attempted theft of personal property from vegetable factory staff hostel is what it's about.'

Silence ensues while Mother thinks what line to take, and when she speaks again her tone is different. 'He's grown up fatherless. His army captain dad was killed on the firing range. All my time goes on his invalid brother. No sooner do I get home than it's off with him to the medics . . .'

'Right,' interrupts the sergeant. 'We could settle for hooliganism – *climbing* in isn't the same as *breaking* in.'

'Wait outside!' Mother orders.

'Who's the sergeant now?' I ask myself.

Five minutes later I am marched back in.

'Next time, use your head, think of the consequences,' urges Mother, and leaves.

I get banged up for ten days, which involves sweeping the yard, mopping both floors of the District Militia, and playing sly games of blackjack with sixty-year-old Zyama, who is doing fifteen days for crapping on the step of a woman who chalked 'Yid' on his.

24

Kiev, May 2015

My physician listens attentively to my new heart, then applies the cold chromium of his stethoscope to my lungs.

'Freckles not going yet?'

'Will they ever go?' I ask hopelessly.

'If they are a symptom of illness, yes. Otherwise not. Spontaneous appearance of freckles in mature years is not sufficiently understood.'

'So what do our clever medics study, with the funds we give them?'

'Not freckles. Cancer, Aids, sarcomas. But if I'm honest . . .'

I wait for him to continue, this ex-army MO, recommended by Nikolai Lvovich.

'Pure supposition,' he says at last, 'but I think Western pharmacists introduce new forms of flu and asthma in order to launch new drugs. Rather as computer anti-virus experts produce new viruses to launch updates against.'

'So is there an anti-freckles available?'

'Not that I've heard of.'

'Keep your ears open, and when you do hear, tell me.'

After my physician, Nikolai Lvovich appears with a sheaf of documents.

'For signature,' he says plumping it down on my desk. 'And something else, so you're not caught on the hop . . . When you were out of action, we, the Cabinet, enacted a reform . . .'

'You did, did you?' I ask, gazing into the round empty plate of his face.

'Prime Minister, as such, no longer exists,' he says. 'Ministers discharge the role in turn, giving their own a temporary spell of priority. At the moment it's Sinko. He's Economy. The documents are here and it was authorised by you.'

'Right, I'll read it. Give me ten minutes.'

It is good, sensible stuff, except that it's his idea. Still, he's attributed it correctly. I tell my aide to fetch him back.

All smiles, I congratulate him on his mauve tie, offer cognac, and wave my aide to join us.

'To reform!' said Nikolai Lvovich, raising his glass.

'Ukrainian reform!' I echo.

25

Kiev, October 1983

My ten days' sweeping proved of benefit, and not only on the score of the useful friends I made. Above all I had ample time to reflect on human values and morality. Or less grandly, in the language of detention, not just to lament my lot but to consider my future. Borne on the stream of life to the District Militia, I could now either drift with the current, or strike out for myself. The past: school, ten or so jobs, none of which I had kept for more than three months, and marriage. The present: ten days' arrest. The future: a lifetime. How, then, to start afresh? By divorcing?

Svetka had herself talked of divorce, and when I got home, her things were gone from our room.

'She's left you a note. I haven't read it,' Mother said.

The envelope was sealed but slightly torn, but there was a fishy smell about the contents, herring being what Mother and I enjoyed twice weekly, with sliced potato and onions.

Dear Sergey,
    Sorry, but I see the death of our child as an omen, and for our marriage a bad one, like your ten days' arrest. We

should, I am sure, divorce. Ring me, if agreeable, at my parents'.

Love,

Svetka

I rang to say I was and she seemed happy, and thanks to friends of her parents' at the registry office, the divorce proceeded apace.

'Calls for celebration!' said friend Zhenya from two floors down.

And that evening I took a bottle of fortified wine to the District Militia, and had a pleasant session with my arresting sergeant. A young Dagestani lieutenant, Marat Husseinov, joined in drinking my health.

'Any problem, just look in,' he said when I left.

26

Kiev, October 2014, early hours

Rain lashes my Desatinaya Street windows, while I sleep. The dying wood fire crackles. Through the veil of sleep I hear both sounds, the one blending with the other. It's been a hard day. Nothing wearies me more than my monthly TV address to the nation, live. Followed by a press conference, also live. Each question jollier than the one before.

'Will Ukraine invoke sanctions against Poland for banning the entry of diesel transport?'

'Your thoughts on the bill providing for the naturalisation of illegal immigrants?'

'When will the government bring order to the power sector?'

And then, at 2 a.m., a gentle knocking. Getting up and throwing on a dressing gown, I go to the door to find Colonel Potapenko, Head of Security.

'Sorry, Mr President,' he says quietly. 'Nikolai Lvovich insists on seeing you. It's urgent.'

'Well?' I demand, entering the suite where Nikolai Lvovich is waiting.

'Kazimir's upping electricity charges tomorrow by 50 per cent! You know what that means.'

'Seeing it's his private electricity and we have a market economy, what can we do about it?'

'Sit down,' says Nikolai Lvovich, then addressing the duty bodyguard, 'Don't just stand there, go and make coffee.

'This is just a beginning,' he continues in a nervous whisper when we are alone. 'He'll have another go at disconnecting non-payers. And who's most in arrears? The state. He'll disconnect you! That's why he bought up Regional Power – at the right moment he plans to switch the whole country's lights off, make himself President, and switch them back on again. And there you are . . . You can imagine the consequences. All because electricity is in the hands of one man!'

'It was Fedyuk who allowed that to happen –'

'And he's now in prison for the financial loss he caused the state . . . and while we're on the subject, you might just sign the amendments raising the threshold of liability.'

'Don't confuse me – it's two in the morning! I'll get angry.'

'Very good, very good,' Lvovich nods. 'But we need to take immediate action on this.'

'What do you suggest?'

'Summon a sitting,' he says cautiously, as if expecting a rebuff.

'When?'

'Now.' He glances at the grandfather clock. 'For 4 a.m. Not everyone. Just the opposition – who loathe Kazimir – and the centrists. They'll provide the votes we need. You attack Kazimir's plans and you present a bill . . .'

'What bill?'

'One I've prepared. "Cheap Energy Production and the Restructuring of State Liability for Energy used", putting a moratorium on price increases before the next presidential election.'

A security guard escorts in a sleepy maid bearing a coffee pot.

'Right, go ahead.'

He dials a number on his mobile, says simply, 'Plan A,' and rings off.

As I drink my coffee, I wonder what plan B may have been.

A sleepy Parliament is the best sort to address. True, I am a little sleepy myself, but not to the detriment of my cause, and there is an air of heightened expectancy in the chamber. Night sittings could be just the thing for getting us into Europe, except that in two years we have had only two.

The result exceeds expectations. The bill is passed, to take immediate effect.

General Svetlov, clearly another who hasn't slept all night, draws me aside afterwards to suggest trumping the other side's aces by removing all paperwork relating to non-payment for electric power.

'Good man!' I say. 'Do it.'

From a first-floor window I watch three hundred Mercs, Jaguars and Lexuses convey sleepy opposition and centrists to their homes, forming a beautiful double line of yellow headlights, heading, like predawn bees, to the scent of distant flowers. 'Well?' asks Nikolai Lvovich.

'First-rate! Ask of me what you will.'

'Your signature to the amendments.'

'Right,' I say, beginning to see and think more clearly. 'Only not with retrospective effect. Those sentenced for exceeding the old threshold stay inside.'

'Of course. The future's what matters.'

'And what I need is an instant state visit. Departing before 9 a.m., so as to miss the Kazimir bust-up.'

He thinks for a moment. 'Right. Go straight to Borispol. I'll contact Foreign Affairs and the airport. There'll be a plane standing by. Meanwhile, we'll think of a country.'

27

Glukhovka, Chernigov Region, August 2003
It's 6 a.m. and after a night of thunder the air is full of ozone and a pleasure to breathe. Mother and I sit in an ancient Opel, the car doors wide open, but the gates of Nursing Home No. 3 for the mentally sick are still closed – at least to visitors. The patients are asleep and are not to be disturbed before breakfast, no doubt already under way. Five little women of indeterminate age have been let in through a checkpoint beside the gates.

'We should have started later,' I tell Mother.

With a sigh she bends forward and takes a sachet of kefir from her bag, and tearing a corner off, puts it to her lips, then passes it to me.

'I'm scared every time of not making it,' she says at last.

I wasn't sure what she meant. Dima is physically in good shape, it's his mind that's sick. Mother is seventy-five, getting on, but as yet with no major ailments.

'And you, not to put to fine a point on it, could come in a better car with a driver,' she adds, adjusting her pink headscarf.

'And you could come better dressed,' I reply, casting a critical glance over her red cardigan and long black skirt. 'If I use an official car, the whole Ministry will know my brother's in a nuthouse.'

At 9 a.m. when we are let in, I go straight to the doctor-in-charge, give him my card and $100 in an envelope, and tell him to ring in case of difficulty.

He nods appreciatively, and asks how long I am taking him for.

'A week,' I say.

Mother and Dima are outside together, she saying something, he shading his eyes against the sun. My gaze wanders over the grounds and I become aware of a beautiful, elegant, distraite young lady in a curious mauve dressing gown and silvery Armenian slippers with turned-up toes coming slowly across the lawn – like the rest of the inmates: a cosmic satellite pursuing an infinite course past other planets and stars.

I take a step towards her and ask quietly, 'What's your name?'

She stops and turns towards me, a puzzled expression on her face. 'Valya, Valya Vilenskaya.

Calling to Mother and Dima that I wouldn't be a minute, I nip back to the doctor-in-charge.

He is alone in his office, bright sunlight streaming in at the window, portrait of Shevchenko on the wall behind him, on the desk before him, an open file and a glass of tea.

'You've got a woman here, Valya Vilenskaya. Who is she?' I ask.

'Mild schizophrenia,' the doctor shrugs. 'Her sister takes a keen interest in her and visits every month. She's beautiful too.'

'I hope your male staff don't give her any trouble.'

'Good gracious no,' the doctor gasps. 'We're very strict about that sort of thing.'

The doctor's white coat and Valya's purple dressing gown are left behind and it's home to Kiev in the ancient Opel, with Dima happy in the back.

'We'll stop for lunch on the way,' Mother says, then asks Dima what he had for breakfast.

'Porridge with jam.'

'An English,' I say with a grin.

'Will we go fishing?' Dima asks. 'Like you promised last time?'

'Yes. In the estuary. Plenty of fish there.'

In my mirror I see Dima's smiling face and it occurs to me that he and real life must have come to an agreement to remain independent of one another.

28

Kiev, October 1983, evening

It's been raining non-stop. Zhenya from two floors down brought up his video player and a porno tape. Mother is at her dressmaker's.

'Abroad they show this sort of thing on telly all the time,' says Zhenya. 'When all we get is news and gardening programmes.'

All it shows is a breasty middle-aged female swimming nude to the side of the pool fondling her bosom, smiling strangely.

'Would you want to watch this all the time?'

'It hots up later.'

But it doesn't, though in the end a man appears, strips off and dives in. They talk in English – no subtitles, of course – then have sex, but because of the water, you can hardly see anything.

'That it?'

'Wrong cassette,' he apologises. 'They promised something else.'

Disconnecting the bulky video player from the telly, he carts it and the video off, leaving me alone. It's not all that late, but the rain makes it seem like night already and a never-ending one.

29

Over Ukraine, October 2014, early morning

The crew of the presidential airliner are clearly tense. Twice in thirty minutes the captain has asked what, failing any flight order from the ground, he should do.

'Keep circling till we get one.'

The flight attendants, both young and blonde, having put on their make-up in a hurry, are now standing at the rear of the cabin whispering nervously together, clearly affected by the pilots' anxiety. But the pilots are sensible chaps, they'll have realised something is up, a military coup or similar. And a coup there has been, a little one, of my and Nikolai Lvovich's making. Kazimir might, of course, attempt to counter it, but hopefully he is still asleep and ignorant of events.

Leaving my seat, I walk the broad, pristinely carpeted gangway, deep in thought. The girls fall silent as I approach and wait attentively.

'Where would *you* like to go to?' I ask.

'Turkey and the sea,' says the bolder of them.

'Maybe we will. I'll think about it,' I say, turning and ambling back. Through the open door of the flight deck, a multitude of blue, red and green lights, and a windscreen, beyond which utter darkness.

'The order's come, Mr President. Mongolia,' says the captain emerging from the flight deck. This surprises me. Turkey would have been better and only just across the water.

An hour later comes the news that Nikolai Lvovich and a hastily formed business delegation are following in the second presidential aircraft.

Just as well there is only one President and two presidential planes, I think to myself, before falling asleep to the drone of the engines.

30

Kiev, June 2015, Sunday

'Why not go to Koncha-Zaspa and relax?' asks my aide, clearly anxious on my account. The apartment is kept agreeably cool by three silent air conditioners, but outside it is murderously hot.

'No,' I say, trying hard to think of some task to take him off my back. 'But there is one thing you could do for me. Strictly on the q.t.'

He stiffens, all eagerness to respond.

'Take a car, get hold of about twenty kilograms of good quality ice and bring it back here.'

He takes himself off and the doorway is now free for the passage of cool air again.

At midday my physician comes to check my heart and lungs.

'Care for a whisky?' I ask him.

'Not allowed,' he sighs. 'My liver.'

'How about me?'

'You can, increasing the amount gradually. Your heart will tell you when to stop. A donor heart's more sensitive than one's own. It applies to other organs. I've got the liver of someone who went teetotal. So that's why I can't drink.'

A man after my own heart in all senses.

'So how do you relax?'

'By never getting stressed,' he laughs. 'In case of need, I fish, go mushrooming or ask friends in for a drink . . .'

'But you don't drink?'

'They make up for that. I fill glasses and listen. You can button up your shirt. All's well. The main thing's to keep your head cool and not get excited. Any sort of sudden excitement or rapture is dangerous.'

'I'm a quiet sort of person.'

A security guard sees my physician out, and at that moment my aide reappears.

'Where shall I put it?'

'The bath.'

'All of it?'

'Yes.'

'Then?'

'Call me.'

And in no time I stretch my heat-jaded self blissfully out on the ice-strewn floor of the jacuzzi. After five minutes on icy coals, I turn the cold tap on and searing jets of water lash my body, washing the various-sized cubes of ice out from under me and whisking them into whirlpools.

I shout for my aide to bring whisky.

'With ice?' he asks, looking round the door.

'Without.'

A curious sort of pleasure: whisky with ice, but separately.

Feeling the need of some other elemental stimulus, I get my aide, a good judge of my mood and taste, to play some music.

'O, could I but convey in sound!' comes from the ceiling speakers in the virile bass of Chaliapin. Enough there to stir bodily resonance. I am trembling slightly, a sure sign that I am hearing not only with my ears, but through my skin, with my whole jacuzzi-with-ice-cooled nature.

Would Chaliapin have beaten women? I wonder idly. Possibly. In the heat of the moment. Only his nearest and dearest, of course. In anger and passion. Fist raised to a frightened, delicate creature on her knees before him, begging forgiveness for something she had not even done – imaginings interrupted by my aide with a letter.

'Mr President' reads the envelope.

'Who brought it?'

'Security gave it me, says he found it on the floor.'

'Bring more whisky.'

Opening the envelope, I gaze in wonderment. Not for ten years have I received anything written by hand.

49

Dear President,

I trust you are recovering and will soon agree to meet. It is of great importance to me, though for the moment I am content with the five metres between us at night. Wishing you inner equanimity and goodwill to those about you,

Yours sincerely,

Mayya Voytsekhovskaya

It is like being run over by a tractor. The sheer effrontery of the woman is disarming. Her handwriting recalled primary-school lessons bent over an exercise book with sloping lines across the page so that you wrote at the correct angle.

The aide brings whisky.

Standing the glass on the edge of the jacuzzi, I capture two little cubes of ice and pop them in.

'Find out who found this letter where.'

As I drink, I compare the brownish-yellow liquid with the colour of my freckles. Afterwards I examine the sole of my foot. That too is freckled.

31

Kiev, October 1983

It's 7.45 p.m., and behind Block 16, we're preparing for battle. There are about fifty of us, mostly boys from Blocks 16 and 17, plus ten boys who live near School No. 27. Most are sixteen or seventeen.

At twenty-two, Zhenya and I are the commanders. We are considering strategy and tactics.

'Let's have three roubles,' says Vitya Lysy dashing up to us. 'I'll get some port – the shop'll be shutting!' Reluctantly I part with three roubles, and off he runs. A wind is getting up, stirring and rustling the trees in our park-cum-garden. There's a distant clap of thunder.

'You take over, while I nip off to organise some backup,' I whisper to Zhenya. 'Only use chains as a last resort and if the other lot play dirty.'

I skirt round a gathering of our Shcherbakov Street opposition, playing spy. I strain to catch what they're saying. What I hear is enough to send me back to Zhenya.

'It's bad,' I tell him. 'They've got metal bars and are going for legs, so we use chains.'

Fifteen minutes later I arrive breathless at the District Militia.

'And what can I do for you?' asks Marat Husseinov, leaning on the duty desk.

'There's a gang fight brewing. Block 16 and Park Area. Park have iron bars.'

'And you?'

'Bicycle chains.'

'Iron bars hurt more. Do we stop it starting?'

'Give us ten minutes to see how it goes.'

Husseinov looks at the clock.

'It's Dynamo Kiev v. Dynamo Tiflis in half an hour. Mustn't miss that.'

'I'll nip back. Give us fifteen minutes?'

'Will do.' He turns back to his mini switchboard.

*

The battle begins. A half-brick lobbed from their side, a yelp of pain from ours; bicycle chains immediately start whirling in the air, and charge!

'Call the militia, somebody, I haven't got a phone!' shouts a man in a white singlet from a second-floor balcony.

Headlights flash on from near the vegetable factory. A siren wails.

Busy dodging iron bars, I have no idea who is winning.

'Cops!' comes a shout.

Action ceases abruptly. Both gangs scatter and melt into the darkness.

The militia, in no mood to make arrests that will involve paperwork and care of prisoners at the expense of football, were slow to reach the scene.

From behind a cherry tree I watch two officers gather up weapons in the light of their van's headlights, then they haul out from under a bush someone I recognise.

'He's Vasya Bely, the schoolmistress's son,' I tell them, breaking cover. 'I'll see him home.'

'What's it got to do with you?' comes the reply. I don't recognise this cop.

'Are you one of them?' a sergeant challenges me. I don't recognise him either. They nab me. The police van turns and sets off with Vasya and me looking out the back window as our five-storey apartment blocks, garden-park trees and the vegetable-factory hostel disappear from view.

I have an idea that we are in the hands of officers summoned by the enemy; our lot having forgotten us.

But then there is the familiar much-swept courtyard, and Husseinov waiting for us. Vasya gets antiseptic for the cuts on his head, and we all sit down together to watch the match.

At half-time the score was 2–1 in our favour.

32

Kiev, September 2003

'Sergey Dmitrievich Dogmazov to see you,' says my secretary. I nod and in comes the two-metre-high Doctor of Historical Sciences, President of the Intellectual Resources Foundation, to mention only two of his many titles. To get his visiting card into my card holder, I had to cut off the edge. But his titles are his life achievements; let him shout about them. 'Strasbourg one minute, Brussels the next, you're hard to get hold of. Do you never tire?'

'I'd like to, but can't,' I smile, 'though it means never properly relaxing.'

'No problem, then,' he smiles, lowering himself into the visitor's chair.

The more serious the business, the longer the preliminaries.

'Your mother, how is she? On the mend?' he asks, to my surprise.

'You know about that, do you? After a fortune's worth of medication, yes . . .'

Not wanting to drag things out and having other plans for the day, I glance at my watch.

'Don't you feel a bit cramped here?' he asks, surveying my spacious office.

'No,' I say, not sure what this is in aid of: a test of my general contentment or of my readiness to accept promotion.

To me, now a Deputy Minister, the next rung holds no appeal. Deputies tend to survive longer than their Ministers. And I don't crave the limelight.

'I wouldn't have thought you were sufficiently extended. I can tell who's not up to a job, and can also see who can do so much more. And lately I'd say you're in the latter class . . .'

'Coffee?'

He nods.

I ask Nila to serve mocha.

'We've a vacancy at Bank Street,' he says sotto voce. 'Same money, but more joy, more responsibility, of course. Give it thought, and I'll ring' – producing his electronic notepad – 'on Wednesday at eleven.'

Finding the coffee too strong, he takes three teaspoonfuls of sugar.

'Sweet tooth. Family trait,' he says with a smile. 'None of us diabetic, though.'

He goes off, leaving another of his cards – a strange habit of his, like something out of a detective story. I pick it up and am about to bin it when it occurs to me that I don't know where my rubbish goes after the cleaner has emptied the bins. It could end up on some-body's desk. Never forget: the nearer the sun, the greater the heat!

Glancing through the lengthy list of titles and appointments, I spot one extra: Academician of the European Academy of Management. That does it. Tearing the card in half I insert it over the one already in my card index.

'Sergey Pavlovich, Vasya's waiting with the car you ordered for three,' Nila informs me.

'I'm out for the rest of the day,' I say as I leave.

*

Sitting waiting at a table in the USSR restaurant behind the Caves Monastery, Svetlana Vilenskaya is so like her sister as to be instantly recognisable.

I apologise for being late, and when a waiter sporting a Young Pioneer red scarf appears with the menu, I ask what she would like. We settle for a salad and a glass of muscat.

She looks in her mid-thirties, but whether she is older or younger than Valya is hard to tell.

'You know my brother is also in the home at Glukhovka. The doctor-in-charge said that the diagnosis for your sister and my brother is similar,' I begin.

She is watching me attentively. Very attentively. Under a stylishly short, unbuttoned jacket, she wears a close-fitting jumper and skintight jeans.

'Has your brother been there long?' she asks.

'He was in a home near Kiev, but he's been in Glukhovka for three years now. And Valya?'

'Not so long, a little over a year. Nikolai Petrovich said –'

'Yes, when he mentioned the similarity of the diagnosis, I thought that we might try this new therapy together. Do you know anything about it? I'm not a doctor, let alone a psychiatrist. Apparently colour therapy was developed by the Germans. They select a colour that has a calming effect on the patient and one that stimulates the patient to focus on reality. During treatment patients live in a special apartment decorated in those colours.'

'Money's not a problem,' says Svetlana calmly. 'I'd just like it to work.'

'We might be able to manage without money. I'll try to do something through the Ministry of Health. It's a new clinic, only just got its licence. What do you do?'

'I deal in honey,' she replies. 'Honey export.'

'Really?'

'Yes. The market's there for the taking. I could sell three times what I do – demand is huge.'

'So if you have nothing against my suggestion, leave me your card and I'll let you know how things go?' I conclude, suddenly feeling a bit tongue-tied and foolish.

Her card is simple: name, telephone and fax number.

33

Moscow, October 2014

To fly to Mongolia and not pop in on Moscow on the way back would have been foolish, given Russia's keen interest in keeping tabs on the strategic plans of its neighbours.

'What is it exactly that makes Mongolia a strategic partner for Ukraine?' asks the Deputy Speaker of the Duma, genuinely surprised. 'What, apart from leather, have they got?'

'We've signed seventy-two contracts,' I announce with pride. 'Half of them for leather and the leather industry, yes – one's governed by the possible. The leather field is equally open to you.'

Where do they find these giants? I ask myself, gazing up at the Deputy Speaker who is blond, blue-eyed, red-bearded and two metres tall: the pure Aryan Hitler dreamed of but never achieved. My neck aches from looking up at him, an unbecoming situation given my superior status.

'Shall we sit down?' I ask, seeing he is not going to take the initiative.

'Yes, of course,' says the Russian Aryan. 'We'll go to the parlour. The Prime Minister's with the German Chancellor in the audience chamber.'

The *parlour* – local parlance! – is simply a small sitting room like fifteen or so others in the Kremlin Palace, with leather armchairs and a smart dark-suited servant in attendance.

A nod from the Deputy Speaker, and in no time an enormous bowl of fresh fruit appears, together with mineral water and crystal goblets.

'That flap a couple of days ago – what was it?' he asks out of the blue.

'The night sitting?'

'The night sitting, Mr President.'

'The prescribed response to a call for urgent measures,' I say, suddenly realising that for two days I have heard nothing. 'And all's quiet now.'

'A statesmanlike solution that worked,' he says approvingly.

Instant relief. My spirits rise. Now we are seated, Aryan no longer seems so enormous. Indeed the reverse. Fancying an apple, I take the largest, and seeing neither fruit knife nor plate, bite into it with a crunch that fills the parlour. The Deputy Speaker looks on clearly amazed by the boldness of his guest.

Having finished my apple, I suggest that he should consider opening a couple of joint leather-processing plants in the free frontier area above Kharkov.

He promises to come back to me within a week, and on that we part.

★

'All's well at home, as I should have told you earlier,' says Nikolai Lvovich sitting with a glass of mineral water opposite me on the plane. 'Cheap energy's gone down well. Even been a demonstration in support.'

'What about Mongolia? Is that going to be all right?'

'The Mongolians need an outlet into the European market to distribute fur and leather. Turkey is the only competition. We're closer to Europe; we've a good workforce, and our own market's not that bad . . . potential sales of three to four billion dollars a year, at a rough calculation, six thousand new jobs . . .'

'Good.'

Laboriously we lift off from Russian soil. Could it be there are buried magnets? My one thought is home and to bed as quickly as possible.

34

Kiev, October 2003

Dogmazov is driving me from office to office in his black Volga, introducing me to new people, parading me like a marriageable girl before suitors, although mercifully without my having to show the state of my teeth. Our next port of call is a block of flats at the top end of Vladimir Street. On the second floor we stop before an armour-plated door bearing neither name nor number. We are received by a security guard in camouflage fatigues. A young man in suit and tie then appears and conducts us along the long corridor of what must once have been a communal flat. At the end of it, a vast office with framed diplomas on the walls, and seated behind a polished desk, a bald, slightly hunchbacked man of about fifty, both hands resting on the tabletop, displaying two massive rings on podgy fingers, beside his right hand a large calculator.

'Here he is, the one I mentioned, Bunin, Sergey Pavlovich,' says Dogmazov.

'Good name,' says the bald man. 'I've heard it somewhere before.' Then, 'Adaptable?' he asks, abandoning the attempt to remember when it was he heard it.

'I believe so.'

'And in five years' time, still under fifty?'

'Yes.'

'No chronic illnesses?'

'No.'

'Good.' He turns to Dogmazov. 'We'll speak tomorrow.'

And that is the end of our eighth visit of the day, all similar in tone.

'Home or to work?' Dogmazov asks when we are outside.

'Home,' I say.

35

Kiev, July 2015, Monday, 7 a.m.

Waiting in my sitting room, a silver coffee pot and silver dish of hot pirozhki. And as the coffee entered the delicate china, the bells of St Andrew's ring out as requested. What better on so fine a sunny morning than to feel closer to God and earning His approval.

No, I haven't become a believer, but I have ceased to be an atheist. The importance of the Church and the importance of faith are, I realise, two different things. The Church, as part of the state system, is very important at election time. Faith provides the grounds and stimulus for believer voters to put their trust in the Church. Apart from which it's beautiful and like foreign theatre – incomprehensible without translation, but still a pleasure to watch.

And, on the subject of theatre, in two days I go to see Zdoba, the sculptor – presidential concern for the arts being the agreeable side of home politics.

'Nikolai Lvovich to see you,' announces my aide, and I think I know why.

'Sorry to be so early, but there's been a nasty kidnapping in Russia I thought you should know about: Maritime Region Governor, five deputies and twelve heads of departments, eight of them ethnic Ukrainians. If it's a Chechen job, we could step in and show the Russians how to negotiate.'

'But they'll all have Russian passports, so why get involved?'

'In situations like this Russia is grateful for help. I'll keep you briefed.'

'Do.'

Much as it jars against the sound of the bells, Nikolai Lvovich's visit does nothing to spoil my mood. I send for Svetlov, and twenty minutes later he joins me for coffee.

The Maritime bunch are, as I suspected, at that moment on their way to Ukraine by air. Other Hands Op success No. 1. The *other hands* being ours.

'We've built them a nice little prison in the Carpathians. With a capacity for three hundred,' says Svetlov. 'We used Turkish builders

– told them it was a hotel. So first-class accommodation. The perimeter is the work of the finest army engineers.'

'So now we're Russia's Cuba,' I laugh.

'How so?'

'Guantánamo for their Taliban.' But the joke is lost on Svetlov.

'I must make up the list for their operation. It'll be in Zaporozhe region. High time we introduced some order there.'

'Good. And replacements for the resulting vacancies?'

'In hand. Mainly former State Security people.'

'Fine, only give the army a thought, so they don't feel left out.'

'OK, we'll have a few from the army.'

'Have some of these nice fresh pirozhki.'

As we sit enjoying the refreshments it occurs to me that Monday, properly begun with bells, coffee and strawberry pirozhki, could be the very best day of the week.

36

Kiev, 31 December, 1984

It's a blizzard and a half; the street a stinging, blinding wall of snow, all blackness, lamps no more than blurred fairy-tale yellow flowers on concrete stalks.

The collar of my sheepskin coat is raised tight against the ear flaps of my rabbit-fur cap, leaving only my eyes exposed to the blizzard; that is just bearable.

With two bottles of cognac and one of Cypriot muscat in a carrier bag, I am on my way to see the New Year in at the District Militia –

my best and only option. Zhenya was called up for military service a month ago. And the romantically minded girl where I bought vegetables scared me stiff by agitating to celebrate New Year *with me and my folks*. So rather than flee ignominiously, I told her I thought I had syphilis, at which she shot off home to Vinnitsa. That was a week ago, and I still shiver at the thought of having ever got to know her. Was I drunk?

So only the militia are pleased to see me. Of course. I'm known to them, and I've even helped solve their end-of-year informants quota deficit by signing on as unpaid part-time militia officer, and gladly, seeing how they had helped over our battle. Now I am reaping my reward, and Husseinov has just been promoted to Senior Lieutenant.

The militia, in the shape of Sergeant Vanya, take charge of my bottles and there's a clink-clink as they join the vodka and champagne already in the fridge. It's 10 p.m.

I help move two desks to form a great square tabletop, and ask for a cloth.

'Coming up,' laughs Sergeant Vanya, darting away and returning with an enormous laminated political map of the world.

It fails, when laid, to overhang the edges in the approved fashion, but it does cover the desks, which is the main thing.

At eleven we sit at table, awkwardly side-on, because of the desk drawers.

Before us, sliced sausage, smoked pork fat, bread, bottles and glasses. Another sergeant brings in huge bowls of salad.

Fifteen minutes short of midnight sees us all well oiled and merry.

'Forgotten something!' declares Husseinov suddenly, clutching his head. '*As New Year is begun, so will it be lived!*'

And off he marches with a spring in his step, blue tunic open almost to his belly button on account of the heat.

'Look lively!' he calls, and I look towards the door to see who he is ushering in. Two heavily made up, scantly clad girls appear.

'Sit yourselves down, girls. How could we have forgotten you?' Husseinov clears a space for the 'girls' who turn out to be two of five prostitutes arrested that morning, the others having been transferred to District Internal Affairs and now I understand why.

Sergeant Vanya pours them vodka.

'Begin the New Year with those you'll live it with! You've some catching up to do, girls, and champagne's on the way.'

The girls drain their glasses and set about the smoked pork fat. Husseinov opens the champagne, and switches on the television just as the Moscow chimes ring out.

'A happy New Year to you!' booms the mighty bass of an announcer hidden behind a wintry view of the Kremlin.

The party begins to take off. To Alla Pugachova's 'Sorcerer's Apprentice' on tape, the girls, at Senior Lieutenant Husseinov's request, strip off and dance on the table.

Seeing the wretched girls being given my cognac while I get vodka, I make a show of indignation.

'Look,' says Vanya, 'they've a hard life – don't begrudge them a bit of New Year happiness. They're of the proletariat – you're not. It's them who get fucked, not you.'

I am about to object to this drunken codswallop, but another vodka, and I am in full agreement.

By 4 a.m. peroxide-blonde Sonya is in my lap, with me gazing into the pink mist of her red unfocused eyes.

Husseinov makes strong tea to sober us up.

'The party's over,' he announces wearily, 'Get out of here, you, before the major turns up . . . You girls sod off too. General amnesty! No charges, but leave your phone numbers.' Then, turning to me, 'Bin the bottles and rubbish, and thanks for coming . . .'

I try to stand, and after a tremendous effort manage to.

The early hours of 1985 feel amazingly fresh like the freshest of fresh Doctor's Health Sausage. Done with celebrating, the city sleeps. The snow sparkles in the light of the street lamps.

I feel joyously weightless at heart, heady with champagne, and my legs the worse for the vodka, borne up, carried forward towards a bright future.

37

Kiev, October 2003

The sun is blinding. My ancient Opel, after two days' servicing, is a different car.

'Thirty-five thousand Swiss francs sounds a lot, but in euros that's 23,000,' I say, looking to see how Svetlana takes it. Her beautiful face is a picture of calmness.

'No problem,' she says.

I am struck more by the music of her voice than the sense of what she says, though, on reflection, I am relieved by her words. For me it would be problematic, not to say painful, to lay out that sort of money so that Dima can attend some Swiss clinic. I will have to learn to be equally generous. Is honey really that profitable? Maybe that's what I should be going for, rather than power?

Thirty kilometres short of Glukhovka, with my stomach rumbling, we decide to stop for a bite to eat.

Parked by the roadside café are two lorries with trailers, and sitting together in the café, the drivers. There's a smell of borscht and fritters.

'How do they make a living with prices like these?' I ask, looking at the menu.

'Small business is on its uppers, no one has any money. For me, cabbage salad and apple juice.'

'That all? It is lunchtime.'

'I always have that for lunch.'

For me, borscht without garlic rolls and a cutlet with buckwheat.

We exchange a few glances while we eat, but the conversation goes no further than mere pleasantries.

We have coffee at the nursing home with the doctor-in-charge who is a bit taken aback by our decision.

'But what about the last session of colour therapy?'

'It's a rare case,' I begin, retelling what the doctor from the private clinic told me. 'Neither of them notice colour at all. The only colours they react to are orange and red and those drive them into a corner.'

'That's normal,' says the doctor, and now I am surprised. 'For them, I mean, not to notice things is normal.'

Svetlana sits drinking her coffee in silence, contemplating the polished wooden floor.

The doctor goes over to the window.

'They have become inseparable,' he says, beckoning us to join.

They are crossing the lawn together, apparently hand in hand.

'Is it possible for them to form relationships?' I ask.

'Attachments occur, and more intensely than with the healthy. I can think of two cases, but their complete recovery was followed by relapse.'

'How so?' asks Svetlana.

'Personal involvement acts like a drug, but lasts only as long as the illness. The patient's perception of the world is altered.'

I listen, while continuing to watch them, Dima in his blue woollen tracksuit, Valya the same mauve ankle-length dressing gown. Halting suddenly, they turn to each other, looking into each other's eyes, as if about to kiss.

'They complement each other,' says the doctor. 'Therapy may not have helped so far, but it's brought them together. And now they're attuning to a common perception of their environment.'

'Do they eat together?' asks Svetlana.

'They sit opposite each other.'

'Talking normally?'

'If they could do that, they wouldn't be here.'

'Time we were heading back to Kiev,' says Svetlana. 'I've a meeting at five thirty.'

'I'll have the release papers ready by Monday,' the doctor says as we get up to leave.

38

Kiev, July 2015, Friday

'What's the oil?' I ask Sonya, removing my shirt.

'A mixture. Nutmeg, milk –' and dropping to a whisper – 'opium poppy and propolis.'

Naked, I lie face down on the couch.

Sonya strips to bathing costume, washes and dries her hands at the little basin in the corner. My back senses her approach. Heavy oily drops descend onto my shoulders for powerful fingers to rub in ever widening circles into my flesh.

Sonya is a former world champion gymnast, and world champion gymnasts pass on as easily into Health as former People's Deputies into prison or government service. Yet more proof that sport is better for you than politics.

'Relax!' The fingers proceed along my arms stretched beside my body.

After my massage I stand for some minutes before the wall mirror in the recovery room examining my naked body, wondering whether my freckles really were, as Sonya claimed, a lighter colour. But now my chest hair shaved for the operation is back; some of it has a reddish tinge. That's all I need. I am in the process of plucking out the really red hairs when Nikolai Lvovich calls through the door, 'Mr President, the Albanian Ambassador.'

Reluctantly I dress, increasingly depressed by the thought of my red hairs.

The Albanian Ambassador proves to be a pleasant lady of forty. She presents me with her letters of accreditation, we exchange set phrases about improving Albano-Ukrainian relations, and that is that.

'You have agreed to have coffee with Mayya Vladimirovna today,' says Nikolai Lvovich.

'Where?'

'At home in Desatinaya Street. She's there already.'

'She's waiting for me in my apartment?'

He purses his lips, clearly not in a good mood, which is usually the case when Mayya Vladimirovna is the subject of discussion.

'She's waiting at your official residence as President,' he says grimly.

'How long will this coffee drinking last?'

'Half an hour. And you smell of nutmeg,' he adds, softening.

'So?'

'Nothing women like better.'

I have a very strong urge to box his ears, but presidents have to ignore their urges, at least sometimes.

39

Kiev, January 1985

'When are you going to find yourself a job?' is Mother's morning call.

Opening my eyes with difficulty, first I see the clock – it's 7.45 – then my brother peacefully asleep in the bed opposite. Being less than normal has its plus side. 'Dima, drink your nice milk and honey! Dima, eat your nice buckwheat porridge and butter!'

He is sleeping with his face towards me, and seems to be dreaming, widening his nostrils like a horse.

How can that be my twin? I wonder, watching his face twitch. We have nothing in common. Well, not quite nothing. There are points of similarity – same forehead, same dimples, same eyebrows meeting in the middle. But not in the way we laugh and smile. There we differ totally. His voice, which is that of an aggrieved thirteen-year-old, is peculiarly his. I didn't sound like that even at thirteen, or at twelve or ten, come to that.

'Get up! Now!' orders Mother, returning. 'Doctor's coming to see Dima at ten, so see you're here to let him in and remember whatever he tells you!'

Slowly I lower my feet to the floor and sit on the edge of the bed. I yelp as the cold linoleum stings my feet.

'Not much of a help with the draught-excluding, are you?'

With Mother the rhetorical is the norm. Only when giving instructions does she await some sign of response, if only a nod of the head.

After eight, she's gone to work, peace. I can go back to bed, but I sit in my pyjamas on a cold kitchen stool. Ultimately I shiver myself into activity, and light the gas under the frying pan of kasha and two sausages which Mother has left ready for my breakfast. Later, when he wakes, I'll boil Dima a couple of eggs and see that he doesn't eat any shell, which he never does, being neither a fool nor a halfwit. In all likelihood he is normal, brighter than me even, and simply playing the harmless nutcase. That way he is less of a burden to Mother than I am. She expects nothing from him, though she does receive some sort of an allowance. It is me who is the parasite, the forever layabout with no position in life. I find every job I try a bore.

Once again Mother has left the blue booklet that is my Work Record on the sideboard for all to see. Right then, I'll take it and have another shot at qualifying at something – only something that

I have not so far done. I've done manual work, loading and unloading trucks, laid asphalt – stunk of tar for three weeks after. So now what?

As I light the gas under the frying pan, a cockroach scuttles out in alarm. Seeing me, it doubles back and nips into a crack between the stove and the dirty green tiling.

'Don't worry,' I tell him. 'I'm as much a parasite as you are. Just look different.'

Suddenly more cheerful and filled with an urge to do something, I start cleaning the tiled area around the stove with a rag soaked in a solution of household soda and water. The smell of burning sausage reminds me to turn off the gas, by which time the tiles are free of grease and gleaming. We'll see what Mother has to say about *that* when she gets back!

It is snowing, and everything is astonishingly white and clean. Pressing my nose to the cold pane, I look down. Our caretaker has dug narrow paths through the snow, along which warmly clad women with shopping baskets are making their way, like so many tiny, plump, black hedgehogs, in quest of herring or sausage. All leading valuable Soviet lives.

40

Kiev, July 2015, Friday

'Freckles suit you,' says Mayya Vladimirovna with the ghost of a smile.

She is wearing a blue summer frock patterned with tiny pale

70

yellow flowers and drawn in at the waist with a narrow belt, neat chestnut hair fastened by an enamel butterfly pin, no make-up evident on her face.

'If in doubt, wear the same colour,' my mother advised, helping me to prepare for my first grown-up date. The girl, whose name I forget, didn't turn up. Instead she sent her younger brother with a photograph inscribed *'Remember me like this. My fiancé got back from the army today. Love.'*

'Did your husband have freckles?' I ask.

'Very slightly. You had to look hard,' she says with a little laugh and, at last, a proper smile.

Setting down a tray on the little table between us, a maid served coffee in exquisite china cups.

'So, what can I do for you?' I ask, stirring my cup.

'For me, nothing – Igor's heart is what concerns me,' she says, clearly surprised, lowering her eyes to its location.

'Nikolai Lvovich said there was a contract.'

'Haven't you seen it?' she asks.

'No.'

She nods, as if at last understanding my difficulty.

'I could fetch you a copy.'

'No, don't worry. In five minutes I must be off,' I say, looking at the grandfather clock.

'You really ought to see it,' she says sadly.

41

St Andrew's Descent is dreary and deserted. I must have been mad to set off down its ice-glazed cobbles to Podol. I'm only halfway down and I've already fallen three times, so I cross over to the right so as to use the cold walls of the buildings for support, the yellow light from their windows forming great moon-like blobs on the uneven glaze at my feet. Here, all windows ablaze, is Richard's Castle. I've often visited a friend in an enormous communal flat on the first floor – all wooden floors, giant cockroaches and scent of kitchen soap: the brown stuff eternally priced at nineteen kopeks a bar. Automatically I sniff the frosty night air in hopes of catching the familiar whiff of it. But the air smells of nothing. Frost is odourless. Odour comes with thaw.

I fall twice more before reaching the bottom of the Descent, where I take a left turn into an alley, and straight ahead is the artificial limb workshop and my rendezvous with Nadya. I knock on the wooden door and peer through a window at an unusual greenish light. Nadya looks about thirty, which would make her six years my senior; though only in years, not wisdom. Talking to Nadya on any subject makes you want to ruffle her auburn hair, and tell her to read more and wake up. But otherwise, silent or sighing, Nadya is lovely.

The door opens, and Nadya, still in working overalls, drags me in and flings her arms around me, smothering me with kisses, while telling me how cold I am.

The bottle of dessert wine, three cabbage pasties and two patterned glasses standing on a stool by the glowing spiral of a primitive home-made electric fire formed as fine a still-life subject as any painter could have wished for.

'What if someone comes?' I ask.

'They won't. The boss has gone to his mistress, the limb-maker's on the bottle and won't be seen for three days.'

It doesn't take long to finish a bottle of dessert wine, and covering the protruding springs of the busted couch with three thicknesses of canvas, we soon snuggle down under a striped rug. Just for a laugh I take an artificial leg in with us. In turn I stroke Nadia's leg and then the future leg of an invalid. We both find it funny. We're both cheerful and warm.

'Wouldn't you like to marry?' Nadya asks.

'You, do you mean?'

'Well, yes.'

'What would we do if we did?'

'The same as we're doing now,' she says happily.

'So why get married?'

We both laugh and I throw out the wooden leg which falls with a crash onto the wooden floor.

'How come you've got such small breasts?' I ask.

'Better small and firm than big and flabby. You can kiss them. But gently. Gently!'

I am learning, though by now I should have known more, if not everything.

'That's right. And now here,' she whispers, guiding my hand down.

How easy it is to do what a woman wants. How easy and natural!

Someone taps at the window. I freeze. We should have turned the light out.

'Who is it?' calls Nadya.

'Vasya there?'

'At home, boozing.'

Getting up, I turn off the light, leaving only the red glow of the heater.

I slip back under the rug to continue our wonderful winter evening. The falls and bruises suffered on the way here no longer matter. Going back would be easier than coming down. The pain of the descent was worth it!

42

Borispol Airport, November 2003

Yesterday's trawl round the shops with Svetlana to fit Valya and Dima out for Switzerland had the makings of a film. Neither, to begin with, showed any interest. But when Svetlana brought Valya out of the dressing room wearing a short leather jacket with a fur collar, I saw Dima's eyes light up. Guided by Valya, he tried on suits, sweaters, blazers, and all we had to do was present our credit cards. Svetlana won in the generosity stakes, by my calculation, laying out a good 10,000 hryvnas to my 6,000. But then I did resist Svetlana's advice to buy Dima a dozen Italian ties.

When at last the boarding call for the Zurich flight comes, we set off down the green corridor, having, on the advice of their consultant, arranged that Dima and Valya should not be asked the normal questions such as purpose of journey.

I embrace Dima, promising to fly out and visit him.

'Will Mother visit too?'

'Of course.'

Svetlana and Valya are hugging each other in tears.

'Dima, you will look after her?' I ask.

'Shan't let her out of my sight! I'd do anything for her,' he declares with a look of determination that I find alarming.

'Within reason, of course,' I whisper, but he shakes his head.

43

Kiev, July 2015, Sunday

At dawn it was sunny, then an evil vast black cloud descended, casting gloom over all. I've come to look out of the bathroom window, the only one in the end wall of the block, made at the whim of a previous first lady. Seen from the outside, it looks odd, but it gives onto the dome of St Andrew's, now especially beautiful in the strange light heralding a thunderstorm.

Turning away for just a moment, I tell my aide to bring me my coffee here. The window ledge is deep and smooth; I could use it for lunching off occasionally, just me, on my own. You only realise how valuable your solitude is when you find yourself beginning to gag at the sight of certain individuals; you become so sick of their constant presence. Then the simple pleasure of breakfast in isolation seems priceless.

As the sky darkens, the dome loses its lustre, and suddenly hailstones the size of hazelnuts are bouncing off the copper cornice. We are under bombardment. A handful of tourists standing by the Pronya Prokovna Serkova monument sprint to join others under the blue awning of a beer tent. I look up at Desatinaya Church, in which hundreds once sought sanctuary from the Tatars, now hideously rebuilt on its own ruins and their bodies.

Watching the hail rain down, I can see what might have led to the invention of the bomber.

The silver coffee pot looks remarkably fine on the greenish marble of the window ledge. Moving back a couple of steps, I stoop and align coffee pot and dome. Beautiful!

My aide pours coffee and leaves a hot croissant.

Feather-light, it melts on the tongue, delightfully replacing the fifty-year old Martell cognac lingering on my palate from the night.

'Telephone call from Nikolai Lvovich, Mr President,' announces my aide.

'What about?' I ask, without turning from the window.

'He says there's a hailstorm.'

'That all?'

'No, he's anxious to see you for ten minutes. Now.'

He is improving. Two days ago I kicked him out when he came to my bedroom at half past midnight with 'papers for my signature'. Experience dictates never sign anything in the small hours. In your desperation to get back to sleep, it's far too easy to miss something (if you read the documents at all).

I receive him in the bathroom. He is carrying a leather folder. I wonder simultaneously what papers are inside and where I should ask him to sit. There's only the bidet and the toilet and the bidet has no lid.

'Have a seat,' I say, indicating the toilet.

He looks round at the seating I propose, barely hiding his indignation.

'Go on. Sit down!' I insist.

With ill grace he sits, but quickly jumps up again.

'I wanted to apologise for the other night,' he says.

I nod.

'I've got some new government proposals,' he says, opening the folder. 'This one from Mykola is of interest.'

'And what is the Deputy Prime Minister suggesting?'

'A regional experiment to raise the level of patriotic awareness . . .'

'Like a coming-of-age presentation of ID cards in church?'

'But just in the western region to begin with, and just Greek Catholics.'

'Show me.'

He has done well, my Minister of Humanities, this three-page plan is a great improvement on his last effort.

'Good. Very interesting,' I say, placing the sheets on the window ledge. 'Let him go ahead. Not all churches, only those in the regional centres. Sort of mass baptism. And you had better make a note,' I add, noticing that Nikolai Lvovich seems slow on the uptake today.

Perking up, he perches on the toilet with paper and pen.

'"In accordance with the proposals of the Deputy Prime Minister charged with Humanitarian Affairs, to be organised in Lvov, Ivano-Frankovsk and Rovno two days in advance of Independence Day by the Greek Catholic Church, a solemn presentation of Ukrainian ID cards passports to all who this year, 2015, reach their sixteenth year. Oath of allegiance to be submitted for approval within the week. Mykola to execute, you to oversee." OK?'

'And something else to do with identity,' he says, pulling out a sheet of paper. There's a new fashion for German passports in Parliament. To date, twenty-seven Deputies have got one, and Kazimir the electricity oligarch.

'How about Israeli?'

'Israeli: eighteen; Panamanian: three; Costa Rican: two; and Venezuelan: one.'

'So put your thinking cap on,' I say beginning to feel angry. 'It's patriots we want, not rats about to jump ship. I'll see Svetlov tomorrow at one.'

'At one you're lunching with Mayya Vladimirovna.'

'Sod that! Make it breakfast, and bring me that bloody contract so I know how to talk to her!'

'I have,' says Nikolai Lvovich seeking to calm me, 'taken the liberty of bringing in a specialist.'

'In freckles?'

'No, stress. The best we have. Treats Luxembourg bankers.'

'The ones who work here?'

'Yes.'

'Have him here tomorrow after breakfast. And the Voytsekhovskaya contract on my desk by this evening.'

He gets up off the toilet seat and proceeds to dust himself down as if fearful of being somehow contaminated.

Through the window I see that the hail has passed.

44

Kiev, February 1985

'I'll finish drinking then jump to hell out of here!' says Husseinov, leaning far out over the bridge rail.

I pull him back by the collar of his short ratine overcoat. The wind, there on the footbridge, is murderous, threatening to blow over our second bottle of vodka, of which we've only drunk half.

'How can I look my father in the face?' he asks in despair.

'Don't talk like that. They could have put you inside. You're not going to be a militia officer, that's all.'

'What am I going to be? They've taken my gun. They'll not have my uniform, even though I can't wear it!'

'Home in Dagestan you can wear it, as much as you like.'

He seems somewhat reassured by this.

'It was the only thing I could do, you see. Imagine if it had been *your* first cousin once removed in the cooler, and *you* his guard. He'd tell your folks. Let's face it, you'd do as I did, let him go.'

I shake my head.

'You wouldn't?' He is flabbergasted.

'No.'

'Not if it was someone you'd grown up with?'

'No.'

He sighs, recovers the bottle, takes a long swig and passes it to me.

I drink, though revolted by the stuff, gazing sideways towards Trukhanov Island, a strange land of bare trees and an indistinct snowy shoreline.

'With us it's different,' said Husseinov. 'The younger ones who get caught for something, we belt or punch, and let go. The older ones we just let go. We Dagestanis can't lock up our own, we just can't. We're thin on the ground as it is, and almost all related.'

'Well, we're thick on the ground and practically nothing to each other. Tell you what, when I'm General Secretary of the Communist Party I'll get the militia to reinstate you.'

The empty bottle rolls, tinkling away across the deserted bridge. The bridge itself seems to be rocking. Or maybe it's us.

I figure we're exactly halfway across the bridge.

'Come on,' says Husseinov, nodding towards the island.

'Right.'

The island is closer now, but it is beginning to snow, so we crack on, so as to keep it in sight. It snows harder. The snow thickens. The cold is bracing, helping clear the head but doing nothing to steady the legs.

Then a whiteout. And nothing. I have no idea where Husseinov is or where the island lies.

I recover and press on, not knowing where, until with a sudden loud crack, my feet break through into icy wet and sink a good metre and a half deep before touching terra firma. Stretching out my arms, I rest them on the ice around me. I feel good – horribly cold, and good.

'Getting this drunk could be the death of you!' comes an elderly voice from above. I'm no longer standing upright in an ice hole, but lying on a camp bed under a rug, a blanket and a sheepskin jacket. Beside me, the comforting warmth of a tiny stove and, sitting on a stool, a hook-nosed old man.

'To think – destroying a good healthy body like that! Falling asleep in an ice hole! Dreaming, were we?'

I stare uncomprehendingly.

'What is it? Unhappy love? Trouble at work?' he continues, pressing me to speak.

Unhappy love? Yes! Yesterday Nadya didn't let me in, and I heard a man's voice. So I went back to Nivki and the District Militia in search of a bit of comfort, only to find trouble. Husseinov had released a Dagestani, a distant relative of his, caught red-handed rifling a flat. So there it was, a chain of events: from unhappy love to the Trukhanov Island ice hole.

'Drink this.' The old man thrusts a little glass at me.

I don't want to, but do and it leaves a strange sweetish aftertaste.

'What was it?' I ask.

'Nettle tea.'

'And you pulled me out?'

He nods. 'I did, then I came back for the sledge to bring you back here. Took two hours. Never thought you'd live.'

'What about Husseinov?'

'There was just you, no one else.'

The old man is, it emerges, Trukhanov Island's last inhabitant, living in this dugout to commemorate the now defunct settlement, and by way of protest. His wife and daughter accepted the offer of a room in a communal flat, but not he.

'May I ask your name?'

'David Isaakovich.'

45

Leukerbad, Switzerland, February 2004
Shown around the clinic by a nurse in belted blue uniform with starched collar wearing her watch like a medal, I suddenly feel like a patient myself.

Gleaming floors, artificial scent of spring flowers, views of snow-covered mountains. Pausing by one of the windows and pointing, the nurse speaks in German. That, Natasha, our embassy interpreter translates, is the covered area for patients to walk in. Swiss mountain air is amazingly beneficial. I, in the manner of the fool intelligently and authoritatively addressed, nod. Svetlana asks what cultural programme or therapy is offered.

'They're not cutting edge technologically, but do have a lot of pictures,' reports Natasha, gesturing, as the nurse had done, at the wall where hung the most banal landscape possible: mountain background, meadow, grazing cow, shepherd boy sitting against tree.

Maliciously I ask Natasha to enquire about the breed of cow.

'Brown Alpine,' comes the answer.

Again I nod, again feeling a fool. And wishing the tour would end, knowing it won't until we have been shown every detail of what we're paying for.

Another half-hour, and we are left in peace, in leather armchairs so deep that when Dima and Valya come in, we are hard put to get up.

Dima embraces me with tears in his eyes. Rosy-cheeked, the picture of health, he must have drunk daily of Brown Alpine milk.

'How are you getting on here?'

He presses me to him with all his strength.

'Well, really well. Except for the German. I've asked for a tutor, but they won't provide one.'

'Maybe they've not understood you.'

'I asked in writing which they faxed to a translator, and the answer was no. Tell them they must give me one.'

'It's not for me to tell them what to do. I just pay.'

'Well, pay for a tutor!'

'I can't without their OK. I'll speak to them.'

'More important, though,' his voice drops to a whisper, 'is that Valya has agreed to marry me . . .'

I look to where Svetlana and Valya are whispering together.

'And you'll help,' Dima insists.

'I'll talk to your doctor,' I promise, seeing that my answer does not go down well.

I need time to think, and so does Svetlana judging from her expression as she whispers with her sister.

The professor-in-charge, whom we consult ten minutes later, is optimistic.

'It's a striving for normality,' he says, 'which should, so far as possible, be supported, only that would require the written approval of you both. Initially, I would leave it at civil marriage. They could move to a double room, create a family-flat atmosphere, care for the room themselves . . . Interesting study. Material for a paper . . .'

Aged about sixty, hair *en brosse*, thin, he looks as if he had stopped growing at thirteen.

'What do you think?' Natasha translates.

'I'm against civil marriage,' says Svetlana. 'They'll have no sense of responsibility.'

'The sick have a more developed sense of responsibility than the healthy,' says the professor. 'But if you insist, the legal side of the matter will be your decision.'

The legal side involves no more than verification of the first pages of Dima and Valya's passports before a notary, and other documents which our embassy obliges over.

46

Kiev, July 2015

Within a quarter of an hour of my receiving the Mayya Voytsekhovskaya contract, the stress expert appeared, a two-metre giant of a man of non-Slav appearance in a close-fitting suit. Meeting him in the street you would have taken him for an Italian male model. Not that I ever did meet people in the street, my thoroughfares being of the indoor carpeted variety.

'Nikolai Lvovich will have told you –'

'He has,' I cut him short, laying aside the idiotic contract, 'so get on with it.'

'What?'

'Ridding me of stress.'

'I would need first to determine the cause.'

'So read that,' I said, indicating the contract.

Donning his glasses he picked up the first page. His at first 'intelligent reader' expression was suddenly replaced by a 'scared boy' one and he only just saved his glasses from falling.

'I can't . . . It's secret . . . Don't tell Nikolai Lvovich that I read it! '

'Then treat me without reading it.' I sighed, realising that it was now he who was most in need of stress relief. I offered him a drink.

'Have you had a transplant?' I asked, after a second glass of cognac.

'No.'

'Well, don't.'

The cognac was working and I stopped thinking about the contract for a while. 'Tell me, which other of my people are you treating?'

'Apart from Nikolai Lvovich . . .' his eyes rolled up as if his memory had dissolved in the cognac, 'Pyotr Alekseyevich, and Semyon Vladimirovich –'

'Who's he?'

'Your premier adviser on marriage and family matters.'

'Really? And Nikolai Lvovich, is he a frequent sufferer?'

'He suffers daily.'

'And how do you treat him?'

'Sometimes like this.' He nodded towards his glass. 'Sometimes acupuncture. But he's afraid of needles.'

'And Semyon Vladimirovich?'

'Also, daily.'

'What's his problem?'

'Persecution mania.'

'Who's persecuting him?'

'He thinks you are.'

'I don't even know the man. How long has he been with us?'

'A year.'

'Good grief!' I looked towards the door and shouted for my aide. 'Get Nikolai Lvovich in here now!'

When he arrived, I demanded who the hell Semyon Vladimirovich was.

'Mayya Vladimirovna's brother.'

'Have some,' I said, indicating the bottle.

I watched his hand as he poured. It was shaking more than the stress specialist's had when he raised his glass.

'So one whole year before my operation, *you* took on an adviser whom I have never since seen!'

'Calm down,' said Nikolai Lvovich, hurrying from the room, 'think of your heart. I must just pop out. I'll be back.'

I picked up the contract and read aloud: '*Success or failure of operation notwithstanding, the heart shall remain the property of Mayya Vladimirovna Voytsekhovskaya, and be returnable when no longer required.*'

'An extremely stressful situation . . . traditional methods are of no use,' said the expert, blinking and staring at the cognac in his glass.

'Such as?'

'Drink,' he said, eyeing the bottle, 'or vigorous sex.'

'So what is the answer?' I demanded.

'Well, there is aggressive work therapy.'

'As in the army?' I asked, interested. '"Dig a ditch for as long as it takes"?'

'Something of the sort, but I'd have to check with Nikolai Lvovich.'

'Fetch him!' I told my aide, who two minutes later reported that he was in his office but unable to stand up.

'Hit the bottle, has he?'

He nodded.

'Managing his own stress, but what about mine?' I was getting angry and gave the stress expert a filthy look. He turned pale.

'If you really want to, I can . . . But there's the question of security. We need a vehicle, a driver, a bodyguard and powerful lights.'

'Don't tell me what's needed,' I yell. 'Get in here.' I shouted for my aide. 'Tell him.'

For a while aide and stress expert stood, staring at each other as if hypnotised, in silence, until restored to life by my hammering my fist on the desk.

And beyond the window, a silent city that couldn't care less about me, my stress or my someone else's heart.

47

Kiev, February 1985

Absolute silence, and a clinical sanitary feeling of peace, as if I lay, closed in a refrigerator, on a shelf with all that is cold and fresh.

That was, as I realise, opening my eyes, a dream. The dugout is warm and dark, apart from ruby reflections from the gently crackling stove.

There is something heavy over me. I feel to discover what it is: not a blanket, no, but a greatcoat, and here was the sleeve. Returning my hand to the warmth of my thighs, I wonder at their concentration of bodily heat. I would, I decide, drifting back to sleep, get a book, maybe study at medical school to be a medical auxiliary.

On the brink of sleep, I think of the drunken medical auxiliary we had in our unit, a construction battalion, where the only non-drinkers were the barrack rats. What had we been constructing?

A coffee factory in Lvov, suggests my sleepy, reluctant brain.

I disagree. No, not a factory. It was a storehouse . . .

At last I go back to sleep, sliding on an invisible shelf back into a clean, cold refrigerator, the door shutting with its familiar click.

48

Leukerbad, February 2004

Amazing thing, democracy. Especially the Swiss sort, which seemed created specially for the sick and aged. 'For our youth this land has a road to everywhere,' we used to sing, which the Swiss didn't, though they always made way for the aged, rather as we gave them our seats on city transport.

The professor smoothed the way with the civic authorities to the extent of arranging for the town hall formalities to be conducted in *absentia*. But so engaged was the mayor by the couple's being given in marriage by siblings, that he appeared in person to shake us by the hand and wish the newly-weds well. Once or twice in the course of a brief address, he forgot that Svetlana and I were not the happy couple, until put right by Natasha.

The main ceremony, however, began at 6 p.m. at the Château d'eau, a water castle in the true sense.

We were driven there in the clinic minibus by courtesy of the professor, who promised to look in later, when he was free.

Among the pictures adorning the walls of the foyer was the mandatory sign of a crossed-through camera, prompting a reluctance to check my Minolta in at the cloakroom.

We followed the maître d'hôtel to changing cubicles, one for Dima and Valya, the other for Svetlana and myself, where towels and the whitest of sheets were laid ready.

Svetlana, shedding her garments, turned, elegantly draped in her sheet, to me still standing fully clothed. I quickly followed her example.

The solemn, church-like silence of the place seemed intensified by a pleasant humidity, and the maître d'hôtel in dark tailcoat and swimming trunks might have been a priest leading the young pair and us to the altar.

Suddenly – though I had long ceased to be surprised by anything – we were splashing through water which became deeper with every step, and there before us was the restaurant, with marble tables and stylish plastic chairs, the water now knee-high and higher when we were seated.

The maître d'hôtel explained in English where we could take a plunge, and now it was Svetlana who translated, English to Russian, having let Natasha go after our visit to the town hall. After nine, he said, we could dispense with our sheets.

A waiter, wearing bathing trunks with more formal upper attire appeared, drawing a boat-like tray with champagne in a silver bucket and a plate of dainty sandwiches.

'*Gorko!*' I called, my voice strangely muffled by the humidity.

Dima and Valya kissed, radiating happiness in a way that was rare. Svetlana and I exchanged glances.

'Shout here, and no one will notice,' I told Dima.

He laughed, and did his best to shout to Valya that he loved her.

At nine we threw off our sheets and bathed at the deep end of the restaurant, where a bar took the place of tables.

Dima and Valya dived in and played about, oblivious to us.

I turned to Svetlana and whispered, 'I love you.'

'What's that?' she shouted back, leaning towards me.

'*Gorko!*' I cried.

We drank only champagne. At eleven I quietly retrieved my Minolta and got a lady at a nearby table to snap us, up to our knees in mineral water – a wedding *à la Suisse-Ukrainienne*.

When Dima and Valya retired to their five-star bridal suite, Svetlana and I set off to our separate rooms one floor lower. I was suddenly sad, foreseeing the lonely night ahead. But my melancholy thoughts were misplaced. Svetlana asked me into her room and now there were two couples enjoying their wedding night. The doctor had told us about the high metal content in the local water and I could taste it on Svetlana's skin. I was happy.

It was not until late next morning that I remembered that the professor had not after all joined us for dinner.

49

Kiev, 23 February, Defenders of the Motherland Day, 1985

'Were you in the army?' asks David Isaakovich, from under the table, retrieving a bag of potatoes. 'Well, were you or weren't you?' he asks, looking me straight in the eye, while I fix my gaze on his hook nose.

'I did my two years.'

'So today's our day,' he smiles. 'I hoisted our flag in '45.'

Five potatoes roll out onto the table.

'They're frozen, but they'll be all right mashed. And I've something else, so it's good you've come,' he says, eyeing the bottle of strong red I've brought. 'You're a practical chap, and you don't forget a kindness.'

'Was it over the Reichstag you hoisted it?'

'No, I never got to Berlin. The pity is I've forgotten the name of the place. But I know it was in Germany, and if I could remember where, I'd write to their embassy. I might get invited to visit. If our bloody lot would let me go. You married?'

'No.'

'"The unique one and only", then, like the Party. Parents?'

'Just Mother. Twin brother, but he's got brain damage.'

'And no sweetheart,' says David Isaakovich, nodding sympathetically. 'In that case, open the wine and fetch our delicacy from the freezer.'

'Which is where?' I ask, seeing, in the chilly realm beyond the stove, no more than a crude home-made bed, a table, two stools and a box of saucepans and plates.

'Outside, two paces left of the door. Brush away the snow and you'll see a box.'

In the five or six degrees of frost outside, I find a half-litre jar of stewed rabbit. All around, trees bare and silent, an air of abandoned cemetery, and, though still only early afternoon, a general greyness deepening, merging with a leaden sky threatening snow.

Having nothing to open the jar with, we break it with the iron frying pan, and pick the resulting fragments of glass from our jar-shaped rabbit. We then wash the potatoes in snow, bung them in with the rabbit and put the pot on the stove.

'I have a daughter, Mira,' says David Isaakovich, sipping his wine. 'You must meet.'

'We must.'

'Intelligent child, intelligent family. Mother is wardrobe mistress at the Opera. And me, well, I was fifty when I fathered her.'

So how old, I wonder, is he now?

'I'm just her dad, Mum's the clever one – makes trousers to measure, and a lovely job of it. Don't even need ironing, if properly hung after washing. I'll give you her address and a note. Time was we had everything here on the island – our own wine shop, our own cemetery. My brother's buried in it.'

It's dark. The wine's all gone, but I don't feel like leaving. It's cold and snow is falling again.

'Share the bed,' says the old man. 'I don't take up much room any more, and two sleep warmer than one. And tomorrow I'll write you that note for Mira. You'll like her.'

50

July 2015, early hours, whereabouts unknown

Heart pounding as loudly as the helicopter's engine, I am flying somewhere – where doesn't matter – to get rid of stress.

Ahead of us is another helicopter, with security guards and a special communications colonel.

Looking across the dimly lit cabin to where my stress expert in a leather upholstered seat is trying not to catch my eye, I motion my aide to pour him a glass of cognac too.

Suddenly alert to something on the ground, the stress expert turns to me then quickly back to the window, only to be distracted by the aide with his cognac.

'What is it?' I ask.

'I think it's the landing area.'

Seeing nothing from my window, I go over to his, and see flashing lights marking the corners of a square, the headlights of several vehicles, and the lead helicopter hovering.

'How long have we been in the air?'

'An hour and a half,' he says quietly.

It's dark and windy on the ground, and there is a murmur of voices from the shadowy figures, brought by my stress to this mysterious spot. A little later we are speeding along a rough country road in three Mercedes, me in the back of the second with my aide and the driver in front.

As four men with powerful torches set about placing phosphorescent green marker flags, the stress expert appears out of the darkness to hand me a light spade with a shiny white blade.

'There's thirty square metres,' he whispers, avoiding my eye. 'If you feel tired, stop immediately.'

The unploughed stretch of earth is lit by invisible men. My eyes now used to the dark, I can see a peasant dwelling in the distance, and beyond it, others.

I dig with a will, my razor-sharp spade slicing the hard dry soil as if it were meat.

Twenty minutes later, palms pleasantly calloused from metres of soil turning, I am taking physiological delight in the way dynamism battles with fatigue inside me, and the surge of energy to arm and calf muscles at the turning of each spit, oblivious to all else – guards, freckles and men with torches.

'Time to pack it in,' comes a familiar voice. It's a special communications colonel. 'Nikolai Lvovich has just rung. It'll be dawn in thirty minutes. He's afraid you'll be seen.'

There are just a couple of metres left to dig.

'Over to you,' I say handing him the spade and making for the cars which, as if at a signal, switch their headlights on as one.

Back at the Residence, my bleeding palms are treated by the physician, Nikolai Lvovich standing by, looking the worse for drink and a sleepless night. Suddenly he brightens and hurries out, returning with a digital camera which he focuses on my hands.

'What are you doing?'

'Ne'er a misfortune that can't be turned to advantage,' he mutters, snapping away.

'I rid myself of stress entirely of your making, clot that you are, and you want to photograph my hands. Get out of here.'

'It's for the archive,' he says, taking two more snaps and tiptoeing out.

The ointment applied to my calluses and broken blisters smells of mutton fat. I ask what it is.

'Ostrich grease.'

'I might have known,' I say with an equanimity that surprises me.

The sleepless night has not been in vain – the stress is gone, my mood much improved. I feel generous.

'Any children?' I ask the physician.

'A daughter.'

'How old?'

'Sixteen.'

'Wants to be a doctor too, eh?'

'No, a model.'

Concealing my disappointment, I take off my Philippe Patek watch and hold it out to him.

'Take it as a thank-you present.' The doctor is aghast, but he takes it, mumbling something about having a son by his first marriage.

'I'm not interested in your son,' I say without aggression. 'You may go.'

51

Kiev, 24 February, 1985

The door was opened by a plump moon-faced girl in a blue tracksuit. She had very blue eyes and an amused smile.

'Who do you want?'

Knocking the snow off my boots, I produced the envelope from my pocket.

'I've a note from your father.'

'For me? From Father?' The smile was now mildly foolish.

'You are Mira?'

'A-a-a-h!' She pointed down the long corridor behind her. 'Third door on the left.'

Thank God for that, I thought, entering the communal flat.

Mira proved to be more attractive than expected – dark gypsy eyes, ample figure, and nothing of her father's nose.

Having read the note, she asked anxiously after her father, then set about making tea.

It was a large room with a great number of portrait photographs in wooden frames. The two iron beds were neatly made and decorated with plumped-up cushions. On a lace napkin on top of the television set was a crystal vase of artificial flowers. It was all very clean and tidy.

'Do you like music?' she asked.

'Yes.'

'Mother and I work at the Opera Theatre. I'm due there in half an hour. You can come if you like.'

I said I would.

Snow crunched underfoot, as we walked in silence up

Saksagansky and Vladimir Streets. I kept looking at her felt boots with black galoshes over. I had thought that no one in Kiev wore felt boots any more.

Just short of the Morozov House, she said she must pop into the food store for cheese and sausage because the sandwiches at the Opera buffet were expensive.

I nodded, and she disappeared inside. Snow collected on my nose. At four in the afternoon it was growing darker as I looked, and car headlights were yellow blobs in the snowy murk. We were ten minutes from the Opera and I wondered what we would do until the performance at seven. Then Mira came out, bringing such pondering to an end.

We entered by the stage door. The old man inside gave me a disinterested look, and nodded in reply to my 'Good evening'.

I received a guarded reception from Larisa Vadimovna, Mira's mother, but having read the note Mira gave her, she was all smiles.

She was standing at an ironing board, iron in muscular hand, over the shining emerald velvet of some regal garment. The air was heavy with naphthalene.

The iron was lowered to its rest as if light as a feather.

A Samson of a woman in black flared skirt and wine-coloured blouse with sleeves rolled up to the elbow, I wondered how she managed to get through doors.

'Mira, show our visitor round,' she said distractedly, lowering her eyes to the note.

Our tour of the Opera ended in the attic, reached by a wooden stepladder. Mira struck a match, and lit a candle, in the light of which a secret room was revealed, complete with an occasional table, on which were empty glasses and cups, an old busted couch, a thread-bare carpet and tatty posters peeling from the wooden partitions.

'Here's where the cast have secret assignations,' said Mira, so tenderly and romantically that I just had to draw her to me.

The busted couch gave hardly a squeak. We stripped off, she leaving on her felt boots divested of galoshes, Just as I, though cold, was beginning to get somewhere, Mira broke off and whispered that someone was coming.

Gathering our garments from the scrap of carpet and extinguishing the candle, we hid, clutched shivering together for warmth and watched the other couple who relit the single candle. I thought the woman very beautiful. I found her taut, slender body much more attractive than the warm, cuddliness of Mira's. It was bitterly cold and had it not been for the brevity of the couple's assignation we would have caught pneumonia.

'Principal dancers,' whispered Mira as the lovers climbed down the ladder. 'And did you see? He was doing it from behind.'

I nodded.

We went back to the divan, now the worse for the others' perfume and smell of sweat.

The ballet was Khachaturian's *Spartacus*, and not to my liking.

52

Kiev, March 2004

Damn this winter! I think, then maybe not – our champagne breakfast in a five-star Swiss hotel was also a feature of this winter.

At first I was angered by the snow stinging my face. But now, sitting at my desk with mocha served by Nila, tapping out Svetlana's telephone number like a secret code, I have to admit that so far God has been kind with His winter.

'Hello, where are you?'

'In the car, on the way to the salon.'

'Going to be made beautiful?'

'Wasn't I yesterday?'

I laugh. I have never learned to say the right thing, but at least I am no longer ashamed of it.

Yesterday morning, however, my conversation with Svetlana left me mystified.

'We've never talked about us,' she said, as if, clever as she was, only just aware of the fact.

'Maybe because we're so concerned with Dima and Valya.'

'Perhaps, but I did wonder if it was Valya, not me, you were interested in.'

'How could you! You, always you! all the time.' I realised, as I spoke, a falsity in tone had given me away.

But ignoring me, she went over to the window and, drawing the curtains, stood for a moment in all her beauty. Then turning she said, 'I think I'm going to have a baby.'

'Your first?'

'My first.'

I imagined her standing like that, only with a baby in her arms, a beautiful picture.

'How's the honey business going?'

She shot me a look of surprise and I was shocked by my own stupidity at attempting to change the subject.

'Sales for this year were completed in January, I'm on holiday.'

'Holiday? So let's go to Rome.' I laughed.

She shook her head.

'I don't know yet what I want,' she whispered.

I must buy her an expensive present, I thought.

53

Kiev, July 2015

When you sleep on your own in a king-size bed, inevitably you dream that you are not alone and not sleeping. No matter how the dream starts it always ends with the same sad, uncomfortable feelings and, already half awake, you imagine another woman, some presidential chambermaid changing the sheets, and this image makes you want to reach for the cognac and to wash away thought altogether. Yes, you're the President, but that doesn't mean you're impotent. The nation does not replace a woman.

A careful, but persistent tapping at my door breaks through my dream. I open my eyes and run my hand over the sheets beneath the duvet. They're dry. So it was a dream.

'Wake up, Mr President!' urges my aide. 'It's General Filin, Internal Affairs. There's been an incident.'

'Give him coffee,' I say, thinking, as I slip on my dressing gown, of Mayya Voytsekhovskaya, or whatever she's called, beyond the Shishkin forest scene adorning my wall.

I enter the sitting room and pause at the window. The General, who smokes like a crematorium, coughs. I swing round and look him straight in the eye.

'Well?'

'I hardly know how to tell you, Mr President – case of abduction, planned operation . . . The whole Zaporozhe regional government, all thirteen, but one jumped to her death out of a window.'

'Who?'

'Kalinovskaya, Deputy Finance.'

'And?'

'I've sent a crack team to investigate, set up roadblocks, but so far nothing.'

'Good man. Report again at 0800 hours.'

'You must have nerves of steel,' says the Minister on his way out.

'I have steel everything,' I murmur under my breath. As the door closes I allow myself a smile.

No longer sleepy, I order a car 'of the plainer sort', and half an hour later the black Audi with somnolent driver has drawn up at the main entrance of Night Club X. Bouncers try to approach the car, only to be discouraged by my own bully boys, and I am able to observe the faces of departing customers, some beautiful but weary, others tough and determined. I drink chilled sparkling New World muscat and think of future generations as I watch.

At six, a tap at the window. Nikolai Lvovich I would have told to go to hell, but it's Svetlov.

'Ours are already in Russia. There's a purpose-built sanatorium in the Urals for them.'

'Hop in. Care to celebrate?'

Wearily but gratefully he gets in.

'Tell me, Valeri,' I say, providing us both with cognac, 'have you ever really been in love?'

'I tried, but she wouldn't let me.'

'What a fool,' I blurt out. 'If you don't mind me saying so.'

'Right as always, sir,' Svetlov replies quite calmly. 'It's rare for a woman to love. More often than not she chooses whoever it is loves her. Mine was courted by a businessman, a good deal taller than me. He was killed by a protection-racket gang.'

I nod in sympathy.

We drink.

'Will you ever marry?'

'I am married. Two grown children. Typical family set-up.'

I feel flattered in a way that Svetlov would not have understood. His talking to me as to an equal is not only reassuring, it raises me to the level of those sure of the rightness of their own views, sympathies and thoughts. And self-assured is what I have not been that night, skulking behind tinted glass, incognito, avoiding the beautiful anonymity of life.

54

Kiev, 27 February 1985

The icy wind seared my face and there was nothing I could do to protect it. My rabbit-fur cap pulled down, ear flaps fastened tight, prickly angora scarf, the raised collar of my sheepskin jacket doing nothing to create warmth. Trukhanov Island as I approached over the footbridge was trying its damnedest to repulse me. But I was thinking of the old man alone in his dugout and maybe out of wood for the stove. Not, of course, that I was bringing any wood for the stove. In a sports bag hung from my shoulder, I had food and two bottles of red. The bag was quite heavy; even so, the wind kept lifting it and letting it drop back against me.

Mira had been bought the food, and persuaded me to bring it, while refusing to make the journey herself and now I could see why. Still, I was more persistent than the wind, and the harder it fought me, the harder I fought it.

Next it was deep snow, but I was not to be stopped.

Winter dusk was deepening, the sky bending lower and lower, like a drunken giant no longer able to stand. In a matter of minutes that great black bulk would fall upon me, except that already I could see the tiny candlelit window of the old man's dugout.

'Second Pavlik Morozov, that's you!' was his cheerful greeting.

'Didn't he denounce Daddy to the OGPU for helping the kulaks?'

'Second Volodya Dubinin, then – anyway, a real hero for braving this terrible weather. And by way of thanks . . .' He produced an open bottle of Moscow vodka.

'Now there's a right lordly repast!' he said helplessly, seeing what I had unpacked from my bag. 'What's the occasion, young man? Getting married?'

'No. It's from Mira!'

'She's a good girl!'

Thinking of the theatre, I nodded.

'Good, but best not marry her!'

'Why not?'

'You'd grow fat and lazy, and never do better than average! She takes after her mother. Can't grasp that the soul of man is forever in flight. A woman's an airfield, a man's a glider. Her job is to wait for him, not to ban him from flying. You follow me?'

'Where did you fly?'

'Figuratively, to other women. It's not only women who are in search for happiness. But listen!' he said, lifting a finger for silence.

A blizzard was raging.

'No sort of flying weather, this,' said David Isaakovich. 'But a time for family consolidation in advance of spring. Still, that's all done with . . . There comes a time of other values, when it's not curler-curled lovelies you'll look for, but like-minded companionship . . . A couple of days from now I'll have friends here. Come and join us – *Pravda* doesn't tell all, you'll find. There is another life!'

55

Kiev, March 2004

For two days I tried to imagine what form our talk about us might take. With nothing to ask Svetlana about, there was much concerning life, thoughts, relatives and friends to be asked about me, and I prepared to answer fully and truthfully. Lies were out. For a man of my age in my position to concoct new tales for old was as ridiculous as it was to be so nervous.

In no mood for work, I told Nila to transfer my appointments with tax-paying and tax-evading businessmen to the following week, and near the end of the day I asked her to join me for coffee. This she did with more than usual alacrity and the air of a diffident young actress quite at odds with the firmness she showed unwanted callers.

'Forgotten the sugar,' she said, springing up light as a feather. 'One spoonful?'

'A bit less.'

Reducing the heaped teaspoon to a level one, she stirred it in.

'What sort of a present does a man give a beautiful woman?' I asked.

'Are you intimate?'

'Yes.' I replied, realising with surprise that I had not found the question impertinent.

'Have you got any cognac?' Nila asked.

'She doesn't drink cognac.'

'No, I mean for now, with coffee.'

I went to the drinks cabinet and took out a bottle.

'You're not expecting anyone else today, are you?' Nila asked, sipping her cognac.

'I told you to postpone everything.'

'Yes, I did,' said Nila, jumping up and going towards the door. 'I'll be back in a sec.'

Savouring the taste of the cognac and coffee, I thought of Svetlana, suddenly aware of the hush that had fallen over the building usually abuzz with the sound of paper being pushed in different directions, like so many billiard balls scattering over the smooth green table, some disappearing into a pocket for the boss's final signature, others getting stranded in the middle of nowhere, lost and unsought forever. Mine was a miserable and lucrative job. I was well compensated for my isolation from real life.

Nila came back into my office and I just had time to notice that she was no longer wearing tights.

'The best present for your sweetheart is lingerie.' Her voice went into a whisper and with a playful twirl of her body she whipped off her suit and there she stood, in some really very fetching red undies which made her look incredibly seductive. I held on to my glass as if it were a lifebelt.

'Nice?' she asked, glancing down at her panties.

'Yes,' I answered, looking round. 'Did you shut your door?'

'Of course I did, I've been meaning to tell you something.'

'Fire away.'

'I've had people in asking about you.'

'Who?'

'Dogmazov and two others.'

'Asking what?'

'Do you have women in, who you hobnob with, how much you drink, what papers you read, who you dodge on the telephone, who you see without appointment. Maybe they're trying to undermine you, push you out.'

'Would it matter if they did?'

'Yes. You're good to work for – you're kind, don't shout, don't expect sex.'

'And some do?'

'Your predecessor, Ivan Semyonovich did, almost nightly . . .'

I felt terribly sorry for Nila. She looked so fragile standing there in her underwear – why had she got undressed? Oh yes, I asked about a present for a woman.

'Could I have some more cognac,' she asked.

I refilled her glass and she perched on my desk, tears in her eyes.

'What's wrong?' I found myself stroking her hair.

'You're going to buy her some nice things, but you know how much I earn?'

I shook my head, I had never thought about anyone else's salary.

'Two hundred hyrvnas!'

'You live on that?' I can hardly believe it.

'I only manage because I live with my parents and they help.'

'With your parents?' Once more I'm shocked and moved by Nila's gentle self-pity.

Rummaging in my drawer, I picked one of several sealed envelopes which I judged to contain a couple of thousand dollars at least.

'Take this and buy yourself whatever you like and think of it as a present from me.'

'You love her very much?' she asked suddenly.

'Probably,' I said, not wishing to hurt her feelings.

'I'll always tell you everything,' she said, taking another sip of cognac. 'If you treat me properly. You know I have everything necessary for happiness,' she went on, looking down at her lovely body. 'Only no happiness comes along.'

56

Stary Sambor, Lvov Region, August 2015
'I, in assuming Ukrainian nationality, swear faithfully to love this, my native land, to defend its social and political interests, and to apply my every effort towards developing and strengthening my country and enhancing its world respect. I promise to fulfil all my obligations as a citizen, honestly to pay my taxes . . .'

Sonorous Ukrainian, solemn grandeur of the cathedral, first-rate acoustics notwithstanding, there was still something artificial about the ceremony. And it wasn't the procession of Indian, Bangladeshi and Afghani illegals diligently reading out the oath (some pointedly attired in the embroidered shirt or blouse seen as de rigueur by their adoptive country). Psalms were chanted. A ceremonially robed priest muttered away in a baritone voice. An official of the Lvov regional government stepped forward supported by a female secretary bearing the ID cards for the ceremony.

'Ahmed Zahir Shah,' called the official reading from the first passport handed him by the secretary, surveying all the other Ahmeds drawn up before him.

It was just like the presentation of school-leaving certificates in Soviet days.

'Who wrote the Oath of Allegiance?' I asked of Mykola who had persuaded me to attend.

'Vasily Kazansky, singer, People's Artist of Ukraine.'

'Why didn't you get a writer to do it? '

'Kazansky was bursting to contribute. He's a great patriot.'

'Is that a profession?'

'No.'

'A vocation?'

'No.'

'Well, just make sure that oath has had its last hearing. Either write one yourself, or find a writer patriot.'

From clusters of votive candles, a pleasing scent of wax. From the choir, a bouquet of sound rising into the cupola and echoing beautifully back.

'So the Archbishop made no difficulty over the differing faiths of the recipients?' I asked, turning to the hapless Mykola.

'They've all been baptised. That was one of the conditions attached to Ukrainian citizenship.'

'The others being?'

'Sitting a Ukrainian-language exam and writing an auto-biography in Ukrainian.'

'On whose authority?'

'Yours. I put the order in for signature, it came back signed.'

'I want to see that signature. One of us must have been ill . . .'

'It was when you weren't well . . .'

The official continued to call forward one new Ukrainian after another.

The regiment's reinforcements, I thought, feeling a sudden unpleasant tightening around my heart.

On my way out I noticed the predatory lenses of three TV cameras. So all this would appear that evening on all main channels. How will that affect my image?

Face caressed by a weary summer sun, I did my best not to think of the ceremony and the reaction that would not be slow coming. 'Ukrainian Greek Catholic Ahmed Zahir Shah' would provide a good laugh. Not so good would be for the original order to surface in some wretched newspaper, signalling an assault on me!

57

Kiev, 1 March 1985

This morning Mother took Dima to see yet another psychiatrist, and I put on a white shirt, pressed trousers and warm sweater, and then as many layers as possible on top so as to keep out the March cold which was no improvement on February's.

I had known that there were some who, wanting to live differently, neither welcomed nor backed the Party's politics. I had heard of meetings at night in kitchens and the telling of political anecdotes. Though none struck me as especially amusing. But how could an old man in a dugout be involved? He didn't even have a kitchen. Still, interest aroused, I set off once more for Trukhanov Island.

No wind. Bridge steady. Creak of snow underfoot. The winter isolation of this footbridge never ceased to excite wonder and respect. I looked for evidence of other feet, but there were none. Maybe there was some other, secret, way to the island.

Indeed, there must be as others were there before me. The dugout was warmer than usual, and on the table, in place of strong red, three bottles of non-alcoholic kefir. Sitting on the old man's bed was a bearded, solid-looking man with a prominent nose, far from old, but with a markedly venerable air. On a stool to his right, one leg crossed over the other, a lean man with aquiline nose and incipient bald patch. Blue wool tracksuit with white-striped trousers notwithstanding, clearly no sportsman. The third visitor was short, plump, smiling-faced and rubicund.

'This is Sergey whom I've mentioned,' said David Isaakovich by way of introduction. 'Father Basil,' he continued, pointing deferentially at the one with the beard. The others he introduced more simply as 'Ilya' and 'Fedya'.

I sat down on a stool, ready for intelligent discourse to follow.

But instead, David Isaakovich dragged out from under the bed a bundle of rough towels which he placed on the table with the kefir.

'Well, God be with us!' boomed Father Basil, beginning to undress. The others followed suit.

'Aren't you joining us?' said David Isaakovich.

'In what?' I asked, alarmed at the general undressing, mindful of what I had read of male rape.

'We've got to hurry.'

'Where?'

'The ice hole. I cleared it this morning, but if it refreezes, we'll get cut.'

So not buggers – walruses! My sense of relief was infinite.

In single file we set off barefoot across the snow, each with his rough towel, me bringing up the rear, contemplating a wobbly whiteness of bare bottoms, all too conscious of my own exposure and fear of cold water to worry about the sub-zero temperature.

'Baptism, in a state of intoxication, is not valid,' confided Father Basil at the ice hole's edge, gently pushing me in.

The cold burned into my flesh, and as I thrashed about in the mush of ice and water, the naked, almost blue David Isaakovich gazed down from the edge of the ice hole.

'Don't dive!' he cried. 'Or the current will carry you under the ice!'

Quite the contrary, I doing my best to get out and eventually did, and gashed my right elbow in the event.

David Isaakovich passed me a towel. The roughness reddened my flesh, but as the feeling of cold diminished, physical lassitude and mental apathy took over.

Father Basil hung a silver cross about my neck.

'Saved, by a miracle,' he said, with a meaningful look at David Isaakovich. 'And now a servant of God, upon whom the Lord's blessing.'

Longest to stay wheezing and oh-ah-ing in the ice hole was David Isaakovich himself.

'It's good for me,' he announced. 'Cold *preserves* you, as it does tomatoes!'

The notion of a new healthful regimen was quickly dispelled on our return to the dugout by a general quaffing of vodka, 'to the glory of God', David Isaakovich, unlike the others, drinking his with kefir.

'And now to politics?' I ventured to ask, as we sat at table, only to receive strange looks.

'Politics is for earthworms,' declared Father Basil. 'Life is what we talk of – and life is love.'

58

Kiev, March 2004
All night long, the wailing of tomcats, and where dogs would merely have kept me awake, the cats stirred my subconscious into a stampede of thought which I chased from one corner of my mind to the other until dawn.

Next morning, to an aroma of coffee from my espresso, Svetlana rang. 'I've got some news,' she said seriously, prompting thoughts of Dima and Valya's bills at the clinic

'The scan says I'm having twins . . .'

'Congratulations! We must celebrate,' I said, stung by the 'I' as opposed to 'we'.

'But that's not all. Valya's expecting too.'

'Only Valya?'

'Dima and Valya, your brother, my sister.'

'How about the Déjà vu at seven?' My mouth was suddenly dry and I could hardly get the words out.

'Fine.'

By the evening it was drizzling, bestowing a mother-of-pearl-like lustre on the Opera Theatre cobbles. I dismissed my driver. Convention dictated that he should sit in the BMW awaiting my return reading rubbish, till the small hours, but I hated such conventions and I only followed rules that were posted in writing.

'She rang you then?' I asked, kissing Svetlana hello.

'And would you believe it – we're due on the very same day!'

The waiter brought a bottle of Moët and glasses.

My spirits soared. Svetlana had obviously ordered it herself and that meant I had been wrong to fear that she would be in a bad mood.

'That's a pretty necklace.' I noticed how the coral beads matched her sweater. Svetlana always dressed according to her mood and today she was obviously happy with herself and with life. I pulled the gift-wrapped lingerie out of my jacket pocket, once more stunned by how light modern underwear is.

'This is for you,' I said, placing the rectangular box in her hand.

Svetlana smiled knowingly, slipped it into her bag and raised her glass.

'To you and the twins!'

The champagne was pricey and not to my taste, but I managed not to show it.

'A stupid question,' said Svetlana, 'but *are* you related to the writer Bunin?'

'No. Bunin dates from the Siberian orphanage my father ended up at, having lost parents and documents in bombings. The Director chose the name and he was obviously well read because Father's friends in the orphanage were called Gorky and Ostrovsky!'

'That's a lovely story.'

'One of many, with Leukerbad the best.'

We touched fingers.

'Move in with me.' I leaned forward trying to look humble and pleading.

'Let's wait,' she said, withdrawing her hand and picking up her glass. 'I can't see you liking children.'

'Any more than I see you liking honey. And anyway, I do like children.'

'So we'll drink to Valya and Dima,' she said, looking at the smear of lipstick on her glass. 'I have the feeling only they are capable of real happiness.'

As we stepped out into the street, the rain stopped. Yellow headlights flashed by in the dark. I raised a hand, and with dog-like obedience, one pair of lights bent towards us.

We were approaching my flat when Svetlana remembered that she had forgotten her umbrella.

Dialling 09 on my mobile, I obtained the number of the restaurant and asked them to leave the umbrella in the cloakroom. A trivial success, but one that put Svetlana in an even better mood.

59

Kiev, 1 September 2015

'I did like the way you put it,' gushed Nikolai Lvovich. '*Learning, learning, learning!*'

'I didn't make that up, that was Lenin.'

'Doesn't matter. No one remembers him any more! It's what every pupil in Ukraine will be thinking of today.'

We were returning from a New School Year celebration at a school on the corner of Vladimir and Desatinaya Street, opposite my Residence. I had said a few words for live TV, taken the handbell and rung it. We were now on our way to Bank Street.

'What's next?' I asked.

'General Filin reporting on the state of the country and the Zaporozhe local government affair in particular . . .'

'They've still found nothing?'

'Not for want of trying. They've checked every reservoir in the region for bodies,' he said clearly concerned.

'Then what?'

'Medical examination and massage 1400 hours. National Opera prima donna 1500 hours. After that, Cabinet in closed session.'

We drove the rest of the way in silence. Today Potapenko would once again come running up to bemoan my excursion without motorcade and outriders. But to hell with him. My one concern was how to get Filin to be brief and avoid hearing the ins and outs of his battle with corruption in the ranks of the Militia Ministry. The figures were becoming an irritation. Officers discharged: 80,343. Officers charged on administrative or criminal grounds: 35,000. So having calmly disposed of 115,000 officers, is there anyone left on the job? Could they cope? And how many prison places are there?

General Filin had been waiting half an hour for his moment, and on seeing me he performed his customary act of greeting, a snapping to attention reminiscent of a high-voltage spasm.

114

'Take a seat,' I said, indicating the Melnichenko ottoman, knowing that he wouldn't sit on it. Military and militia shunned it – whether from superstition or fear of some low trick on my part, I never knew – preferring the soft well-sprung beige of the armchair beside it, whither General Filin now directed his rear.

'What have we got?'

'On the Zaporozhe regional government, nothing. We even got our crooks to check things out, but they found nothing. So it's not a criminal job. A guest performance by some special group, possibly, but there's nothing to go on.'

He's not stupid then, I think to myself. He's figured out it was a guest appearance.

'I've got two hundred on the job. Zaporozhe enigma apart, things are normal. Deaths at work: thirty-seven; fatalities attributable to counterfeit vodka: eighteen; contract killings: three; murders: thirteen.'

'Anti-corruption?' I prompted.

Filin positively blossomed; he told of the arrest of two generals and three colonels, and the discovery of a racket on the Odessa clothing market involving a group of militia.

'Right. That's it,' I said. 'Mykola has an idea to discuss with you now, if you could give him twenty minutes of your time . . .'

'Of course.'

As the door closed behind him, I summoned my aide.

'Get me a prawn-and-mozzarella pizza. Bring it here in whatever you like, but no one must know. You've twenty minutes.'

He shot from the room, and I bounced up and down on the ottoman, like a pupil fresh from the New School Year ceremony.

My pizza came in a special postal delivery bag, and I enjoyed half an hour of peace consuming it on the ottoman, having directed

Nikolai Lvovich to admit no one. I tried to recall when I had last so enjoyed a pizza.

My medical examination was quickly over. There was, the physician said, no advance in the freckling, examination showed my skin to be healthy, and he was happy with my heart. My massage, as performed by a young Chinese lady, was both enjoyable and invigorating.

It was now three thirty. Ten minutes to the prima donna of the National Opera. We would talk – it would be interesting to see about what – duly recorded for National TV 1. An interest in the arts was expected of the President, even if ballet and opera did made him spew.

60

Kiev, March 1985

I spent half a day wandering a chilly Podol, looking first into the Bacchus wine bar, then a Fraternal Street café for a warming glass. I was in no special sort of mood, but game for adventure. A chance acquaintance in the shape of a nice girl would not have come amiss. I hadn't the money for the other sort. A five-rouble note – what did that amount to? Enough for five days at a stretch, but what fun would there be in that? I was already familiar with the fifteen-kopek carrot cutlets at the Lenin Street health-food eatery, but what I always fancied was the meat variety. And meat cost dear. I was sick of begging from Mother. Which I wouldn't have to, of course, if I went off and studied. She'd give me money then. On top of my grant. But where to go? It would have to be something not too complicated leading to something not too boring. Still, it was the education part itself that mattered; you could switch to something more interesting later. Mother, having trained as a lathe operator, was now head of distribution at a large factory. That was career advancement. Not something I was threatened with.

I came out into Lower Wall Street. Hands in the pockets of my artificial fur coat, my hood pulled so tight as to leave only an apple-sized portion of face, I might have been taken for an Eskimo.

I wasn't far from the paper-recycling point run by red-haired Senya. He and his wife lived right next to it, so she hadn't far to drag him when he overdid the drink. She was a powerful woman, half a head taller than Senya, twice his size, but not what I would have called fat. It was more that Senya was thin.

I hesitated at the entrance to Senya's yard. Should I try my luck today or not? Senya was a kind of lucky dip. I'd give him the odd three roubles, and for that he let me rummage through the waiting bundles, helping myself to anything the bookseller in nearby Konstantinov Street might buy off me. And occasionally I made sales on my own account, as when a woman grabbed off me two volumes of Dumas for ten roubles. Remembering the Dumas, I made up my mind and entered the yard.

The recycling point was much like the usual brick-built hut for rubbish, only better smelling, damp paper being offensive to the uninitiated.

I found Senya sitting on a chair. On an old bedside table to his right, a cut-glass tumbler and a half-eaten sausage-filled roll; on the concrete floor at his feet, massive, blue-painted scales.

'Hi!' he said, looking up with bloodshot eyes. 'Bored? Short of books?'

'Can you take three out of this?' I asked, producing my five-rouble note.

'I'll get the cobbler to change it. If anyone comes they're to wait.'

Looking behind the bedside table and finding a half-full bottle of Moscow vodka, I poured a shot into the empty tumbler and downed it at a gulp, warming the hungry inner man.

Now I could get to work! The place was packed with bundles. Just the job! A Kilimanjaro, no, a veritable Everest of newspapers and books!

An hour later I descended, well pleased, from the summit to the scales and a more cheerful Senya, now with full tumbler, sliced liver sausage and two three-kopek rolls.

'Any luck?' he asked.

I laid my find of books and bound numbers of Niva for 1904 and 1907 on the concrete floor.

Taking the topmost book, he examined it, screwing up his eyes.

'Hound of the Baskervilles. Keen on dogs, are we?'

'Always wanted one, but Mother said no.'

'Like me wanting a poodle but Anka said she'd kick us both out.'

Anka, the wife, had red hair too, but unlike Senya's mop, it suited her.

'How about my change?'

Reluctantly he fished out two crumpled one-rouble notes, keeping them clutched in his hand.

'What say we get a quarter-litre of vodka and sit on for a bit? There's sausage enough for three.'

'No,' I said, easing my two roubles away from him with difficulty.

Clutched in my pocket half an hour later, were sixteen roubles – six apiece for the bound sets of Niva and four for the books.

To get rid of the tang of damp books and in celebration of my haul, I went so far as to regale myself with coffee and a cognac. The café wasn't exactly crowded – a couple of men, and some obvious students, slyly topping up their coffee with strong red of their own provision, but no young beauties with whom I could share my expansive mood.

61

Kiev, 9 May 2004
On Victory Day Svetlana and I celebrated our move to a new flat. She had done well not to come and live with me straight away in March. In the morning, after she'd left, I had gone around the flat, noticing with surprise how dilapidated the place was. The flat could, of course, have been restyled more to our taste, but money and the time involved could be better spent on our happiness together. With this in mind, I spoke to a few folk around the Ministry, including Dogmazov, and as if at their own prompting, those charged with the welfare of senior civil servants busied themselves with mine, very soon offering me a new flat in Tsarskoye Selo, on Staronavodnitskaya Street. In a tall block commanding Lesi Ukrainki Boulevard I was given a choice of floors and I opted for the twelfth.

The Head of Housing, handing over keys to a spacious flat with fully fitted kitchen, quietly, and to my surprise, advised that we register our marriage at the earliest opportunity. I was surprised that he knew so much, but then I had not tried to hide anything.

Svetlana and I had looked at the flats together and she was beginning to show.

Svetlana's office was also in Pechersk, near the House of Furniture. She, astutely managerial, had recruited a couple of businesslike girls from among her acquaintance to manage her honey business and the recently introduced new lines in herbal remedies and food supplements and so she had no need to be in constant attendance.

Back at the Ministry, I told Nila to ring Pechersk registry office and book me and Svetlana in for 2 p.m. next day and soon she popped her head round the door, obviously excited, her smile more charming than ever.

'It's all arranged,' she whispered.

'Fine. How about a coffee?'

62

Kiev, September 2015

I rarely derive much pleasure from meeting the creative and intellectual – I tend to forget them in far less time than it takes them to shut up and go. Though my latest encounter, the day before yesterday, could well linger in the memory. I'd been all set to switch off my brain and assume the proper TV smile with which to accommodate TV journalists as they ask their questions. The prima donna turned out to be a ballerina who was past-her-prime. Not that that would have been apparent to the viewer. She was slender and elegant, with a fine nose and a theatrically haughty profile. But seen at close quarters over arm's length, her face was more studio make-up than flesh and blood.

The picture was all that mattered; sound was not recorded. So while she might as well have been telling an amusing story, she was in fact speaking of unpaid salaries and how old the decor and costumes were. But I was prepared. Culture is always impoverished; that is its nature. At least in our country, and hence such a meeting; so that the President can be seen tackling the problems. Indeed after this conversation, I did instruct the Finance Ministry to make funds over to the Opera and Ballet Theatre to cover salaries owing and cost of decor for a new production.

She had, she told me, come straight on from rehearsal without so much as a shower, the one at the theatre having been long out of order – this revelation was lumped in with the others but it revived a memory, supported as it was with a whiff of perfume and sweat. A bitter-sweet female sweat, light, but with the power to drive you mad. I stared at the ballerina, deaf to her somewhat harsh voice, turning the pages of my memory, seeking out that combination of female sweat and professional perfumery – perhaps it was a particularly pungent talc or face powder. And then I remembered. Still staring at her fine lips, my mouth dropped open, and she, thinking this evidence of my heightened interest in her words, spoke more animatedly.

'Tell me,' I said when at last she stopped speaking, 'there was an attic with a busted couch – you reached it by ladder. Is it still there?'

The ballerina stared back at me, not even blinking, as if hypnotised. Inside my head I replayed that wonderful episode of my youth. Mira and I making love in that attic with no walls or windows. Everything steeped in that cocktail of odours – sweat and perfume and suddenly we are interrupted by a couple from the ballet troupe. We watch them making love on the same broken divan, the ballerina so finely holding her body.

I lower my head a little in concentration, straining to see, one more time, the profile of that ballerina. I am almost certain it was her, only younger.

'There was, a few years ago,' she said eventually in a hardly audible voice.

I nod, noticing on her face a trace of live skin. She is blushing and that blush shows through her make-up, like the first snowdrops appear from under the snow.

'How do you know about it?' she asked in a whisper, leaning forward.

'I went up there once,' I whispered back.

'The theatre is life,' she said no longer in a whisper. She was confident again, sure that she had caught me out with her question, not I her. After all, I had admitted to visiting the attic. She had not.

63

Kiev, March 1985, evening

'We must talk,' says Mother, frowning and serious, gesturing towards the kitchen.

She came home from work earlier than usual, changed into her blue velveteen dressing gown, and put on knitted socks and old slippers. She was in a good mood to begin with, even humming to herself as she opened a large jar of stewed fruit. But she started to look worried towards evening and now I would learn why.

Through the glass of the closed kitchen door we can hear the television in the sitting room, where Dima is watching his favourite *Avengers*, which he knows by heart, and is prone to quote from, sometimes correctly.

'I'm being given a spa voucher for Truskavets,' Mother says, as we sit opposite each other at the kitchen table.

'You must go.'

'But you were going to look for a job. Who would be with Dima?'

'I don't have to look for a while.'

'It would be better if you went in for a bit more study . . .'

'But courses begin in September, and now it's March.'

She nods thoughtfully.

'The voucher's from the 25th. I need treatment. My heart tells me I can't take much more.'

'Much more' of who or what, I don't ask. She looks worn out. She has clearly been sleeping badly and letting herself go.

She sits thinking for a while in silence, then with a sigh, says, 'Right. Call Dima.'

'You're going to tell him?'

'Yes.'

I have to shake him several times by the shoulder to get him away from the TV.

'Mother wants you in the kitchen.'

Most reluctantly he gets to his feet and goes into the kitchen, and I sit down on the warm patch he's left and watch the programme, just for a minute or so, and then I hear a shout and the tinkle of breaking glass. I rush, crossing with a furious Dima carrying a ladle, and just as I meet the icy blast from the broken kitchen window, I hear glass shattering in the sitting room. Mother is sitting, ashen-faced, numb with fear, her back against the stove.

Hardly knowing what to do, I return to the sitting room, now open to the cold with splinters of glass everywhere. Dima has shut himself in the bedroom. Pausing only to put on my GDR artificial fur, I look in at him. He is sitting on his bed, staring at the ladle at his feet. I pick it up and go back to the kitchen.

Half an hour later we are sitting in the kitchen of a neighbour, warming ourselves and drinking hot tea. Dima is yawning, and soon our neighbour takes him in to sleep with his own children in a sleeping bag on a mattress on the floor.

Our neighbour's wife has gone to bed, but he sits up with us in the kitchen.

Mother weeps. For her this is the end.

'He'll have to be put away,' she sobs.

'Get him a wife,' advises our neighbour. 'That'll knock sense into him. Being married steadies you fast.'

'*He* was married once, and where did that get *him*?' says Mother, pointing at me. 'No steady job, no steady friends – that's where!'

'Once isn't enough,' says our neighbour, fortifying his tea with cognac. 'You need another go. Keep looking until you find the one you can live happily with!'

With each gulp of tea his voice grows louder, I want to hush him, but he's doing us a favour, giving us shelter – Dima the family bedroom, us the kitchen.

The door opens a chink and his sleepy wife put her head round it.

'Not so loud, you'll wake the kids.'

'You go back to bed,' says our neighbour, throwing her a menacing glance. 'These good people are in trouble.'

His wife goes obediently away, closing the door.

All the same, for the next two hours we converse in whispers. Full of tea and starting to doze, our neighbour takes himself off, saying he has to go to work in the morning, and Mother and I are left to sit on in a kind of semi-slumber.

64

Kiev, 13 May 2004

At just before two I looked in at the ceremonial hall of the registry office. Seated at a massive oak table, I saw a woman in a wine-red velvet dress with the weary look of one trying to lose weight.

Approaching smartly, I leaned over the table and handed the registrar an envelope containing $100 and said firmly that I hoped she would keep the official stuff to a minimum, just a few warm words was all we wanted. Momentarily thrown, she consulted her papers and having noticed something scribbled beside my name she became helpful.

'Any other special requests?'

'Sweet or semi-sweet champagne.'

'How about red?' she asked, entering into the spirit of the thing and naming a brand very much to my taste.

'And the bride?'

'On her way.'

I went to look and was surprised to see Svetlana standing by her BMW talking to an elderly traffic policeman. Going over, I asked what the trouble was.

'Traffic offence. Failure to give precedence to a vehicle with right of way.'

'She was hurrying to the registry office – a big day for this young lady. And haven't I seen you somewhere?' I asked, producing one of my official gold trident-adorned cards.

Snapping to attention, the captain saluted.

'On behalf of the Militia and the State Vehicle Inspection, permit me to offer congratulations,' he said solemnly.

I thanked him and wished him good luck in his hunt for traffic offenders.

'How about witnesses?' enquired the lady in the velvet dress.

'We don't have any.'

'You must have,' she said.

'Could you be one?'

'I could,' she said after a moment's thought, 'but you will have to have another.'

I fetched in the militiaman, who was happy to oblige with an ornate signature of ministerial proportions.

'Weren't you at Nivki District Militia?' I asked, now more certain of having seen him before.

'I was.'

'Would you care to join our celebration?'

'I'm on duty,' he said without great conviction. 'Still . . .' Walking to the other end of the room, he spoke into his walkie-talkie.

'I've three other couples waiting,' the velvet-clad registrar reminded us.

'One more glass and we're off,' I reassured her.

'All's well,' announced the captain, rejoining us. 'So long as I'm not celebrating in public.'

'You won't be.'

65

Kiev, October 2015, early hours

In my dream I am in solitary confinement in a cell doubly lockable from both sides of the door with different keys, of which those to the inner locks hang from a nail on the wall. The iron door has been unlocked from the outside, but in spite of insistent knocking, I am letting no one in. I look at my two keys hanging from their nail. They are the keys to my inner freedom. I could be locked in from the outside, but I can also decide who to let in.

'Parcel for you, Sergey Pavlovich,' calls a woman's voice.

For me? In prison? I don't believe it. It's me they want something from, though surveying the miserable contents of my cell, I'm at a loss to know what. It can't be the Ukrainian Bible on the bedside table. The woman is talking Russian. Perhaps it's my tiny Samsung TV in the far corner? Too small to be of use to them. The fridge the TV stands on? That, too, is small and old. I shrug. Maybe there really is a parcel. With ill grace, I rise from my bed, unhook the keys, and open the door to a woman standing with a cardboard box, and beside her a security captain.

'Really, Sergey Pavlovich, our legs ache with standing waiting.'

Having signed for the parcel, I double-lock myself in again.

The parcel, a New Year gift box from Internal Affairs Minister Filin, has a card attached showing Grandfather Frost in militia garb. Pinned to it is a questionnaire requiring the inmate to report to Prison Management on the conditions of custody and quality of catering, and to suggest in writing how his term of imprisonment might be better and more usefully filled.

With the biro enclosed I first write that every cell PC should be on the Net and completely upgraded. My cell PC, for example, has Word 92! We'll be a laughing stock in Europe if Brussels gets to hear about it! Again an insistent knocking at my door, and just as I want to open my New Year present. Again I lower my feet to the floor, and open my eyes. Total darkness. I must have been dreaming. It's not prison, it's my Residence, and someone actually is tapping on my bedroom wall. Bloody cheek!

'H-i!' I bawl.

The tall double door opens a little, throwing a faint shaft of light across the parquet, and there is the sleepy face of my never-off-duty aide. I should reward him with something or other – a toaster, say, or an electric kettle, only not from me personally.

'Hear that?' I demand, gesturing at the wall. 'Well, do something! It's ruined a dream I was having – a prophetic one of state importance!'

I go over to the window. And still the knocking, now as of a hand grown weary – an uneven, sick-heart-like beat, like a call for help. And suddenly it dawns – Mayya Vladimirovna! She must be hammering. Something must have happened to her, alone there, poor thing, with no domestic help – at least not from my reading of the contract.

The hammering stops. Silence. And outside, total darkness, except for a distant twinkle of lights from the Troyeshchina or Raduzhny Districts where I have never been.

My aide coughs discreetly from the door.

'She says she saw smoke from a wire and panicked,' he reports woodenly. 'There *was* a smell of burning rubber.'

'You've alerted someone?'

'No. There wasn't a fire.'

'It's my bloody Residence we're talking about!'

'Regulations require a complete electrical shut-down, which means waking Nikolai Lvovich to switch video surveillance and communications to emergency power –'

'Do you think I need a lecture at this time of night!' I am not really angry, I want only to renew my dream which I hope is still waiting for me, every vivid image of it. 'Get out!'

The door closes, I return to my duvet and essential-oil-impregnated feng shui pillow, and in no time I'm again rising from my bed to take down the keys and open my two locks of the cell door.

66

Kiev, March 1985

Scrunching under foot is an icy layer left by slapdash snow-clearers to give pedestrians something to remember them by. And remember them I do, each time I slip and fall, as happens at least once a day while the ice thaws. The evening freeze is an aid to keeping one's balance, but by bath time I am never short of fresh bruises.

It will soon be spring and there'll be a general thaw, but even in the heavy snows of January our block caretakers clear paths to each block with their big shovels. Where are they now? Have they all been sent to Truskavets spa?

Mother didn't take up her union's offer of a free voucher. After the windows were replaced, it took more than a week to restore the flat to 20°C. The only draught now was from the balcony door. The windows I sealed myself.

For three days Dima has refused to talk to us. The doctor has told Mother that he must go into a mental hospital for a minimum of three months, his condition being now so acute as to require constant specialist observation.

This news cheers me. Let him watch his *Avengers* there! Retribution, as I see it, for his ruining Mother's chance of recuperation. And for three months I'll have a room to myself.

I am just approaching the Academic bookshop in Lenin Street, where I agreed to meet Mira. She rang this morning to say that we were both invited by friends. Three in the afternoon seems a funny time to be invited, but I suppose her friends are way-out opera folk or something similar.

Mira appears on the dot, carrying a cardboard box which I took to be a present.

'It's Chekalov Street, not far,' she says.

We walk arm in arm. The pavement is free of both snow and ice and a pleasure to walk on.

In no time we are climbing to the first floor of an old pre-revolution block and ringing at a battered door.

The passage, full of enormous cases, some bulging and bound with leather straps, is anything but welcoming. The flat reeks of naphthalene. Wondering what we'd got into, I turn to Mira, who indicates that we should go on, and on we go into an enormous room furnished only with a table and chairs. Unfaded squares and rectangles show where pictures or photographs have hung. The table is laid, no one is about, but we can here voices.

'They're in the kitchen,' says Mira, leading me down the next passage to a spacious kitchen and a surprise in the shape of Larisa Vadimovna, who greets me warmly as though I were her son-in-law already. Three women and two old men standing at the window stare, as if looking for some defect in me.

'This is Sergey,' says Mira.

Staring done, they quickly resume their conversations. Then other guests appear, among them a lad of fifteen called Lenya.

'I've been expelled from the Young Communist League!' he announces indignantly. 'When I get over there, I'm going to join some other league that none of them can get into.'

'There being where?' I ask.

'Israel,' whispers Mira. 'They're emigrating. This is their send-off.'

Replete with garlic chicken and stuffed herring, we take ourselves off, and dutifully I walk Mira home.

'Would you like to get out?' Mira asks suddenly.

'They wouldn't let me. I'm not a Jew.'

'They would if you married one,' she says half jokingly, looking me in the face, just as her feet slide from under her and I only just manage to save her from falling.

'Thanks,' she says, regaining her balance. 'You can come in and sit. Mother will be another three hours with the Lichters. She's known them twenty years.'

Why not go in and sit, or lie, come to that? Life goes on and must be properly enjoyed. For one's own well-being and the happiness of others.

67

Kiev, May 2004, Sunday

I sat with espresso coffee in the warmth of our glassed-in loggia.

Svetlana was out doing antenatal exercises which she preferred to do in the company of other expectant mothers, rather than at home. Gentle exercise, massage, a swim, then coffee and a chat about morning sickness which Svetlana was happily free of.

Valya's pregnancy was also going well. They were expecting just a daughter, and Dima rang once to tell me as much, his voice shrill with joy. But he ended by asking for money – over and above the 40,000 Swiss francs I paid annually in advance.

Do you believe in miracles? I don't but I do believe in the amazing coincidences. When I got twenty days' social work for hooliganism and spent it sweeping the yard of the Nivki District Militia, the officer put in charge of me had been none other than Captain Murko, our witness. In those days I had thought him twenty years older than me, rather than the seven or eight he actually was.

As our non-public venue we settled on a billiards café at the corner of Lower Wall and Glybochitskaya Streets, which Svetlana at first was not all that struck with. We drank champagne with cold appetisers, and Svetlana and I had a game of billiards.

'If I win, will you grant me three wishes?' she asked.

I said I would, and anxious to know what they were, I played to lose.

'The first,' she said, potting the last ball, 'is that if you ever stop loving me, you will still love our children. Second, that we won't interfere with each other's professional affairs or try to give each other useful advice. And third, that you never again buy me gaudy underwear!'

She smiled and rising on tiptoe brought her face close to mine. We kissed, but were interrupted by the Captain's choking on something. A slap on the back did the trick, and he called for vodka and a chop.

'Ever see Husseinov after he was slung out?'

'The lads have seen him. I haven't . . .'

'Ring, if you hear of him,' I said, giving my card, 'to use in evidence if you get into trouble at home for drinking. And if you hear anything of Husseinov, let me know.'

'Thank you,' the Captain nodded. 'I'm afraid they don't give us visiting cards.'

'No problem,' I said, pouring him more vodka. Now I know what my wife wished for and the Captain's desires were catered for, it only remained to think about what I wanted, but I was horrified to discover that there was nothing I wished for. I remembered how a doctor had told me that the absence of desires is actually an illness, he even told me the name of it . . . something beginning with 'A', I think. Perhaps I have the same thing as Dima – after all we like the same kind of women.

When his chop arrived, I poured the Captain vodka and, seeing that Svetlana had had enough of the billiards café, placed two hundred hryvnas on the table in front of him.

'We must be off, but you drink on to our health and happiness,' I said.

'What month is she in?' he whispered in my ear.

'The third.'

'And that's why you've married?'

133

I let out a raucous laugh that brought chef and both waitresses to the kitchen door.

'No. I've tried that sort of marriage. This time it's for love.'

68

Kiev, October 2015

A morning of drizzle, the masseuse and the barber, leaving me spick and span and presentable, although today I have no public appearances scheduled. Just a few low-level encounters, as Nikolai Lvovich put it, before nipping off somewhere, leaving me time to peruse my latest edicts in solitude. After all, I do occasionally need to know what I am ratifying, lest Nikolai Lvovich take it into his head *per pro* me to free for privatisation some jealously preserved little factory. At 10 a.m., still sleepy-eyed and having difficulty focusing, I switch on my desk lamp. Just as the edicts are becoming more intelligible, the yellow light of the lamp starts to flicker irritatingly. I send for Nikolai Lvovich, who comes running and gawks.

'What the bloody hell's up with this?' I demand.

'Cheap energy.'

'Meaning?'

'Remember the Cheap Energy Production and the Restructuring of State Liability for Energy Bill? Kazimir was upping prices. You convened a night sitting.'

'But not to have this happen. So ring the bugger and tell him –'

'I can't. His secretary hangs up on anyone from the government or presidential administration.'

'Is he off his rocker? Does he think he can do what he likes here –?'

'He doesn't think, he knows he can.'

'I want Svetlov, today.'

'But you're meeting with Filin.'

'Can't have them together – oil and water.'

'So Svetlov for 4 p.m.,' says Nikolai Lvovich noticeably softening, as if in preparation for some manoeuvre.

'Oh, the Russian Ambassador rang to request a meeting. "Matter of vital importance." He'll be here in ten minutes.'

'So did he request a meeting or demand one?'

'Both. You know what the Russians are like.'

No sooner has he gone than he returns with Ambassador Poyarkovsky, a demoted oligarch, a grabber of all there was to grab, until the President grabbed it off him, leaving him to choose between emigrating and serving his country. He is grabbing still, but now for Russia, and forever poking his nose into our economy, about which there is really nothing to be done. It may be staffed by Ukrainians, but the whole thing belongs to Russia, Germany, Lithuania and Cyprus.

'Mr President,' he says by way of greeting, slightly bowing his head, then turning haughtily to Nikolai Lvovich, who immediately leaves the room.

I motion him to the ottoman, of which his profession has no fear, and for a while we sit, me at my edict-covered desk, he, legs crossed, adjusting his narrow emerald-green tie, holding the pause like an actor.

'Is there a problem?' I ask.

'Something very serious, Mr President. I feel the need to enlighten you since others are concealing the facts, vital as they are to the state of the country.'

'Who is concealing them?'

'Your entourage,' he says calmly. 'We know more about developments in western Ukraine than your press reports. And we are disquieted.'

'What developments?'

'Catholic resurgence.'

'There aren't enough Greek Catholics there to worry about.'

'But these aren't the Greek sort. Special Service agents of the Vatican have been seen in Lvov. Something else of interest we're on to is that the Roman Church is at present debating whether to authenticate a miracle in western Ukraine.'

'And you see a miracle as potentially dangerous? What is it, a weeping icon?'

'Mr President,' he says, unwaveringly firm and confident, 'miracles always have consequences! Get your people to keep an eye on these spies and what their Church is up to in general. This is the birthplace of Russian Orthodoxy! No ground must be lost. The people would never forgive you.'

I am inclined to send this oligarch manqué packing, but since he is an Ambassador of the Russian Federation, the easiest and least costly way of indicating the end of our conversation is for me to rise from my desk, and this I do. It's now 11 a.m. Time for Filin.

69

Kiev, March 1985

'Do you know, I'm being watched,' was the first thing David Isaakovich said, as I deposited a bottle of strong red and two tins of Traveller's Luncheon in a paper bag on the dugout floor.

'Watched?'

'By them. Security.'

'They've actually been here?'

'Here and all over. Even cutting an ice hole near ours.'

'Why?'

'To keep an eye on us, while pretending to walrus.'

'And do they walrus?'

'Not that I've seen. Real walruses leave naked footprints, they only leave boot marks.'

Half rising from the bed, he put a couple of logs in the stove.

'Brought something to drink?' he asked, eyeing my paper bag. 'Well, let's have a warmer, then go for a dip.'

Feeling the benefit of my first glass, I took off my GDR fur. David Isaakovich was sitting in just a blue sweater topped by a quilted jacket without sleeves.

It was getting dark.

'Father Basil was coming,' David Isaakovich said, looking at his watch.

His voice betrayed his longing for company. Genuinely glad as he was to see me, he would have been even gladder to see Father Basil as well.

Half an hour later, as we were finishing the wine, the crunch of snow and a knock announced Father Basil's arrival.

'Let's see what they're up to, these unbelievers,' he boomed, when told of the KGB interest in us, and pulling a green towel from his anorak, stripped off and went barefoot forth, the towel about his loins. Pausing only for David Isaakovich to produce a towel from somewhere, we followed, still dressed.

Here, in wind and a temperature of -10°C, it was still very much winter, a far cry from Kiev's melting icicles, drip-drip of water and puddles where ice had been.

The worrying new ice hole was a good fifty metres downstream, and it was hard to see how anyone splashing about there could hear what was being said in ours.

But there was no sense in arguing with David Isaakovich, who, knowing life as he did, couldn't possibly be mistaken.

Letting his towel fall, Father Basil plunged in.

'Splendid!' he cried, waving his arms to emphasise it.

David Isaakovich started undressing. I followed suit, and we were soon all in the intensely cold water together.

'Splendid!' I lied cheerily, frozen to the marrow, but unwilling to admit as much to these he-men.

'No,' said Father Basil, looking towards the other hole, 'if they were wanting to check up on us, they'd have made it closer. They're not idiots.'

'They've no need to listen, they can lip-read.'

'Won't get far with me, then,' said Father Basil who, as I noticed for the first time, barely moved his lips when he spoke.

The flow of water – or talk of the KGB – stirred a kind of boldness in me. With a look to fix its direction and a great gulp of air, I dived and let the current carry me towards the other ice hole. After what seemed several minutes and still no hole, I panicked. Had I missed it? Bloody fool that I was! Then suddenly a great bright patch, and up I shot, breaking through a thin crust of ice and grasping the side of the hole so as not to get carried further.

With a feeling more of pride than confidence in my achievement, I climbed out onto the ice and saw Father Basil and David Isaakovich standing anxiously by their hole. Then they spotted me.

'Really!' said David Isaakovich, gesturing helplessly as I approached. 'One tiny drink, and you're away! And not even for a bet!'

'Well done,' boomed Father Basil. 'What matters is not where you dive, but where you come up! You have the makings of an interesting fellow. And since God swam with you all that time under water, He loves you. Don't go thinking it was luck. It was God!'

70

Sharm el Sheikh, May 2004

'All for you!' I said, indicating the star-studded night sky.

A camel snorted. Bedouin were spreading a canvas groundsheet on the sand.

'The stars at home are fatter,' said Svetlana in a comical put-on voice.

'Like everything else. We've black earth where they've got desert.'

The windless chill of an Egyptian night made me sorry I'd left my sweater in Kiev.

A match scraped, and a fire flared into life, dully reflected in the bronze of a cauldron suspended from an almost invisible tripod. One of the Bedouin was crouched, filling the cauldron with water.

I put my arm around her and we gazed up at the bright stars together.

'I want to kiss you,' I whispered.

'Only not in public in a Muslim country, we were told.'

'The desert's not public,' I said, putting my lips to hers.

The four Bedouin now settled by the fire looked away, and struck up a strange, slow spine-thrilling song.

Our kiss lasted minutes.

'I love you,' I said softly.

'And I love you.'

While the men sang on, we sat by the fire, watching the reflection of the flames on the cauldron. The fairy-tale atmosphere of that desert night cleansed us of all our worries. We were lovers travelling in time, youthful, free of past and future, made for each other and this night together. Watched over by guardians who sang mournfully to our happiness.

Squeezing Svetlana's hand I felt its warmth and responded to its gentle pressure on mine.

'Ya saidi! Ya saidi!' called one of the Bedouin to wake me.

Above the grey-yellow desert, the sun was rising. Tripod, cauldron, flames were gone, and the men were standing by their camels ready to depart. The groundsheet was removed and folded, and we watched the hotel jeep approaching across the barren plain.

Majid, the driver, tipped each of the Bedouin, and, without a backward glance at us, they mounted their camels and set off across the desert.

71

Kiev, October 2015

Filin is amazingly cheerful, and a pleasure to talk to after Poyarkovsky.

'Re reform,' he begins. 'Mykola and I spent two hours drawing up a programme, an experimental one initially, the budget allocation falling short of what would be required for all prisons. The main task, Ukrainianisation, falls of course to Mykola. I get –'

'A cognac, if you'd like one,' I suggest warmly. I have maintained a respect for the militia from my youth and here I have a particularly charming representative.

'To prison reform!' I propose, and after a little cognac, conversation flows with river-like fluency. Mykola was pushing for compulsory Ukrainian courses in every prison, and punishment for refuseniks. This seemed inhumane and with a little assistance from me it has been dropped and replaced by plans for voluntary courses and the possibility of early release for those who pass, with an option for first-time, less serious offenders to be recommended for teacher training.

Filin, however, is more concerned with material provision, filling libraries with books and instructing prisoners in the basics of business and management.

'I've hundreds of letters from prisoners who don't just want to sit their time out. It's training they ask for. To acquire new professions. They are still our citizens.'

'And voters. So that's it, you put your training programme on paper, present it as Mykola has his, and we'll give it effect and maybe extra funding.'

Filin, sitting to the left of the ottoman as stiffly to attention as if he has swallowed a sword, smiles, and for a moment there is silence.

'Do you know,' I say, 'I dreamed recently of being in a prison cell that had a little fridge, a little Samsung TV, an ancient computer and a hook on the wall with keys to the two locks of my inner door.'

Filin listens attentively and frowns.

'That's Kazimir's cell, right down to the fridge and the Samsung telly.'

'I didn't know he'd done time.'

'Just a couple of weeks. When he was found with drugs and a Kalashnikov. First he was the defendant, then a witness and, in the end, the prosecutor general ordered his release so as not, you understand, to upset the balance of power in the shadow economy. A new slicing up of the cake would not have been in anyone's interests.'

'But he went and cut himself another huge slice including all our electricity!'

Filin sighs.

'Why did I dream of his cell? I've never even been in prison.'

Filin shrugs, then as if startled, consults his watch, looking up guiltily.

'Right,' I say, rising. 'You prepare your basics of business for the prisoners' course.'

72

Kiev, March 1985

It's three days since Dima started living in the Hospital for the Mentally Sick, Row 1, Pushcha-Voditsa, facing Pioneer Camp Dawn, now all silent shabby dormitory blocks, with a lone watchman sitting bored at the gate forever shouting at a slow-witted dog.

Mother and I crossed the road to board the number 30 bus back to Kiev.

Dima, I knew, was at the fence watching us go. There were tears in his eyes when we left. But with him tears could mean something quite different. As different as he is.

Mother had talked for the sake of talking about an upcoming business trip to some factory in Dnepropetrovsk. She had asked what Dima wanted her to bring back for him, but he had just looked thoughtful and nodded, his shoulders raised as if he had intended to shrug and then left them up high, straining towards his ears.

'So?' Mother had said insistently.

I had wanted to answer for him. He doesn't want anything and he's happy the way he is. But Mother had persisted, and in the end roused him to reply.

'Halva,' he'd said, leaving me to wonder what halva had to do with Dnepropetrovsk.

'I'll get you some,' said Mother, all smiles, clutching him to her, kissing him three times, and telling him to do what the doctors said.

In the evening, with rain lashing the window, I sat on my bed wondering what the ice would be like underfoot the next day.

Dima's neatly made bed under its grey-check rug made me strangely sad. It's as if I no longer had a brother, as though he had died. My pity for Dima returned, with a measure of sorrow for myself. Lying in my own bed, looking across at his, I thought how we had been like two puppies in a kennel. But our master had decided to keep only the strong one and had taken the weakling down to the lake, to drown.

73

Paris, July 2004

'It's those beige ones I like,' said Svetlana pointing to some elegant and amazingly expensive shoes.

'You might fall with heels as high as that.'

'No I shan't.'

Taking one of the shoes, she sat down on a pouffe to try it on, but her eyes filled with tears. Now her legs were swollen, her body was no longer what it once was.

'You'll soon be as you were,' I said.

'I know. But I've had friends who never were the same again. One was beyond recognising!'

'You won't end up like that. Not after all your books and exercise videos.'

'But do I use them?'

'You must. Make sure you do.'

Seeing her eyes return to the shoe shelves, I sought to distract her.

'Let's look at baby clothes.'

She got up from the pouffe with alacrity, her swollen legs and itchy feet forgotten.

So through Perfumes we went without so much as a glance, and purposefully on past the assistant-attended trial stools of Cosmetics.

'Look,' she said, picking up a transparent pack of romper suits marked 'o–3 months'.

And in no time we collected any number of purchases that could just as well have been made in Kiev.

'Where now?' I asked, heavily laden.

'The hotel to dump this lot.'

'And then?'

'I'd like to see the prostitutes. They're supposed to be ugly.'

I laughed. 'The beautiful become call girls, the less attractive streetwalk.'

We sat at a pavement table, Svetlana busy with a Turko-Greek version of a hot dog liberally sprinkled with ketchup, and watching a mulatto prostitute on the other side of the road.

'What do they charge?' she asked.

I went over and used my broken English to find out.

'For twenty minutes, thirty euros. With her' – indicating Svetlana – 'watching, fifty euros. Video, one hundred euros,' she explained, and presented me with her card. She was Lulu and could be telephoned.

'And I thought Paris was expensive,' Svetlana laughed, when I told her.

74

Kiev, October 2015

'Ah, at last,' I say, getting to my feet as Svetlov comes in. 'Take a seat.'

He sits, instantly attentive, instantly ready to act.

'Care for some cognac?'

'No, thanks,' his refusal accompanied by an apologetic smile.

'To business then,' I say, switching on my desk lamp which quickly reduces itself to a flicker. 'See that?'

'Loose wire?'

'No, cheap energy – Kazimir's revenge for our making him charge less for his kilowatts.'

'We've no direct leverage,' says Svetlov gloomily, having thought for a while, eyes on my desktop. '"Leave him alone, let him develop," was your predecessor's line, but that was when Kazimir could be reasoned with. Now he has *developed*, with a vengeance . . .'

'What about indirect leverage?'

'Not possible. We couldn't pull it off quietly; any noise would frighten away investors.'

'So meanwhile I ruin my eyesight?' I say, switching off the lamp.

'I'll give it thought.'

'Put him on the Other Hands Operation list?'

'He's not a civil servant. Only those of middle and senior rank qualify under the agreement.'

'B-l-o-o-d-y hell! We've an oligarch with a criminal past taking liberties, and nothing I, as President, can do? I've even dreamed of the cell he spent two weeks in, so Filin tells me.'

'What was he in for?' asks Svetlov, suddenly animated.

146

'Filin can tell you.'

Svetlov looks quietly hopeful.

'What, do you suppose, made me dream of that cell?'

'No idea,' he says. 'But I could find you a good parapsychologist. One of ours.'

'Yes, do. Something else: Poyarkovsky was here, beefing about a flare-up of Roman Catholic activity, and the Vatican's debating the authentication of some miracle which occurred here in Ukraine.'

'I'll look into it and report back tomorrow,' says Svetlov, quick as ever to know when it was time to rise, snap briefly to attention and depart.

The working day is over, though it could have been continued indefinitely, given the twenty or so kilograms of freshly baked edicts and documents awaiting signature on my desk. But a spell alone at home in Desatinaya Street is what I want. Today I've had enough of them all. Poyarkovsky especially. Today has felt like a week.

Loosening my tie I call my aide and give him various instructions. Nikolai Lvovich can take control of the spider's web. I'm so tired I'd rather sleep than eat.

The door opens to reveal Nikolai Lvovich, looking worried.

'Mr President, don't forget you've a dinner tonight.'

'Who with?'

'Mayya Vladimirovna.'

I'm speechless. The only words that come to mind would leave me rinsing my mouth out for hours afterwards. I don't like swearing. It leaves a bad taste, but I'm sure my facial expression says it all.

'At the Residence, just for half an hour. She's not in the best of moods. Some wiring in her bedroom burned through.'

'Has it been attended to?'

'No. We've no electricians we can rely on not to talk.'

'Then get the Minister for Energy to see to it himself.'

'Is that an order?'

'Yes. And another thing, if this lamp starts flickering tomorrow, there'll be no more dinners with your precious Mayya Vladimirovna, or breakfasts either! So get cracking!'

75

Kiev, April 1985, Thursday

'It'll be knee-deep in mud!' I protest.

'But it's very important,' says Mira, looking uneasily at my broken-zipped Polish half-boots. 'I'll wash them off at my place after.'

'How about me?'

'We've got hot water.'

'And ten neighbours queuing for it!'

After ten minutes I give in, and we go to a food store where she spends ten roubles on sausage, cheese, a twelve-kopek loaf and a box of fruit pastilles. She is about to buy barberry-filled chocolates too, until I stop her.

'What about something to wash your sausage down with?'

'Such as what?' she asks sheepishly.

'Port wine at the very least. Beer does in summer, but not now.'

She thinks for a moment, and then we go to the wine and vodka counter. Here, after counting her change, she looks helplessly at the bottles.

'That's the one,' I say, pointing.

We take the metro to Post Office Square, then walk, me carrying the groceries and carefully avoiding puddles.

The footbridge is still icy and it's blowing hard.

I walk, wondering what the hell this expedition is in aid of and why today. That it would end badly seems more than likely. He is her father, but as she said herself they'd not seen each other for years. Why not wait for spring proper?

'It's not his birthday, is it?' I ask, indicating the weight of the bag.

'No.'

No easier in my mind, I slip and fall, bruising my right hip but managing to keep the bag with the old man's bottle clear of the ground.

David Isaakovich is not so much surprised as puzzled.

'What's up?' he enquires in a trembling voice, looking anxiously at his daughter. 'Is Mummy ill?'

The dugout is surprisingly warm. The top of the stove is glowing red and logs lie ready.

'We've just brought a few things,' she says, taking the bag and handing it to her father.

Looking inside, he wrinkles his brow, as if troubled.

'What's the date?'

'The 4th,' I tell him.

Reassured, he livens up and fusses about. It isn't every day his beloved only daughter comes to see him!

We lay the food on the table and start to cut the sausage. David Isaakovich fills three glasses with wine.

All seems to be going well, but I still have doubts. I just can't see why, on a working day and in bad weather, Mira has dragged us both out to Trukhanov Island. Still, the old man is happy, and that is the main thing.

But no sooner are we munching Doctor's Health Sausage to the spreading warmth of the wine than Mira announces that she and her mother are emigrating to Israel.

David Isaakovich chokes at the news. I give him three good thumps on the back, and as he struggles to regain his breath, Mira prattles on.

'Don't worry, we'll be all right. There'll be the sea and mountains just like in the Crimea.'

So this is it.

Father and daughter sit looking at each other, while I help myself to cheese and sausage and sip my wine, feeling utterly superfluous.

For near twenty minutes they look at each other in silence, then suddenly he spits out, 'You're traitors, you and Mummy!'

Mira sobs, shoulders heaving. Perhaps I should comfort her, but I don't want to get involved and I am not sure who is the dearer to me: David Isaakovich, the teacher and father I'd never known; or Mira? We are good together, she and I, sometimes *very good*, although she makes as poor a job of life as she does of washing cups. True, communal flat conditions provided some excuse for that.

'We'll write,' she says through tears.

'Where to? I've no address here.'

'We'll write care of someone,' she says, looking at me.

Damn that, I think. Not a word to me about going to Israel, and here she is expecting me to play postman in all weathers on that footbridge!

David Isaakovich stares long and hard at me before refilling our glasses.

'We'll get through, like in the war,' he says.

At which it dawns on me that he assumes Mira and I are in cahoots and I am here to defend her.

'Couldn't you stay?' I ask Mira, looking into her tear-filled eyes.

She tries to answer but can't and just shakes her head.

Again we fall silent. It's getting dark now, and I'm not relishing the windy walk back, half-boots squelching water.

'Please, Daddy, let us both go,' implores Mira.

'Go where you like,' he says quietly.

Mira is incredulous.

'Go,' he whispers.

'So will you sign this?'

She gives him a small sheet of paper rolled into a cylinder.

Screwing up his eyes, he looks uncomprehending at his daughter and then at the paper.

'What's this for?'

'A statement for Visa and Registration that you have no objection to our going, Mother and me.'

Surprisingly calmly David Isaakovich writes to her dictation and Mira tucks the paper away in her jacket with its artificial-fur-trimmed hood.

'How about a statement from me?' I taunt on the way back.

'Do you think I like it? It's Mother who wants to go, now her friends have gone. So what do I do? Stay on my own? Move to the dugout? I've cried over it for nights.'

The wind turns my face to ice, but my step, strong red notwithstanding, is firm, and we arrive at Post Office Square without fall or misadventure.

'Pity I live in a one-room in a communal flat, or we could have had a night together,' says Mira, in an effort to make amends.

'There's always my place. Mother's in Dnepropetrovsk.'

'Fine,' says Mira without much conviction.

Heading home to my flat on the metro, I wonder which it should be: Mother's couch in the sitting room, or my and Dima's beds pulled together.

76

Kiev, July 2004

'You'll never guess what's been going on here!' wailed Nila as I entered the office.

'What?'

'People shutting themselves in your office, and going through your drawers, I shouldn't wonder –'

Having come straight from the airport, dropping Svetlana at the flat, and with Paris still coursing through my veins, I felt distinctly uneasy.

'OK, Nila, I'll check. Meanwhile I'm taking no calls.'

Everything, files, documents, water-wheel-like name-card index were as they should be.

Nila's phone rang. Mine stayed silent.

I looked through my drawers. All were as they should be, everything in its place. Even the envelopes of dollars I never found time to open. Exactly where they'd come from I couldn't remember. Deputies and businessmen would turn up with queries or requests, I would promise what was required, and in a flash they were gone, and there would be an envelope on my desk. One visitor who had been holding a copy of *How to be a Millionaire* the whole time, left that on my desk when he went, and as I picked it up, meaning to run after him, an envelope fell out – heavy, but not so heavy as to contain a million. I had to laugh.

I must do something about them, I decided. Whoever the visitors had been, they obviously weren't interested in money, but I couldn't be too careful. There were Secret Service folk. I must be more vigilant.

I got them out. There were eleven, and slitting them open, I sorted the contents into $100 and $50 piles, putting a comic wad of forty-eight new one-dollar bills to one side.

Counting money is pleasant, but doing it for too long makes your fingers lose sensitivity, as if sanded and varnished over.

The final total was a laughable $13,800. Was I really that cheap? Still, I hadn't asked for this money. It had been left in the manner of a tip by clients not wishing to be thought mean or rude. I must get rid of it! I glanced towards the window. No, Pechersk had no need of money. Even the caretakers were plumper here.

I called and Nila came, sweet-faced, green-eyed, attractive as Eve – a baby doll with intelligent eyes.

'This is for you,' I said. 'Buy yourself a flat.'

She took a step back.

'You must be joking.'

'I'm not. You shouldn't still be living with your parents.'

Sweeping the dollars into a large brown envelope, I eventually got her to accept it.

Having at least made one person happy, I sank into an armchair. What else had I got today? I could have rung through to Nila, but preferred not to trouble her.

77

Kiev, October 2015

'Freckles suit you,' observes Mayya Vladimirovna.

We are eating at a round table in the small dining room, served by a blonde slip of a girl in brown frock and white apron, Zoya I think, a product of four or five generations of presidential service.

'Do you know, I'm even glad now that it turned out like this.'

'How do you mean?' I ask although I could hardly care less.

She is very sensitive. It's as if she sees right through you. Her face, no longer lined, looks decidedly more cheerful.

'May I?' Zoya asks and, receiving a nod, removes Mayya's untouched sturgeon in aspic. And while I finish my own horseradish-doused turbot, Mayya sips her Chardonnay.

'How did it all start? Who actually suggested using your husband's heart for me?' I add, seeing her not with me.

'Let's not talk of that,' she says apologetically. 'For one thing, I've signed an undertaking to say nothing; and two, because I prefer not to talk about it.'

She has dressed well for our dinner – black tights, black-belted frock, generously slit skirt, elegant platinum earrings, and projecting from behind each ear, pure thirties-style, a curl.

I am in her debt. I owe her my life, or, more precisely, my heart. It behoves me to be more affable, my own dubious character and the shock of my new heart notwithstanding.

'Nice perfume,' I say quietly.

'Pardon?' Mayya looks genuinely surprised. 'I'm "au naturel" this evening,' she whispers.

Zoya sets before her a plate of baked strips of calf's liver and a vegetable terrine and the scent of perfume grows stronger.

I realise the perfume is Zoya's. She has good taste. I throw her a respectful glance before returning my gaze to Mayya.

'Did you love your husband?'

'No,' she says calmly. 'He loved me for a while before we married. Which was why I accepted him. Better a love you don't reciprocate than to love in vain.'

'What about loving and being loved?'

'Easiest of all things to pretend. Have you ever really loved?'

'Seeing as I'm nearly fifty, yes, of course,' I said with a smile. 'Really, passionately.'

'And was it mutual?' The irony in her voice is barely disguised.

'Yesterday I would have said yes. Now I'm not so sure. Probably, regarding the last few love stories, I would have to say "no".'

'A man loves and is truly loved only twice, they say – the first time and the last.'

'So I've missed out on the first,' I say, leaning back and putting down my fork. 'That was just first sex.'

'Life's not kind to all of us,' she says, apparently genuinely sympathetic.

'And I'm not so bad as you may think,' I say, my gaze wandering to her lips, which I noticed were also 'au naturel' this evening. 'State service takes a man progressively further from the norm. The higher you get, the less normal you are and I'm the President! Normal is the last thing for him to be – normal is too straightforward, too stupid, too naive, too good, and not what we as a nation ever elect.' Zoya removes our glasses, and fills fresh ones with red wine.

'What I think,' says Mayya Vladimirovna watching the fragrant Zoya's progress from the room, 'is that you are suffering from stress.

Hence your present candour. And if I were your wife, I'd seek help –'

'Psychiatric?'

'No, I put that badly – stress consultancy.'

'I've tried it. The last course of treatment left my hands aching for a fortnight. True, it did rid me of stress. Incidentally, I appear to have a marriage guidance counsellor too, despite having no marriage. I give you one guess who.'

'My brother,' she says quietly.

'Sheer coincidence?'

'There's no such thing. Still, it's nothing to do with me. We're not on the best of terms, my brother and I. He didn't care for my husband, and I never cared for my brother and his crowd, half of whom are from his school year and now hold posts in your office . . .'

'Say no more,' I say, raising a hand as if to have my palm read. 'They are not of my choosing. I only ever see them by chance, and the more I hear of them, the more depressed I become.'

'So we should see each other more – a good heart-to-heart does away with depression.'

My garrulity, this bursting forth of a sense of guilt or obligation towards Mayya, alarms me, but like all my outbursts I know it's temporary. And what if I'm unpleasant next time we meet? I suddenly feel sorry for her.

'That burnt-out wire of yours will be seen to,' I say.

'It's already fixed.'

'When it started to smoke, I was dreaming a strange dream and your knocking became part of it – our rooms adjoin.'

'I didn't know what else to do. I banged on the door first, but no one came. They lock me in at night so I won't come out and set the alarms off.'

'Who locks you in?'

'No idea. Nikolai Lvovich told me they would.'

'So you called for help and no one came . . .'

'Yes, but as Nikolai Lvovich said afterwards, this is the one building in the country where there is never any need to summon help, since security is total.'

I begin to wonder how many other secrets my official residence is keeping from me.

Zoya comes in with an envelope.

'*Sergey Pavlovich,*' reads the card inside, '*You can send HER away now. Time's up. Goodnight. Nikolai Lvovich.*'

Taking my pen I write '*Get lost!*' and return the card to its envelope.

'See he reads this,' I instruct Zoya, whose expression admits the shadow of a smile. She has obviously been well trained. One of the golden rules of the job: never smile in response to a tease or compliment. Turning to Mayya, I say, 'I'll tell them not to lock you in. We're not in the Middle Ages.'

In my mind's eye, I see again the iron door lockable from both sides and the ring of keys hanging from a nail to the left of it. Keys, doors – like riddles and the answers thereto.

78

Kiev, April 1985

Mother really does bring Dima halva from Dnepropetrovsk, a whole kilo of it. She returns on Friday, and early on Saturday we go out to him in a half-empty bus.

The sun is shining. Mornings are still cold but by midday there is warmth that is lost towards evening.

To left and right, snow-floored pine forest, as slow to thaw as Kiev is quick.

'What's this?' asks Dima, examining the halva.

'It's what you asked for. I promised,' says Mother, nervously concealing her disappointment.

He pops a piece of halva into his mouth and his face takes on a look of quiet childish delight. Relieved, Mother breaks him off a larger bit.

'Aren't you cold?' she asks.

It's by no means warm – 12°C, or so. I am in my jacket, Mother her coat, and he in his hospital or, rather, nursing home blue flannel suit.

'Yes,' he says, darting off to the two-storey brick block, and returning wearing a blue dressing gown.

'You two wait here and talk,' says Mother, 'while I have word with the doctor.'

Dima and I stand facing each other in silence. Every so often he dips into the bag I am holding to break off a bit more halva, puts it into his mouth and chews, all the while looking through me.

Talk? What about? I don't know. When we shared a bedroom we talked sometimes. Now it's different. I am the surviving puppy, he the drowned one. For as long as he is out of sight I feel sorry for him, but standing with him, knowing him to be alive, living his own peculiar life, my pity vanishes.

79

Kiev, August 2004, Saturday

I take cocoa to Svetlana still in bed. She attempts a smile, but is clearly unwell.

The bright blue sky beyond the window is like an extension of the blue of our bedroom walls.

Sitting up in bed and placing a pillow behind her back, she takes the cup from me.

'Let's go for a drive today.'

'You'll get car sick like last time.'

'Not if I have no breakfast.'

'But you must eat more than just tablets.'

'Did you get the calf's liver?'

'Zhenka got it.'

Zhenka was our home help. Aged fifty, she always comes while we are out.

'Right, I'll eat, and then we'll go for a drive. To the Ring Road.'

Cutting the liver into thin strips, I fry it. The extractor fan hums quietly away above the stove, my stomach rumbles, but through the open window vent, not a sound of bird or of traffic on the Lesi Ukrainki Boulevard, which a glance through the window shows to be almost deserted.

Feeling my chin, I decide to shave. Why is she so interested in prostitutes – in Paris, where they were supposed to be so ugly, and here? This is the third time she has been drawn to the Ring Road.

'In Kiev it's twelve midday,' the car radio tells us as we enter Odessa Square, Svetlana sitting beside me, legs awkwardly splayed, supporting her stomach with both hands.

'Not one to be seen,' she says, as we drive through one of the market areas.

'Sleeping off exhaustion. What's the fascination anyway?'

Usually she shrugs off such questions, but today she says unexpectedly: 'I think they know something.'

'About men?'

'About life. Troubles . . . Danger . . .'

'Yes, they would know about all that.'

'And it's the oldest profession.'

'Not much scope for career advancement.'

'Stop.'

I brake and find myself looking at a slim girl in a T-shirt inscribed 'Fuck You' and skintight trousers, wearing a tiny locket on a cheap chain and looking haughty and defiant.

'Get her name and telephone number,' says Svetlana.

'Want a threesome?' asks the girl.

'My wife would like your name and phone number,' I say lamely, beginning to wonder about Svetlana.

'What sort is she?'

'Kind and loving.'

Having nothing to write on, I hold out my hand and with my pen she writes 'Zhanna 444-0943', while I become aware of her pleasant perfume. Straightening and with an amused look at Svetlana in the car, she quickly kisses me on the lips then runs her fingers down my unshaven cheek.

Returning to the car I show Svetlana my palm.

'Careful you don't rub it off,' she says, and then, 'I wonder why she kissed you.'

80

'Not my doing!' Nikolai Lvovich protests. 'She has no right to be in this building! She's not your wife.'

'That's rich coming from you!' I snap. 'It was you who discovered her and her heart, you who brought her to me in hospital, and you who now bangs her up at night! Is this some slave state we're running? "Woman hostage incarcerated next to President's bedroom" – is that the headline you're after?'

His eyes flash, but not with fear, more inspiration, as if I have given him an idea. Like everyone here he is vengeful. He'll say nothing now but one day he'll stab me in the back. I must practise more restraint.

'Right,' I say, 'get her to agree not to leave her room at night without good cause, and be gentle about it.'

'I am always more or less gentle, unlike . . .' He leaves off and I wonder who he means. I'm never really rude.

It's Sunday. From my bathroom window I see it's snowing, and through the snow, St Andrew's – a beautiful subject for a little calming meditation.

Nikolai Lvovich having gone, I tell my aide he is to come to me only in case of dire necessity. Putting my whisky on the window ledge, I run a cold bath, and to the sound of tumbling water, look out at the snow and the cupolas.

A living landscape such as the Good Lord, if He exists, could not fail to take pleasure in. A sight to show Mayya, though not from a presidential bathroom gleaming white with the remarkable sanitary engineering of Spain – bidet a good two metres from lavatory pan and even further from the bath, all so wonderfully clean and sterilely tiled that I feel like a surgeon about to slice up the dead land beyond the window.

The double velvet of my bathrobe gives kindly warmth. Navy blue suits me as well for bathrobe as overcoat.

Bath full, ice in tumbler melted, I feel no need of extra cold. Today I'll bath 'au naturel' – without ice.

Slowly I lower myself into the cold water, finally immersing myself totally for just a moment. Too long for me to touch the end, the bath is wide enough for me and another to face each other.

Once again, a sense of animal inadequacy and incompleteness. Double bed, double bath, and alone in both. Space enough to heighten a sense of loneliness, create a semblance of moral pressure, with Mayya Vladimorovna, semi-incognito a wall's width away, completing a cruel *Arabian Nights*-like situation.

What do I really want? Why do I take a bath so cold it arrests thought, slows the blood in my veins, freezes my desires, which, terribly banal as they are, I cannot satisfy? I am not allowed to satisfy them. A president can't go to a striptease bar, sit in warm, pleasant surroundings contemplating the seductive. I can't, as I once took special pleasure in doing, book tickets to Brussels or Paris for an attractive lover, flying out the day before to be at the airport to meet her and carry her off with all about us dancing to the tune of my secret passion. Paris and Brussels would keep my secrets forever. Here I have no secrets, except her in the bedroom next to mine, and any number know of that.

Downing my whisky, I emerge from the chilly solitude of my bath, throw on my robe, and go again to the window, below which is a mighty radiator whose warmth penetrates the double velvet.

It is still snowing, and soon it will be dark.

Calling my aide, I instruct him to tell Mayya 'Dinner in half an hour'.

'What would you like to eat?'

'Anything, so long as it's tasty.'

81

Kiev, May 1985

What a state of affairs! It is not, it appears, quite so easy to sever ties and obtain permission to emigrate. The Visa and Registration Office has spent a whole month chewing over David Isaakovich's statement which was duly certified *per pro* by a notary, a sometime classmate and old friend of Larisa Vadimovna. And now it appears that a statement is insufficient. A husband cannot simply renounce wife and daughter, particularly if still in a state of lawful matrimony.

'You must get divorced,' Visa and Registration told Larisa Vadimovna.

'But we've been living apart for the last ten years!'

'On paper he is still your husband.'

Mira and her mother have invited me to supper to put me in the picture.

I'm relishing the chicken in garlic sauce rather more than what they have to say. They are like a couple of chickens themselves, one young, one old.

'I simply do not know what will happen now,' Larisa Vadimovna says, sighing a sigh that brings her breast nearly up to her chin.

163

She is sitting oddly and awkwardly at table in a pink knitted blouse that doesn't suit her.

'But don't stop eating,' she insists, returning my gaze to my plate of chicken and fried potatoes. 'These Hungarian broilers really are juicy, aren't they! Whatever do they feed them on?'

From broilers she returns to David Isaakovich.

'He's so difficult, so impossible!' she declares, smacking her lips. 'And I don't know anyone at the registry office. Maybe Sofa Abramovna does,' she suggests turning to Mira, but Mira merely shrugs. 'If only he'd agree to come to the registry office, it could all be settled. And we wouldn't be here sitting on what's no longer ours!'

I give her my attentive-pupil look.

'We've sold everything! Table, chairs, beds! We've taken the money and people are waiting to collect it. What do we tell them? "Sorry, my husband won't divorce me"?'

By the tea and gateau, I have grasped what is expected of me: the disagreeable mission of persuading David Isaakovich to come to the registry office and divorce his wife.

Still, the splendid garlic chicken, complemented by sweet Crimean muscat, has done its work.

82

Kiev, August 2004
Beyond the office window, a blaze of sunlight. Yesterday I was worrying how to spend my leave, now the Chief has taken holidays off the agenda. Leave is postponed, and that is all to the good.

Summer working is three times more relaxed than winter. The Cabinet only sits for the TV cameras. Serious questions are deferred until September or October, and general policy discussed instead. Such matters as the restoration of greenery to suburban settlements; payment of unpaid wages; promises, resolutions even, concerning improvements in the investment climate and the easing of fiscal pressure on small and middle business. Big business being problem-free and ever the friend of pressure. And now, out of the blue, an extraordinary Cabinet meeting. With presidential elections in the offing, our Guarantor of the Constitution, the President, is demanding that we 'accumulate positive image'. And that being less difficult than combating a negative one, accumulate the positive is what we'll do. I'm to read a speech in place of the Chief which has already been written by his aides. The Chief having had the good sense to go into hospital for treatment and there keep a finger on the pulse of events. The Cabinet meeting is tomorrow, and I have today to read the speech and, if need be, summon the aides to revise.

'Sergey Pavlovich, you've a visitor.' Nila's announcement is made almost in a whisper, her eyes signalling me a warning.

Short. Slim. In a dark suit, plain, but perfect fit. I can't place him. You can tell a People's Deputy from a mile off. He obviously isn't one. Too fit and slim-faced, apart from which Deputies never leave home without their little lapel badges.

'Come in, take a seat.'

He seems a little awkward. He sits looking at me as if he has already asked me a question and is awaiting my response.

'What can I do for you?' I ask.

'Major Svetlov,' he says, rising from his seat and extending his hand. 'Department of Internal Security.'

'Bunin,' I respond. 'Was it you who came when I was not here?'

'It was us, yes. It's our job.'

The room goes quiet. So that is the message Nila's green eyes were trying to give me.

'Nothing to worry about,' he continues, placing his right hand on the table and drumming his fingers on the wood. 'Just one or two questions I have to ask.'

'Go ahead.' I sound calm, but inside I am desperately running barefoot through snow, howling wolves at my heels.

'Sergey Pavlovich, you will appreciate that as a state official rising high in his career, you attract special attention.'

'On your part?'

'Yes, and as is perfectly normal. We have to make sure that those admitted to high office recognise that they are accountable for all that they do – as well as for their nearest and dearest and friends – and do not for an instant fail in their loyalty to the interests of the state.'

I nod in agreement, thoughts racing as to the reason for this visit and the search that preceded it. My one and only serious departure from the straight and narrow is the envelopes, and as I see it, the straight and narrow is not something that anyone keeps to, in life or in work.

'I've not lobbied for anyone, if that's what you mean,' I say with as much assurance as I can muster. 'There are things which I do not entirely understand, but I can assure you that I will attend with the utmost –'

'No, no.' Major Svetlov dismisses my words with a wave of his hand. 'There are just a couple of points I would like to clear up, more for my own interest, in order to be able to understand you better. There's a child on the way, isn't there?'

'Twins.'

'You have a charming wife. But I'm puzzled by these excursions to the Ring Road.'

'I don't use my official car.'

'No, thank God, but why go at all?'

'For some reason,' I begin, lowering my voice confidentially, 'my wife has become interested in prostitutes. I don't get it, but the pregnant are not to be crossed – they get funny ideas.'

'Well, try and get her to see reason. And it's time you changed your personal car. You're not strapped for cash.'

'No,' I say, reminded again of the envelopes.

'Right,' says the Major, rising and extending his hand. 'Keep in touch. Any problems, ring me.' He places his card on the table.

'Would you care for coffee?'

'Next time.'

All day my conversation with the Major went round in my head. As I was driving home I suddenly realised that it wasn't a conversation at all, only the opening phrase of one. The moment I entered the flat the phone rang, the sound augmented by the sparsity of furniture.

'Can I speak to Svetlana?' asked a pert female voice.

I shouted that she was wanted, but there was no reply.

'She must have gone out.'

'Tell her Zhanna called.'

83

Kiev, December 2015

'He's out of his mind!' I explode.

Filin nods. 'We can't go giving valuable prizes to prisoners. We'd have to keep them back till they've served their sentence. And that top prize of his! That'll just make us a laughing stock!'

'Absolutely! That one's out for a start! I'm not having a knowledge of Ukrainian linked with a pardon! What's wrong with a diploma?'

'Diplomas are what he doesn't want. He's got two whole pages describing what's on offer, some of them constitute direct interference with prison rules. I mean, for example, transferring successful learners to Ukrainian-speaking cells!'

'Actually I think that might be all right. Why don't you have another look at his proposals, crossing out what won't do, then the three of us can meet to finalise things.'

Filin's expression and the jerk of the head leave me uncertain as to what he thinks about that, but it is high time he went. I have a lot on my plate, most importantly Svetlov's belated report on the Vatican's 'Ukrainian miracle'.

I glance at my watch. Svetlov must be on his way, and meanwhile I must take a dose of the sedative herbal concoction prescribed at my last medical. The doctor didn't like my heartbeat. 'Too fast,' he said, 'you're overworking.' But it's not *my heart*, nor am I overworking. Suffering for the country, yes, but doing as much work as Nikolai Lvovich steers my way. I have the impression he is shielding, too much so; taking on a number of my engagements and functions himself.

On the dot of four Svetlov appears looking nervously about him, gaunt cheeks shaven so clean as to make him look thinner. He is carrying a leather folder.

'It's a serious matter,' he says, eyeing my herbal drink.

'Cognac?'

He nods.

'The miracle happened here,' he says, taking from his folder a map of western Ukraine, on which a dot indicating a hamlet is ringed in red. 'Ternopol Region, Terebovlyansky District . . .

'One summer night angels came down from heaven, lighting with heavenly radiance the long-uncultivated kitchen garden of Granny Lukiv, Orysya Stepanidovna, whose husband and children were victims of the NKVD after the war. She, having lost the use of both hands, depends on a younger sister living nearby for meals. The "angels" dug over her kitchen garden, planting an unknown, but apparently very superior variety of potato. I've got one in the car.'

'A miracle potato?'

'Like to see it?'

He calls his driver on his mobile, and in no time I am examining a potato the size of a football.

'I've sent two that size for analysis. Granny has turned Roman Catholic, along with all her neighbours, and is selling the potatoes off at fifty hryvnas a piece, and the Vatican's got Polish workers there digging foundations for a church.'

'So you keep digging also – miracles like that don't happen.'

'Will do,' he promises, eyes flashing. 'Oh, I meant to tell you – Kazimir's ill.'

'What ails him?'

'Don't know, but it sounds nasty: puffy eyes, two hours the longest he can see for, bad headaches . . .'

I switched on my desk lamp. All was well.

'Think he'll recover?'

'Can't say. He's flying off to some expensive Swiss clinic.'

'Switzerland didn't do me much good,' I say sadly, remembering my experience of eleven years ago.

'And maybe it won't him.'

Getting up from his armchair, Svetlov reaches for the potato.

'Leave that, could you? Take the map, but I'd like the potato.'

Never one for unnecessary questions, he folds the map, taking care not to spill soil on the table.

The Catholic potato is conveyed by my aide to Desatinaya Street for the chef to fry for a dinner with Mayya. We'll see what happens to people who eat a miracle.

84

Kiev, 9 May 1985

After a thunderstorm in the night, bright sunlight. I receive a most opportune phone call from Father Basil inviting me to visit David Isaakovich with him.

It is, God be praised, Victory over the Nazis, and so I might, over a glass, at last have a chance to discharge my promise to Mira's mother of a few days back.

So here we are, descending Vladimir Hill in the funicular, Father Basil in mufti, bushy beard and flowing hair the only clues to his spirituality, and me lightly clad, without even a windcheater. The people around us are happy and a bit tipsy already, and it's only midday.

The footbridge shakes under our feet. Today we are not alone. Everyone is off to the island, carrying bags of clinking bottles and paper bags of sausage and pork fat. Free of snow and ice, the island is again drawing picnickers, and Father Basil and I are for all the world one of their number.

It's strange to see parties of merrymakers gather where I nearly drowned, and later walrused with David Isaakovich, Father Basil and the rest of them. One fat fellow, clearly enjoying inner warmth, is standing up to his waist in the Dnieper, splashing his tummy with water.

'We must love our fellow men,' Father Basil rumbles following my gaze 'swine though they are – we *must*, lest they get even worse.'

David Isaakovich is in excellent spirits. In one corner of the dugout is a host of empty beer and vodka bottles.

'From the May Day celebrations,' he says proudly. 'There's about twelve roubles' worth of deposits there. The essential thing is to get them back to the mainland.'

Where to picnic, is the question. Dugout or beach? We decide on a spot between the two.

Spreading an old coverlet, we unpack the food and bottle of vodka we've brought. David Isaakovich fusses over plates and glasses of different sizes, while we cut thick slices of wheat loaf and sausage.

Not far away a tape recorder is playing.

As if from nowhere, Father Basil produces a canvas-covered

flagon and, unscrewing the cap, he fills our glasses with a dubious brown liquid.

David Isaakovich looks puzzled.

'What's this?' he asks.

'All in good time,' says Father Basil, taking from his pocket three small tumbler-like receptacles in German silver which he sets besides the filled glasses.

'We're not drinking to get drunk, we're drinking to converse,' he says, nursing the bottle of vodka. 'Wine by the glass – fine, but vodka calls for a more measured approach.'

'But what's this you've given us?' asks David Isaakovich indicating his glass.

'Can't you see? – kvass! National drink since time immemorial!'

The word had a mollifying effect on the old man, and I at once reach for my glass and take a good gulp. Kvass isn't sold in winter, and I've not seen any barrels lying around.

'Right, then,' said David Isaakovich, seizing the initiative, 'to Victory!'

We clink glasses, drink, and eat.

'Victory, my friends, is a serious matter,' says Father Basil, mouth full of sausage.

'You can say that again,' says David Isaakovich. 'So much bloodshed!'

'It was a different victory that I had in mind,' says Father Basil. 'The one that stays forever. In the soul of man, living in harmony with God.'

David Isaakovich shakes his head. He looks pained. 'Give God a rest today. We're here to celebrate, not pray.'

'Same thing. Prayer, too, is a form of celebration. Still . . .' And so vigorously did he shake his head as to set hair and beard swinging.

'Very well,' he says. 'Except, David, that you're mistaken. God does love you, you see. How often have you had the militia here threatening to fill in your dugout to send you hell? But they haven't, have they? And why haven't they? Because God is with you.'

'All right,' David Isaakovich agrees wearily, 'God is with me, and that's the truth.'

He pours further tots of vodka and Father Basil tops us up with kvass.

'David Isaakovich,' I venture at last, 'I've a favour to ask on behalf of your wife and Mira.'

'What is it now?'

'They're not being allowed to go.'

'I can't help that. I'm not stopping them.'

'But you're not officially divorced – that's why Visa and Registration won't let them go.'

'God is against divorce,' interposes Father Basil.

'You really should divorce,' I add quickly, trying to stick to the temporal plane. 'It just means a trip to the registry office.'

'And going there?' he demanded indignantly, gesturing to the Dnieper and beyond.

'Where's the difficulty?'

'It's five years since I went there.'

'You were thinking of collecting on the bottles!'

'I was going to ask you to do that.'

'Their furniture's sold, they've only their cases to sit on, things are difficult!'

'It's the 9th of May,' David Isaakovich reminds us. 'Let's not talk to no purpose. It's Victory we're drinking to – to victory over the Nazis and to all victories. And happiness to all the victorious,' he adds, turning to Father Basil.

As we sit, I feel my cheek lightly touched by sunlight through the trees. Conversation has moved on from Victory Day and for a good five minutes David Isaakovich and Father Basil have been arguing about who lived above the Passazh Arch: a famous tailor or, as Father Basil insists, Korneychuk's mistress, who was in fact living there still.

'The Korneychuk who wrote children's verses?' I ask.

'That was Korney Chukovsky. Korneychuk wrote plays.'

My interest subsides. Theatre leaves me cold.

Astonishingly the vodka lasts over four hours.

When I return to the subject of a divorce, David Isaakovich hears me out, no longer protesting but nodding understandingly. At the end, he gives a deep sigh and says, 'It'll be a chance to get the deposits on my bottles.'

'I'll do that for you,' I say happily.

His look of gratitude turns suddenly to one of concern.

'Registry office calls for respect,' he says. 'And I've nothing to wear. No suit, no shirt and tie, no shoes . . .'

'He's right,' said Father Basil, 'some dress better for the registry office than for church.'

So another problem, but a spirit of conciliation. He *has* agreed to come and get divorced, and that is the main thing.

'Let Larisa Vadimovna buy what you need,' I say. 'It's she who wants the divorce, not you.'

'Exactly! Let her buy what's needed, and I'll be there.'

Which is great, except for my then having to cart away two sacks of empty bottles, protesting vainly that nowhere will be open to receive them.

'Bell-like, the jangle of empties,' remarks Father Basil, walking, unencumbered, beside me over the bridge.

85

'My new card,' says Dogmazov dropping it on my desk. 'New office, new home address. The country's taking a turn for the better all round.'

'Coffee? Tea?'

'Tea.'

'Two teas,' I tell Nila over the phone.

'It's a long time since I've been here,' he says, looking about him. 'Nothing changed, everything the same.'

'It suits me as it is.'

'"No good resting on our achievements," as one of the great Marxist-Leninists said, and you, Sergey Pavlovich, are doing just that. Time to be considering the future.'

'So what are you suggesting?' I ask bluntly, thinking how horse-like his face is.

'In two weeks' time there's a vacancy in Presidential Administration. Not, if I'm honest, the one I had in mind, but I think you should take it.'

'As what?'

'Deputy Head of Internal Politics.'

'You see that as a step-up?'

'You have to lengthen your run to jump further,' he says in the edifying manner of elderly mentor. 'You've a very good dossier at present, but it could date fast, or pick up the odd nastiness, and then you wouldn't even have this job.'

Not the best words for Nila to overhear as she comes in with the tea, and her green eyes flash as much at the back of Dogmazov's head.

'I'll have to think it over,' I respond, realising that I should not react sharply to his gentle blackmail. Blackmail being long the means of obtaining highly positive results.

A gulp of tea, and Dogmazov rises to go.

'Ring me before the end of the week. I'm aware you have family commitments, but this can't wait.'

'How about a coffee now?' asks Nila when he has gone.

'Please,' I say, moving to the window and looking at the grey walls of the Stalinist building opposite.

I am fed up with this place, I decide, looking down at the manoeuvrings of black Mercedes in the car park, like the preparations for a funeral procession, only where is the hearse and the coffin? I need a change, but the arrival of the twins in October will supply that and too much change isn't good for you.

86

Kiev, December 2015

Mayya Vladimirovna is at a loss what to make of our complementing common fried potato with Bordeaux *premier cru*, while I drink and eat, offering no explanation.

'Is there something special about today?' she asks.

'No. Just that this potato has Vatican associations,' I say grandly, and pushing my plate aside, I tell her the story, omitting my part in it.

'But was there really a miracle?' she asks.

'Granny's neighbours and folk from other villages reported seeing heavenly radiance and hearing a strange noise. A local history teacher took photographs, thinking extraterrestrials had landed, only to find the negatives blank.'

'Might it not have been Vatican-inspired provocation? Their planting someone, then blowing it up into some kind of miracle? Western Ukraine's chock-a-block with military – anyone can get the use of a helicopter for fifty dollars.'

Reaching for my glass, my hand shakes. I remember the digging and the damage to my hands, but not the planting of potatoes . . .

'You're worried, aren't you? And it's not worth it,' she observes. 'All churches have their importance, all fulfil needs,' she says with a disarming smile.

She's right again, which is something that I've got used to. But not always, more so over the last two or three months as our relationship's improved.

Today she is wearing a tweed skirt and a loose-fitting, green-and-dark-blue, ribbed, check-patterned sweater that would do as a chessboard.

'Are you warm enough in your apartment?' I ask.

'Except for a draught from the window, yes.'

'Have it sealed.'

'No, I get a strange pleasure out of it – as if it's the touch of my dear husband from the other world.

Having just taken a gulp of wine, this last comment by Mayya nearly induces me to spit it out all over the table.

'I think maybe you need to see a psychiatrist,' I splutter.

'I said it was strange myself. Anyway, there's no doubt a certain pleasure can be derived from pain. It makes me more aware of life and everything around me. I often, as it were, try on other people's pain, see what it might feel like, how I would cope. When Igor died I desperately wanted to experience his pain, I was ready to have his heart transplanted into me, so that my pain would be made physical, so I could carry it with me for the rest of my days. But that's over now. That pain has lost its significance for me and no new pain has appeared.'

Mayya's final phrase makes me want to recommend a psychiatrist again, but instead I suggest we go and have coffee in her room, to experience this peculiar draught.

Her reaction is one of fright. She refuses, saying she doesn't want coffee and five minutes later leaves.

What was that about? I ask myself, when left alone. Could she have found my innocent suggestion ambiguous? This thought makes me roar with laughter. She must have thought I expected something of her. Nothing could have been further from the truth. But I had better not tell her that. She would be upset.

87

Kiev, 11 May 1985

Mira, her mother and I arrived at Ukraine Universal Stores half an hour before opening and joined a group at the main entrance.

'Number 115!' called a voice. 'Name?'

'Ivanchenko,' a woman answered.

'You are now 104.'

I watched the woman lick a stump of indelible pencil and write her new number on the palm of her hand.

'Refrigerator queue,' murmured Larisa Vadimovna knowingly, and we moved away.

The stores opened on the dot of nine. Men's suits were First Floor.

In two minutes we found the right department, and wandered around, noting the tedious sameness of men's suits, varying only in size. True, you could get dark, navy, blue, even grey, but all of the same cut.

'What is he now?' Larisa Vadimovna asked Mira.

'About this,' said Mira embracing an imaginary waist.

'Thin as that?'

Mira shrugged.

'How about you?' asked Larisa Vadimovna, peering narrow-eyed at my tattered denim jacket bought three years earlier from a friend who dealt in foreign goods.

'I'm 48 or 50.'

'Would you say he's thinner than Sergey?' She turned again to Mira.

'Thinner and shorter.'

'His height I remember. So we'd better have a 48,' she said, giving me another look.

And fifteen minutes later she settled on a mousy grey suit from the Salute Garment Factory. Nothing special: four-buttoned jacket, zip fly. Just right, except for the colour.

Shirt and tie took no more than five minutes, but shoes had us marking time for a bit, no one knew what size he took. Larisa Vadimovna applied logic. The commonest size was 42. He – meaning me – took 42. But David was a good half-head shorter. Men's sizes proper began at 40. So David was most likely 41.

Brown shoes being two roubles cheaper than black also played its part.

'And now to relax,' said Larisa Vadimovna wearily, and down we went to the ground floor, for three glasses of tea and three rum babas.

88

Kiev, August 2004, evening

'Where are you?' comes the crackly female voice from the speaker in the corner of the lift.

'I'm stuck in the lift!' I shout back.

After Dogmazov's visit it was downhill all the way. Missing documents concerning the privatisation of the Sukhodolsk brick-works turned up in my office. The brickworks were worthless, but the Minister went so far as to say that I was deliberately impeding the process for personal motives. After which I permitted myself a couple of whiskies.

'Press Stop,' commands the crackly voice.

'I'm stopped already!'

'Press Stop.'

I do as I'm told.

'Now press for the floor you require.'

I jab 13, but the lift goes down, stops, opening its doors for a girl with a white poodle on a lead.

'What floor's this?' I ask.

'Fifth,' said the girl.

'I wanted up but got taken down.'

'You must have been up already.'

'Which floor for you?'

'Ground floor. Pavlik's going for his walk.'

As I enter the flat, quiet music and light in the hall from the open door of the sitting room. I long to see Svetlana, to hug her and stroke her tummy with our two little ones swimming inside. I wash my hands and go into the sitting room where, to my amazement, I find a smiling Zhanna sitting opposite Svetlana at the table.

'You're late, but we've waited to have supper,' says Svetlana.

I'm lost for words. Not only is there a prostitute in my front room, but she's staying to dinner. Great! What should I do? Throw her out? What would Svetlana say? After all, she invited her. I don't like rows. I heave a sigh.

'How about making us coffee and phoning for prawn pizzas?'

'You're not allowed coffee.'

'There's decaffeinated in the kitchen. Zhanna brought it. She'll have ordinary.'

89

Kiev, December 2015, Monday

Two weeks. Two more weeks and the country will slide into the season of heavy drinking – Catholic Christmas, New Year, Orthodox Christmas and old-style New Year, then a hangover . . . For now my difficult times continue, with fifty a day seeking interviews on matters of state, and not all them of the they-can-sod-off category. On Friday, another unannounced visit from Ambassador Poyarkovsky, and hot on his heels, his US counterpart to warn of the latest perfidious Russian plans – the Demo-Russkies, as he calls the Democratic Russia Party, have been discussing Ukraine with the Communists. Followed by the usual deplorable bunch of oligarchs, all knifing each other in the back. Why do they hate each other so? We're a big country, with scope enough for all. But no, not with each bent on outprivatising the other!

'I can't find him,' reports my aide looking guilty.

'So get Nikolai Lvovich to find him! Immediately.'

Enjoying my interlude of peace, I am contemplating the Melnichenko ottoman, when Nikolai Lvovich bursts in.

'What do you want him for?'

'That is no business of yours,' I say, standing up behind my desk and looking at him as a general would look at a drunken subaltern. 'You brought him. Where is he?'

'He's quit.'

'Sit,' I say, indicating the ottoman.

Reluctantly he sits.

'Who picked the spot for my digging?'

'He did.'

'Where exactly?'

'I don't know.'

'Who does? The pilots? Security? I want a map of our route, here, on my desk, in the next five minutes!'

'Cognac?' enquires my aide appearing in the doorway.

'Yes, and General Svetlov.'

Svetlov arrives first. In mufti.

'We'll find this stress expert of yours,' he says confidently. 'But it may not be his fault at all. It could well be that someone just used the opportunity to stir up Roman Catholic fervour. Maybe the lab has something already,' he adds, getting out his mobile phone.

'Svetlov here,' he says in a fierce voice. 'Right. Put that in writing and I'll send a driver.'

'Well?' I ask impatiently as he puts his phone away.

'Agronomical miracle, genetically modified, all iron and vitamins, superior to the ones the Americans produce.'

'Good. A miracle of science I can handle, and the Blessed Mother of God has nothing to do with it.'

'Quite. But we don't want to spoil relations with the Vatican. We have their respect. We need their support in certain international matters. Why row over potatoes?'

'Maybe you'd like to be Foreign Minister,' I say with dry sarcasm.

'You're joking.' Svetlov is alarmed.

'Yes, I'm joking. What do you suggest we do about this miracle then?'

'Play them at their own game. This miracle is nothing to us, one way or the other, but it'll keep the Papal Nuncio busy, and it'll draw pilgrims, tourism – just what they need in those godforsaken parts.'

'So we'll leave it at that.'

'One more thing – the Other Hands Op will have to be closed.'

'Why?'

'I've got word that our Russian colleagues intend to float some politicians and a couple of oligarchs our way in the guise of corrupt civil servants. It's a much tougher job to put and keep such folk in custody than local government riff-raff. We might be putting our men in hot water.'

'And the rest of Ukraine with them,' I say, the subject of miracle potatoes already falling to the back of my mind. 'How do we pull out?'

'I think I know, but it would mean losing our illegal detainees.'

'How do you mean?'

'So as they never resurface.'

'That's inhumane.'

'Which is why I'm not anxious to enlarge. Your OK is all I want. You say you trust me.'

'I do.'

Smilingly he relaxes.

'What if the Russians spill the beans about the op?'

'We get to find out what's become of our Zaporozhe officials.'

Svetlov takes himself off, as ever, on cue.

90

Kiev, 13 May 1985

Life's a funny thing. A fortnight or so back I lost my watch, and today at the bus stop I found one. The glass was cracked, but it was going. I picked it up, checked the time with a passer-by, gave it a wind and put it on, glad that the strap was leather.

Bright sun, not a cloud in the sky, but a keen breeze is blowing.

Still, no matter, it's early, just eight, and the sun will soon assert itself.

I am carrying a bag containing David Isaakovich's suit, white shirt, black tie, brown shoes. We are due at the registry by ten, and have ample time.

As I cross the footbridge there are fishermen on the far shore with rods, and others heading back to the mainland.

'Catch any?' I ask one, who by way of reply holds up a transparent bag containing a few tiddlers.

Standing outside his dugout is a wet-haired David Isaakovich towelling himself after a swim in the river.

'Must be clean,' he says, with a meaningful look.

I, too, have made a special effort to the extent of wearing the navy blue suit Mother bought for my school-leaving evening, which, amazingly, still fitted, I having neither grown nor filled out since I was seventeen. I have on a clean beige shirt, but no tie. I'm not keen on ties, and didn't wear one for my school-leaving party either.

'Anyone would think it was you getting divorced,' says David Isaakovich with a merry twinkle.

'I divorced by proxy, didn't even have to go to the registry office.'

'You were lucky. Well, let's see what you've got. Don't want to have washed and scrubbed for nothing, do I?'

The dugout is still warmed by the stove.

'Don't you ever let it out?' I ask lightly.

'I need it at night. And if I don't keep it going, I freeze.'

He is pleased with the suit, feeling the material between finger and thumb with a look of concentration. He then unfolds the shirt, and that, too, is to his liking. The shoes trouble him.

'Was there no other colour?' he asks, examining them closely.

'There was black, but your wife went for these which were two roubles cheaper.'

'She did right. How about socks?'

'Socks?'

'Socks, to put the shoes on over.'

No one thought of socks. We slipped up there.

'Don't you have any at all?'

'A green wool pair, but nothing clean without holes.'

From between his bed and the wall he brings up a greatcoat, a blanket and various bits and pieces of clothing from which he extracts several odd socks, all with holes in the heels.

'You see,' he says, showing me, 'I don't walk properly. People who do, get holes where their big toes are. With me, it's always the heels I get holes in.'

Laying the socks out on the bed, I make a pair of one black and one navy blue.

'Got needle and thread?' I ask.

'Of course.'

From an old tin of fruit drops he produces both, and in no time I sew up the holes with black thread.

'You're a marvel,' he says. 'It takes me five minutes to thread the needle!'

In next to no time David Isaakovich stands transformed before me. The suit fits, shirt and tie are just right – Larisa Vadimovna chose well – and there in his socks he contemplates the brown shoes.

'All right?' I ask.

'Splendid.'

Brown shoes are wrong with the grey suit, but that, against the generally satisfactory picture, is a mere detail.

Sitting on his bed, he puts the shoes on.

'The damned things are tight!'

'New shoes always are. They'll ease with wear.'

The breeze, as we climb up onto the footbridge, is, if anything, keener.

Halfway across, he stops abruptly.

'I can't,' he says quietly, looking towards the mainland.

'But you promised! Your wife's waiting!' My 'new' watch tells me that we will never make it by ten.

The bridge trembles. Grey hair ruffled by the breeze, David Isaakovich looks frightened and unsure of himself. Seeking something to hold on to, he finds the handrail.

'Now we've bought all this for you, you must! Come on!'

'What about the suit – was it bought or hired?' he demands.

'Bought. I've probably got the receipt in my bag.'

Calmer, he takes a few cautious steps forward, then walks on beside me.

'You should mark your divorce by going to a restaurant,' I say, in an effort to distract him from further foolishness. 'Suggest it to your wife. Father Basil can join us. Your suit will be just the thing for that.'

'Good idea! I haven't been to a restaurant for ages.'

It's 10.45 when we get to the registry office. Larisa Vadimovna comes hurrying towards us.

'Where *have* you been? I've twice arranged for us to be let in without queuing.'

The queue numbers no more than about twenty in all, mainly young couples.

'Who's last?' asks David Isaakovich cheerily.

A tall chap in a denim suit raises his hand.

Larisa Vadimovna clasped her hands dramatically. 'David, you're a war veteran! We don't have to queue.' Then, turning to those waiting, 'Is that all right?'

The queue nods. It is good that senior citizens are shown such respect.

Larisa Vadimovna goes in with her husband, and I remain

studying the young ladies who are getting divorced. Lovely and naive, they will soon emerge as free women. I could take my pick and carry one off.

In thought, yes, but in fact I don't care for any of them, and I'm not in the mood. The morning has been a strain. I feel like a rest.

Still the same breeze, but warmer now. I look around for a café or a little square to sit in, but see no more than a bakery.

Right, I thought. I'll wait. Congratulate them. Get Larisa Vadimovna to treat us to coffee and pastries. However you look at it, it's a serious event in her life. Now she really will be able to emigrate.

91

Kiev, August 2004, morning

Good grief! 6 a.m. and everywhere the scent of Zhanna's damned perfume! It was midnight before she left, and but for my yawning my head off, she would still be here.

Svetlana is asleep, lying on her side, face to the window. Two more months, and that's it. We'll begin a new life. Peace will be a thing of the past. To start with our babies will cry, then learn to talk, ask for money and sweets, and for the next fifteen years banish our childless silence.

I can still taste the ketchup I tried to make the dried-up supper pizza palatable with. After Zhanna, I didn't have the energy to clean my teeth. Now I force myself to, using my lazy man's electric toothbrush. That disposes of the bad taste, but not Zhanna's persistent perfume. Professional perfume of intentional memorability.

'What are you stomping about for?' Svetlana asks sleepily as I look into the bedroom.

'Not asleep?'

'Silly question.'

'Like some cocoa?'

'Please.

'Why did you have her here?' I ask, as we sit together at our breakfast bar.

'I'm giving her a job. Public relations. She knows how to talk to people.'

'To men, you mean.'

'No, people. She's practised on men.'

'Under them, you mean.'

'Skip it.'

'So in her time off, she'll be back to the Ring Road?'

'My employees' own time is their business. Apart from which, she's now onto something different.'

'What?'

'Telephone sex. Evenings.'

'Great! I've never tried it.'

'I'll get you free sessions.'

Thinking it well to remove Zhanna from our conversation, otherwise she'll cause an argument and it's a crime to argue with your pregnant wife, I gradually move the conversation round to Dogmazov's proposal.

'Whatever you decide, I'll support you. Maybe it is time you got a new job,' she says, carefully getting down off the high bar stool. 'I'm squashing them,' she says, patting her tummy.

I carry our cocoa to the table by the window. I like the bar because you can not only talk, but also kiss across it. You can't kiss across an ordinary table.

92

Kiev, December 2015

Far from stupid, Nikolai Lvovich can, on occasion, be smarter than a mating hedgehog. No sooner has cognac with Svetlov faded on the palate, than there he is with a photocopy of a map marked with our course from Kiev to near Ternopol.

I fix him with an accusing look which he can interpret as he wishes.

'You know what the important thing is?' I ask.

He makes no reply.

'That this flight remains secret.' It's wonderful to watch his thoughts rushing about behind his little eyes. How desperate he is to figure out what's going on.

'The original map – the route to the potato field – and all copies are to be destroyed. Do you understand?'

'Yes. I'll see to it,' he says, though with rather less than the appropriate alacrity.

'And see I've nothing on tomorrow evening. I'm dining with Mayya Vladimirovna.'

'Where?' he asks anxiously.

'At my Residence.'

His relief is evident, but then he notices my unfriendly expression.

'You do trust me, don't you?' he says.

'What do you think?'

Beads of sweat appear. His eyes dart this way and that. If he ran away now, he would only be able to return as the prodigal son, and maybe not even as that.

'How do I prove my loyalty? It's for you that I –'

'I have a little plan.'

His eyes grow round.

'It was you who shut the princess in the tower . . .'

'Meaning?'

'Mayya Vladimirovna.'

'It just happened like that . . .'

'Did she bring anything with her?'

'Two suitcases.'

'I want to look at that flat when she's not there.'

'No problem,' he mutters. 'Security will tell me when and where she goes. We could order a medical . . . Flu epidemic, danger of infection . . . Give me a couple of days. The maps shall go. Every last one.'

'That's it then. Off you go!'

'You should take it easy,' he says in the doorway. 'You look tired.'

93

Kiev, May 1985, Friday

Larisa Vadimovna's response to the suggestion of a meal in a restaurant to mark their divorce had been calm and positive – at least that was how David Isaakovich put it as we again walked over the footbridge together.

Again there was sun, but every now and then it was obscured by wispy cloud.

Again he was wearing his divorce finery. He was limping ever so slightly in his overtight shoes, but keeping up a good pace so as not to be late.

Father Basil was waiting outside the Philharmonic Hall, Mira and her mother opposite, by the entrance to the Dnieper Hotel where a table was booked.

David Isaakovich had decided against inviting Ilya, Fedya and his other friends.

'No need for hangers-on,' he said. 'We'll have a quiet session, eat more ourselves, and have a clearer, firmer memory of it all.'

Father Basil was also in a suit, a dark green one, making our meal a truly smart occasion. Larisa Vadimovna had made a real effort: long black velvet dress, brooch at her breast, gold wristwatch and bracelet, hair amply pinned into something resembling a tall bowl of fruit. Mira was more simply attired in a white, lace-collared blouse and black skirt narrowing slightly at the knees.

'You might have brought some flowers!' was Larisa Vadimovna's greeting to her husband, but she immediately turned to Father Basil and me with a smile which remained on her face until the end of the meal.

Our table was by the window, and every so often I looked down on those passing in front of the hotel.

We spoke little, and ate with moderation. Green salad, chicken Kiev, Ambassador vodka for the men, Moldovan Cabernet for the ladies – nothing special, but a pleasant atmosphere, unlike the small celebration of a shotgun wedding at a table ten metres from ours. The bride was clearly six or seven months gone. The youthful groom gave her the occasional bewildered glance, while imbibing beer, champagne and vodka, indiscriminately. No fine toasts. No '*Gorko!* Groom-kiss-the-bride-and-let's-drink!'

'Don't worry,' I said, bumping into him in the toilet. 'Another month or two, and you can divorce. No problem. I've been there.'

He gave me the same trusting, respectful look I must sometimes have given David Isaakovich while listening to his musings on life in which some moral would suddenly spring up and then be lost in the weave of the next thought.

Towards the end of the meal, David Isaakovich's only too sober ex-wife rose to speak, patting her brooch, smoothing her dress and picking up a glass of wine.

'David,' she said, 'for some years I've thought badly of you. But I see now that you are still a good man. You have done for us all that you could. Not a lot, of course, but I would like to drink to you and wish you long years of health and happiness. We will send you letters. Try to change your way of life and become a normal member of society.'

She reached down into her bag hanging from the back of her chair, and came up with a small envelope containing something metallic.

'Take it,' she said, 'and think well of us. We are as close to each other as any could be. You have none closer.'

'What is it?' asked David Isaakovich.

'The keys of the apartment in your name which you have never lived in,' said Larisa Vadimovna, shaking her head. 'Now you can move in and begin a new life.'

The 'apartment', it occurred to me, was their one room in a

communal flat, but luxury in comparison to the Trukhanov Island dugout, which he was hardly likely to abandon.

'Now let me kiss you.' With tears in her eyes, Larisa Vadimovna made her way around the table to where David Isaakovich had risen to his feet. They embraced and remained so for some minutes. An improvement on the lack of action at the wedding party.

94

Kiev, 1 September 2004

'In six years' time they'll be off to school,' says Svetlana, as I stand tying an Italian tie at the mirror. Foolishly happy, I smile.

What Dogmazov and his pal in Presidential Administration will tell me today is not important. My mind is made up. Life is thrusting me into the jaws of a golden-toothed lion. A soft metal gold, but capable of cutting throats or dashing brains out.

I spent the night in a strangely wakeful state constructing opposites along the lines of: silence is golden – no answer is consent; oil is black gold – sugar is white death . . . In an earlier age I would have spent the hours of darkness alone at a card table playing patience and sipping champagne.

'Will you be back early today?' Svetlana asks. 'Zhanna's coming this evening,' she adds warily.

'Good,' I say, surprising even myself.

Maybe I'm missing her perfume. There has been an article on prostitution in one of the papers. Enough to make one weep. Life could thrust you where it liked. And here, in the shape of

Dogmazov, it's setting me off on a path I would hardly have followed of my own free will. Zhanna must have been driven to the Ring Road by poverty and hopelessness.

'Where does she live?'

'With her mother in Borshchagovka in a one-room flat.'

I might have known.

'What are you wearing?' Svetlana exclaims suddenly. 'You're not going to the theatre. Haven't you seen the President and his entourage on TV? Dull black suits and white shirts. That's what they all wear.'

She's right. The idea is to be colourless so as not to threaten or irritate. So, one, two, three, and there I am in white shirt, black tie and the suit I bought for funerals.

95

Kiev, December 2015

It's odd to be following Nikolai Lvovich up the uncarpeted, badly lit back stairs of my Residence in Desatinaya Street, as well as stuffy and claustrophobic.

Reaching the equivalent of my floor, we stop at a CCTV-monitored bronze-handled wooden door which Nikolai Lvovich quietly unlocks.

'Where is she?' I ask, aware that evening is not the time for a medical.

'Gone to a restaurant with a school friend from Donyetsk who we arranged should just happen to be passing through.'

Mayya's little flat is nothing special – small hall, tiny kitchen, larder, bedroom. Scrupulously clean, at least in the kitchen, where we start.

Nikolai Lvovich switches on the lights.

Curious to see what she eats, I look in the fridge: a litre jar of pickled cucumbers, another of tomatoes; in the door compartment: a half bottle of Nemiroff vodka and some Pepsi-Cola; in the bottom vegetable tray: black radish and beetroot.

I turn, as I think, to Nikolai Lvovich, but he isn't there. The bathroom contains the basics: soap and the usual Bulgarian shampoo. Odd for the widow of an oligarch!

'Mr President!' Nikolai Lvovich calls from the bedroom.

One side of the room is taken up by a rather larger than single bed. Against the opposite wall, a desk, and on a small table in the corner, a TV.

'What is it?'

I follow his gaze to the wall above the bed and a framed photograph of I can't see exactly what – a lot of red lined with silver.

'What is it?'

'Hold on.' Removing his shoes and climbing onto the bed, he takes down the picture and hands it to me.

The light in the bedroom being weak and flickery, I take it to the table in the kitchen.

If I cut my finger as a child, I would suck the wound, and now, bending over the picture, I seem again to taste blood, for what it shows, exposed and held so by shiny forceps and clamps, is a chest cavity. And there is the heart with its main arteries and veins and other blood vessels, of which the upper have little blue and yellow clips attached like the circuitry of a deactivated mine.

'Whose do you think it is?'

'His . . . I mean hers, I mean her late husband's . . . I mean . . .'

'Shut up! Make me a copy.'

'What for?'

I turn sharply towards him.

'Right. Yes. I will,' he says, saved by the ring of his mobile phone.

'They're leaving the restaurant,' he reports.

'Good man. Keep an eye on everyone, do you?'

'That's the part of the job. I watch on behalf of the state.'

'Well done! Keep it up.'

96

Kiev, July 1985

'Straight on,' the old lady told us, 'turn left and you'll see it, a three-storey building.'

It was spotting with rain, and Mother looked up at the sky wondering whether to open her folding umbrella.

We were on our way to City Hospital No. 17, where Dima was taken the evening before. Happily it was no distance from the mental hospital. Mother was worried.

'Casualty? Ground floor,' said the caretaker, pausing in his sweeping. 'But don't go through reception. Door to the left, that's the one.'

We soon found Dima in Ward 3, a small ward with only three beds. One had a crutch lying on it, another was neatly made, obviously free, and in the third was Dima with a bandaged head.

Mother went for him. 'You must have been mad, taking two drunks on bare-handed!'

Dima's doctor from the Psychiatric Ward gave us a full account yesterday evening over the telephone. Dima had been standing, as he often did, by the fence looking out at the tram stop, where a girl was waiting. Two drunks had started to pester her and then dragged her into the wood. Dima had vaulted over the fence to the rescue, seizing one by the hair and tugging out a handful. The drunks had then started on him, resulting in concussion, bruises, scratches and torn hospital garb.

'You were lucky,' said Mother. 'You might have been killed.'

Dima looked nonchalantly from one to another of us.

'There's room in life for deeds of valour,' I said softly, and a wan smile crossed his lean face.

'You'd best keep quiet,' said Mother. 'Dima here is not well. You're well, but idle and a burden.'

'From September I'll be studying. So not long to wait.'

'Where?' she snapped cynically.

'Institute of Light Industry – Public Catering.'

She screwed up her eyes for a moment as if putting what I'd said to the test of reality.

'How will you get in there?' she asked after a brief silence. 'You've got to pass exams.'

'Which,' I said calmly, 'I shall.'

With a wave of the hand she turned to Dima.

'Taking your medicines?'

He nodded.

'Doing what the doctors tell you?'

Another nod.

It seemed a good way of conversing. There wasn't much to take exception to in a nod.

For which I was again envious of Dima, small thing though it was. In reality my life was infinitely fuller and more interesting than his. The evening before, for instance, with Father Basil, I had helped carry into the one-room flat, now David Isaakovich's, the furniture we had bought second-hand: sofa, bed, round table, sideboard, two easy chairs and one bentwood chair with ply seat. I couldn't believe he would actually live there, even after Father Basil's helping with the money: a hundred roubles for the furniture, plus ten for the lorry driver.

'We shan't be keeping him here long,' said the doctor at the end of our visit. 'Three days, and if he's free of pain and hasn't a temperature, we'll move him back.'

Mother nodded and slipped a three-rouble note into his smock.

'Thank you,' she said, 'I was terribly afraid he might have fractures.'

97

Kiev, September 2004

It's hard to describe that strange, painful state of being unable to think any thought through completely. Logical, clearly verbalised fears and conjectures enter the old-fashioned mincer, but what drops into the bowl beneath, which is your head, is nothing.

I'll ring, I think, ask to delay my next appointment until the twins arrive, and when I do, Dogmazov sounds indifferent.

'OK. Carry on where you are. I'll be in touch.'

So goodbye, ministerial career, and back to the desk I've already said goodbye to. I've no idea what to do next.

'Can you spare a moment?' asks Nila looking even smarter than usual.

'Take a seat.' I smile, glad of the distraction.

'Friday's my flat-warming,' she says. 'Do come, if you can. It will be nothing without you.'

'Where?'

'Sevastopol Square.'

'One-roomer?'

'Two-,' she says proudly. 'I was lucky.'

'And may you go on being.'

'I shall, so long as I'm working with you.'

'How so sure?'

'I've been to a fortune teller.'

After Nila the day rushes by. I see two colleagues, and dutifully resume the role of Deputy Minister. Amazingly, no one, not even Nila, notices how like an empty jeroboam I am, awaiting a refill.

'Well?' says Svetlana.

'They'll be ringing. We must decide when to fly.'

'Within a week, the doctor says.'

Good, I think, the Minister knows about the babies, so there'll be no problems. Soon we'll be off.

98

Kiev, December 2015

Strangely, I am beginning to look forward to my dinners with Mayya, and the opportunity of normal conversation about human problems. 'Human' being the operative word. With her I don't feel like a man, or possibly I'm not aware of her as a woman. For me she is just a person suddenly become pleasant to talk with. So long and unceremonious has been the thrusting of her upon me – or, more precisely, so blatant her establishment as neighbour – that, while not thinking badly of her, I do, even now, shoot the odd suspicious sidelong glance that, happily, passes unnoticed. Or if noticed, passes without comment – the noblest of all reactions.

Again we are dining, again served by blonde, white-aproned Zoya, as attractively perfumed as earlier. It is a Thursday and potluck is fish: fillet of salmon, crab and prawn salad, with a good white wine, after a little thick, spicy sturgeon soup.

'I can be wrong sometimes,' she says apropos of nothing, pulling her emerald jacket more tightly about the wine-red blouse.

'We all can.'

'No, I've a particular time in mind . . . We could this evening have coffee at my place,' she says, and seeing my surprise, 'Last time I had no coffee and no coffee pot.'

I accept gladly. I'll now see a little more of the building.

We go down a floor, then through a number of rooms, passing lines of washing machines and cupboards with dozens of drawers, before coming out onto the familiar back staircase.

We sit in the pleasantly snug kitchen, with the lights of Podol beyond a tall, narrow window, the warmth of its triple radiator and an aroma of coffee from a bubbling Siemens machine.

'You're not so badly provided for here.'

'You haven't seen my own flat,' she laughs. 'Four hundred square metres living space, thirty-square-metre kitchen with bar area. Have you ever breakfasted at a bar in your own kitchen?'

'I've not always been President, you know. I've got a flat with kitchen bar too. Lesi Ukrainki Boulevard. What's beyond your bedroom wall isn't mine either!'

'What will you do when you're no longer President?' she asks, producing a bottle of Crimean cognac.

'Be nobody with a capital N – like all ex-presidents. Some make prison and the history books simultaneously, some just in the former.'

'Having each contrived two terms in office, as if one wasn't hard enough.'

'Especially since the extension of term. Still, there's always a Nikolai Lvovich to shove work off onto, before coffee and cognac in agreeable company . . . Aren't you lonely here?'

'A year is the usual period of mourning, so I shall spend a year by Igor's heart, and then we'll see.'

Before I have fully taken that in, the phone rings in the hall and she hurries out to answer it.

'For you – you're wanted,' she says, returning.

'General Svetlov has urgent information,' reports my aide.

'And he's where?'

'Here, in the Residence.'

'Give him coffee and tell him to wait.'

The telephone brought an end to a cosy kitchen chat.

202

'The state calls, I take it,' says Mayya sadly, helping herself to cognac.

'But first I shall finish my cognac,' I say, and to her surprise, I sit down again at table.

I really am in no hurry. Svetlov can wait and his information keep, while Mayya and I talk of matters of the soul, leaving the physical well alone.

99

Kiev, July 1985

The door into the communal area is opened by a man naked to the waist, unshaven and wearing baggy-kneed tracksuit trousers, and, I notice, David Isaakovich's divorce shoes.

'Is David Isaakovich in?' I ask, looking suspiciously at his feet.

'He'll soon be back. You can wait in his room.'

I make my way along the corridor, passing the door of the toilet, memorable on account of its seven light bulbs and seven controlling switches outside to the right of the door.

On my first visit I turned on the nearest switch, but no sooner had I locked the door than the light went out. Some eagle-eyed neighbour wasn't going to let me use his electricity. The room is still on the empty side, although there is now some furniture and the bed is even made, with its two pillows propped up to increase the effect. All the same, something is missing. But what?

I look around. Pictures, photographs?

Looking at the window, I realise what: the blinds. Larisa

Vadimovna sold them with the furniture. They were heavy, greenish, striped with grey. Just before they were taken, Mira and I had closed them, shutting out the sun and creating night. Larisa Vadimovna, knowing what we would be up to, had pointedly gone for a walk, 'to bid her childhood farewell', as she put it.

At six, while we were still disporting ourselves on the divan, the same bare-bellied neighbour knocked to announce that Mira was wanted on the telephone. So we had to get up and dress, and half an hour later the divan went literally from under us. Buyers turned up with their loaders, and ten minutes later, not a stick was left. Mira and her mother spent the night with friends.

Next morning I met Mira at the corner of Comintern and Saksagansky Streets outside the food store.

At the station, a pile of belongings on the platform and a hubbub of well-wishers, of whom most were speaking well of Vienna, where every emigrant got given sandwiches and a bottle of Coca-Cola. Mira and I, looking for the last time at each other, said nothing. A wall was going up between us, though as yet with no actual sense of distance. We had grown accustomed to the idea of our paths diverging. Our very last kiss seemed feeble, forced even. She didn't cry. Nor should she have. Their going had been long in the making, with me assisting all the way, entreating David Isaakovich to divorce and buying him clothes. In short, my part had been played. And for the last month or so, Mira's kissing and loving had been more of the mechanical order, though not perhaps lacking in gratitude. Only who could tell? What I did know was that there was nothing in life – be it love, be it passion – that did not come to an end.

'Ah, here already,' says David Isaakovich, coming in with a bag of provisions and wearing slippers.

'Your neighbour's pinched your brown shoes,' I tell him.

'No, he hasn't. I've given him a rouble to wear them in for me. They'd rubbed the skin off my heels. Like something to eat?'

We sit at the round table.

'Believe it or not,' he says, looking up from the sliced Doctor's Health Sausage lying on its grey wrapping paper, 'the state appears to owe me 1,500 roubles.'

'How so?'

'It's my pension. I've not drawn it for years, and so it's mounted up. Now I just go to District Social Security, get a chit and I'm a millionaire. I'll buy forks and spoons and plates.'

'Why not bring them from the island. You've everything there.'

'That's now my dacha. For holidays in summer, and ice-hole swimming in winter. For here I'll need to buy separately. We might go along to the Haymarket, where it's cheap.'

'International phone call, David,' says his half-naked neighbour, poking his head around the door.

David Isaakovich hurries out and comes back looking puzzled.

'Bloody foolishness!' he says. 'Operator says they were ringing from Vienna, but couldn't get through. If she knows where they are, how come she doesn't know why they couldn't get through, silly cow!'

'Maybe she didn't want to put them through.'

'Could be. Could be. Anyway, it's all right. At least we know they've got to Vienna.'

100

Kiev, September 2004, Friday

'Could I see the green one.'

Mounting a stool, the assistant fetches down a plate.

'Turkish?'

'French. Hence the price.'

'For how many persons?'

'Four, six or twelve.'

I stop to think. A dinner service was the first thing I thought of as a present for Nilochka's flat-warming. No doubt other guests will have thought the same, so why risk duplicating? Leaving the china shop I go to the Central Universal Stores where I am pleased to find a big selection of toasters, until it occurs to me that a toaster will be everyone's second choice of present.

I buy myself a cappuccino in the café and, trying to think of something original, find myself thinking of Zhanna's perfume. She was with us last evening, bringing a grilled chicken, with which we drank white wine, and I felt neither irritated nor resentful. She was smartly and tastefully dressed. 'Why is it Svetlana always rings, never you?' were her parting words at the door. When had we become so familiar? I ask myself.

'Buy us a sandwich, guv,' says a gypsy boy no older than ten plucking at my sleeve.

'Try washing cars,' I tell him.

'You wash 'em, stupid!' he says shrilly, passing on to the next table.

With half an hour to go, and certain to be late, I find myself looking at cameras. Just the thing.

So complete with Olympus camera, film and a large bunch of roses, I take a taxi to Nila's.

'Not first, I hope?' I ask as she opens the door.

'The first and only,' she says, relieving me of the aristocratic pale yellow roses. 'Come on in. I'll fetch a vase.'

There is a general smell of newness, cleanness, fresh paint. In the sitting room, a round table with pink cloth laid for two. A select flat-warming indeed! Still, given the pleasant smell of spices and roast meat, and in a bucket a bottle of my favourite semi-sweet red champagne, I feel hungry and in good spirits.

The meal is enjoyable, and when I reach the point of being able to manage no more and Nila clears the table, I sit watching the door and wonder how I will manage even the smallest piece of the cake which she is bound to carry in any second now.

But at that moment Nila appears in the doorway wearing a blue silk dressing gown. She looks teasingly at me and then at her bare feet and says: 'You like sweet things, don't you,' before letting the gown fall to the floor, leaving her standing before me like Venus de Milo. My blood rushes and I feel a bit dizzy, the red champagne dulling my thoughts, but hastening the normal male reaction to a naked female. I sit there and try to think of a rational reason for wanting to throw myself on her and I realise that so long as I keep searching for this reason, I won't move and that will save me. I just have to keep asking myself questions like 'Why do that? Where might it lead?' And at last the saving thought comes into my head: 'In one month my wife will give birth to twins.' I breathe a sigh of relief, but Nila stands watching me, uncomprehending.

'I'm sorry, Nila,' I say, trying to sound gentle. 'You do understand, don't you? We're expecting twins.'

Her face is a battleground of emotions. The smile remains, but her eyes are desperately seeking a way out.

'I just don't know how to show you my gratitude,' she whispers at last.

I want to help her find a way out too, but can't, and then Nila's gaze falls on my present.

'Sergey Pavlovich,' she speaks more brightly, 'perhaps you could take some photos of me. Then I won't feel so stupid about showing you all like this.'

I imagine how I would feel standing naked in front of a woman who had no intention of taking her clothes off.

'That's a great idea,' I say, springing up to load the camera.

Nila amazes me with her erotic grace as her body takes on the most amazing, but not unnatural poses. She lies on the floor, flays her arms and legs and commands: 'Now take one from above . . . now from the doorway.'

At some point I realise there's music playing, some intimate night blues, and we move round the room, as in a dance.

When thirty-six exposures have been used, Nila jumps up off the floor and we both stand catching our breath as if we had been up to more than photography. Nila runs over and gives me a kiss on the lips and then on the chin, saying, 'I'll be back in a sec.'

Left alone, I place the camera on the table. I enjoyed the dance, but I sense a strange residue of feelings, maybe because I have subjugated my desires or maybe it's jealousy over Nila's youth and charm. Not my jealousy so much as that of all other women who have lost their freshness and ardour.

101

Kiev, December 2015, early a.m.

'You've come about potatoes at this time of night?' I am not really angry, just surprised.

'Yes, but this potato miracle turns out to be very curious indeed,' says Svetlov.

I invite him through to the sitting room, where we sit in green leather armchairs either side of the newspaper table.

'The potato is of a variety stolen from an American laboratory – absolutely top secret.'

'So who stuck it in our kitchen garden?'

'Min. of Ag. Intelligence Service.'

'Since when did we have one?'

'We had one in the old days until it became unnecessary and uneconomical; then we broke it up and specialists from there were scattered among various other ministries, where they continue pinching the odd secret – but our concern is how to feed the people.'

'And that's what they did – pinch the Americans' new potato?'

'Legalised now by the Vatican's authentication.'

'Brilliant! Let's drink to it!'

My aide brings champagne.

'So someone has pulled off a brilliant operation allowing us to grow these extra special potatoes with the Vatican's approval.'

'Exactly.'

'Have you any idea who's behind it?

Svetlov shook his head.

'If we knew we could reward him.'

'Have a word with the Minister of Ag.'

'Artillery General Vlasenko?'

'The very same,' says Svetlov with a polite laugh.

'Then let's reward him.' I am surprised and delighted by this turn of event, though I don't cross paths with Vlasenko very often. One or two more like him in civilian life, and one or two fewer in the army is what we need.

So we drink to him and his minions.

Soon after Svetlov leaves, I shut myself in the bathroom and, putting my glass down on the window ledge, feast my eyes on St Andrew's. The Descent is deserted, ice-glazed cobbles glistening in the yellowish light of the street lamps. A few cafés and boutiques have lighted windows. Then suddenly I'm caught in full glare of the powerful headlights of a Hammer Jeep climbing the Descent. I step back in alarm, taking my champagne with me.

102

Kiev, August 1985

It's odd, but sometimes what you blurt out in haste becomes reality before you know it! When Mother was getting ready to go to work, I was still asleep. She came into my bedroom and shook me, but decided not to waste any more nervous energy dragging me out of bed and dropped an envelope on my pillow.

Much later, over tea in the kitchen, I was astounded to find it contained a glowing, officially signed and sealed Military

Commissariat testimonial recommending that I be admitted, on preferential terms, to the Institute of Light Industry. The references said that while in service as a private in the Soviet Army, I had received many commendations, and been decorated 'For Success in Military and Political Training'.

How much had that little lot cost Mother? I wondered. Very likely no more than a couple of bottles of cognac, seeing what a simple, boozy lot military commissars were.

Although a wry smile crossed my face, an inner voice told me that this was my chance and I shouldn't miss it.

I tried to remember when the idea of Public Catering had cropped up. Not on the score of a deprived childhood. So there it was: Light Industry, here I come!

103

Kiev, September 2004, Saturday

It was 1 a.m. when I returned to the flat, and opening the door as noiselessly as possible, tiptoed along the corridor. All to no purpose. Svetlana was watching TV.

'I thought I'd be asleep before you got back. Like something to eat?'

'I ate at the flat-warming.'

'Valya rang,' she said, pointing to the phone as if she expected the receiver to nod in confirmation. 'Let's sit down. It's such a struggle for me to stand.'

We sat down on the sofa.

'And guess what? We're due on the same day, 27th of October. It's a miracle!'

'Well, the babies were probably conceived on the same day,' I said, attempting to explain the miracle in scientific terms.

Fortunately Svetlana took no notice.

'She's found a good clinic in Zurich, not too expensive. She'd like us to give birth there together if you don't mind.'

'Of course I don't.'

'And can you imagine, Dima wants to be there at the birth! But I'd rather you weren't, OK? There's a little hotel attached to the clinic and you can wait there. All right?'

'Fine.'

'There'd been some trouble with Dima,' she said, suddenly sounding guilty. 'He went missing for two days, he'd walked forty kilometres, then sat for hours at a bus stop until suspicious locals called the police. Just as well, or he might have caught his death in the rain . . . They prescribed a course of ten injections, and now he's all right. Like some tea?'

'Not on top of champagne. I think I'll open another bottle. Care to join me?'

'Only a tiny spot for me, you know how it is.'

'I know I know,' I said getting up off the sofa.

'Really, just imagine it. Our three babies all coming into the world on one day, in one place. It's so wonderful, so beautiful. Conceived on one day and born on one day!' She laughed, raising her palms to her mouth and hiding her lips with her fingers. I had never seen Svetlana happier or sillier.

104

Kiev, December 2015

> *Beyond the mind's grasp our Russia is,*
> *not measurable by common measure . . .*

was how Tyutchev put it, and he was right.

It's half an hour since Nikolai Lvovich came running with a video cassette, plunging me into a world in which all Andersen's fairy tales were rolled into one, with Moscow the scene of action.

'Would you like to watch it again?' asks Nikolai Lvovich.

'Yes.'

Again the troika news logo of the Russian TV and Radio channel, then, through the wintry streets of the capital, street lamps bright spheres in the frosty murk, a vast procession of people carrying crucifixes and banners, and the proud voice of a hidden commentator.

'*Millions of Orthodox Russians have welcomed with great enthusiasm the decision of the Supreme Synod to canonise that true Protector of the orphaned and wretched, victim of Jewish assassin Fanya Kaplan, Vladimir Ilyich Ulyanov-Lenin, henceforth to be known throughout Orthodoxy as the Great and Holy Martyr Vladimir. And by consent of the President of the Russian Federation and the Patriarch of the Russian Orthodox Church, the holy relics of St Vladimir will continue to repose in granite at the Kremlin wall. The word "Mausoleum", at variance with the canons of Orthodoxy will be removed. Already, as you see, amongst this throng of pilgrims there are many carrying icons of the Great and Holy Martyr Vladimir. And now, today's sport . . .'*

Nikolai Lvovich switches off.

'Some reaction on our part seems called for,' he says without much conviction.

'Why not wait and see? As is our tradition.'

'But we do need to decide on our general attitude, find out how our patriarchs regard this saint!' Nikolai Lvovich persists, and I sense that he is right.

'Right, take the Chairman of the Religious Affairs Committee with you, do the rounds and report back.'

With the look of a man sent to cross a minefield, he makes slowly for the door. He's the bearer of bad news and is worried about it. He'll try and get to the bottom of the situation with all the makings of a fairy tale: a prince in a glass coffin and God-possessed 'idiots' out of Pushkin or Dostoyevsky bearing icons and banners, beneath the yellow haloes of street lamps.

While God looks on from above.

105

Kiev, October 1986
A good thing about life is that, you can, as on a motorcycle, U-turn and head off in a more interesting direction, much as I did in becoming a student, a form of existence that was a pleasure beyond imagining. You scrape satisfactory, or sometimes slightly better marks, and spend your evenings in discotheques and the girls' hostel and all on a grant of thirty-six roubles, with coffee, in a little place adjoining the Institute of Light Industry, only seven kopeks a

cup! It's a question of doing the right thing at the right time, as I did in making my decision. The other students might be years younger than me, but I have the army behind me and a future before me. They look on me rather as we look on old soldiers on the verge of demob. And the lecturers aren't too bad. The fundamentals of public catering duly assimilated, I am now onto the outline history of the CPSU. Our Marxism-Leninism professor likes neither Stalin nor Brezhnev. Khrushchev, arch-cultivator of Indian corn, is his hero, and now and again he tells us about him and how unjustly he has been treated by Brezhnev and other members of the Politburo. So much for study. Justification, rather than goal, of a happy student existence.

I continue to visit to David Isaakovich, now recovered from the trauma of finding his dugout flattened by a bulldozer. It had not been in anyone's way, yet it survived no more than a year. We went there in winter with Father Basil, got the stove going and walrused in an ice hole. Then, to our sorrow, someone took it into his head to flatten it. It was a shame, but our feelings were not so much for the dugout as for David Isaakovich, who for two months went about utterly downcast, and planted a cross on the spot, as if it were a grave. As indeed it was. Buried there, as he put it, was his independence from odious reality. Against that, he has become the richer for receiving his back pension and now draws it monthly. He drinks little. He has bought himself two carpets second-hand and hung them on his walls. Little by little the room has filled up and grown dusty with junk, acquiring – you noticed the moment you entered – a homely, long-lived-in smell about it.

Brother Dima is still in his mental hospital at Pushcha-Voditsa. Mother takes chocolate marshmallows out to him every week. I accompany her a couple of times a month, but with small pleasure beyond that of finding books he wants, he having developed a great taste for reading. His two favourites right now are Voynich's *The Gadfly* and the blind Ostrovsky's improving *The Making of a Hero*. By no means healthy reading, but then Dima did not think of himself as normal.

Books like that are not by choice read by the normal. And as I see it, the normal don't read anything anyway, unless it's newspapers or the weekly *Ogonyok*.

So there we are, Mother and I, travelling to Pushcha-Voditsa, glimpsing autumnal forest from the window of a half-empty bus, me nervously clutching the latest *Moscow News*, containing three articles of interest: life in Stalin's labour camps, computers and the growing menace of syphilis.

106

Kiev, September 2004

Our Monday meeting with the Minister was the most tedious ever. For the umpteenth time he called on us to combat abuse on the part of subordinates, and strive for complete transparency over the privatisation of large- and medium-scale industrial concerns. I looked him in the eye, expecting any minute a broad wink inviting us to wink back, as if to say, 'Piece said, now back to work as before!' But no wink came, leaving us all perplexed.

'Tea or coffee?' Nila enquired cheerfully as I entered the office. Her happy mood assuaged my fears of a change in her attitude after

Friday night. But all was well and before I could answer the telephone rang.

'Try again in fifteen minutes, when he'll be back,' Nila told the caller, smiling at me as she did so.

Well done, I thought.

'You didn't get into trouble for being late?' Nila asked as we drank coffee together.

'Why should I have?'

'You must come for another meal.'

'It will have to be after I get back from Zurich. Which reminds me. Please book two business-class seats to Zurich for Friday with return date open. You won't forget?'

'I never forget anything, especially kindness,' she replied with one of her bell-like laughs.

'You shouldn't laugh so nicely or they'll transfer you to someone else.'

'Never!'

At that moment Nila's phone rang and she went to answer it.

'It's the militia for you,' she said looking around the door.

'What militia?'

'A Captain Murko.'

'Ask him what he wants.'

'To speak to you. He was at your wedding.'

'Put him through.'

'Sergey Pavlovich, you were asking about Husseinov – I've found him. Here in Kiev, dealing in refrigerators. Like his number?'

'Please, and remind me of yours – for the christening in a month or two.'

Looking at Husseinov's number I suddenly felt sad. I remembered the footbridge, covered in snow, the blizzard, the old man who pulled me out of the ice hole. It would be quite interesting to meet Husseinov now, to find out what he'd been up to. But first I'd have to punch him really hard. True friends don't behave like that, and back then I had thought we were true friends.

'Sergey Pavlovich, there's a call from the Mayor's office about the Obolon concrete works,' called Nila. 'Shall I put him through?'

'Yes,' I sighed.

'Your tie's askew,' she said, righting it for me.

107

Kiev, December 2015

The very next day Nikolai Lvovich's concern proved well founded. At first light the Communist Party of Ukraine, in conjunction with neo-Communists and neo-Young Communists bombarded the Embassy of the Russian Federation with sour apples and pickled tomatoes, and set up pickets. But by eleven the Ukrainian Party of Toiling Orthodoxy had come to the Russians' aid. More than a thousand young 'toilers', some with home-made icons of our brand-new Great and Holy Martyr, formed a double cordon around the building, singing psalms and praying to his eternal memory and that of other victims of Jewry. Meanwhile in Podol the Congress of Jewish Communities was in session, demanding that the Synod amend the wording of its proclamation.

Cancelling my engagements I summoned all the top people to Bank Street at noon.

'Mobilise all forces, bring all unpredictable elements under control and restore order immediately. The Mayor must . . .' I looked around for the Mayor.

'Where is he?' I demanded of Nikolai Lvovich who shrugged in reply.

'Inform him that from dawn tomorrow he's to close the city centre and area of the Russian Embassy to traffic, lay on festive street gatherings, amateur performances, that sort of thing. Make the beer and vodka factories sponsor it. Drink to flow till old-style New Year – but I want order and no major crimes.'

I turned to Filin.

'The cream of our criminal fraternity will take themselves off to the Canary Islands at their own expense.'

He nodded gravely.

After the meeting I asked Nikolai Lvovich whether he thought the Lenin canonisation a stunt aimed at us.

'At everyone, but it's more dangerous for us.'

'So, carte blanche. Unofficially, strictly on the q.t., no press involvement, get an anti-provocation committee going. Any problems, straight to me. Svetlov will assist.'

'I'd rather he didn't.'

'Why?'

'Too closely watched by Russians and almost everyone else.'

'All right then. It's up to you. Plan of action by tomorrow morning.'

Once alone I collapsed on the ottoman, weighed down by a great invisible burden, and filled with doubt and dismay. It was as if peace was departing from my far from peaceful life forever.

Snow was falling in great fat flakes. Joyless winter, but I was alone in seeing the joylessness of it. Everyone else seemed completely satisfied.

'You should go and have a rest,' came the voice of my aide practically in my ear.

I opened my eyes in alarm. I had neither the strength nor the desire to swear at him.

'Call a car for Desatinaya Street.'

'At once. There's an envelope for you from General Svetlov.'

'Mr President,' ran the note, '*Bad news is better conveyed by messenger: stress expert found hanged in the forest near Lutsk. Hands tied, so not suicide. Your obedient servant . . .*'

So now I'll never know the connection between a kitchen garden, stress and genetically modified potato, I thought mournfully.

108

Kiev, December 1986

A second week of snow, and everything beneath a soft white carpet. In the dark of early morning, the scrape of caretakers' shovels freeing paths. Our balcony has snow to the top of its railings. But no matter. The door is now well draught-proofed, so it will be March or April before I will be able to go out on it.

Mother has gone off to work, and unpleasantness she hasn't told me anything of. Something's going seriously wrong with our country – it's just too big. From one of Mother's telephone calls I gathered with half an ear that two truckloads of parts from Kazan had failed to reach Kiev, days had been spent trying to find them, bringing a production line to a halt. Clearly a shambles, and one I could do nothing to help with. What I could do, I have done: ceased being a source of grievance by enrolling at the Institute. I am now a Soviet student. A disorganised creature, I am a young specialist of the future.

But today I propose being my old self again, walrusing with David Isaakovich and Father Basil on Trukhanov Island. My fellow students, the girls especially, are much impressed by my winter bathing. There are nine girls and three males on our course. The two collective-farm-sponsored males got in on 'Satisfactory' passes, like me. The girls go all out, poring over textbooks, never letting up, writing notes and cramming, where we three take the easier line of swotting only for exams. What I particularly enjoy are our field trips; I like the food-processing plant and equipment and the general soundness of our light industry. And only by actual contact with it and its components do you grasp the vital importance of feeding the people. One, because if you don't feed them, they get drunk on an empty stomach and do things that take ages to remedy. And two, because if hungry, they are unlikely to go to work at all. Thus it is, consciously or unconsciously, that I have become more closely acquainted with the root sources of our nation's labour, and am impressed by what I have found.

David Isaakovich listens open-mouthed when I speak of macaroni extruders, having never before pondered where macaroni came from. Now that he knows, it adds greatly to his regard for and interest in what we eat. Father Basil is not so impressed. For him all food is from God, and no matter who stands at the extruder, Lord of all extruders is God, who is baker, fisherman, macaroni grower and sausage-maker.

I do not argue. There are two attitudes to food. Not God's or the scientific, but those of the hungry and the replete. And for as long as I have known him, Father Basil has never in my hearing admitted

221

to being hungry. Ready to eat, and with relish, that's Father Basil, with not so much as the offer of a sandwich, let alone an invitation to table, from him. David Isaakovich is the one for that. Father Basil opens bottles and pours.

Looking out through the frost-patterned window, I wonder how we are going to get across the snowed-up footbridge and walk barefoot to the ice hole, hoping to God it wouldn't be frozen over.

The telephone intervenes.

'Sergey?' It's Mother. 'Don't forget we're going to see Dima tomorrow. So get the latest papers.'

'Today's won't be the latest tomorrow.'

'So get today's and tomorrow's. You remember what the doctor said.'

What the doctor, who is new and on the young side, said is that Dima was making progress, conversing about almost anything and asking intelligent questions. He has seen him smooth out and read papers discarded by visitors, and with a marked improvement of mood. As an experiment, he has given him numbers of the weekly *Ogonyok*, and discussed his reading of them. Told which, Mother beams. Dima is as good as well, his problems being more emotional than psychological. Hence our taking him more newspapers. Gradually to bring him back in touch with real life, make him feel like returning to what he reads so much about. Especially as it is so rapidly changing for the better.

I wonder. 'WOMEN MURDERED AT RAILWAY STATIONS BY MANIACS' was a headline in the last *Literary Gazette*. Would I, if I were Dima, *want* to come back to that?

109

Kiev, September 2004, Tuesday evening

'Fancy telling me to meet you at a place like this.' Husseinov waved disgruntled at the large, yellow 'M' above us. 'With such a beautiful church nearby, why couldn't we meet there?'

'Maybe if it had been a mosque, I would have suggested it.'

'I'm not a believer. But Hello anyway.'

'Hello, Lieutenant,' I said and we embraced.

'Not Lieutenant any more,' said Husseinov loosening his grip. 'So where shall we go?'

I looked around. At that time of day Post House Square was a beautiful sight. Across the road, carriages of the funicular railway were making their way up Vladimirski Hill, while identical carriages made their way down, illuminated by the occasional street lamp. On the other side of the square neon lights decorated the river port terminal with its busy terrace restaurant emitting the sound of music for the over forties. To the left, at the quay a river cruise ship was also lit up and full of life.

'Let's go to the Americans,' Husseinov suggested.

'You mean Arizona?'

'Yes.'

We turned off the Embankment road into the cosy, but brightly lit courtyard of the restaurant and I was at once struck by my old friend's taste in clothes. Everything he wore was of the latest fashion.

'The best table you've got, young lady,' he commanded and the waitress led us to a table in the left-hand corner of the restaurant, turning away to get the menu.

'What's your name?' Husseinov asked her.

'Vita.'

'Vita, we don't need the menu. I don't like reading. Why don't you just tell me about the most expensive and tastiest thing you got.'

'And if the tastiest is not the most expensive?' asked the waitress, intelligently I thought.

'Then the tastiest.'

'Mutton à la Argentina.'

'So two portions of that with a variety of salads. Is that OK with you?' He turned to me.

'If you're paying, I'm easy.'

'Of course. I owe you. And to drink?'

'With mutton, a Chilean or Argentinian red.'

'Fine. But that's no good for me, the Koran forbids it. I'll have vodka.'

'But less than half an hour ago, you were a non-believer.'

'Yes. A non-believer, but nonetheless a Muslim.'

'You used to knock back our port.'

'That was in USSR days when all were equal and drank on equal terms.'

While Husseinov ordered, I called Svetlana on my mobile so she wouldn't wait up for me.

'Another flat-warming?' she asked, but with no trace of irritation.

'Met an old friend. We're in Podol. Restaurant on the Embankment.'

'Say a few words to reassure my wife,' I said, passing Husseinov the mobile.

'Good evening. My name is Husseinov. I've known your husband since childhood, when he was first brought into the police station. We're here all by ourselves. Not a woman in sight. So goodnight to you.'

Husseinov returned my mobile to me and I said goodnight to Svetlana.

'Is she beautiful?' he asked

'Very lovely. We're expecting twins.'

'I promise to give them a pram.'

The wine and vodka came, then the order, the latter remarkable for a preponderance of meat over chips, and as we ate Husseinov held forth.

'Well, I went back to Dagestan, and there made Militia Colonel rather more easily than I could have done here. But then Chechnya got going, and things got nasty. They started blowing up militiamen and ministers. No peace. I told Father I wanted to come back here. He let me. I brought money. Bought a flat on Chokolovsky Boulevard. Got a business going. Lead a decent life. Thinking of marrying . . .'

All very well, I thought as I listened, but how about that drunken winter night on the footbridge after which we lost sight of each other.

'. . . But here's you, married already. Wife expecting twins! A proper man. Let's drink to our friendship!'

I raised my glass, but something in my manner got through to him.

'What's up?'

'Remember our last meeting? Winter of '85? Perhaps an explanation?'

'When I got sacked from the militia? Yes. We marked the event by drinking vodka on the footbridge.'

'We were drinking vodka on the footbridge when you left me to my fate.'

Husseinov's lips moved. He seemed to be mumbling something

to himself, some Muslim prayer. His gaze turned inwards. Maybe he really had forgotten.

'You know, it's like this,' he said eventually, looking back at me. I see guilt in his eyes. 'I am ashamed. I've often remembered that night. I was leaning out over the bridge throwing up. When I'd finished, I turned and saw you going off towards the island. It was snowing. Damn you, I thought. If I come after you I'll freeze to death. You would be all right – someone would help you out, but not me, a Caucasian, I'd be left to die like a dog.'

I listened and was amazed by the clarity of his memory and the courage it must have taken to admit his shame.

'Forgive me, if you can,' he continued. 'And let's drink to Bruderschaft. We'll be brothers and it will never happen again.'

'If it hadn't been for an old Jew who dragged me half dead out of an ice hole we wouldn't have met until we got up there.' I pointed heavenward.

'What am I to do? It's not good to hold a grudge like that for so long.' There was genuine concern in his voice. 'We were both drunk. You could have abandoned me.'

'Maybe, but I didn't. You abandoned me.'

'Maybe I should let you whack me one.'

'I've long wanted to.'

'Only not here, seeing there are foreigners present.'

He got to his feet, swaying a little and made for the door. I followed.

It was already dark on the Embankment road. We stopped by the entrance to the restaurant courtyard.

'Make it a real punch and get it out of your system once and for all. Don't worry, I've been hit before. I'm tough. Hang on.' He pointed to a couple leaving the restaurant. They walked to their black BMW and we waited until they had driven away.

'Come on then,' he said, having glanced round once more.

I punched him in the face with all my strength. He fell backwards, landing on the asphalt. He lay there motionless.

I stood for a few seconds, calmly waiting. I knew he couldn't have hit his head very hard. I couldn't possibly have killed him.

What an idiot! What about Switzerland? The babies? The headlines will read: 'DEPUTY MINISTER KILLS DAGESTANI BUSINESSMAN'.

What horror I experienced in those few moments. But then I noticed Husseinov move. He raised himself on his elbows, sat up and eventually stood up, all without a word.

'If I'd known I'd have worn jeans,' he said holding the right side of his eagle nose. 'I thought I should get dressed up to meet an old friend. I put on my best.' He brushed down his right sleeve and trouser legs with his left arm. 'Nothing torn, I think.'

I walked round him, brushing his jacket and trousers.

'No. All in one piece,' I said, immediately aware that all my anger towards him had disappeared.

'You've broken my nose,' he said calmly, his eyes, glistening above his hand, full of self-pity.

I took his arm and we went into the toilets. Blood was dripping from his left nostril. I handed him some paper towels.

'What's happened to you?' asked the waitress noticing his dishevelled clothes.

'Slipped, going out for a smoke,' said Husseinov.

'You can smoke here, I could have brought you an ashtray,' she said.

'You can bring us dessert. What is there?'

We made our choice, then Husseinov filled our glasses and we stood and drank to our undying friendship. Knocking back a whole glass of Chilean red in one is a heathen act, but that's what Husseinov wanted and he had respected my desire to thump him. Thus one long-held grudge was forever erased from my biography.

110

Kiev, December 2015

With the festive gatherings in full swing, memory of the Great and Holy Martyr Vladimir faded. Passions cooled, but the calm was bound to be temporary – the lull before a storm, and whence and in what shape that storm would come no meteorological report could tell us.

In honour of the Catholic Christmas I received Papal Nuncio Grigory in the Mariynsky Palace. We exchanged gifts in a subdued, almost sorrowful atmosphere before a seasonally decorated Engelmann spruce. His Russian was good, and at a moment when the attention of my aide and of the official interpreter was elsewhere, he contrived to whisper, 'Beware of Magi bringing gifts!'

I nodded, but after he had gone, wondered who exactly he meant. His was the only present I'd received: a sixteenth-century painting of St Peter's Square in Rome.

By twelve I was back at Bank Street, summoning Nikolai Lvovich, who, with a spring in his step and a clear sense of his own worth and importance, came, carrying a brown leather folder.

Motioned to the ottoman, he plumped himself down and crossed his legs.

'All quiet at present, but here's what you wanted,' he said, taking from the folder a photocopy of the photograph in Mayya Vladimirovna's bedroom, which he placed on the desk before me.

'Ah! And?'

'It appears the canonisation business is just a bit of Russian internal politics. With a presidential election imminent, they used it to split the left opposition. Cunning move! "If what you want is a Leader, Church sanctified and authenticated as Protector of the orphaned, wretched and captive, join the Presidential Christian coalition! Or get stuffed." Our Caves Monastery got an order last night from Zagorsk for 20,000 icons of the Great and Holy Martyr. Otherwise, all quiet. By the end of January our festivities will end and our new saint will be old hat and forgotten.'

'So we're in the clear?'

'I wouldn't go so far as to say that, Mr President.'

No, I thought, or he'd be out of a job.

'Ukrainian Orthodoxy is refusing to recognise the new saint, and expressly forbidding veneration of his icons.'

'Where does that leave us?'

'It gets the Church deeper into schism, but that's no skin off our nose. The more they fight among themselves, the less they'll interfere in affairs of state.'

'You're a wise man for your years. How's the ID card experiment going?'

'Fine. We've expanded the project into five regions and the Crimean Republic. Future citizens can choose, from the churches on offer, where they wish to take the oath. There is one snag with the Tatars – we haven't approved the oath they have drawn up in Tatar, but they refuse to alter it.'

'What's the difficulty?'

'No mention of Ukraine, just a promise to be a good Muslim and live by the Koran.'

'Let Mykola deal with it.'

'He's at a health resort,' said Nikolai Lvovich with a laugh.

'Which is where I'd rather be,' I said, placing the heart photograph under my desk lamp, meaning to examine it. 'A resort specialising in cardiology.'

So saying, I switched on the lamp, the flickering of which set my heart fluttering.

'Weren't you supposed to sort this out?'

'Yes,' he said, no longer so confident. 'This must be a loose wire.'

'Try the top light,' I said icily.

Getting up, he reached for the switch. The top light flickered just as badly.

'Are you *trying* to give me a heart attack?' I demanded, jumping to my feet. 'Go straight to Kazimir, and if, in thirty minutes, we're not back to normal, I'll put Democracy and the Constitution on hold for five minutes and sort it out by force!'

He was gone in a flash, leaving no more than a depression in the ottoman.

My heart was really paining me. This poor heart was obviously not so healthy. I turned to the photograph which must have been taken as a souvenir before the closing and stitching of the chest cavity. I told my aide to find and bring me my heart transplant surgeon. After which I lay down on the ottoman and fell asleep.

111

My head is still buzzing with exams. Really buzzing. In the lead up to them I drank hardly anything, but now it's nothing but celebrations at the hostel, now for a 'Good', now for an 'Excellent'. It beats me how easily people manage to get marks like that, I certainly can't do it, but 'Satisfactory' is good enough for me.

Mother and I communicate via written notes. I pop home while she's out and write: *'Sorry, not home tonight, preparing for exams at the hostel.'* Next time I find the reply: *'You rotten pig! You'll know better when you have children! Come straight home. Hostels are all filth and syphilis.'* 'Not to worry,' I reply, *'No syphilis for me! Back after the exams.'*

But I do feel guilty. It is rotten of me. But it takes over an hour to get home from the hostel, and more than two and a half hours there and back. I am now well used to student chaos. I had no idea that study was such fun. And, given that I am already twenty-six, I might never have known, but for a happy chance. It's Mother I have to thank for getting a testimonial out of the Military Commissariat. I must do something to show my gratitude.

On my next visit home I leave a bunch of red carnations on the table, seven at fifty kopeks a bloom, and a tube of hand cream, my feeling of gratitude coinciding with a present of ten roubles from David Isaakovich.

'I've money to spare,' he complained, sipping his tea. 'But no vodka, no wine, the doctors have told me, and what else is there to spend it on? So take this and drink my health!'

Ten roubles was enough for a bottle of red. I didn't feel like vodka. It's not something we students go for. Strong red or equally strong 'Liquid Sunshine' white wine is our student tipple. The carnations and hand cream were bought with the change. I wonder what Mother will write in response.

112

Ukrainian Airspace, September 2004

On the plane I adjusted my watch. Every ten minutes a stewardess appeared to enquire anxiously if there was anything we needed, all the time gazing at sleeping Svetlana's tummy.

In spite of my assuring them that the babies were not due for another three weeks, the airline had required me to sign a paper confirming that Svetlana was flying at her own responsibility and absolving them from any.

'Concerning what?' I had asked.

'The possibility of there being no doctor or midwife on board, and the expense of making an unscheduled landing,' a representative of Ukrainian International Airlines had explained.

Taken by minibus from the VIP lounge to the aircraft, we had settled ourselves in our business-class seats, and for ten minutes, until the economy passengers arrived, we had the whole aircraft to ourselves.

From a gloomy Kiev midday we were soon lifted into sunnier regions. Offered drinks, Svetlana took fruit juice and I champagne.

'To success!' I said, clinking glasses.

'And happiness,' said Svetlana.

Soon Svetlana fell asleep and I went over in my mind the events of the day before.

I'd called on Mother, she'd tried to give me a sweater for Dima. 'If he hasn't a sweater, I'll buy him one!' I kept telling her, but she insisted. In the end I took the sweater home, but didn't pack it.

'Then come back home, all of you,' she urged, trying hard not to cry. 'Don't stay out there. I'll help. I'll look after the grandchildren. Tell Dima, they're to come back. I'm miserable on my own. I only see you once in three months, and then for no more than five minutes! Dima must be better anyway, seeing they've decided to have a child. His treatment must be costing you the earth!'

She was right about that. My savings were dwindling. Planned expenses plus those for the clinic would leave a balance of about $15,000 at the Ukrainian Export-Import Bank, and the next invoice for Dima and Valya would be for $30,000. By Western standards I was bankrupt, and Valya and Dima would be booted out of their clinic.

I'd have to talk to Dima before the birth of their baby, which wouldn't be easy. I had done all I could for him. More, even. But now, with wife and child, he was on his way to normality. Fortunately Mother's flat was a three-roomer, and in Kiev he could always count on help from me if need be.

Svetlana was still asleep. The flight attendant asked if I had seen the menu. I said that I had, and ordered salmon and still mineral water.

Yesterday morning at the office Nila had given me a turquoise cross on a red cord. 'To bring you luck,' she said. I felt like laughing, but kissed her instead.

Of the pile of documents on my desk I endorsed the most important, to which I had no objections, and put them in a folder marked 'Minister, for attention'. The rest I had no inclination to deal with.

'I'll tidy those,' said Nila.

'Yes, do it so no one ever sees them again!' I said half jokingly.

'Oh, and I forgot, Dogmazov rang yesterday. Wants you to call him.'

'When I get back.'

I gave her a hug and promised to ring.

113

Kiev, December 2015

By evening my heart had settled down, but my mental unease remained and was even increased by Svetlov's reporting that Kazimir had flown to Moscow and was meeting government officials.

I was left wondering why I never flew anywhere. Leaving out Mongolia, it was months since I had made a foreign visit. I got myself put through to the Foreign Minister. He muttered timidly that before my operation there had been no opportunity, and that now was too soon after my operation. State visits were physically demanding. I had to build up my strength. 'We are,' he said finally, 'planning a visit to Albania for early March next year.'

Albania! Honduras was what I wanted. And now!

By 9 p.m. I was bored beyond bearing. I wanted beauty. Mayya was not in her flat. I told my aide to organise a museum visit.

'Where?' he asked, startled, with an eye on the clock.

'Where there's beauty.'

He shrugged.

'The Great Patriotic War Museum by the Mother Ukraine monument is the only one I've been to.'

'Paintings are what I want . . .'

'Russian Museum, then?'

'OK.'

Forty minutes later saw me treading the parquet of the Museum of Russian Art. Standing by the staircase with my bodyguard were the Director and his curators looking decidedly frightened. What I wanted was to be absolutely alone, communing with something of beauty. So ever deeper I went, into Russian art I went on until I found myself in a room hung with enormous and truly beautiful Shishkin forests. Shishkin was someone I was very fond of. A canvas of his adorned the wall above my bed, watching over me in sleep.

That's where I wanted to be! I thought, sitting down on a wooden bench. There in those sunny glades. To hell with its being Russian forest! He must have painted here in Ukraine. Or else Russian and Ukrainian forest are exactly the same!

114

Kiev, June 1987

Life is wonderful and also delicious! This much I realised on our first day of work experience. Viktoria Kozelnik and I were sent for a month to the canteen of the Central Committee of the Young

Communist League. True, it would have been more logical to send someone from the School of Cookery, but then Viktoria and I would have missed an experience and ended up in some factory canteen or meat-packing and -processing factory.

Clad angelically in white, we place our food out on plates and garnish it, keeping the portions equal, check-weighing chops and sliced meat, contriving to pop sausage and cheese into our mouths as we do so.

Time passes quickly. Lunch is when we are at our busiest. The Young Communist leaders are a cheery, mad keen lot, with no money problems. And no wonder, when a red caviar sandwich costs only thirty-two kopeks and a black one costs forty-three.

Yesterday, Georgiy Stepanovich, the Young Communist leader whom everyone calls Zhora, came up to me and asked if I was the sort of chap who could be relied on. I nodded that I was. 'Then you won't go hungry,' he laughed, slapping me on the shoulder.

Viktoria, too, is happy, though for a different reason. Towards the end of the day she surreptitiously extracts cheese and sausage from the unsold sandwiches, and wrapping them in napkins, stuffs them into her capacious handbag. Living as she does in the hostel, she has breakfast to think about and that of her friends as well. I'm free of such concerns. After a week at home I have had another row with Mother. I was sick of going to visit Dima. 'Once a month, and no more!' was my ultimatum. 'When you've children of your own, you'll know better,' came the stock reply. 'Don't worry, I won't have any!' I said, banging the door behind me.

Since then I've been living at David Isaakovich's, fetching him his medicine, and frying potatoes in the communal kitchen, where it's whispered that I am a distant relative of David Isaakovich's, brought in to establish a claim to the room before he delivers up his soul.

And a soul he certainly has. He's so delighted by a letter from his wife and Mira and some Polaroid prints which he can't stop gazing at. They show Mira and Mummy outside a shop, of Mummy and Mira standing by a fountain with a fine car just stealing into the picture. 'So they're settled in,' he says with a sigh of relief. 'I did well to agree to divorce. They're all right now.'

'Like us,' I threw in.

The grittiness of our over-fried mashed potato is the fault of the neighbour, at whose request I went to replace a lavatory light bulb, in the middle of the cooking process. Seven bulbs stick out of the wall and the neighbour wasn't there to tell me which was his. So I switched six bulbs on and off before discovering the seventh to be the dud. Thus my potatoes got burned. Good deeds come at a price. But had I not obliged over the bulb, the neighbour might throw some muck into my next fry-up. With one kitchen and three refrigerators between seven tenants, it was vital not to put anyone's back up.

115

Leukerbad, September 2004

In Zurich it felt as if we had flown from September into August, and the fresh Alpine air so warmed by the sun that I felt like removing my jacket.

Our taxi driver was amazingly helpful, and hearing where we wanted to go – a good 300 or 400 Swiss francs' worth by my calculation – waxed doubly so. Gathering that we had no German, he went over to broken English, and finding we were from Kiev, broke into a Russian folk song. As the road climbed into the mountains, he stopped several times for us to admire the view, and even treated us to tea in a tiny village.

Svetlana kept dozing off, the flight had taken its toll on her. There was a puffiness about her eyes that I found worrying. How much further? I asked. 'Soon, very soon,' shrugged the driver. But it wasn't. On a narrow bridge between Leuk and Leukerbad we stopped to contemplate the abyss. Svetlana joined us out of politeness or curiosity, but to our concern, immediately felt sick and dizzy. I was alarmed and so was the driver. Half an hour later, our two cases and travelling rug were unloaded and carried up to our room by a bellboy. The meter showing 370 francs, I gave 400.

'Before we see Valya and Dima I'll have a lie-down,' Svetlana said wearily.

'Of course.'

I helped her off with her shoes, brought a robe from the bathroom, then went out onto the balcony. We were on the first floor. Three hundred metres from the hotel complex, the bare rock face reared up, and I had the impression of being at the bottom of a beautiful and gigantic glass tumbler, at the mercy of the elements, but clearly under the protection of Swiss gods, and as safe from rock fall or avalanche as from flood.

Svetlana was still peacefully asleep, breathing regularly. Taking a bottle of beer from the minibar, I went back to the balcony and the soaring Alps.

116

Kiev, December 2015

That night I dreamed of a Russian forest. I knew it was Russian because somewhere, a long way off, among the lofty spruces, someone was constantly effing and blinding in Russian. A wheezy-voiced man was calling for Dusya. I was gathering mushrooms, keeping a wary eye on columns of reddish-brown ants. Squatting to pick penny buns, I noticed that the hairs on the back of my hand had turned reddish-brown. Pulling up the sleeve of my quilted jacket – a further indication of the Russianness of the forest – I saw to my amazement that I had reddish-brown hair everywhere, on top of my freckles.

'Dusya?!' came a man's voice from the trees.

Changing direction so as to avoid him, I pressed through a tangle of young spruce, cutting myself a dozen slippery jacks with my wooden-handled knife in passing. Then out into a clearing to find myself staring at a brand-new shiny yellow Hammer Jeep with no one in it. It sported an impressive Kiev number plate: oo IIII NN, and growing around the offside front wheel was honey agaric. Into my plastic bucket went the mushrooms, and after a glance back at the strangely familiar-looking jeep, I walked on, coming almost immediately on two lovers sitting on a dark green rug, picnicking on savoury pirozhki and a bottle of champagne. The woman, blonde, mid-twentyish, regarded me with curiosity, the horse-faced man with arrogance and irritation. Reaching into his grey tweed jacket, he produced what looked like a TV remote control, pointed it at me and pressed the button. I dissolved into thin air, my agreeably heavy bucket of mushrooms dissolving with me. Opening my eyes, I looked about me. It was dark. I was in my king-sized bed in Desatinaya Street, heart racing in my dream-troubled breast. I put a hand to it, tracing the scar with my fingers, before leaving my hand to warm it and be warmed.

Only a dream, but my mind remained troubled. It was, I remembered, two weeks since my physician's last visit.

I shouted for my aide and heard what sounded like a book falling on the floor.

'Tell Nikolai Lvovich to get my physician here thirty minutes from now!'

Motionless on my back, I listened to the heart that he would be listening to.

117

Kiev, May 1990

Something odd is happening to the country. Especially in the shops. No butter, no soap. Still, Mother gets both from somewhere. We are OK at home, and the fridge is never empty thanks to what I bring back from work. Zhora having persuaded me to go extramural, I'm now working at the Young Communist Central Committee café full-time. 'To hell with study,' he kept telling me. 'You're bright. You'll qualify all right, and this way you'll stay in the warm and in good company.'

I agreed. With no regrets. It's all the same to me what goes down on my Work Record. There are more important things in life. Moreover, even Mother shows respect for my contribution to the family fridge, and Dima is happy with the slightly dried up but still tasty caviar sandwiches. An off-site luncheon could bring home anything up to twenty such sandwiches as well as other things. And we do off-site catering increasingly often – to Koncha-Zaspa, Pushcha-Voditsa, Obukhov – practically every week. They call them 'seminars' or something similar, but they always finish with a full buffet, cognac and drunken dancing.

'Remember that nice girl you studied with?' Zhora asked a few days ago.

'Viktoria?'

'That's the one. How is she?'

'No idea.'

'Look her up. She's not from Kiev?'

'No, the hostel.'

'We've a stag party on, it'd be good to ask a few girls,' he confides. 'Have a word. Maybe she could bring a few friends.'

I said I would, Zhora slapped me on the shoulder and went his way, singing.

They must be fed up of Young Communist girls, I thought, watching him go.

At the end of the day, while I was removing cheese and smoked sausage from the unsold sandwiches it occurred to me that there were rather fewer Young Communists of both sexes about, and remembering faces I had not seen for weeks. Where were they all? On leave? It *was* very nearly summer.

118

Leukerbad, September 2004

Dima and Valya we saw only the next morning, when they came to the hotel, worried at our not appearing. But Svetlana's lie-down extended into her sleeping until morning and I was glad. A three-hour taxi journey on top of the three-hour flight is no joke for a woman about to give birth.

I think we must have been the last guests to have breakfast because there was only one table still laid when we went into the restaurant. The waitress kept glancing at Svetlana's tummy with what looked like a mixture of respect and envy, but when she brought a vase full of miniature red roses to our table, I decided it was a gesture of devotion, not to us, but to our as yet unborn children.

As we emerged from the restaurant, we caught sight of Dima and Valya standing at the reception desk. I was amazed to hear Dima speaking fluent German. He had flatly refused to learn English at school. The receptionist nodded towards us and soon it was hugs all round: a somewhat difficult task for Valya and Svetlana. I hugged Dima too, but we were both more taken up with the meeting of our wives.

'There's a fine cable-car railway here,' said Dima. 'We could go up. There's a lake with a path round it. It's beautiful. Like paradise.'

Valya and Svetlana were not so struck with the idea.

'You two go. We'll sit and chat in the café. It's ages since we saw each other.'

Dima looked disappointed, but I backed Svetlana. Especially as Dima's paradise would be a good place to discuss his plans for the future. Dissuade him from living in Switzerland indefinitely at my expense.

There was a twenty-minute wait for the next car, during which the man in the ticket box tried vainly to dissuade us on account of the weather.

But when, only two hundred metres up, the wind set the car swaying, I was horrified to think how Svetlana and Valya would have reacted. Certainly only a madman could have suggested such an excursion to a woman in her ninth month. We swayed for another fifteen minutes before bumping the terminus buffers.

Here, high above Leukerbad, the sun was brighter and warmer, and now a thin layer of cloud intervened between us and the tiny town in the valley. The shores of the lake were dotted with remnants of last year's snow.

We followed the narrow path, walking side by side when it was broad enough and with Dima leading when it was not.

'How do you see the future? Any plans?' I asked cautiously.

'Yes, wonderful plans: have our baby, feed, clothe it, bring it up, come and see you in Kiev.'

'And that's seriously it?'

'Nothing wrong with that, is there?' he asked, puzzled. 'Normal life's just beginning.'

We walked on in silence for a while, before I said, 'There's something I've got to tell you.'

Turning from the path, Dima sat on a felled tree.

'The truth is you'll soon have to come home to Ukraine, both of you. I just can't go on paying. Neither can Svetlana. Mother's miserable without you. She's got a big flat. She'll help with the baby.'

'Why can't you go on paying?' he demanded, voice trembling as if he was cold.

'I haven't the money. I don't take bribes. And what does now and then come my way won't keep two families.'

'Why don't you take bribes?' he whispered, staring, shielding his eyes from the sun.'

'Because then I'd be stuck having to hobnob with bribers to the end of my days.'

'So take just from the decent who wouldn't pester you later.'

'They don't exist. The plain truth is that this stay, these babies will clean me out. When we go home, Svetlana will have enough to keep you here three or four more months, and that's it. Have I made myself clear?'

He nodded, looking down at the thick, iodine-coloured moss growing over the rocks at his feet. I had said what had to be said, but was far from happy. Still, just as well to get it over on our first day, then carry on normally for the rest of the time. The hard fact of what I had told him would remain, inescapable, however much he might try to disregard it.

119

Kiev, December 2015

Outside, darkness; sunrise still some time off. Dawn at this season being well after the beginning of the working day. Only this day I don't feel like work, lousy as my work is, affording neither satisfaction nor happiness.

'Your physician's here,' announces my aide.

I switch on the corner standard lamp. The soft light extends to the bed but not to the other half of the room. The power, I notice, is not of the cheap sort. No nasty, shameful flicker.

I sit in my warm dressing gown on the bed. Footsteps on the parquet.

'Worried about something?' asks my sleepy-eyed physician.

'Very. Unless no examination for a fortnight means I'm completely fit.'

'I'm sorry. I've been off with a cold . . .'

'So to work.'

From an old-style leather bag he produces a stethoscope.

I open my dressing gown. The stethoscope strikes cold to the line of the scar, then to the left of it.

'Not feeling too good?'

'One way of putting it. Bloody awful is another. I have weird dreams.'

'Nerves. Let me listen to your back.'

Throwing off my dressing gown, I turn round. Again, the cold metallic searching.

'Hold your breath.'

Holding my breath, I listen to the silence, and as though today gifted with unusually acute hearing, become aware of a rustling, a ticking and a distant hissing. The ticking seems to come from Mayya's bedroom on the other side of the wall, the rustling from the other side of the door where my nameless aide is on duty. Uncertain about the hissing, I continue to listen. The silence is broken by the physician.

'You need peace and quiet. I'm not happy about your heart.'

'Neither am I. Especially, seeing it's not mine . . .'

'I'm sorry. I put it badly.'

'Care to see it?'

The doctor gives me worried look, obviously concerned about my sanity.

'No need of a further op, I've got a photograph.'

'You have?'

'Taken on the operating table. Care for a drink?'

'I would.'

I order Hennessy and two glasses in the bathroom.

The physician now has a hand to his own heart.

'Yours a transplant too?'

'Who am I to warrant that sort of attention?'

While the aide sets down a tray on the bathroom windowsill, he studies the photograph in silence, hunched under one of the halogen ceiling lights with it.

'It can't be!' he says with a sigh.

'Can't be what?'

He went on studying the photograph, his expression a mixture of confusion and fear.

'Well?'

Returning to the window ledge he pours himself a full glass of cognac, of which he downs half in a gulp, only then turning his gaze, like someone turning away from the sun, towards me. Avoiding my eyes he seems to be focusing on my nose.

'So what is it?'

'I could be wrong . . .' he begins uneasily, 'but this hasn't the look of a healthy heart . . . More like your original. Did you have a pacemaker inserted?'

'No. What's the trouble?'

'There's a typical pacemaker scar.'

'Who was the surgeon?'

'Professor Khmelko.'

I tell my aide to get Khmelko here immediately.

'What else can you tell me?'

'I don't know . . . It's a heart much like any other . . . Some fattiness . . . Maybe no other was available.'

In search of solace, I look out at St Andrew's Descent where a woman in headscarf or shawl and a coat to her ankles is coming slowly out from behind the church carrying a candle.

'How old would you say *she* was?' I ask the physician.

'Who?'

'The woman with the candle.'

'What woman? There's no one there.' He shrugs, but his eyes again show fear.

I look again. She is there all right, large as life under the street lighting.

'Have you got eye trouble?' I ask the doctor.

'No. Ah, now there she is – just come round the corner – in a long overcoat. How could you see her before she came out from behind the church?'

I turn and look at him attentively.

'Can a doctor cure others if he's ill himself?'

'According to medical etiquette, a doctor must cure others first.'

'So he'll never get sorted himself?'

Before the doctor can reply, there's a knock on the door and my aide comes in.

'Mr President,' he announces, his voice slightly shaky. 'Professor Khmelko died yesterday evening!'

'Died?'

'Liver failure . . .'

'He never got to cure himself.'

120

Kiev, May 1990, Sunday

At nine two minibuses bearing the logo of the Sputnik Travel Bureau moved off from in front of the Stalin-era columns of the Central Committee of the Young Communist League building. Aboard the first were our forty-year-old 'Young' Communists carrying briefcases and looking anxious, as if they were going anywhere but on a picnic. I was in the second with four girls from the hostel and all the food and bottles.

When we got to the Desna, Zhora told me to get a fire going, see to the kebabs and other food, and keep the girls amused while they dealt with Young Communist business.

Which they did with gusto, making themselves comfortable on a rug spread on the riverbank, now whispering, now shouting as they passed round documents.

I caught only the odd word, 'credit' and 'transfer' being two that I was not familiar with. The girls, all wearing make-up and in jeans, sat around on the grass. Viktoria, spotty-faced and three months pregnant, had declined the invitation, sparing me the tricky necessity of persuading her not to come.

With a good fire of pine branches going, tickling the nose with its smoke, I could shortly set up the barbecue for our mass of marinated meat.

Checking the drink, I found we had ten bottles of Napoleon cognac and a magnum of Soviet champagne. Champagne was right to start with, but what when it ran out? Cognac for the girls? Very likely. Or Zhora, mainspring and organiser of all such excursions, would have seen to it that there was wine. He had packed the drinks bag himself and hoisted it into the back of the minibus, signalling to the driver to get the show on the road.

121

Switzerland, 13 October 2004

The doctor who examined Valya and Svetlana recommended against returning to Zurich by car, Dima explained.

'Do we walk there then? Or do we have the babies here?'

Dima spoke again with the doctor.

'A helicopter could put us down on the roof of the hospital in Zurich.'

'And what would be the pleasure of that cost?'

'Three thousand francs,' said Dima, clearly already informed.

So here we are in the helicopter. The red cross on its white fuselage makes me think of the Swiss flag: the same, only vice versa. Maybe this country was one big first-aid centre. It had certainly become one for our family.

The pilot, a man in his early thirties with an extremely neatly cut little moustache and large headphones, every now and again looks over his shoulder towards us. Svetlana and I sit with our backs to the side opposite Valya and Dima.

The helicopter rises up and out of the rock tumbler, and flies along the valley and over the little town of Leuk where we see the twisting line of the road to Zurich.

The helicopter shakes and I see Valya's tummy shaking too. It seems strange that Valya is about the same size as Svetlana. Is her one baby going to be as big as our two put together? I don't like the idea. I want our babies to be big and strong too. On the other hand, we are producing two children at once. Valya will have to go through all this again if she wants another baby.

I take Svetlana's hand. Her palm is burning. We exchange glances and I can see she is nervous. Suddenly I'm nervous too and I don't let go of her hand until we are safe on the ground.

The helicopter alights gently in the centre of the landing platform. A white-clad nurse, sporting her watch like a medal, helps us out of the helicopter. Svetlana holds both her hands to her head and I feel myself being pushed along by the backdraught even though I am carrying two heavy cases and a leather portmanteau over my shoulder.

Within half an hour we are established in two-room luxury in a rehabilitation centre with its own little park with an exit to the lake, its own ambulance, and a duty doctor and nurses in attendance, and – just as in a good hotel – phone, satellite TV, bathrobes, bath slippers provided.

From the balcony I watch the yachts, then spot Dima sitting on a bench at the water's edge, also watching.

'How about coming to the lake?' I ask Svetlana.

'I don't feel too good. I'll just lie down.'

I wait until she is asleep, before joining Dima on his seat.

'How's Valya?'

'Resting,' he says, looking back at the yachts.

'Isn't today the 13th?' I ask, knowing perfectly well that it is.

'So? Lovely day. Warmer sun, warmer breeze than Leukerbad's. And across the lake, that villa with white columns!' he says, with a new, nervous note to his voice, as if afraid.

He continues for a while to extol the white villa, then falls silent.

'I shan't come back to Kiev!' he says suddenly, eyes still on the distant shore.

I'm watching a tiny learner's yacht and a little thirteen-year-old girl in a red life jacket doing her ineffectual best to gybe, learning much in the process.

I feel there's nothing more to say. I'm content to remain silent until 27 October. Then we can congratulate each other on the births, and prepare to return to Kiev.

122

Kiev, December 2015

The events of the previous night allow me no peace. Or rather not so much the events, of which I know nothing, as their scandalous result of which the press must learn nothing. While I was peacefully asleep in Desatinaya Street, someone made off with the ottoman from my study.

I now sit contemplating where it once stood, waiting for Svetlov.

Astonishingly, my Office Security saw nothing. True, there are still the CCTV tapes, which, as Nikolai Lvovich assures me, will have recorded everything.

Svetlov appears at long last, breathless and dishevelled.

'I've heard what's happened, Mr President. We're searching the Writers' Union at the moment.'

'What would they want with my ottoman?'

'We're searching all over.'

'Another job for you: find out what Surgeon Khmelko has died of, and have this photograph of my heart expertly examined.'

'The photocopy, examined?'

'No, the heart. I need a discreet, reliable opinion.'

Half an hour later, Filin turns up, looking around as if the ottoman has been shrunken and tucked away somewhere.

'Outrageous!' he says, shaking his head. 'Office Security should be subordinated to the MVD.'

'Is that all you've got to say?'

'Yes, Mr President.'

'Well, go and find it for me!'

In the lull that follows, I drink mint tea, said to have a calming effect. But I need a tranquilliser. I need to relieve the stress, but not in such a way as to cause another miracle.

And what, I wonder, of the Ternopol miracle?

Outside it's snowing, great milky flakes trying hard to stick to the window, only to be displaced by following flakes.

The New Year will soon set the pieces out again; an end to the present shambles. But that is just an illusion. Nothing will change, the chaos will remain the same; for things to change we need new people, and they are impossible to get. Anyone entering this world of power is reshaped, all courage and decisiveness is extracted, any sense of humour frozen.

Remembering Shishkin, I yearn for the forest! For inner peace. I must either commune with art or go mushroom picking. It occurs to me that these activities have much in common.

'Eh!' I shout for my aide. 'That museum near the Russian one, what is it? Western Art?'

'I think so.'

'Tell them I'm looking in at ten this evening. With Mayya Vladimirovna.'

'Nikolai Lvovich won't like it,' my aide responds in a whisper, his voice fading as he realises what he has said.

'You can tell Nikolai Lvovich . . .' I begin, but he's already left the room.

123

Kiev, 20 December 1991
David Isaakovich greeted the break-up of the Soviet Union with malicious pleasure. From then on his health improved, and he decided to float a party on his pension money, telling me to invite Father Basil, which was easily done.

Set before us were two herrings, decorated with rings of sliced onion and dressed with sunflower oil, a saucepan of boiled potatoes, salad, the freshest of Doctor's Health Sausage and two bottles of vodka.

'What are you so down in the mouth about?' Father Basil asked, pouring vodka.

Reaching into my shabby jacket, I produced my Work Record.

Putting down the bottle, he leafed through it.

'*Discharged due to reorganisation*' he read. 'Well, so what? You'll find a decent job.'

'I shall,' I said, reaching for my glass.

'Don't be in too much of a hurry, that's the main thing,' Father Basil advised. 'It will soon be New Year, and then we'll have a better idea what sort of country we're in. God's abundance may come to us without any sort of work. You'll see what changes there are!'

'Changes!' grinned David Isaakovich. 'Last year when I called an ambulance, it took an hour to arrive, this year it was an hour and a half! So it's change for the worse.'

'It can't be any worse,' said Father Basil with a wave of the hand and looking at me.

'It can,' I contradicted. 'Anything's possible.'

'To hell with you,' declared the bearded priest with a toss of his head. 'Herring and vodka on the table before us, and here you are grumbling! Is that what we've gathered for?'

'It was me who brought you together,' said David Isaakovich. 'Because I'm feeling well. The moment I stopped taking the medicines, I recovered. So let our toast be "No repeat of the past!"'

Father Basil frowned. 'To the general good and the good times returned for good is what we should drink to, not to the past not repeating itself!'

'Keep that for your old women,' said David Isaakovich. 'When you're my guest, you drink to what I tell you!'

I sat understanding nothing of this verbal crossfire, catching the drift, but the vibrating edginess of it more than the sense. It was tension. And I was no less tense myself. The proximity of the New Year failed to cheer. Just as the past had. Indeed, for some time I had been aware of a trembling apprehensiveness affecting everyone. Even Mother. Who for no apparent reason had been crying in the night. Probably the only one not affected was Dima. With him all was well.

Drinking my third glass, I remembered how, from force of habit, I had popped into the Central Committee building and saw men carrying files out and doors being sealed off. I asked about Georgiy Stepanovich, only to be told, 'In America. That's where your Zhora is!'

'It'll all sort itself out,' said Father Basil suddenly, adopting a velvety, almost singing baritone. 'Wait and watch, that's the thing.'

124

Zurich, October 2004

A week before the babies were due, Dima went for another of his long walks. Svetlana and I sat watching the yachts on the lake when Valya staggered up breathless. Resting heavily against the back of our bench she gasped: 'Have you seen Dima?'

'See if you can find him,' Svetlana said quietly, persuading Valya to sit down and wait.

Last time it had been forty kilometres, now, with the sun beating down and leaves rustling underfoot, he might have gone into Zurich. He could be anywhere. When I got to the road my inclination was to head for the city, until I remembered that Dima's last walk had been *away* from civilisation. So I set off in the opposite direction, speeding past elderly walkers, glimpsing, between restaurants, hotels and boarding houses, the lake and its yachts. It would have been quicker to get a taxi, but I was quite glad of the exercise. All that sitting on benches was beginning to get to me. I would have liked to run, but I was not wearing sports shoes. I had not brought any with me. Eventually I was tempted to take a break at a café with a terrace. Only to find, sitting with his back to me and the world, Dima. He was writing on a piece of paper, coffee cup beside him.

I sat down at the nearest table. A dark-skinned waitress appeared: Albanian or Greek perhaps. I ordered coffee and Coca-Cola. The last thing I wanted was to upset Dima, but seeing it was one thirty, I went over to him.

'Dima, they're waiting for us back at the hotel,' I said quietly.

His head turned and for a second I saw terror in his eyes. Then he said: 'You? All right.' And a dry smile crossed his face.

Rolling up what he had written and putting it into an inner pocket, he got to his feet.

Tipping the waitress generously, I asked for a taxi.

125

Kiev, December 2015

The idiots have closed access to Tereshchenkovsky Street except to trolley buses and all because Mayya and I are sitting at a mahogany table in the Lesser Dutch Masters Room. There's a guard on every door and, no doubt, Nikolai Lvovich is pacing about behind one of them.

'Your Igor,' I say, pouring Mayya a glass of dry red, 'was he often ill?'

Our dinner on this occasion is somewhat lacking in refinement. I ordered a picnic, so everything is cold: dried salmon, black caviar tartlets, stuffed quails' eggs and every kind of other delectable items.

For the third time this evening Mayya adjusts the low-cut front of her black dress. The cloth is soft and falls straight down, concealing her natural figure, supposing she has one. I am no authority on fashion, but I would advise my wife against such purchases. True, having no wife, I am spared the trouble.

'I don't like talking about him, as you know . . .'

'His health, not him, is what I want to hear about. Whether he had trouble with his heart.'

'All men who drink and work in business have trouble with their heart.'

'Did he ever have a heart operation?'

'Not while I was his wife,' she says thoughtfully, clearly troubled by something. 'And that was for two years. What happened before that I don't know.'

I may as well relax, make the most of this picnic in these lovely surroundings. I'm not going to find out anything from her.

Getting up, I go over to a small canvas showing oddly dressed Flemish peasants drinking wine from ladles.

'Life was simpler then,' I say, and when she says nothing, 'Would you believe, someone's stolen my ottoman. It must be a first: a burglary from the President's office.'

Doing her best not to, she laughs.

'Nothing funny about it. It's a circus, with me the clown.'

'Oh come on. Everyone in this country steals. It's an old Byzantine tradition. And this is petty theft at the very summit of Power.'

'Hardly petty. That ottoman weighs a hundred kilograms at least. Whose side are you on?' I ask gloomily.

'You do know, don't you, they're collecting signatures for your impeachment?' Mayya asks quietly.

'Where did you get that from?'

'A newspaper.'

'Who?'

'Communists and combined Right Opposition . . .'

'You mean Kazimir?'

'Yes, and he's going to head the Opposition.'

'Enough! Of politics not another word!' I say, my mind at once on quails' eggs and stringing Kazimir up by his bollocks.

'You're so unhappy,' Mayya says softly, eyes moist with sympathy.

'Don't cry,' I urge. 'All 45 million of us are unhappy. You should feel sorry for the entire population, not just the President.'

There is a lot left uneaten, but our picnic is over. I have lost the urge to talk. We finish the wine in silence.

Mayya is driven off to Desatinaya Street, and I hang on. Svetlov is due, and I hope he will have something to report.

126

Kiev, 12 January 1992

'You're late,' says Father Basil as I join him in Quinta, the cellar café in Great Zhitomir Street.

We agreed to meet at one, but conditions are icy and transport almost in abeyance.

He fetches me a shot of vodka, and I sit down still wearing an old sheepskin unearthed from a cupboard at home. With the temperature -15°C, I regret having neither mittens nor gloves.

'What news?' I ask.

'Drink first,' he says gloomily.

I raise my glass, expecting to clink glasses with Father Basil, but he holds his in front of his lips in silence, like at a wake.

I get it. Someone's died. Surely not the old man? I think, watching Father Basil toss back his vodka. Then he speaks quietly.

'David Isaakovich has departed from us. He had a stroke.'

'When's the funeral?'

'That's for us to decide. We being all he had. No sense in telling his ex and his daughter just yet.'

From a pocket of his own ancient sheepskin he takes a bunch of keys which he lays on the table. 'He's to be collected from the mortuary tomorrow. But I don't think he would have wanted a funeral,' he says gazing in earnest at me.

'What would he have wanted?'

'With you helping we could make him happy.'

I struggle to formulate a question, but Father Basil has already read it on my face and he goes on.

'You remember how he made a mound and put a cross where his dugout had been? Let that be his grave. It was where he most loved to be, his real home – no neighbours, no shared kitchen.'

I nod, wondering how we would get him to Trukhanov Island. How we would dig the frozen earth? And how was he to be buried? In a coffin? Or as he was?

'Is it allowed?' I ask.

'God alone is our judge. He will not forbid it!'

I shrug.

'I've been to his room,' Father Basil says, indicating the bunch of keys. 'There was money there. It should cover a burial and a wake . . .'

127

Zurich, 25 October 2004

Svetlana's final check went well and left her feeling more confident about the days to come. The doctor said that she and Valya should check into the hospital the next day to be on the safe side. And that evening he asked to speak to me and Dima separately. I went in first with Valya as interpreter. I had never ceased comparing Valya with Svetlana, whose face had been particularly pale since our arrival in Zurich. Valya's cheeks were positively rosy. It must be much harder to carry twins than just one baby, I told myself.

'Will you be present at the birth?' asked the doctor.

'I'd like to, but my wife prefers not,' I said.

'There's a rest room by the labour ward where you can sit and we'll keep you informed.'

'How?'

'In English.'

Dima's interview was considerably longer, and I, waiting outside, caught one or two explosive exchanges between him and Valya.

At dinner – Dima having taken himself off to the lake – Valya told us that Dima had been told he could not be present at the birth, and this on the advice of his Leukerbad psychiatrist, to which Dima had replied that he would punch the psychiatrist on the nose as soon as he got back to the Alps.

'He'll calm down,' Valya said. 'I have some tablets they gave me in Leukerbad. I've already slipped some into his tea. They work like magic.'

It was hard to believe that she was as mad as Dima. I recalled the delayed reactions and slow-motion gestures which characterised her behaviour back in the home in Glukhovka. Now sitting at the table with us was a normal, healthy, beautiful young woman whom pregnancy had made even more attractive. Again I could not help noting that this was not so in Svetlana's case.

'I've got lots of things together,' she said proudly, 'although I've been told you get given a set of what's needed free. You'll probably get two.'

Svetlana smiled. It was a tired smile, but at least she was eating properly.

'Oh my, they're running about!' she cried, happily. 'Here, feel.'

Placing my hand on her tummy, I felt the movement of little feet running over my palms. Svetlana's smile was now quite radiant.

I kept my hand on her tummy. The unseen feet, or perhaps not feet, continued to drum on my palms. It was a wonderful feeling. A miracle. It was as if they were warning us that they would soon be out, that they were in a hurry to see their parents and create a real family.

128

Kiev, December 2015

Last night I left the museum after midnight, having spent some time contemplating *Portrait of an Unknown Man* and envying him. I wished I could be unknown. Even without a portrait. Every president we've had has been a national disaster. School textbooks already make do with just their dates. Not a word about the country's achievements during their presidencies. Children had to be protected from history. Recent history especially.

I can imagine my own entry in a hundred years' time. *'President Bunin, S. P., was given the heart of an oligarch who perished tragically. The heart was not entirely sound and only worked thanks to a pacemaker implant. President Bunin's attempt to elucidate the details of his own operation revealed that his surgeon had died, that the latter's two assistants had been killed in the same car crash, that the anaesthetist had disappeared, and that no theatre nurse could be found who would admit to having assisting in the operation. After which, the President himself died. His pacemaker had run down, and could not be replaced.'*

Then schoolchildren would be asked:

'Who was S. P. Bunin?'

'The president who had his ottoman stolen.'

'Correct. By what name was the piece of furniture known?'

'Major Melnichenko's Ottoman.'

'Correct. Who was Melnichenko?'

'Hero, man of mystery. He bugged President Kuchma. The bug was concealed in the ottoman whereon the Major liked to sit.'

'Excellent! Thank you.'

Nothing to worry about, but today I'm going for heart

tomography. I have the feeling that my heart knows something I don't. They say that a dog can anticipate the death of a master, even at a distance. Likewise, the irregular beat of my heart signals that something is amiss.

My body cries out for a cold bath, but it will have to wait – doctors first.

129

Trukhanov Island, 13 January 1992, night

Tonight feels like a cross between an American horror movie and a Soviet film about the Siege of Leningrad. We collected David Isaakovich in an ambulance, not in the morning but just after 3.30 p.m. in the gathering dusk, Father Basil having persuaded a sociable driver and orderly 'to assist in achieving the last request of our dear departed'.

After first dressing him decently in his divorce suit, we laid him out in the minibus and set off without flashing light or siren.

We negotiated the snow of the footbridge with surprising ease, but, once across, the driver would go no further. We eased David Isaakovich from the hospital stretcher onto the snow, practically picked up the ambulance to help it make the turn, back up onto the bridge. Now we stand sadly watching its rear lights disappear into the murk of a January evening.

I am growing increasingly cold and irritable as Father Basil fetches from under the bridge the child's sledge he secreted there, and on it we drag David Isaakovich to his dugout in the wintry waste of the uninhabited island.

Fifteen minutes sees us there, and it's then that the practical side of Father Basil becomes apparent. A great pile of firewood stands ready, and nearby, hidden in the snow, are a crowbar and a spade.

We get a fire going to unfreeze the ground, and some five hours later, after two breaks and a warming bottle of vodka, we have fashioned a shallow grave, and Father Basil is reading the burial service over the body. His deep resonant voice striking a mournful but affecting note in the darkness, the tiny circle of light created by the fire now moved to one side. I barely understand what he is reading. Close to weeping, I listen more to the voice than the words. The yellow waxy face of David Isaakovich, no longer the man I had known, is fitfully lit by spurts of flame from the fire.

Gently we lay him in his earthy niche.

'David Isaakovich, till our next meeting,' says Father Basil, taking him by the hand, before turning to me. I too grasp his icy hand, but cannot say a word.

Crossing the footbridge, the icy wind is in our faces. We walk in silence. We are on the Embankment now and have reached the river port. All around is silent. Not a car, nor a lighted window. Blocks of flats are few and far between here anyway.

'Cold?' Father Basil asked.

'A bit.'

'Let's go to his place. I've got the keys. We'll drink to his repose.'

Chancing on an all-night kiosk and waking the young man inside, we buy Hungarian salami, two bottles of beer, a jar of red caviar and a bottle of vodka. After that the going is more cheerful and the wind less cruel.

130

Zurich, 26 October 2004

Time is in no hurry. By the hotel's digital alarm it's 00.20, and though our window opens to the freshness of the lake, there's not a sound from outside. No country can sleep more quietly or serenely than Switzerland.

Svetlana is asleep, face and distended tummy towards me. I lie on my back pressed close to where our little ones are, quiet one minute, stirring the next.

Tomorrow or the day after, our lives will change, though exactly how proves beyond imagination. I try the logical approach. A nanny, they'll need a nanny, maybe two. Svetlana can't manage them alone. She'll be exhausted and look it, and that will upset her more than anything else. I must avoid that.

By the digital alarm it's now only 00.30. Maybe it isn't working, and dawn is about to break. Why can't I sleep?

The twins have been extremely active, kicking, kneeing me in the ribs. I'm amused by their antics and find myself playing a sort of game with them: I move my hand from one position on Svetlana's tummy to another trying to catch the babies' movements. I'm playing with them even before they are born.

'Don't worry,' I tell them. 'I'll see you soon.'

By about 03.00 they have settled down and gone to sleep. I wish them well. They have a couple of difficult days ahead.

Sleep still refuses to come and I get up, and donning a bathrobe, address myself to the minibar, selecting a small bottle of Moët. Tomorrow I will buy a large one, but this would do for now.

Barefoot, I tiptoe out onto the balcony with my bottle and a glass, and close the sliding door behind me.

The silence outside matches the silence within. The lake, the moon on the water, the far shore with its occasional lamp, all Switzerland is asleep. The not very loud pop of the champagne cork is like a criminal act. I'm the frightened guilty child again, but the pop is absorbed into the amazing Swiss night.

When I pour only foam fills the glass, so I raise the bottle to my lips. It's brut again, but tonight I don't mind. I'm not drinking to enjoy the taste, but in celebration of new life. Even the sourness of the drink and the bubbles up my nose cannot detract from my pleasure. I am reminded of a cold New Year's night in the distant past, me leaning against a warm radiator. A teenager with a big bottle of champagne, trying to act grown up. Now I am grown up and the bottle of champagne is small and it suits me fine.

131

Kiev, 30 December 2015

'That's your heart, and that, there, is your pacemaker,' says the doctor, resting his pointer on a tiny rectangle to the left of the heart on its opalescent screen. 'But it's not one of ours.'

'How do you mean?'

'Ours are of simple design, this is different – more intricate.'

Looking around at the consulting room, I wonder why I am here. The Theophania hospital is regarded as our best, but we've come to one of Kiev's twenty or thirty private clinics.

As his mobile rings, Nikolai Lvovich who has been sitting motionless, springs to his feet and hurries out, checking first to see who's calling.

'That's no pacemaker,' the doctor whispers quickly with one eye on the door which Nikolai Lvovich has left slightly open. 'I didn't say this, but get that photo to a computer buff!'

I nod and take a good look at the doctor's face. White coats depersonalise people, conferring a uniform appearance of saintliness. This doctor is about forty, hollow-cheeked, stubbly-chinned, hook-nosed, probably Jewish, as those who cure us usually are.

'Thank you. And you are?'

'Rezonenko, Semyon Mikhaylovich.'

'Can I trust you?' I ask, but before he can reply, the door squeaks, Nikolai Lvovich is back, and the doctor is left to imply trustworthiness with a look.

So the doctor can be trusted, but is afraid of Nikolai Lvovich, which seems to imply that the latter is not to be trusted.

Having pronounced a few formal words of thanks to the doctor, I dismiss him and turn to Nikolai Lvovich.

'A job for you personally: get me a few more consultants' opinions on that photograph. In writing. And that phone call, was it to do with my ottoman?'

'No, no news on that front.'

'Have the CCTV tapes been found yet?'

He shakes his head.

'Tell me, how many of my staff would have to have been in on this in order to pull it off?'

The question was not intended seriously, but Nikolai Lvovich clearly took it to be.

'Five or so.'

'Well, find them . . .'

'We're trying to,' he assures me and I notice an unusually cold-blooded glint in his eye.

132

Kiev, February 1992

Thinking of David Isaakovich, I recall the French proverb, 'To part is to die a little.' His wife and daughter left him and seemingly died a little. And he has died and left forever.

For a month now David Isaakovich has been lying in his earthy freezer on Trukhanov Island, while Father Basil and I frequent his room. Yesterday I went so far as to pay his rent and electricity bill. His neighbours seem to regard us as his heirs, having enjoyed three generous wakes at his expense.

'When his money's gone, we pack it in,' was Father Basil's response when I voiced some anxiety.

Still, at all three wakes we've heard nothing but good of David Isaakovich, who seems to have been as generally liked as he is now generally missed. At the last wake, one Valentina Petrovna, who I couldn't remember ever seeing in the flat before, declared in a voice throbbing with emotion, that the room 'would probably now go to some down-and-out or alcoholic', straight away turning to me with a pleading look as if I was their last hope. Still I failed to catch on until one of our mournful toasts, with no clinking of glasses, was followed by a silence long enough for the forest birth of a bastard militiaman, or the leaking of a major state secret. What ensued was more in keeping with the latter. After conferring in whispers, the people living in the communal flat came up with an amazingly tempting proposal. Unregistered occupancy of a flat for more than six months, duly confirmed by neighbours, entitled the occupier to be registered as resident. They had therefore decided that it would be better for me to live in David Isaakovich's room than to have some stranger turn up there. None of them could apply for it as they had no right to additional space, being without children.

'And bear in mind,' Father Basil said, when Valentina Petrovna had finished holding forth, 'that David Isaakovich would be pleased if you did. He looked on you as his son.'

'As we can confirm,' whispered the wearer-in-of-shoes.

I promised to think about it.

As we take our leave, Father Basil reminded the friendly people at the communal flat that forty days of mourning would soon be up, and that the wakes to come would be of a different, strictly religious order.

I did indeed think about it, and even consulted Mother, who proved to be well up on laws affecting living accommodation.

'Which district? Old Kiev?' she asked, addressing her memory more than me. 'I've a friend in the District Committee there.'

The future of the room in the flat was settled.

133

Zurich, 27 October 2004
The rest room is an improvement on our waiting facilities at home

– ample space, three settees, each with its own newspaper table, a great window giving onto the little park and expertly trimmed verdure, and vending machines dispensing nine variants of instant coffee for a mere one franc fifty, as well as more modest beverages, some without charge.

Dima, on a settee by a standard lamp, is reading a German book.

'What's it about?' I ask.

He shows me the cover. 'Old men's ailments. Fancy living long enough for that sort of thing!'

'What sort of thing?'

'Senile dementia. You go back to your childhood. He's a good chap, this Martin Suter,' he says, glancing at the cover. 'Puts it well.'

'He's probably old himself,' I mumble looking around.

My settee seems too soft. Something to do with my being nervous. I envy Dima his Olympian calm.

A woman doctor who brought us and left us here like a couple of schoolchildren said, with Dima interpreting, that she would keep us informed and that for a hundred francs we could book a room for the night. An offer we declined.

God, how I hate waiting!

I pick up a magazine. All patterns and photographs. Knitted sweaters for middle-aged women. Another, with Madonna on the cover and Britney Spears and Christina Aguilera inside.

Getting up, I listen, and hearing nothing, press the soup button of the free drinks dispenser. A steaming green liquid savouring of Knorr cubes emerges, and I, in no hurry to drink, warm my hands around the cup.

Half an hour later, a woman in a blue smock, who could have been Chinese or Thai, appears and proceeds to mop the floor. She is oblivious to us, though, curiously, she leaves the area around our feet unmopped, finally squirting an aerosol ceilingwards, creating an artificial minty freshness.

Again we are alone. I look at my watch. It will soon be midnight, and still no baby crying its first cry. Maybe in Switzerland babies don't cry. Out of respect for the law forbidding nocturnal disturbance.

At twelve thirty the woman doctor comes silently in, now in carpet slippers and addresses Dima with something approaching a smile on her face.

'It's a daughter!' he declares proudly, before going off with the doctor.

Left to myself, I put one franc fifty in the machine for a cup of coffee. Then Dima looks in to show me a tiny red face peeping out of a pink blanket.

'Isn't she a pretty little darling?' he exclaims, before carrying her out.

Any minute now they'll bring me two.

A quarter of an hour later, Dima looks in to say goodbye. He's taking a taxi back to the hotel. He wishes me a short wait.

Time moves at a snail's pace as if fearful of the dark and of colliding with something in it. Getting up, I look out into the long corridor. Nobody. Just silence. And the impossibility of imagining my wife here somewhere groaning, screaming in labour. How *did* the Swiss manage to soundproof so efficiently?

Head buzzing, I have to lie down.

134

State dacha, Foros, 31 December 2015

Here on the south Crimean coast our rough winter sun seems kindlier. Temperature 4°C. The sea a gentle monotonous whisper. We take the lift down to the shore, Mayya in a blue sweater and skintight jeans emphasising the youthfulness of her figure. I think of past romantic New Year celebrations that will never come again.

Strange the noise the waves make though barely lapping the beach. The water, when I feel it, is pleasantly cold. Oh for a swim! But Mayya will think me mad.

'Like a swim?' I ask.

Mayya looks at me with curiosity.

'No, but if you want to, go ahead,' she says, then, nodding to where men are skulking behind a shelter, 'You'll be rescued whatever happens.'

'Could be it's their job to do the opposite,' I laugh.

Stripping off, I walk slowly into the salty chill of the Black Sea.

The waves, tiny as they are, nudge me back to the shore, while the undertow draws me towards deep water.

Immersed to the chin, I long for someone to share the wonder of it with. Father Basil, David Isaakovich – they should have been here!

I swing round. Mayya waves.

Someone by the shelter is watching with binoculars. Perhaps I should show him my willy. It'll be a new experience for him. Give him something to tell his wife and children.

I have the amazingly harmonious sensation of becoming a natural part of the sea and its fauna. With the cooling of my blood within seems to come a cooling of any desire to return to dry land.

Amphibian-man! Is that perhaps my proper orientation in life – as in a Soviet fantasy film of the not so distant past? Perhaps I should be kept in a barrel of seawater, comfortable, undistracted by thoughts of the constant disharmony between my body and my element which give rise to persistent mental unease and suspicion. True, my suspicion is justified. I woke up to find myself operated upon and provided with a donor heart! Computer-chipped to discharge some unknown purpose! Then my ottoman is stolen from under my nose, together with all the CCTV tapes! How can I sleep at night with all that on my mind?

Seeing I am heading out to sea, I turn, now about three hundred metres from the beach. Binoculars are still watching. Mayya is standing, looking down at something near her feet.

From the direction of Turkey, I can make out the throb of a vessel, and bobbing up above the shallow waves, a white rescue cutter bearing down, and Nikolai Lvovich in dark suit and life jacket leaning over the side.

'Sergey Pavlovich,' he shouts. 'I've Governor Zelman with me carrying an important secret message for you. Could you come aboard?'

Zelman is a dwarfish Crimean Tatar Jew whom I like and have got on well with in the course of five or so meetings.

A white nylon ladder is dropped, and I clamber aboard. Zelman hands me a towel for me to girdle myself with, Nikolai Lvovich a tumbler of whisky.

'Where's the ice?' I ask.

'Aren't you cold enough?'

'Where's the ice?' I repeat.

Nikolai Lvovich nips below and returns with a plastic ice-cube mould straight from the freezer. Struck by something odd about the two cubes I dropped into my glass, I pick out another and see it to be in the shape of a bust.

'Grushevsky, first President of Ukraine,' explains Nikolai Lvovich.

'Wasn't that Kravchuk?'

'Of New Ukraine, Grushevsky was Old.'

'So?' I say, turning to Zelman.

'The Russians are tunnelling under the strait to Kerch.'

'How do you know?'

'No secret about it. On their side it's all fences, plant and security. According to a Ukrainian-born defector who has seen the plans, it's a second Channel Tunnel, with two tunnel-boring machines already on site.'

'With no word to us?' I ask turning to Nikolai Lvovich.

'Not even a hint. On the contrary. We've spent seven years negotiating with them over a double swing bridge.'

'So think of something before they pop up saying "Here we are together again!"'

'I *am* thinking. We've got a few ideas on the go already.'

'Report this evening. Found my ottoman?'

He shakes his head.

'Right. Pour me another, and head for the shore. Mayya will be getting worried.'

At my insistence, Nikolai Lvovich pours himself whisky. Zelman, who has recently converted to Islam and is trying to make a good start by observing its precepts, drinks Pepsi-Cola, although the Koran says nothing specifically about whisky.

135

Kiev, 8 March 1992

For some it's International Women's Day; for Mother there are more significant grounds for celebration, my ID card having the day before acquired a new stamp, making me officially resident at what was formerly David Isaakovich's address, though at the cost of some sweat. David Isaakovich, it appeared, should have nominated me in writing, and so it fell to me to make good his omission.

'Put some effort in!' urged Mother, hanging over me as I set about my third attempt. 'He was old, so it's shaky letters we want, not rounded prep-school stuff!'

Outside it was rain one minute, soggy snow the next, and thoroughly nasty. No one rang. Our entrance stank of cat's piss, for which Mother held our neighbour's Siamese to blame, saying she favoured our doormat.

The smell hit me that morning as I left the flat. But as I had a cold, smells were in the order of muffled noise, and not an irritant.

Outside the food store flowers were on sale for Women's Day, and they were what I had come out for, to show gratitude to Mother rather than keep distressing her with a show of independence, though she had not seemed to mind my moving away.

'How much are tulips?' I asked.

'Tulips are three hundred kupons.'

'A bunch?'

'A bloom.'

'Happy Women's Day!' I say, noticing the girl's gently provocative stance. 'Any chance of a reduction?'

'Maybe, if you come in the evening!' she says skittishly, clearly a transient worker, one of the hundreds living in hostels hereabouts. A little amber locket on a thin gold chain hung from her neck between the ends of her colourful headscarf.

'I'll take three,' I say, counting out nine hundred in the kupons that serve for currency in our days of inflation.

Wrapped in *Evening Kiev*, I now have a bouquet, and enough cash left in my pocket for a jar of caviar and a box of sweets. Parents deserve the occasional bit of affection. Especially when there is only one left, and she genuinely concerned at your failure to grow up.

Mother is moved, almost to tears.

I feel suddenly spiritually uplifted. I would try to be even better, more concerned, more grateful. I'll start peeling potatoes. I knew how, having a thousand times seen Mother at it. It has the calming effect on her that meditation has on the yogi.

136

Zurich, 28 October 2004, morning
Someone is gently tucking at my shoulder. I pull myself away from a dream in which I am making my way down St Andrew's Descent in winter. Standing over me, a white-coated woman speaking German.

'*Bitte stehen Sie auf.*' Her expression is at once demanding and indifferent.

I lower my feet onto the floor and realise something is wrong. I look down. My shoes. Where are my shoes? I look around and am aware of the sweet smell of mint.

'*Was ist los?*'

I stand up and bend down to look under the sofa and spy a few wet patches. The mint smell is no longer a mystery. The cleaner obviously came in just before I was woken up. And there are my shoes, carefully placed together under the window. I put them on and now I'm ready to listen to the woman.

'*Wir haben für Sie eine schlecte Nachricht.*' She speaks looking straight into my eyes, as if she is trying to hypnotise me and I notice an artificial freshness about her face.

'Sorry. Do you speak English?' I see her hesitate and take a breath.

'I'm terribly sorry but we were not able to keep your children alive . . .'

I've misunderstood. I ask her to repeat, and when she does I realise I heard right.

'What do you mean?' My voice box seems to have closed up and I can't get the words out.

'Your children were born at 4 a.m., they were immediately transferred to intensive care . . . Having breathing and heart troubles. We did what we could . . . Medicine is sometimes powerless . . .'

I look around. I can't understand whether I am standing or sitting. My body has left me and the sensation scares me. I stand up. Now I'm looking down at the nurse.

'I'm sorry, I don't understand.'

She repeats the same phrases about medicine being sometimes powerless, breathing problems, heart problems.

'Girls or boys?'

'One of each.'

'And dead.'

She nods and at last I see sympathy in her expression. Her professional façade is gone. Her tear-filled, hazel eyes watch me in silence.

'A baby girl and boy.' As I say the words I feel myself falling, falling into an abyss from which the woman in the white coat looks like a huge stone giant. I continue to fall noticing how she raises her breast-pocket watch to her face.

And she's gone. Everything around me is huge and moving, moving in my direction. I seem to be moving too. I'm hot. My legs are humming, tired from running in uncomfortable shoes. I'm going somewhere. I see sounds. I see the hooting of cars and buses, all grey. Then nearby a bright yellow bird calls in the voice of a teenage girl, calls and waves to her friend on the other side of the road.

I'm inside the tube of a kaleidoscope. Everyone is in there. But something shakes us and everything changes shape and position. We all freeze while a little child's eye looks up at us with curiosity. I feel hotter and hotter. The sun has already risen over the lake. Where did the lake come from? I look round, still running. Something clicks in my memory. Something whirrs over my head. I look up and see a boy in the most flared of jeans and a blue sweater taking a mobile phone out of his pocket. To my right a huge pit, as if someone has dragged out the house and the sand it stood upon. Beyond the sand, water. I stand still. I'm so hot that sweat is pouring over my brow and my underarms are unpleasantly damp. I approach the water and test it with the toe of my shoe. It feels good even through the Brazilian leather of my shoes. First I go in up to my knees, then further, not stopping until I'm up to my neck.

The far shore is no longer clearly visible. Too much water in the way.

Water embraces me, seeing and feeling me straight through my clothes, suffusing arms, legs with pleasant coolness. I am gaining weight, aware again of my body. I raise my arms, lower my arms, very likely smiling at finding myself again in control of my body.

Looking back at the villas, I see I am being watched from a balcony. I can't see the man's face, but his expression must be one of surprise. No one else is bathing, bright October sun notwithstanding. So bright in fact as to be impossible to look at.

Getting out of the water is a struggle. The watcher from the balcony is on the telephone. I know he's reporting on me.

Phone away. See if I care.

I'm back on the street. Regardless of fatigue and squelching shoes, I'm on my way somewhere and I'm in a hurry.

137

Crimea, 31 December 2015

I would not have believed that the last day of the year could include quite so many pleasant hours and minutes. Away from Kiev and Bank Street, I have relaxed and I have no great urge to return. If one has to be President, then it would be good to be burdened with a somewhat smaller, simpler country like the Crimea. Here it's a different ball game. The local elite is more naive, more sincere in its fawning, and genuinely in fear of incurring my displeasure and being, at a gesture, drummed off to the cells in the wake of the latest lot of venal mayors and corrupt officials. But I bear them no ill will and have no desire to do battle with them. For three years

Parliament has kept returning to the draft of a law on corruption, unable to decide how many categories of corruption there should be, which of them should be punishable and which should be considered a part of everyday culture, a tribute to tradition. But it's Parliament's job to make such decisions. I can't and won't do it for them.

Meanwhile I am sitting before a mirror in a leather armchair while a make-up artist from the Yalta Film Studio performs his magic on my head and face. His task, made lengthy by repeated interruptions from my security staff, is to make me unrecognisable.

I conceived a desire to walk the Yalta seafront, not alone but with Mayya, she with a little dog on a lead. Preferably a golden-brown one.

At 5 p.m. it's getting dark, which helps false moustache and goatee beard pass muster. The pallor, a consequence of sea bathing, is completely natural.

Nikolai Lvovich looks into the spacious bathroom where I am being made up. He is clearly nervous, but says nothing. Guilt born of the ottoman affair prevents him from complaining. Once it's found, he can let rip, but not until.

I can't actually remember the breed or colour of the animal in Chekhov's 'Lady with Dog'. I may not even have read the story. But 'Goldie', another story of his, I do remember. I remember weeping over it. I have always felt sorry for dogs, for women too, but less often.

Twenty minutes later we set off in a modest black BMW. They have closed the lower road for us and I can enjoy observing from behind smoked glass something of impoverished, out-of-season Crimea – the lights of villas and blocks, an occasional street lamp, and garishly lit refrigeratorless beer kiosks.

At my side, Mayya, with miniature dog of the required colour appropriately shampooed and groomed.

Mayya, in keeping with the present season and the epoch of the Chekhov story, is wearing a light brown waisted jacket with turned-up fox-trimmed collar, knee-length slit pencil skirt and heeled boots.

I have the childish feeling that tomorrow, with the New Year, something very new and important is impending – if not for the country, then at least for me.

The seafront is practically deserted. There are people about but they are almost invisible in the uncertain light of the street lamps. Clearly, cheap power has reached these parts.

'What, my dear, would you really like to do?' I ask skittishly as we walked arm in arm.

'Honestly?' she asks uneasily.

'Of course.'

'Go to the Metropol restaurant in Moscow.'

I conceal my disappointment. She seems serious.

'Do you think Olga Knipper loved Chekhov?' I ask.

The little dog tugs suddenly to get away, forcing Mayya to stop and tug him back.

'No,' she says. 'Chekhov was a bore, and Olga was a beautiful woman who adored attention and fame.'

'You think so? But how is it that talented men are so unlucky with women?'

Mayya laughs. We are again walking arm in arm.

'Clever men are ambitious. They pick women they look good beside. But women who have played these games realise that away from their clever men they look even better. Simple as that.'

'You're destroying my illusions. I want to believe in women – their loyalty, their devotion, their concern.'

'Believe away! But bear in mind that only a less than beautiful woman can love like that, and then simply out of gratitude for being noticed. Beautiful women calculate. All the way – from how they feel to how to respond, given the glad eye.'

'You're beautiful. Are you like that?'

'How do you mean?'

'Do you behave like your "beautiful women"? . . .'

'You see me as I am: neither in first flush of youth nor past my sell-by date.'

'Nice way to put it! I'll use that myself one day.'

At which our little dog slips from Mayya's grasp, and off into the dark avenue of the seafront. Mayya stands at a loss, while I dash off towards the sound of barking, which proves to be that of our dog challenging the Alsatian of three tracksuited figures sitting on a bench.

'Call your puppy off, arsehole, before my dog eats it,' one of the men says, spitting out a cigarette to do so.

'Arsehole? I'll teach you who's the arsehole!'

'Take it easy, Grandad, or you might not live till New Year!' says the man, rising and reaching in his pocket. 'Funerals are expensive!'

A bottle flashes down and he collapses, revealing behind him Nikolai Lvovich. I am bustled away between two security men.

The black BMW drives up, and I get in.

'That,' says Mayya, 'would not have happened at the Metropol.'

'Where's the dog?'

'He ran off.'

138

Kiev, end of March 1992, Sunday

Underfoot, the slush of yesterday's snow. The sky is a brilliant blue and the sun is bright. I have a headache, having the day before been wined and dined by Zhora of my Young Communist League days, now back from America, fatter and balder and smelling a bit sweeter, but still with the same voice and manner.

'I need you urgently.' he said, on the phone yesterday morning, and at twelve we met beneath the portico of the Central Post Office, and went on to a Georgian café.

'Got your diploma?' he asked.

'Not yet. I'm studying externally.'

'Don't worry, you'll get it,' he grinned, pouring cognac. 'I want you for a job.'

'Doing what?'

'Managing a select restaurant for bankers and crooks. Good pay, good perks. Interested?'

'It's not something I've done.'

'So *start*. You look right – affable, trustworthy. You've got our Young Communist buffet experience. This is much the same, only more fun. I'm offering $200 a month. What do you say?'

'Done!' I responded, impressed.

'Done!' said Zhora, slapping my upturned palm and raising his tumbler of cognac. 'Be bold. If I get a leg-up out of this, I'll take you with me. There's nowhere in Kiev at the moment for the self-respecting politician or banker to go for a bit of privacy. Same old story – all dressed up and nowhere to go.'

He gave a raucous laugh, attracting the attention of the grinning servile Armenian in white shirt and black bow tie behind the bar, who imagined we were just drinking ourselves silly, little knowing that I had been offered $200 a month – more than he would ever make, giving customers short measures.

We got through two bottles of cognac, and but for the bottle of Soviet champagne, all would have been well. But champagne on top of cognac was a mistake, and now, although I keep it to myself, my head aches. I promised Mother I'd go with her to see Dima, and I'm all ready, wearing my duvet jacket and looking at the clock. It is 10.45, and Mother will be back any minute from the food store with sausage for Dima. Sausage – Doctor's Health Sausage – is the only thing he has been asking for lately, as if it were doing him good like a medicine. Doctor's Health Sausage! Why not Teacher's, Engineer's or Officer's Health Sausage? As if we haven't enough of doctors!

139

Zurich, 28 October 2004

I shout for another whisky. There are already three squat empty tumblers on my table, and it is odd that they haven't been taken away. What if I drink a dozen of their ridiculous measures? Would I be left with that number of tumblers?

With the obligatory bitte! the barman sets down my whisky, looking askance at the widening pool of water at my feet.

'Sorry,' I say, employing my one English word of apology, before slowly enjoying my whisky.

I put down my tumbler and before long it is joined by another.

The door bangs open. I turn to see two policemen entering. They sit down at my table, one on either side of me. They shake their heads at the tumblers. The barman runs up.

Oh, I get it. You left the tumblers here as evidence against me.

After a brief exchange one of the policemen says: 'Pass. Identification.'

With difficulty I produce what my wet pockets contain: Swiss banknotes, small change, credit card, hotel key. The five stars on the latter's plastic label mollify them a little.

'English? American?' one of them asks.

'Ukrainian. From Kiev.'

'Russian, then.'

'If you say so.'

While the policeman reports on his walkie-talkie, I move the empty tumblers aside, and folding my arms on the table, allow my head to fall forward onto them.

'Sorry to wake you,' says a woman's voice in clear, crisp Russian. 'I'm Mila, here to interpret.'

She is in her early twenties, white hedgehog crop, rings in ears and on fingers, denim suit, leather half-boots.

'Well, feel free.'

'While you were asleep they checked up. You simply had too much to drink.'

'Don't people do that here?'

'It's not that.' She sits down opposite me. 'You told the barman you had killed your children, so he rang the police, who had already been rung by someone who had seen a man walk fully clothed into the lake.'

'I didn't kill them. I've never killed anyone in my life.' Tears are running down my face. I want to bawl, oblivious to everyone.

'They know that now. Your family are looking for you. You left your wife at the clinic.'

'Clinic? What time is it?'

'Four fifteen.'

'Where am I?'

'Reuslithal.'

'How far is it to Zurich?'

'Twenty-seven kilometres.'

'How did I get here?'

'I don't know. They'll drive you back and I'll come with you to the clinic. Don't worry, I'm paid by the police.'

140

Crimea, 31 December 2015

Disconcerted by the seafront incident, I want to be alone for a while, Mayya having considerately gone down to the sea. But bursting into my solitude comes Nikolai Lvovich with a bottle of whisky.

'Phone call from Kiev. Your New Year message went down well.'

'You saw it?'

'The penultimate version. The background has been altered a bit, but Svetlov says it's good.'

If Svetlov likes it, it must be OK. But clearly Nikolai Lvovich has realised that Svetlov's opinion is the one I most trust. So be it.

'I owe you a bottle for saving me.'

'I'd prefer your signature to a little decree,' he says with a smile.

The whippersnapper! On about his decree again, but my mood has already improved and I don't feel angered by his cheek. On the contrary, I fancy having a joke with him.

'If you can get your decree to me within one minute, I'll sign it,' I say, discerning no decree-like bulge about his nattily suited person.

But Nikolai Lvovich whips off his jacket to reveal a transparent folder stitched to the back lining, in which I see is the decree. He passes it to me together with a Parker.

It is, of course, the decree raising the threshold of criminal liability for financial loss to the state, regardless of office. He has just saved me from the criminal element of our society. I sign it, and Nikolai Lvovich beams with delight, until he notices that I have amended the heading to read 'From 1 January 2017, NOT RETROSPECTIVELY.'

'Why that?' he asks, clearly offended.

'It's for you and me, this law, not those before us. Now get pouring.'

With Nikolai Lvovich soon himself again and in suitably festive spirit, I get him to tell security that Mayya should leave off walking on the shore and join us.

Time 6.15 p.m. Ambient temperature 5°C. Country: Ukraine. Occasion: New Year.

141

Kiev, April 1992

'What you should do is swap this place for a one-room flat and pay the extra,' Mother urges, returning in a highly emotional state from the communal kitchen with the kettle. 'The oven's a nest of cockroaches! You'll have to have a serious word with your neighbours!'

'No I won't,' I say. 'I get on well with them. I don't mind their cockroaches.'

Mother shrugs, her expression one of indignation and incomprehension.

'Think about it. For this place you could get a one-roomer in Syrets District without paying extra.'

I don't feel like thinking. She arrives with a litre of *borscht*, and is off lecturing me again about being practical!

Throwing a couple of tea bags into the pot, I add hot water, then put the sugar bowl on the table.

'And high time you improved on the furniture. This lot stinks of old age!'

'What,' I ask, 'does young age stink of?'

Mother makes no reply, but I know: the sickly odour of strong red from yesterday's unwashed glass on top of tobacco smoke, cheap perfume or eau de cologne . . . A period of life now done with. Thanks to Zhora, I can now tie a tie and I look a thousand dollars managing our restaurant club, or was it a million? Manager at the age of thirty and a bit – Mother should be delighted with me!

'Any photographs of him about?' she asks, looking up from her tea.

'Who?'

'That old Jew of yours who lived here.'

From the sideboard drawer I take out David Isaakovich's papers which Father Basil, a great one for order, had made a tidy bundle of.

'Have a look,' I say.

Mother goes through the documents, diplomas and certificates with interest, studying for some time the photograph in some sort of proof of identity, which, when she's finished looking at all the others, she extracts. It is, I see, a Voluntary Collaboration with Army, Airforce and Navy pass.

'I'd like to take this for a day or two.'

'Keep it if you like.'

'Do you know,' her face brightens into a smile, 'I managed to get all my money out of that investment fund yesterday. With interest!'

'The one that crashed today?'

'Yes.' Her expression is one of pure childish delight.

'Now you can get Dima the raincoat you wanted for him.'

'That can wait,' she says, serious again. 'There are more important things.'

What, she expects me to ask, but I don't much want to know what could have been more important than a new coat for Dima. I'd say she needed to buy something for herself. To go on wearing the same long black skirt and old red woollen cardigan for ten years on end is odd. And it's odd that a woman never thinks of buying something new from a shop, but instead keeps remembering her old seamstress in Obolon who thirty years ago made her a fashionable crêpe de Chine dress! I'd seen it! The most beautiful girl ever could be coming my way wearing that, and I'd still cross the road to avoid her. Like a diagnosis, it says it all. As does her present turnout. She is the one who needs curing, not Dima. Only how?

Two hundred dollars in hand, I can see myself marching Mother

289

off to a clothes market and kitting her out with decent wear from Poland – stylish, bright, inexpensive. Or maybe not so bright. She doesn't like bright things.

But Mother is getting to her feet, putting on her old coat with a fox collar stitched on from an even older coat. At the door she stops and again surveys the furnishing.

And suddenly I, too, became conscious of it, the mustiness of old age or, more precisely, the life aura of the late David Isaakovich, and can understand what Mother dislikes about it. But that is the aura of another's life, now completed. I have no intention of renovating. And nothing short of renovation, pogrom, fire, flood or construction work will ever dispose of that smell.

142

Zurich, 28 October 2004

At my request I was driven first to my hotel, where I changed into dry clothes and combed my hair. I thought of shaving, but didn't feel up to it.

At the clinic we were met by the familiar white-coated nurse, who took us down a long white corridor over parquet-patterned linoleum that had an unusual deadening effect on our footsteps. It must be a kind of floor soundproofing, I thought, stopping and tapping my foot on the floor. Mila and the nurse looked round at me questioningly. And here, coming the other way, Dima, puffy-faced from lack of sleep. Seeing me escorted prisoner-fashion by nurse and interpreter, he looked very uneasy, almost guilty. I had the impression he would pass without acknowledging me, but just as we drew level he nodded.

With white walls, white box-file-laden shelves, glass-topped desk and toy-like see-through plastic telephone, the doctor's room smelled of wild mint. Sitting at her desk and donning gold-rimmed spectacles, she consulted a sheet of paper.

'Let me first offer you our condolences,' translated Mila. 'Your wife gave birth to a boy and a girl. The boy weighed 3.1, the girl 3.2 kilograms. Shortly after birth they exhibited difficulty in breathing, combined with irregular heartbeat. Resuscitation was undertaken, but unfortunately without success. Pending the results of an autopsy, cause of death cannot be stated. We'll inform you in six weeks' time of the results.'

'But how, if we shan't be here?'

'If you leave postage and full address, by special delivery . . . Your wife should stay here another two days. She has been given medication to stop the milk supply. Physically she should experience no difficulties, but psychologically she will need all the support you can give. You can spend the two days with her in her room, after which, come and see me again. Now the registrar is expecting you.'

The registrar's office was in a somewhat neglected building next door, and the registrar a woman in her fifties.

'I'm afraid you have some difficult days ahead of you,' she began. 'The law is that a child beyond the term of twenty-four weeks legally enjoys full rights of citizenship,' she said through Mila. 'And your children must be buried in conformity with the regulations. You must give them names, and I will then issue birth and death certificates. You may bury them here, or have them cremated and take their ashes for burial where you live. Is that clear?'

I nodded. It was all I could manage. I felt the tears welling up and it took all my strength to hold them back. I was sure that any second now they would come pouring out over my cheeks, dripping onto the floor and again eyebrows would be raised about the wet pool around my feet.

'Would you care for coffee?'

I shook my head.

'I don't want to hurry you. Take a day, talk with your wife, and come back.'

143

Crimea, 31 December 2015

A small thing, but I find the absence of snow unsettling. Mayya, roaming the dacha, champagne glass in hand, like a queen abandoned by her ladies-in-waiting, is indifferent to the fact. It never occurred to me that it would be tedious having her about all the time, and that apart from me there was no one else for her to be with. It's 9.55, and in the dining room I hear sounds of the table being laid. Nikolai Lvovich is somewhere checking up on the state of the country, and has been for the past half-hour, although any minute now the state of things would be made apparent by the TV news which is firmly under the control of Nikolai Lvovich's trusty minions. There'll be no Old Year bad news tonight – nothing must be allowed to spoil the people's jollifications.

Plumping myself down on the couch facing the TV wall screen, and waiting for the picture to appear, the hardness of my seat reminds me of my dear old ottoman and I shout to my aide, who comes in looking weary.

'Get Nikolai Lvovich to brief me on my ottoman.'

The Channel 1 news logo, and over to the New Year trees of the regional centres – Zhitomir, Lugansk, Simferopol, Lvov . . . The smallest and poorest – of which I made a mental note – is Uzhgorod's. Then a report from the Caves Monastery, after which one from St Vladimir's Cathedral concerning a New Year miracle: an icon of the Great and Holy Martyr Vladimir is weeping. On the screen a close-up view of still wet traces of tears from both eyes, a number of old ladies and a young couple kneeling before the miraculous icon. Here was someone else, crossing himself assiduously as he kneels. Change of camera angle, and staring from the screen, the face of Kazimir, tsar of our power supply – sod him! – eyes moist with emotion.

'Happiness, well-being, prosperity and an economic miracle are what I wish the people of Ukraine!' he declares.

'Ground down as they are by today's government!' says his body language.

'Shitpot!' I yell at the screen. Where's Nikolai Lvovich? Who the hell has he left in charge of TV?

He turns up in time for the weather.

'Did you see the news?' I ask, switching off.

'No, I've been –'

'Been what? What bloody fool put Kazimir on TV wishing Ukraine a Happy New Year?'

Nikolai Lvovich is equally shocked.

'When I find out, their feet won't touch the ground.'

'Whose side are they on at Channel 1?'

'Give me five minutes,' he says, dashing out.

Blast the lot of them, I'm going to find Mayya. Let's hope she can calm me down, or I'll give them all such a hard New Year that they'll wish for the old one.

144

Kiev, April 1992, Sunday

Mother receives me all smiles. It's amazing what living apart can do: not one word of reproach now for a month. On Sundays I go to Mother's for lunch, after which we visit Dima.

In the passage of the Khrushchev-era flat, the smell of veal cutlets and buckwheat porridge, and there, standing ready, her camel-skin bag of things to take Dima doubtlessly reeking of Doctor's Health Sausage.

We finish lunch with some of the Indian instant coffee 'it is so hard to get' – a ten-year-old notion of Mother's which, for the sake of peace, I fall in with.

'You should invite Dima and me to your restaurant one day,' says Mother, pulling on her boots, zipping them up with difficulty, and putting on her coat.

'I will,' I promise. 'It just means picking a free day.'

We are on a number 13 bus approaching Berkovets Cemetery, where we should change to a number 30 which takes us to the entrance of Dima's hospital. The bag, which I am carrying, weighs a good ten kilos and I am wondering what it contains apart from sausage. We cross the road, and I am making for the number 30 stop ahead of Mother, when she calls me back.

'Let's pop into the cemetery for a moment.'

I wonder why, since we have no one buried there. Maybe some cancer victim friend of hers is here. So I follow her in, hoping it won't be far, given the size of the place and the weight of the bag. Once inside, Mother turns from the main path to one that leads past the polished marble and granite of future headstones to a yard shut in by ugly single-storey structures.

'Where's Seva?' Mother asks of an unshaven man in a quilted jacket, standing hammer in hand.

'Seva, someone for you!' he roars.

Seva appears, also in quilted jacket and officer's green trousers tucked into patent leather boots.

'Ready, as promised.'

He takes us to where, on damp-darkened planks under an awning, lie finished headstones, one of which bears, in gold, on sombre polished granite:

BRODSKY DAVID ISAAKOVICH
DEAR UNCLE DAVID
12 OCTOBER 1922 – 9 MARCH 1992
CHERISHED IN MEMORY BY THE BUNINS

Above the inscription is a new ceramic frame containing a barely recognisable photograph of the deceased.

'Where did you get all that?' I ask in amazement.

With the calm, satisfied look of one who has discharged a sacred obligation, she returns his Voluntary Collaboration pass.

'Hang on, though, the date of death's not right.'

'He died *after* he left you the flat,' says Mother lowering her voice, with a look to where Seva stands smoking.

Well done, Mother! I can only applaud the philanthropy and practicality of her documentary evidence in granite!

'Happy?' asks Seva, looking not at us but the patent leather toe working his discarded butt end into the mud.

'Perfectly,' Mother replies and then she tells me to take a walk about for a couple of minutes.

Watching her count kupons from a sizeable wad, I conclude them to be the ones wrested, with interest, from the sticky fingers of investment crooks.

'By the way,' Mother calls over to me, 'this is where he's buried, isn't it?'

Anticipating more kupons, Seva is clearly all set to cart the thing off and erect it.

'Actually, no,' I say.

'So today or tomorrow it must go,' says Seva. 'There's no documentation, if they check.'

'He'll collect it,' says Mother, meaning me.

'When you come make sure you ask for Seva,' he says, stuffing the money inside his quilted jacket, where I would never have imagined there to be any pockets.

But what to do with it? I'll have to ring Father Basil this evening. No, first thing tomorrow. I'll be busy this evening at the restaurant.

Spotting us at the cemetery gates, the kindly driver of the number 30 stops to let us aboard. Cemeteries have a softening, humanising effect on people. Or is it death? The driver might think we are coming from a funeral.

I think of Dima waiting anxiously for his Doctor's Health Sausage and smile. His eyes fill with kindness when he sees us. Ours, no doubt, fill with pity and sympathy. A never-ending human interchange: pity and sympathy, Doctor's Health Sausage and kindness!

145

Zurich, 28 October 2004

I stood outside Svetlana's door for a good five minutes, listening. There wasn't a sound and I went in quietly expecting her to be asleep.

She was lying on her bed looking up at the ceiling. I was struck by the paleness of her complexion. She had been pale all through pregnancy, but now there was a deathly bluish tinge about her pallor.

As she turned her head to me, her face contracted in agony and tears poured.

'Forgive me!' she sobbed. 'For God's sake forgive me!'

Kneeling beside her bed, I took her in my arms.

How long she sobbed I never knew, but when at last she stopped, she looked beseechingly at me, her face no longer so alarmingly ashen.

'I love you,' I whispered.

'They were so tiny, so lovely . . . They brought them to me. All clean, bathed and dressed, our son in blue, our daughter in pink . . . They let me hold them, and I held them, but they were silent. I rocked them, but they were silent . . .'

Tears flooded once more. Sitting on the bed beside her, I laid a hand on her heaving shoulders, and I wept. Here I had no need for restraint. And in the mourning hush of the room we wept together.

'We must think of names,' I whispered after a while. 'You think of a girl's.'

'Vera,' she said after a while.

'Oleg,' I whispered.

'Why?'

'It's just a fine name.'

'Vera and Oleg,' she said to see how they sounded together and nodded approval.

Outside it was dark already. We neither of us spoke. I sat in the armchair to the right of the door. Svetlana lay with two pillows under her head. I watched her eyes, listened to her breathing. Every so often she turned and looked at me.

'Wouldn't you like to go to the hotel for a sleep?' she asked.

I shook my head.

'Put out the light.'

I put out the light and the outside darkness filled the room.

146

Crimea, 1 January 2016

Darkness, warmth and a woman's body wearied by feigning passion. A dream become reality.

She has turned away from me. Am I really of so little interest to her? Listening for her breathing, I hear nothing.

Mayya has not been in the best of moods. She'd rather be in Moscow at the Metropol, and to all intents and purposes, that's where she is; though here in body her mind is definitely elsewhere.

Slipping from the bedroom, closing the door behind me, I switch on the light. My aide leaps out of a chair and stares bewildered at the lower half of my naked body.

'Your President is not down there! He's here,' I say sternly, using my index finger to guide his gaze from my groin to my face. 'Whisky and some ice!'

While I'm waiting, I notice framed photographs that have so far escaped my attention – all the Ukrainian Presidents: Grushevsky, Kravchuk, Kuchma and what the hell is our jailbird Fedyuk doing there? He could come down for a start!

The aide bears in a bottle of single malt, a tiny ice bucket, tongs and my favourite heavy squat whisky tumbler.

'How long have those photographs been here?' I ask, pouring for myself.

'Since the day before yesterday. Nikolai Lvovich had them put up.'

'Then tell him either to throw in a photograph of my ottoman, or shift the whole lot to his bedroom!'

'He wants to establish a tradition . . .'

I've no desire to continue the conversation, especially with an anonymous aide who obviously has not yet woken up properly since he sees fit to inform me of Nikolai Lvovich's wants. I retire with my tumbler to the bedroom.

Perching on the edge of my large bed, I touch Mayya's shoulder with my whisky glass. No response.

Complete insensitivity. I am at once peaceful and bitter. It's as if I feel sorry for the past year. It was full of unpleasantness, but still demands that we regret its passing. No, that year has gone into history while I am still here. True, I'll be going that way too sooner or later, but not now. Now I am concerned with this useless female body with its back to me. I look down at my penis, barely visible in the darkness. We are both relaxed. Only my head is struggling with the lack of even the tiniest spark that could ignite passion between us. She does not want me to be passionate and I take pleasure from the cold, from water, from ice.

But maybe it's worth another try. I put my glass down on the table and slide under the light cover, pressing against her body, without passion or even affection. She probably won't even wake up, or she'll pretend she has not woken up, just as, an hour ago, she pretended she was burning with passion. When was it that I started having kindly feelings towards this woman?

No. Tonight is not the time to calculate cause and effect in a relationship. It's New Year's night. My first, and possibly last, with Mayya.

147

Kiev, 14 April 1992

Father Basil and I are sitting over coffee in my room in the flat.

'Headstone? For David Isaakovich?' He is clearly surprised. 'But he's not in a cemetery.'

'Mother didn't know that. But it's paid for and has to be collected as soon as possible.'

Father Basil smoothes his beard, shedding dandruff on his voluminous black sweater.

'Will she want to go and look at it?'

'I doubt it, but who knows?'

He gestures helplessly, his face a mixture of doubt and bewilderment, fat lips twisted into an expression of regret.

'Well, there we are . . . It would have been better if she had consulted us, and ordered a welded cross. It would have been cheaper, and not such a pity if it gets taken –'

'Graves don't get taken!'

'But it's not a cemetery. Who knows what plans there are for that island. There must have been some reason for evicting the people. They flattened his dugout, didn't they? . . . Know what?' he says at last with the stare of a man who has come to a decision. 'Let's find that ambulance again, and get them to help. So it's just us and them in the know. Granite's worth money, and there's so much poverty about.'

'Can you remember the crew?'

'I'm good at faces.'

It's raining on the Left Bank, and from the metro to the emergency hospital we walk without umbrellas, Father Basil in an ancient mackintosh with chequered lining, me in my duvet jacket.

A round of the minibus ambulances in the hospital forecourt fails to discover our driver and paramedic.

'Do we wait?'

For over an hour we wait, meeting every ambulance that comes in, but none of the faces are familiar.

Father Basil decides to have a word with some of the drivers, but comes back five minutes later disappointed.

'Nobody's willing.'

'Back to the flat – I've an idea,' I say.

We return to the Right Bank, my room and warm ourselves drinking tea at my place. I then phone for an ambulance. It's getting on for five. If my plan works, we'll just be able to pick up the headstone before the cemetery closes. Provided Seva's there!

148

Zurich, end of October 2004

The bereavement counsellor – a title Mila had some difficulty in conveying – had an office in the tiny church next to the clinic. She greeted us pleasantly, motioning us to heavy oak chairs.

'God teaches us to mourn and to rejoice. For you now it is a time of mourning. Obey your heart. Share your grief with those near to you. Pray to God. He will hear.

I threw a perplexed glance at Mila as she interpreted this speech and she responded with a barely visible shrug and went on: 'I have got together some material which will help you and your wife to come to terms with this trauma. The main thing is not to bottle up the grief inside you, not to keep it to yourself.'

She handed me a number of pamphlets.

'You'll find useful advice from a psychologist, also website addresses for parents who have lost children. And by Internet you will be able to make contact with people who have suffered similar bereavement.'

Leafing through, I saw that they were in German and French.

'To speak now of the final leave-taking. You have a choice. They can be buried in a cemetery near here. This is quite expensive, but our clinic receives a small discount. Or if you prefer, they can be cremated. The cemetery has a children's area, the Lewis Carroll

Garden, where you could scatter the ashes and plant two rose bushes on the spot. The roses could have your children's names inscribed on a bronze plate. It would be good if you could come to a decision today.'

I was very grateful to Mila, who seemed affected by our grief and unwilling to leave us until everything had been decided.

'I'll go for a bite to eat, then wait here on this seat. While you talk to your wife.'

Svetlana was sitting in an armchair in front of the window. The bed was disarranged as if she had tried to sleep and not been able to.

'How are you?' I asked.

'Not good,' she said, turning to look at me. Her eyes, no longer blurred with tears, were expressionless.

'There's something we have to decide.'

'What are those booklets?'

'For bereaved parents, from the church.'

'Let me see.'

While she turned the pages, whispering to herself, I stood, now watching her expression, now looking out at the trimmed trees in the park. In the end I made the decision on my own.

Next morning, Svetlana and I, accompanied by Mila, took final leave of our children in the tiny church next to the clinic. Prayers were read by our bereavement counsellor, Svetlana and I sitting tearful and stony-faced, Mila weeping as if she had lost her children.

The two white cardboard coffins – like dolls' boxes they seemed – slid into a suddenly revealed opening in the wall, the closing off of which struck terror to my heart. I thought I glimpsed that other world of light or fire to which all in death pass.

I looked around for an icon, but the tiny church had only a carved crucifix on the wall.

The following day, in the Lewis Carroll Garden where the roses were still in bloom, we scattered the two small urns of ashes, Svetlana and Mila both in tears. A gardener in a dark suit and tie handed us little rakes to rake the remains of Vera and Oleg into the soil, then brought two rose bushes which he planted twenty centimetres apart.

'That's not too close?' I asked.

'They were twins,' translated Mila. 'But I can space them if you wish.'

'No, don't,' said Svetlana, still in tears. 'No, don't separate them – they are twins.'

Mila, after seeing us to our hotel, gave us her card, promising to keep an eye on the roses.

We received a large envelope from the clinic containing Polaroid photographs of our little ones, together with their birth and death certificates, plastic identity wristlets and small cellophane packets with locks of light brown hair.

I went over to the window and looked at the lake. Yachts, someone on a bench at the water's edge – nothing had altered in these several days. But we, who several days ago had been expecting a miracle that would change our lives, were left with nothing more to expect. Pack up and leave was what we had to do, bearing our agony with us, leaving behind in Switzerland only two small rose bushes.

That night I was woken by a baby crying in what sounded like the next room. A nightmare, I decided, then realised it must emanate from Dima and Valya's room. Svetlana was also awake and listening.

We lay in silence, not touching. Remembering how I had played with the twins the night before they were born. Had their frantic kicking been a cry for help? For my help?

I'm a bad father, I concluded, crying once more. I got up, slipped on a dressing gown, and went out onto the balcony.

I tried to imagine the lake frozen hard, but holed close in, and me diving into that hole and diving and swimming under the ice until the air in my lungs was exhausted, and with it everything else, leaving me no longer fearful, no longer cold.

I had now, I realised with horror, three dead children. I remembered the night in the maternity home with my first wife, also Svetlana. My fate, whether in Kiev or Zurich, was one and the same.

149

State dacha, Foros, 1 January 2016, morning

Mayya, now lying face up, is still asleep. I go over to the window. What I see takes my breath away: the sun rising over the sea, flashes of it darting ashore across the still waters to wintry park, dacha walls, trunks of cypress and fig. And far out on the horizon, safeguarding peace and order, a vessel. All so beautiful. Inspiring forgiveness and generosity.

I look over to Mayya. I can forgive her. Firstly because she is a woman asleep and secondly because she is a woman with an unwomanly character. True, very few of the women in my life have had characters typical of their sex. Or perhaps they were typical women and I simply had the wrong idea of what female character was. I had, after all, based my ideas on the *Mona Lisa* or some image of the holy Mother and Child.

Hearing a distant crying of gulls, I open the window a little, admitting a salty icy blast that prompts me to pull the bedding up over Mayya's bare shoulders. Shutting the window, I look into the next room, where, seated in an armchair at an occasional table drinking tea, I catch my aide relaxing.

'I'm not,' I complain, smiling benignly, 'hearing the gulls properly.'

'I'll attend to it,' he says with a ghost of smile, leaping to his feet.

Five minutes later, hearing gulls, but looking out and seeing no sign of them, I decide they must be down on the beach, though their cries are growing steadily louder against the unhurried wash of the sea. An atmosphere for meditation, if ever there was one. I look back at Mayya. Were she to surface now to the cries of gulls, she would spend today and the whole year in happiness and at peace with herself, and perhaps even with me.

It's then that I at last notice the ceiling loudspeakers in all four corners of the room. Gulls in quadrophonic! Miraculous union of nature and acoustics! While Mayya sleeps, the music of the gulls enter her dream of lying in a solarium cubicle at the Metropol.

I feel I am about to have an attack of democracy and love towards all people. Heaven forbid that she catch me in such a mood. That would be the end of me. I quickly go into the adjoining room and, again, my aide leaps to attention.

'Sit where you are, finish your tea, then make me some,' I tell him, noticing that this room also has seabirds calling from four ceiling loudspeakers.

'Would you like the volume turned up?'

I shake my head. He nods and goes out and, as he goes, I notice that his clothes have a domestic look about them. He seems to be more at home here than I am. But then I am naked, while he is wearing black corduroy trousers and a dark blue pullover. Pity I didn't notice what he's wearing on his feet.

My gaze wanders round to the other corners of the room and I see a video camera trained on me. I wonder what part of my anatomy the security are looking at right now. Maybe no one is looking.

Still, I feel I should put something on and the most comfortable of all my dressing gowns is the one I received as a gift from the Russian President on the four hundredth anniversary of the Romanov dynasty. I go into the bedroom, glancing at Mayya, still sleeping peacefully. Robed in my dressing gown, I return to the adjoining room where my aide has already pushed the other armchair up to the coffee table and set ready a glass of sweet tea and a bottle of single malt.

150

Kiev, 14 April 1992, evening

It would seem that I am quite a good judge of human nature.

We phoned for an ambulance, and precisely fifteen minutes later, there was a young lady doctor and a paramedic at the door.

'You the patient?' she asked Father Basil, who turned to me embarrassed.

'The patient's dead,' I said, embarking on an explanation of the situation. But it was a few minutes before they understood what was going on. I was most concerned about the lady doctor. She didn't look hard up with her 'I'm-all-right' air, eyeshadow, manicured nails, false eyelashes and bleached hair. In my book the peroxide blonde was the most capricious creature on earth.

But she proved me wrong and five minutes later there we were drinking coffee and cognac, they the happier for 20,000 kupons.

'Where's the pickup?' asked the paramedic.

'Berkovets Cemetery, then to Trukhanov Island and about four hundred metres on over the bridge.

'I'll go and have a word with Pyotr,' said the paramedic exchanging glances with the doctor. Pyotr, the driver, being the key man.

In five minutes he was back, insisting that we should get a move on.

Seva was soon found sitting drunk on a finished headstone.

'So you've come for the Jew, have you? Take him away then.'

Father Basil's expression showed that he could not see how we were going to move the block of granite anywhere. It did take all five of us to load the headstone onto a barrow and, supporting it on both sides, to wheel it to the minibus.

Sleet made the going slow, and no sooner were we at the bridge than the driver demanded extra, and satisfied with a further 10,000 kupons, drove on.

Curiously it was not snowing on Trukhanov Island, the only snow there being beneath the trees, so the driver, next to whom I sat giving directions, made no bones about driving us to within a hundred metres of the grave. After which he managed another thirty metres before baulking at going any further.

Leaving the doctor seemingly deep in thought aboard the mini-bus, the four of us unloaded the headstone and got it to the grave.

'Want a lift back?' asked the paramedic when the stone was set up.

'No, we'll hang on for a bit,' said Father Basil.

The 30,000 kupons duly pocketed, driver and paramedic set off in the dusk for the minibus.

We stood for a moment by the headstone, newly established in the yielding spring soil, before setting off on the slushy path back to the bridge.

'We must keep an eye on it,' said Father Basil as we walked. 'And come the summer, reinforce it somehow. Maybe with cement.'

He turned to me, but my building knowledge was limited to two kinds of bricks, silica and fire, and which was which I could not say.

151

Borispol Airport, Kiev, November 2004

Early in the morning I had rung Nila from the hotel asking to be met by car. I told her our bad news and, hearing her voice crack, I rang off, unable to pretend any interest in events at the Ministry.

Svetlana and I were the only two in business class, sitting in adjacent aisle seats. It was my grimmest business-class flight ever. Wanting nothing to drink and nothing to eat, I just watched the motionless figure of my wife, wanting to say something, but not knowing what.

The young flight attendant, whose sole charges we were, hovered disconsolate, producing rugs and little pillows for us, anxious to ensure us a memorably pleasant flight, unaware just how memorable it was likely to be.

Reaching out, I put my hand over Svetlana's. Turning towards me she nodded.

It will be all right, I thought, immediately doubting that it could be. Even if it was all right, it would be different from what we had expected: no children's voices, no hubbub of busy domesticity. Just silence.

As we descended from the plane into the autumn chill of Kiev, the passenger coach was waiting, but no VIP minibus appeared for us, just a black Mercedes, which set me wondering, until a very smart chauffeur approached us and said, in a tone more authoritative than you expect from a driver: 'Please get in.'

'Where's my man?' I asked.

'New car, new man,' said the chauffeur.

A few minutes later our luggage was loaded.

'Please accept our sincere condolences,' said the chauffeur, as we moved off. 'I have a letter for you,' he added, passing me a long envelope. First, Dogmazov's card, on which I noticed further additions to the list of distinctions: Honorary Professor, Kiev Mogila Academy, and Co-Chairman of the State Civic Construction Awards Committee. Then the letter, no more than a note.

> Deepest commiserations on your loss. Time, I would think,
> for a change. Your office, as Viktor Andreyevich will show,
> awaits.
> Dogmazov

The paper had an unusual feel about it, and holding it up to the light, I saw it to be watermarked with state tridents.

'Viktor Andreyevich?' I enquired of the chauffeur.

He nodded. 'I'm to take you home, help unload, wait, then show you your office.'

It's just as well, I thought. Being taken out of myself, plunged into something deep and opaque, where I'd not be known or asked about anything, was just what I wanted. Foolish, of course, to expect that of a new place of work. Still, as a new man I'd be treated warily, cautiously, while they took the measure of me. And I could meanwhile rest in spirit, regain my old working rhythm and press express-like on in life. The less time for window-gazing, the better.

152

State dacha, Foros, 1 January 2016, evening
If the whole year is as calm and easy as its first day, I will be content. Dinner at the great oval walnut table with Nikolai Lvovich, the Governor of Crimea and his wife, and Mayya in revealing décolleté evening dress. It was a table for twelve, but where to find so many people worthy of my trust and friendship? I would have had Svetlov here, and maybe the doctor who told me the thing in my heart was not a pacemaker. Nikolai Lvovich's worthiness is uncertain. Still, having entered the New Year with me, he should stay. The overlarge roast turkey could be finished off by the kitchen staff and the aide with whom I drank tea this morning, becoming so involved in what he thought and was troubled by that I almost went so far as to ask

him his name. Fortunately I did not, because that would have been the beginning of the end. His end, I mean.

'Massandra champagne,' announces Governor Zelman indicating the jeroboam. 'The finest. As served to the Tsars.'

'Out with the cork, then,' I say.

Zelman sets about uncorking the champagne, Nikolai Lvovich signals to the head waiter and a veritable corps of miniskirted, white-aproned young waitresses dance attendance serving hors d'oeuvres, to subdued sentimental music from above. An old-style Russian romance, 'Softly Open the Gate to me', followed, sung in a voice like velvet by a female I ought instantly to recognise.

'Who is it?' I ask Nikolai Lvovich.

'Ruslanova.'

'Lovely voice.'

'Would you like the volume increased, sir?' enquires the head waiter.

I indicate that I would not.

We are just raising flutes of sparkling royal wine in a toast, when from the breast of Nikolai Lvovich bursts the musical ringtone of his mobile. Unabashed, he proceeds to clink glasses, leaving it unanswered until he has drunk and put down his glass. What it has to say is plainly not to his liking. Responding in a whisper, he rings off and, avoiding my eye, nervously addresses himself to his sturgeon in aspic. Whatever is amiss could be left till dessert.

Mayya opts for hazel grouse in curry sauce. I follow suit, and to dispose of an uneasy foreboding, call for more champagne. I have the feeling something bad is about to happen, but I push the idea aside. Nothing should be allowed to spoil our homely celebration. The show must go on!

As we tuck into turkey with cranberry jelly, Nikolai Lvovich glances increasingly anxiously at his watch.

'In a hurry to get away?' I ask.

'No, just that in twenty minutes we have another festive surprise for you. But we'll have to go out on the terrace.'

'Fine by me.'

Turning to Zelman's charming Crimean Tatar wife Leyla, I ask how 'New Year' sounded in Tatar.

'Yeni yıl,' she says sweetly.

'Beautiful,' I say.

It is cold on the terrace, but we are in overcoats and sheepskin jackets. The sky is dark, but there are the lights of a vessel anchored close in.

Nikolai Lvovich speaks into his mobile, and the heavens burst into a colourful mosaic of fireworks which even captivates the waitresses who've come out to serve more champagne.

'Compliments of the Russian Navy,' announces Nikolai Lvovich.

153

Kiev, 14 April 1992, night

'Sleeping?' bawls Zhora over the phone. 'Stir your stumps!'

Not easy, having been dragged from my bed. It's about eleven. Not late, but after our day with the granite headstone, all I want is sleep.

'Get here on the double! Slavik and Yulik are on their way. We've customers booked for 1 a.m.!'

And they probably wouldn't be hungry at that hour. Food isn't exactly our line of business. Folk come to our restaurant to talk in whispers and get drunk, behind closed doors. Five are expected. And once here, our job is to serve them until they leave. Or rather, Slavik and Yulik's job. I am the face of an establishment which has no signboard, just an address and a door.

But Zhora, or Georgiy Stepanovich as he insists I call him in public, has grown livelier with each passing day, and now he is positively radiant with joy. He comes along himself 'just to make sure', as he puts it. Though sure of what I'm damned if I know.

Slavik and Yulik look as weary and puffy-faced as I do.

Zhora is flapping.

'Sweep under the tables,' he orders. 'And you, Yulik, wipe them over, polish the glasses and see to the cutlery.'

In the fridge I find mutton, ham and cheeses, including Polish Roquefort, from the day before.

As the ring of the telephone breaks the silence, Zhora springs to answer it, then hurries to the door.

The four men who enter are either in disguise or wearing suits for the first time ever, doing their best to pass for normal human beings, but ham-handed and lacking in confidence.

Zhora sees them to a table before summoning me to take their order.

On his recommendation they opt for Nikolai vodka, and I duly note their other requirements: tomato juice, herring fillets, caviar pancakes, stuffed eggs, cod's liver salad . . . A banal choice as even I could see, but my job is to approve, smile and disappear to the kitchen, where Yulik is already preparing salad and the rest. He is not by profession a chef, but has learned a thing or two serving in an officers' mess.

I bring and pour the vodka. They fall silent at my approach, but after I've refilled their glasses they go on talking. They are getting red in the face. Two have loosened their ties, and one has removed his jacket and draped it on his chair.

'But how to change it into dollars for you?' the man in shirtsleeves demands of his companion in a voice just short of a shout.

'Open an account with Parex Bank – those Balts can teach you a thing or two about covering financial tracks. I'm with Gradobank. Anyway, why do you want it in dollars? Take them in hryvnas, and a payment order's yours tomorrow.'

Withdrawing to the kitchen, I pour myself cognac, and exchange a few words with Yulik and Slavik.

Yulik, sniffing an opened tin of cod's liver, presents it for an opinion.

'Dodgy – needs plenty of salt and olive oil,' I suggest. 'They're on vodka and vodka kills all.'

At least ten more times I attend their table to top them up and see how they are doing, and they are doing well, with ties now loosened and no longer shouting.

'What's your degree in?' one demands of me out of the blue.

'Light Industry,' I say.

'Good for you!' he laughs, peeling off $20 which he passes to the man sitting opposite, leaving me to wonder what the bet has been.

Soon Zhora, the only one impeccable in his suit, becomes one of the party.

'Another bottle of Nikolai,' he orders with a wink.

At three the customers take themselves off. Zhora, a little the worse for drink, slips Yulik and Slavik $20 each, and gets them a taxi. Me he drags me off to a bar.

'You'll like it,' he says getting behind the wheel of his 'German-imported' Audi. 'Ever tried tequila?'

'No.'

'A delight to come, then. They liked you, by the way. They're the Enterprise Committee, or will be. Could be a place for me.'

'And me?'

'You, in case it's escaped you, are my adjutant.'

As the traffic light turns red, Zhora accelerates. There's a scream of brakes near by.

Zhora roars with laughter and I put my seat belt on.

'We'll get through, like in the war,' growls Zhora, taking Kiev's remaining traffic lights at amber.

154

Kiev, November 2004

New car, new driver, new office with new Italian furniture. I still sometimes missed my own door in the long corridor of the Bank Street building, since it was as yet without a nameplate. When I entered the room next door by accident I was greeted with a nasty look from a little man in a grey suit, but when I encountered him in the corridor the next day, he smiled, already recognising me as a colleague. In the first few days, I was beset with nostalgia, not so much for my old Ministry as for the homely atmosphere of my old office. But when I was told that Nila would be joining me the following week I rejoiced. Splashing solo into an unknown lake involves an element of fear. I would feel more confident with a familiar partner, especially one I felt I knew like the back of my hand.

On Tuesday I was introduced to the President, and escorted by none other than Dogmazov, who remained at my side for the three minutes of weary, uneasy scrutiny, followed by a handshake and best wishes.

'Your predecessor made a mess of things. You'd do well to study where *he* went wrong.'

'He will,' said Dogmazov, throwing me a warning glance.

'What happened to my predecessor?' I asked, once outside.

'Made Ambassador to Mongolia.'

'I thought he would have been for the chop?'

'Wouldn't wish my worst enemy four years in Mongolia. Or maybe I would. Roasted alive, drinking fermented mare's milk, riding about on camels! Go through his papers. See what you need to know. I'll bring them after lunch. Sent any number of good men over to the Opposition. Spent two whole years doing damn all. Strong public support is what the President needs and he couldn't deliver, even though the majority of these academicians, professors, sportsmen and arts people would have been for us. Let's go to your office, and I'll enlarge.'

Over coffee in my office, Dogmazov explained my duties for the third time that week, with me listening patiently and nodding.

'There are, you understand, questions the President cannot himself raise without some pretext – a letter signed by eminent scientists, say. You organise the letter yourself, drum up signatories and hand it over to the press department. They publish it and the ball's set rolling . . . By the way, get au fait as of now with our VIP list. The President must be kept in regular contact with the cultural and scientific elite. And we don't want him on camera with the same old opera singer or chess player. Look for new people of obvious quality. We're a young country, and every citizen must see it. "*For our youth this land has a road to everywhere!*"'

'So I shouldn't use the old VIP list, then?'

'Use it, but not exclusively or for official audiences. For awards and receptions, fine. One or two names I'll cross off for flirting with the Opposition, but the rest are normal, decent folk.'

Those crossed out were well-known rock singers, and being myself indifferent to rock, I was glad not to have to hobnob with them.

155

State dacha, Foros, 1 January 2016, evening
Fifteen minutes of the Russian Salute to the New Year and mild heart sensations prompted a return to a table swept of crumbs and cleared of empty dishes for a dessert of pear stewed in red wine, and fried banana soused in Baileys Irish Cream liqueur.

Seeing Mayya fatigued and increasingly irritable, I whispered that she might care to withdraw, perhaps for a massage, whereat, clearly relieved, she left the table, pleading migraine.

Shortly after, Zelman and his wife took their leave, leaving me and Nikolai Lvovich to watch the news and shots of our chief cities' thoroughfares, rapturously presented by a young lady costumed as the Snow Maiden. Celebrations were still in full swing, and of those questioned at random, some were convinced that New Year had not yet begun. All, mercifully, without a whiff of politics. Finally, the Dormition Cathedral of the Caves Monastery, and another weeping icon of the Great and Holy Martyr Vladimir, drawing believers in their thousands. And there, before the cathedral, for all to see, the well-organised queue of those desiring to pray at and, if possible, to kiss the icon. Clearly engaged, the cameraman dwelt for minutes on the fixed, purposeful expressions of the queuing faithful.

'It looks like the Ukrainian Orthodox Church is in the lead as far as miracles are concerned: two miracles to the Russian Churches one,' I observed.

'I don't like it.'

'Nor do I. Especially the weeping Bolshevik.'

'We've a hard year ahead, Mr President – you most of all,' said Nikolai Lvovich, his tone implying that he wanted to enlarge. But whisky and peace were what I wanted, not bad news. And contact with beauty. That of art, not woman. Women aged, art did not.

'Leave it till tomorrow,' I suggested gently. 'We'll start early, kill our appetites. High time we dieted. For the moment, it's whisky, and art.'

'Which whisky?' he asked with alacrity.

'Aberlour single malt. And get some talented, intelligent Crimean artist to bring his work.'

'Tatar?'

'Talent has no nationality.'

156

Kiev, 1 May 1992

'To hell with this!' yells Zhora prancing happily about the restaurant club. 'New management arriving the day after tomorrow! Time for us young 'uns to move on!'

Looking at him, I try to fathom what this grey-templed, double-chinned, flabby jowled fifty-year-old, product of a wild Young Communist youth, means by 'young'. I did in fact still think of myself as young, but kept quiet about it. Young being a transient quality, not like, say, native wit, intelligence, or education, even if like mine uncompleted.

'Hang on a sec,' I call.

The flushed face turns and stares.

'Bit peremptory,' he says. 'Seeing I'm fifteen or twenty years your senior . . . You might just occasionally address me properly, especially when others are present!'

'Yes, Georgiy Stepanovich,' I grin.

I am in a jolly mood myself. It costs me no more to bid this restaurant club farewell than other pages of my life, especially when it's contributing nothing of value to it.

'Oh!' he exclaims, opening the fridge.

Looking over his shoulder at the mass of food, I think of the couple of kilos of best cuts of lamb in the freezer compartment, together with poultry and fish.

Zhora stands lost in thought, no doubt regretting the loss of so much to the May Day festivities. His Young Communist celebrations with girls, campfires and dirty-weekendings in sanatoriums are also things of the past, their glorious primordial free-and-easiness never to be repeated. It's all different now. I try to imagine how those flabby, weary, aged Young Communists amuse themselves these days. Are the girls who come to them as old as they are? Probably not. Oldies wouldn't get invited. Still, today's lovelies wouldn't be as easy and hot-blooded as the pre-1991 Invisible Revolution lot.

'Georgiy Stepanovich,' I call over my shoulder.

He swings round in surprise.

'Might I, as a reward for good service, have this food for a little family celebration? We'll see to all the preparations and clear up later.'

'Reward?!' he says nastily, making a pretence of gazing up at the ceiling and the dusty lampshades, then suddenly relenting. 'Why not? So long as you finish the lot! I might join you. You doing the work?'

'With Mother,' I say, thinking how pleased she would be with the idea. It was so practical it could almost have been her own and, after all, it's not the contents that have been sold, but the fridge.

157

Kiev, November 2004

Returning home deliberately late from work I find, as on two previous occasions, Svetlana and Zhanna at the sitting-room table drinking tea and cognac in silence. I say hello and, disinclined to join them, retire to my study, my temporary bedroom since our return from Zurich, to sit in silence on my own.

I make mint tea. I'm now strongly attached to the aroma. Sitting at my desk, idly examining papers from my briefcase, my thoughts are more on the table in the sitting room. Yesterday evening and the evening before when I went to the bathroom to clean my teeth, Svetlana and Zhanna were still sitting there, both crying.

The first evening, I noticed that Zhanna was not wearing provocative perfume. She still isn't. Maybe it's run out.

At eleven fatigue gets the better of me. Time to turn in. Outside, a chill autumn drizzle. I probably spent no more than twenty seconds in the open that evening, from car to entrance, but in the horrid, icy, marsh-like humidity it was more than enough. Roll on winter proper!

On my way to the bathroom I see Svetlana and Zhanna clinging together, crying softly. The bottle of cognac – admittedly a small one – is empty. They seem not to notice me.

When, if at all, does Zhanna go home? Maybe she doesn't.

She's not here in the morning.

I worry about Svetlana, but something holds me back from returning to our bed. It would have been easy enough to lie beside her and sleep, but dreaming brings moments, when one thing leads to another, making the woman beside you physically desirable. I hug her in the morning before leaving for work, but more from compassion than ardent love. Time would pass, weeping cease, old passion revive. Meanwhile, such looks as I receive from her are either guilty or wary.

I have acquired a humane alarm, one that peeps instead of ringing. At seven I throw on a dressing gown, make coffee and look into the bedroom. Svetlana is sleeping on her stomach, head under a pillow, arm stretched out to where I used to sleep, and I quietly shut the door.

Today I'm leaving early, having told my chauffeur to come at 7.45. Never before have I had a *chauffeur* like Viktor Andreyevich. Before, it was always a Vasya or Petya, modest, jolly men, good for a joke and a laugh. But this one, with his patronymic and top-quality suit, is on a level with me. No jokes, no laughs.

So from Lesi Ukrainki Boulevard to Bank Street we drive in silence, ahead of the rush hour. I'm just happy that in ten minutes I'll be free of the car and the chauffeur and in my office, where I am slowly beginning to feel at home.

158

State dacha, Foros, 1 January 2016

At around midnight a helicopter arrived with the artist and his canvases.

Mayya was resting, and I had no inclination to wake her. I was beginning to cool towards her. Intimacy had brought no joy, but opened my eyes, leaving no room for illusion. No longer a mystery, she had lost her attraction. Women like her grew into capricious old ladies, like the fisherman's wife of the folk tale. So I would have the enjoyment of art and artist without her.

He looked sleepy. Having hung his paintings in the dining room, he was standing contemplating one as if it were the work of another.

I tiptoed forward and looked over his shoulder. Market scales, left pan filled with pocket watches and chains, the other – two alarm clocks and a loaf of bread, making it the heavier. I had never cared for mathematics, but this little problem seemed amusing. I asked the artist's name.

'Vladimir Makeyev,' he said in a quiet voice.

Hair streaked with grey, crow's feet from screwing up his eyes, he was in his early or mid-fifties.

'And the hidden message?' I asked.

'There isn't one. Though you can always seek one,' he added with a shrug.

'Which is what I'm doing. How many watches are there?'

He shrugs, obviously reluctant to count them. I suggest we count together and we both make it thirty-three.

'You see? Two threes! How about that? Two alarms and a loaf making another three. Is that deliberate?'

'No. Chance.'

'Can't be. There must be a secret meaning, It's art! Mystery!'

'There doesn't have to be. You can search for philosophical meaning, but this is art for art's sake . . . Only you're too much of a realist to get it.'

I liked his boldness and preferred to agree rather than argue.

'But I do. "Art for art's sake" is tantamount to "Being President for the sake of being President".'

'Surely that never happens?'

'Nine times out of ten.'

The suspicious look he gave made me wonder what he was thinking.

'Care for a whisky?'

'I don't drink.'

'Tea?'

'Please.'

I ordered both.

'Tell me,' I continued, 'could you, if paid enough, provide a hidden philosophical meaning for each of these pictures?'

'Yes.'

'Which artists do you admire?'

'Shishkin, Surikov, Henri Rousseau, Chagall, Kleist –'

Delighted that we had Shishkin in common, I stopped him.

'Is yours a good life?' I asked.

'Mine is, but not my wife's.'

'How so?'

'She has the family to feed.'

'All right,' I said, patting his arm soothingly. 'I'll buy all these for the Residence. Tea's coming, so sit down, while I take it all in.'

Watches, penny-farthings, scales, tomcats, lonely trees. All very symbolic. But tender, touching work. Far removed from Shishkin, who was all eye, heart and weariness relieved. This was all detail, food for thought. And I was thinking.

'Why no women?' I asked.

'I don't know,' he confessed. 'I did paint women, then stopped . . .'

'Always time to go back,' I said, surprising myself.

'I will,' he said, leaving me to imagine to whom.

Tea came, but no whisky.

'Your favourite malt was there, but it's disappeared,' explained my aide.

'See if Nikolai Lvovich has whipped it.'

My aide left the room very slowly, clearly imagining how Lvovich would react to his enquiry about the whisky, even if it is sitting on his table.

159

Kiev, 2 May 1992, evening

Tomorrow my stomach will probably ache like mad, but tonight it's having a party.

The food goes down well. There's no hurry, no competition, enough of everything for everyone. For Mother, who has prepared all the meat, chicken, fish and salad, and for Father Basil, who keeps busy pouring himself and me Finlandia vodka, and Mother, Dima and the doctor-in-charge from Dima's hospital Bulgarian brandy. Mother, wearing her favourite black dress with beads and gold-coloured snake brooch, is happy. So, too, is Dima's doctor, who probably doesn't often get invited to a family celebration.

For a while he sits quietly, but by his third Bulgarian brandy, he is moved to relieve himself of anecdotes about life in a mental home, along the lines of 'A prisoner, once a patient in a mental institution, is asked what he's in for, and he says "On Lenin's birthday, we in the madhouse paraded under the slogan LENIN IS WITH US! LENIN IS AMONG US!"'

Father Basil grins broadly while continuing to gnaw at a chicken bone. Mother laughs. Dima guffaws.

'It's the truth!' he says. 'One of our medical orderlies told me that the mental hospital that can't show two Lenins, a Gorbachev and a Napoleon loses the doctor-in-charge his bonus and he has to requalify!'

Looking at Dima, I can't think what he is doing in a psychiatric hospital. If sitting him at a table is all it takes to make him normal, what kind of an illness is it?

After the meal we all help wash up and dry. Zhora does not appear, and I'm glad.

With everything back in place and the stove cleaned of grease not entirely ours, Mother, looking into one of the kitchen cupboards, is aghast to find it still full of tins – Polish pâté, Riga sprats, pineapple . . .

'What happens to these?' she asks, standing and staring.

'Let's take them.'

'Why don't *we* take them – for the other patients?' asks Dima, exchanging looks with the doctor.

'Don't be silly!' says Mother. 'Don't I and Sergey bring you enough? No, we'll share it out.'

So we do, but since twenty-seven can't be split five ways, I take two of the tins of pineapple chunks in their own juice for my communal-flat neighbours to enjoy.

'They deserve it,' says Mother approvingly.

'I wonder,' says Dima's doctor to Mother, while I am locking the door for the last time, 'if I as well as Dima might sleep at your place? I live out at Boyarka, and the last train has gone.'

'The trouble is we've only a very small –' begins Mother.

'Come to my place – there's an old sofa with protruding springs but it's bearable,' I tell him, suddenly noticing the quality of his sheepskin coat and leather half-boots. He must feel embarrassed about asking Mother to put him up. For the price of three such coats he could buy a one-room flat in Kiev, or a little house in Pushcha-Voditsa involving no late-train troubles. Or perhaps the clothes were presents from patients' grateful families.

'Is it far?'

'Twenty minutes' walk.'

Father Basil bids us all goodnight, and is quickly lost in the gloom. Mother manages to hitch a lift for herself and Dima.

'You're lucky in your mother and brother,' says the doctor when we are alone.

The pavement and road are wet and shiny. It rained while we were in the restaurant and the air is still heavy with moisture. Every so often there is a clank of tins.

'In your opinion, Igor Fyodorovich, is Dima really ill?' I ask as we walk.

'I wouldn't say "ill",' he says calmly. 'It's that his attitude to reality does not coincide with the majority, and he hates being different from others. That's why he's more at ease with us. He's with educated folk who aren't rude to each other . . .' Saying which, he shoots me the look of one attempting a diagnosis.

Yes, damn you, I'm the healthy one! I think to myself. My attitude to reality is that of the majority! I can be rude, yes, but I'm not soured if others are to me. A plug for your psychiatric game park is the last thing I need!

'You should visit Dima more often,' says Igor Fyodorovich after a while. 'He's very fond of you.'

'I'll try. At the moment I'm out of work.'

'What are you trained for?'

'Nothing medical. Still studying externally. Light Industry Institute.'

'Well, if there's a problem, we've always got vacancies. Not much pay, though.'

I promise to think about it.

But I won't. His earnest concern is laughable. His attitude to reality is plainly not mine.

160

Kiev, November 2004

That Monday proved to be the best day of the week. Waiting at the office I found Nila, more business executive now than secretary. So confident did she look that a stranger would have treated her with some caution. But her smile belied the hard, businesswoman image and right now, it was directed at me. We embraced and, like a schoolboy, I lifted her off her feet and whirled her around

'Really, Sergey Pavlovich! Hadn't you better shut the door?'

Now there were flowers in my anteroom and office, and apart from their scent, a young woman's perfume.

'Coffee?' she asked.

'Please,' I said sitting at my desk. 'And it's good to have you here.'

'Move not a step from your side, my fortune teller said, or there'd be trouble.'

'As you told me, though not in those words.'

'Well, that was what she meant.'

While I was waking myself up with good strong coffee, Nila placed a leather file before me.

'There's an important one on top,' she said, smiling, lips close to mine, looking me in the eye. Then the phone in the front office rang, and she went to answer it, leaving the door half open.

I glanced at the file. A sheet headed augustly 'Office of the President' bore two sentences: '*Submit choice of three theatre personalities to converse with President 12 November, 10.30 a.m. Names to me by noon today.*' Flowing signature.

I had met the Director of the President's Office, a former militia colonel and sometime Deputy Head Taxation. I sensed at once that he was unsure of himself in his exalted appointment, possibly aware that it was temporary, pending a better candidate. Anyway, this directive was clearly not from him, but the work of aides who seem to have been born in the place – outliving all presidents and directors. He spoke drily, trying hard to conceal natural affability behind colourless formality. But there was a vitality about him that inspired confidence.

As I scanned the VIP list, two state prize-winning theatre directors sprang from the page, but the juxtaposition of *male* President, *male* prizewinners jarred.

Here, though, was the answer: a ballerina, the prima of our National Theatre of Opera and Ballet. So I put her first and the male directors second and third, confident that the President's Office would make the obvious choice.

161

Ukrainian Airspace, 3 January 2016
Yesterday it snowed, an impenetrable white wall of it shutting the dacha off from any view of the sea. Winter came to the south Crimean coast, and with it, bad news.

'How is it that our one national TV channel owes three million hryvnas for electricity?' I demanded of Nikolai Lvovich, sitting opposite me in the plane. 'Who's Prime Minister at present? Who's Minister of Power?'

'Ecology's serving as Premier. Power is Safronov.'

'What the hell! Ecology in winter? Don't we budget funds for our TV channel?'

'We do.'

'So why the unpaid bills?'

'No money. We had to use the funds to settle the miners' unpaid wages. It cleaned us out. We couldn't let cities freeze.'

'I don't get it. *Can* Kazimir take our TV to court and bankrupt it?'

'He can according to the law, but the court is a national court and will deny him his action – I've checked.'

'Well, let's see what's happening on Channel 1.'

Apart from the presenter having a lighted candle beside him, the news was as usual, betraying no sign of impending doom until, suddenly, his image was replaced by the words: 'VIEWS EXPRESSED ON THIS CHANNEL DO NOT ALWAYS REPRESENT THOSE OF CHANNEL 1', followed by Kazimir's full face.

'May I, belatedly, wish you a happy New Year,' he began, urbi et orbi. 'Leaving behind with the old all unresolved problems, ills and unpleasantness. Together with all those politicians and members of the government who have failed to justify your hopes. And so onward with new hope, new faces and renewed faith in a bright future towards the long-looked-for spring in the destiny of our nation. On, on into a New Year! One in which we could celebrate twenty-five years of Ukrainian independence renewed and refreshed by impeaching a President who has thwarted all our hopes!'

Lvovich leapt up and switched off the TV, his whole body shaking. I watched him and wondered how it was possible that a person brandished by all as the enemy of the government and the people could make such a speech on the state TV channel. Where was Svetlov? Where were my state security people?

'Radio to Kiev,' I ordered. 'Armed Forces Chiefs to meet in my office in two hours' time.'

The steward observing how pale I had become brought a rug, and asked if I'd like a whisky.

For the first time in years the sensation of cold disturbed me. I felt it flowing into every corner of my body, my extremities aching as the cold rushed in. Only my heart was warm and growing hotter and hotter as the rest of me froze.

When my whisky came, I removed the ice cubes, throwing them on the floor. Now the warmth of the whisky flowed down through my body. It seemed alcohol-free and left a strange taste in my mouth, as if I'd drunk sunflower oil.

'What's the outside temperature?' I asked the steward.

'Minus fifty-eight degrees C.'

'Are all the windows shut?

'Of course,' he replied calmly, but realising I doubted his word, he darted about the cabin checking every window, returning to reassure me that all was well.

I nodded twice; one for 'thank you', one for 'you can go'. He moved away and I realised that the source of the bitter chill was the now blue TV screen. What could be done about it? Perhaps I should turn it off, but Lvovich had done that already. Where was he, by the way?

'Nikolai Lvovich!' My trembling voice sent the steward hurrying towards the cockpit.

It was very quiet, only the purr of the engine in the freezing clear blue sky.

162

Kiev, 15 May 1992

'Get yourself here, with your ID card and Work Record!' ordered Zhora, telephoning me at the crack of dawn.

'Where?'

'Officers' Club, twenty minutes from now.'

'Make it twenty-five! Or better, thirty. Say, at eight.'

'Damn you, eight then!'

So at eight fifteen I'm standing outside the Officers' Club, and still no sign of my grizzled Young Communist. For mid-May it's cold enough for hands to seek the warmth of duvet pockets and eyes to turn from the wind.

The call for documents is encouraging. A job seems in the offing, and a job, in Zhora's understanding and to my liking, is a question not so much of performance one way or the other, as of trustworthiness and quickness on the uptake.

'Sorry! Been waiting long?' asks a voice, and there, clean-shaven, fresh as a daisy, is Zhora, redolent of eau de cologne and mouthwash.

'Since eight.'

'Splendid! Come on!'

He leads me past the cannon adorning the pavement before the Officers' Club, and right into a block of the Stalin era.

A poky little lift takes us to the fifth floor and a shabby double door with a communal-flat-like proliferation of bell pushes.

Scorning the bells, Zhora bangs twice on the door, one half of which opens and I realise that the doors are camouflage. Inside, the flat smells of fresh paint, parquet varnish and decorators' cheap booze. A boyishly cropped girl in tight jeans topped with a stylish blouse leads us along a white corridor to a comfortable office and seats at a polished table.

'Tea? Coffee?'

I opt for coffee, Zhora for mineral water.

I look at the two portraits adorning the white wall: Taras Shevchenko, the poet whose dream was a free Ukraine, and President Kravchuk, the politician who came to personify it. And immediately I see strange parallels, anti-parallels even, in the shabby, bell-studded door false-fronting the Euro-refurbishment. There's conspiracy here. But why, in a conspiratorial flat, do they have the 'correct', *nomenklatura* establishment-figure portraits? What is this? A Second Force, or the secret machinery of one?

'Why so worried?' demands Zhora.

'Worried? Me?'

'Who else?'

I fall to thinking, feeling the temperature and rhythm of my thoughts. No, I am calm, I sense no panic in my head. There are questions, but nothing to worry about.

'Your coffee,' says the girl, setting cup and saucer before me, Zhora having already relieved her of his mineral water.

Now, with our drinks, the silence is comfortable. The coffee is over-strong and less than sweet, but I do not call her back.

'Ah, beaten me to it!' observes a man in a long black overcoat cheerfully, breezing in, the girl in close attendance. Tossing coat, scarf, deerskin cap to her, he joins us at the table.

The expressionless, unsmiling, instantly pliable face is one that I've seen, but can't remember where.

'Well, all going according to plan,' he tells Zhora. 'First-rate renovation job. Computers, phones, faxes, answerphones and the rest arrive tomorrow. So we can get down to work.'

Seeing Zhora produce his ID card, I place mine, together with my Work Record, on the table.

'We've currently no personnel section,' says the man, handing back my Work Record. 'Three hundred dollars a month in an envelope is what you get, but twenty dollars in the books. OK?'

I nod.

'Hours ten to five. Some travel, some rest-day working.'

'Fine.'

'By tomorrow we'll have your visiting cards ready, name as per ID card, phone number the office one. Happy?'

'Very,' I say, at last remembering him as one of the four Yulik, Slavik and I served just before the sale of the restaurant club.

'For the rest of the day you're free. Report tomorrow at ten, in suit and tie. Vera will show you your office.'

Rather than take the lift, I walk down, passing grim, shabby doors thick with bell knobs, wondering what lies beyond: a real communal flat or something like the fifth floor.

Outside it's drizzling. It's still only 9 a.m. At the Kulinariya deli opposite the Officers' Club I order tea and chicken Kiev, and consider my new employment. Pay, hours, they are clear, but nothing else. Odd, but no cause for alarm. Tomorrow I'll find out. Suit and tie suggest something cleaner than labouring. I'll have to buy a tie, though.

163

Kiev, November 2004, Sunday

Zhanna has appeared only twice in the past week. True, Svetlana disappeared a couple of times somewhere, returning as late as eleven. But I did not pester her with questions. She is still not herself. At various times I've seen affixed to her mirror the Polaroid photographs of our little ones, their locks of hair and their name bracelets.

Svetlana usually rises at about ten. On workdays I quietly brew coffee and get my own breakfast. Life continues to play a melancholy tune, which we each hear in isolation. One peculiar to each of us, perhaps, but neither notable for any merriment or ardour. As can be read from Svetlana's face and no doubt my own.

I've grown accustomed to my study couch. I like facing the wall hung with a Hungarian carpet depicting a bookcase of solid old bindings, amusing counterpart of my own bookcase against the opposite wall. It's as if my books were contemplating a group portrait of their predecessors, or taking it for a mirror image. I've even tried to assess how many of my five shelves of books I've actually read. Six at most, and four of those twenty years ago. I consider myself sufficiently well read. I buy bulging magazines, Russian and Ukrainian, and sit on the bog or in the kitchen reading avidly. But just short stories and not always to the end. Lengthy prose has an immediately depressing effect, being so shot through with pessimism as to make me want to find the author and give him money to take at least one joyous look at the world about him!

It's been snowing. The first snow of the year. And good to see it falling in a great white wall of flakes past my twelfth floor window on a Sunday.

The clock shows 9.45. Svetlana is still asleep, but on the point of waking.

And I'm thinking about her as I gaze out of the kitchen window at the snow. Turning to the stove, I set about making coffee for her. I want today to start more cheerfully for her. I want her to smile. It's November, still autumn, but the snow is of winter. A change of time, a change of season. Our children died in autumn, now it's winter. A passage of time. Maybe winter will claim her thoughts, return her to me.

I pour the coffee into a cup of fine Dresden china, place it with its saucer on a tray together with a tiny milk jug. No sugar.

'Good morning!' I call approaching the half-open door.

She is lying gazing at the ceiling, but hearing me lifts her head and smiles. Not her old smile, but still a smile. Sad, weary, faint as a childish whisper.

'Like something to eat?'

She shakes her head.

'I'm going for the papers. I'll be straight back.'

She nods.

There's a pleasant frostiness in the air. Accursed autumn is behind us. I have come out without a hat, exposing forehead, nose and close-cropped hair to the snowflakes' icy touch.

For papers I have to cross to the other side of the boulevard. There are very few cars. Hardly surprising on a Sunday.

The kiosk has only Saturday's papers, Sunday's have yet to come. So not having read Saturday's, I take all there are left. As I look out through the bride-like veil of snow, my eyes light on a café I have not so far visited, and had it been a normal day, would not have visited now, given the scruffy look of it. But such is my mood this morning that I am prepared to forgive that, provided the coffee is decent.

The café is indeed grim, but the coffee, brewed by a hefty woman in an old-fashioned pinafore, is strong and excellent. And there I sit on my own, leafing through the papers.

'*The Director of the President's Office said this, said that . . .*'

He didn't, I think, and flicking through Politics, Economy, Crime, arrive at Sport. More interesting. Less predictable. So who has Klichko thrashed? A German. Serves him right! What about Dynamo Kiev? Drawn again? So be it.

'Another coffee, please,' I tell the woman behind the counter.

'We've some fresh pastries,' she says.

'Fresh yesterday?'

'Yesterday evening.'

'No, thanks.'

Fifteen minutes sees me through the papers. I don't really know what I'm looking for anyway. And if anyone asked what news I've gleaned, I'd be hard put to answer. I do, though, have the sense of a duty done, a wish satisfied.

'Valya rang,' says Svetlana, suddenly more animated, now in her warm, green housecoat, and Armenian slippers that I've not seen before.

'What news?' I ask, hanging my jacket on its hook.

'All's well. They've called the baby Liza. She's already almost five kilograms from four-two at birth. And there was a call from an old friend of yours with a Caucasian name.'

'Husseinov?'

'That's right. He wanted our address, and asked if he might look in for a minute this evening.'

'What does he want?'

'He's your friend – I didn't ask.'

She's right. I just can't see why he should look me up. We've made our peace.

'Did he say anything else?'

'That he understood how we must feel, as if he knew everything.'

'Aha. Did Valya say anything about Dima?'

'He's a different man, she says – helping out with Liza. She also asked for a cash transfer as they were down to 5,000 francs.'

'And how much are we down to?' I ask.

'I've got about $20,000. How about you?'

'Less. In Switzerland, I spoke to Dima and warned him that he would have to come back here soon.'

'How did he take it?'

'He wasn't happy.'

'If Valya was here, I'd be able to help her sometimes,' says Svetlana.

The concierge rang that evening to say that there was a large box for me and the men were wanting to bring it up. I told him OK and a few minutes later there came a knock, and there were four young hefty men with an enormous refrigerator.

'Sergey Pavlovich Bunin?' one of them asked.

I nodded.

'Where's the kitchen then?'

I showed him the way, still bewildered.

'But you've got one already,' said the head removal man. 'Where do we put this?'

I looked around and indicated an empty corner, by the window. The men shifted the fridge into place and connected it up.

'It's a Bosch,' said Svetlana when she saw it, 'an improvement on what we've got. But who bought it, if you didn't?'

'No idea.'

'Could be a bribe,' she smiled.

'For what?'

'I don't know,' she said, opening the fridge, only to reveal an array of food stuff and beverages, all anchored with sticky tape.

At that moment, a ring at the door and there stood Husseinov grinning.

'I just didn't want to put your wife to any trouble,' he said, embracing me.

'So it's your handiwork, this refrigerator?'

'Not exactly. I deal in fridges, yes, but this is by way of a cognac-and-appetiser gift to an old friend, seeing you've not much time for entertaining at the moment. Never leave a friend in the lurch, that's us in the Caucasus. Where've you put it?'

I showed him.

'That other one can go to the dacha,' he said with a disparaging look at our own fridge.

'We haven't got one.'

'If you've the fridge for a dacha, the dacha will follow. Is your wife in?'

'Yes.'

'Then tell her not to go to any trouble. Beautiful voice she's got on the telephone.'

We sat in the sitting room. Svetlana brought sausage, salmon, cheese, olives and the like from the newly delivered fridge, and Husseinov freed a bottle of cognac from inside the fridge door, when she found the tape beyond her. Declining to join us at table, she drank a glass of cognac, then withdrew, pleading fatigue and a headache.

When the bottle was finished, Husseinov unstuck another, and I felt more cheerful.

'Don't worry – you'll have lots more children. A man always has more chances than a woman. Law of nature!'

'Law of the Caucasus, you mean.'

'Father had eight of us by two wives. And may your children respect you as we did him!'

I nodded, thinking suddenly of Mother whom I'd visited only once since returning from Zurich.

'"Kids are the future",' Husseinov continued. 'It's true you know. Sense of life, someone to pass your achievements on to.'

Which would, I wondered, amount to what? And finding no answer, I speared a piece of smoked sausage with my fork.

164

Kiev, 3 January 2016

We land in total darkness. Where are the lights of the city?

'We're using the Gastomel airbase,' announces a pale Nikolai Lvovich. 'Don't worry, our people are there. Everything should be under control.'

'Should be or is?'

'I'll check,' he says, backing away towards the flight deck, as the plane bumps on over slabs in total darkness.

'All's well! Svetlov's here,' he reports, returning. His voice is cold and shaky like the hands of an alcoholic.

'Why the panic? Why Gastomel?' At the mention of Svetlov, warmth returns to my head at least.

'A preventative measure. We have to test Special Sub-Unit loyalty. Kazimir has given some of our Generals interest-free credit.'

'What for?'

'A life-enhancing retainer.'

'Aren't they life-enhanced enough already?'

'Once you're used to taking bribes it's very difficult to refuse.'

'But you can refuse, can you?'

'Yes, I can.' Nikolai Lvovich nods confidently.

Twenty identical black Mercedes all with the Ukrainian blue trident on yellow in place of number plates form our motorcade. Nikolai Lvovich in one, Svetlov and I in another. A precaution against mines. Some cars – like the trolleys pushed ahead of armoured trains – are without passengers.

'He's got three million signatures for impeachment,' Svetlov observes morosely.

'Can't have. He only made the threat two hours ago.'

'Two weeks he's been collecting. He was waiting to get that many before speaking out. We're doing our damnedest to find the list of signatures, but so far no joy . . .'

'But we can't punish three million for wanting a change of President.'

'What they want doesn't come into it. Each signatory got is twenty hryvnas. They'd have signed anything. Burn the lot, and we gain the two weeks it will take him to collect another million hryvnas' worth.'

'Are things that serious?' I look hard into Svetlov's eyes and I see that the answer is 'yes'.

'What else can he do?' I ask.

'Legally bankrupt the country for failing to pay for the power it's consumed.'

'Madness.'

'Mad, but possible under laws concerning non-payment at whatever level, enacted two years ago by Parliament.'

'So what do I do? Resign?'

'Certainly not. Seize the initiative, take him by surprise.'

'And who exactly will do the seizing and taking?' I am suddenly overcome by a wave of indifference. 'I could hand over power to the Premier or Nikolai Lvovich on health grounds.'

'Better Nikolai Lvovich. The Premier's already sold out. But let's not rush into anything. That would look like weakness.'

So now Svetlov is telling me what to do and when to do it. Despite being quite in control of my emotions I feel my heart flutter.

'You all right?' Svetlov asks.

'My heart isn't.'

'Take this,' he says, handing me a green capsule and a glass of still mineral water. The fluttering eases.

'Mayya wasn't on the plane with you?'

'Taking the regular flight from Simferopol tomorrow.'

Svetlov nods approvingly and consults his watch.

'We're a bit on the late side,' he says, consulting his watch.

'Late for what?'

'The meeting of Service Chiefs.'

Our black motorcade winds its way up to Syrets, passing the illuminated sign of the Dubki restaurant on the right.

165

Kiev, 20 May 1992

BUNIN, SERGEY PAVLOVICH

Senior Consultant-Assessor

EXTRA-GOVERNMENTAL

ENTERPRISE PROMOTION COMMITTEE

Telephone/Fax 293-97-93

says my first ever visiting card, its symmetry of layout no less impressive than my appointment. My duties, however, are simple and non-fatiguing.

My role is that of first link in the chain, or, more precisely, first sieve, through which fruits and berries pass into our copper pan to make a potent, glutinous compote reflecting the viewpoint of nascent Ukrainian enterprise. For a small membership fee, novice private traders are offered legal and other aid, including conflict resolution and debt-collecting. I don't in fact know all that we are able to do, but our Extra-Governmental Committee does, I sense, have real power behind it. Zhora is part of it too, but his office is a far cry from my white-walled cell with just room for a desk and a chair for visitors. Even so, I like it and feel rather like a doctor receiving patients. Those who come tell me their problems, I listen, nod and promise assistance. They then fill in a questionnaire and take it to our informal cash desk and girl-boy Vera, with whom I am already more closely acquainted. She, as I discover to my cost, is sharp as glass. On my first day at the office, pay envelope in hand, I ask her out to a bar.

'Look, laddie,' she says, 'if you want to be seen with me, I can supply you with the address of an appropriate men's clothes shop . . .'

Not a brush-off, nor a promise of mutual warmth and joy.

Around 10 a.m., and a lull. I could do with a coffee, but Vera isn't obliging. I can make myself one at reception, but for the undesirability of appearing there. Especially a.m., when the Chief receives visitors of substance.

Zhora looks into my cell without knocking.

'OK?'

'Great.'

'And that's how it must be if you want to achieve more than you are realistically capable of. By the way, as of next week we're no long Extra-Governmental. *Ukrainian* Private Enterprise Association, that's us! Are you with me?'

'Not entirely.'

'Georgiy Stepanovich!' bawls the Chief. 'Ministry on the line!'

With a 'Nose to grindstone, then!' Zhora rushes off.

The holdalls and cases block the door to my room this evening, and a hubbub from the kitchen suggest a sudden influx of relatives.

I look into the kitchen, and am stunned to find neighbours seated in homely attire and slippers at two tables pulled together, and with them Mira and her mother.

Silence falls, heads turned.

'We decided to come back,' says Mira getting to her feet. 'It was too hot and full of . . .' I expect to hear the word 'Jews'.

'Arabs,' she concludes.

166

Kiev, December 2004, Monday

Children are tobogganing. Any number of them. It's some time since I came out to dismiss my chauffeur, saying I was off colour with a cold, and that I'd ring when I felt better. It's now nearly eleven, but better I am not.

There's nothing actually wrong with me. It's just that looking in on Svetlana to say good morning, I found her and Zhanna asleep in each other's arms.

Should I go up, I wonder, approaching my block, or wait a bit? What should I do if Zhanna's still there? The questions make me feel as ill as I said I was. Watching the tobogganers, I find myself counting them. Over thirty. It's good to think that the elite multi-storeys of Tsarskoye Selo are breeding elite children, many with elite steerable toboggans.

A young woman in a short fox-fur jacket is walking two dachshunds. Shifting my gaze from the dogs to their owner, I see her to be pleasant and friendly.

'Do you live locally?' I ask.

'There,' she says pointing to the next block.

'Would you mind if I asked you a silly question?'

Uneasy nod.

'Supposing *you* came home and found your husband in bed with another man?'

'So you know him?' she asked in alarm.

'I know hardly anyone here,' I protested, cursing my own foolishness. 'I was thinking of friends . . .'

'You're lying! You know him.'

To hell with you, I decided, crunching off through the snow, conscious of her eyes still upon me. I remember a line from *The Master and Margarita* that had once appealed: 'Never talk to strangers.'

167

Kiev, 3 January 2016

Politics is a terrible thing. It lures you up into the very dome of its 'big top', up into the limelight, only to leave you teetering on a tightrope, with millions looking on wondering whether you'll fall.

At the long table in my office, thirteen of us.

General Filin is making notes on a sheet of paper, using his left hand to shield them from the Premier, sitting opposite. Svetlov is looking from one to another of the sleepy, undistinguished faces, several of which are new to me.

'Hooked nose, next but one to Svetlov, who's he?' I ask Nikolai Lvovich.

'Minister of Transport.'

'First I've seen of him.'

'Appointed during your illness.'

'And opposite Filin?'

'Yatskiv, new Minister of Defence.'

'Never heard of him!'

'He got in on the quota system, for the Liberals.'

'So now we have a liberal army, do we?'

'It's time we got started,' says Lvovich, ignoring my sarcasm.

I signal Svetlov to start.

'The matter before us is of national importance,' he begins in a base tone that surprises me, 'and – be reminded and keep in mind – it is above Party allegiance.'

Troubled by his thoughts or haemorrhoids, the Premier fidgets.

'The situation is critical. In disregard of people and state, certain elements are bent on destabilising the country in order to further their own interests.'

'Why look at me?' demands the Premier, clearly offended.

'I shall look at you all in turn,' Svetlov says quietly. 'You're not the only pebble on the beach.'

'What beach?'

'Cut the fooling!' I order. 'Continue, General.'

'Our task, in the light of intelligence received and as I shall detail, is, by 9 a.m., to formulate a common policy to meet the situation that has arisen. While we sit here, the enemy is still active. Though just as we have his among us, so we have ours among his.'

With which he shoots another look at the Premier, who is now shaking visibly. A mere lad, not yet in his mid-forties, totally lacking in bearing and composure.

'On information to hand, the enemy is currently meeting with officers of the Kiev District Garrison . . .'

'Please!' interrupts the Premier. 'As civilised human beings, let's drop the "enemy", when what we mean is "right-wing opposition". This is a political conflict.'

A bold little speech. I wonder how Svetlov will respond?

'"Right-wing"? How do you mean?' enquires Svetlov.

'Hold on!' cries Nikolai Lvovich, springing to his feet. 'Let's be clear. Have we, or have we not, the same end in mind? To restore stability?'

'But why pistol-to-head questions, when it's him who's to

blame?' demands the Minister of Agriculture, hoary-headed Vlasenko, jabbing a finger in my direction.

Bewildered, I turn to Nikolai Lvovich, but he is looking elsewhere.

'He failed to sign what he should,' continues Vlasenko. 'He did away with exemption from agricultural VAT. He brought in export duty on grain!'

'Come off it!' I say, jumping to my feet. 'I sign what the Cabinet approves! And *you*, what are you doing here anyway? I wanted to meet with the heads of the Armed Forces! Did *you* invite this tractor driver?' I enquire of a deathly pale Nikolai Lvovich, jabbing a finger back at Vlasenko. 'And who invited our ecologist Premier? Waste of space both!'

Nikolai Lvovich mutters something about 'the seriousness of the situation', but I cut him short.

'General, your findings, please.'

Getting to his feet, he unfolds a paper from an inner pocket.

'In the last fortnight alone, Kazimir has paid into the Premier's Credit Bank of Andorra account: €2,000,000; and into the City Bank account of the Premier's daughter: $500,000. At midday yesterday, the Premier met with Kazimir's aide Burenkov, concerning the line to take in discussion of the crisis. Further, Minister of Agriculture Vlasenko –'

'I've had enough of this game,' protests Vlasenko, holding his hand to his heart. 'Count me out.'

'Not so fast,' said Svetlov. 'There's still the eight million you've whipped from the state, three million you've taken from Kazimir, and the suit you're wearing which he paid for –'

'In short,' I interrupt, 'we're wasting time on traitors who ought to get up and go.'

'While you stand down!' shrills the Premier.

'That's enough – *out!*' I roar.

He and Vlasenko make for the door, followed by Transport, then Health, leaving, as intended, only Armed Forces.

'Found my ottoman?' I ask Filin.

He shakes his head.

Retiring to my sanctum, we open bottles of whisky.

'We've got to beat them to it,' says Nikolai Lvovich.

'Exactly!' confirms Svetlov.

Filin and Yatskiv say nothing.

'What are they after?' I ask.

'Power and Kazimir as President,' says Svetlov.

'And how can they achieve that?' I ask, trying to form a complete picture of the situation in my head.

'By way of chaos, your resignation, a provisional government and fresh elections,' explains Nikolai Lvovich.

'So?' I ask, taking a swig of whisky, and suffering a pang in the chest. Head reeling, vision blurred, I find myself tumbling, as if down a well, not caring whether there was water at the bottom.

168

Kiev, 20 May 1992, night

There is a bright full moon, and the voices, banging of doors and other sounds heard through the small open window suggest a lively response.

Mother and I are sitting in the kitchen thinking. More accurately, she is thinking while I meditate idly, sometimes aloud, quickly to be cut short.

'What exactly is their plan?' she asks.

'We only talked for ten minutes. I said I'd go back tomorrow morning.'

'That was a mistake. They're not registered to live there. You've been feeble!'

'Feeble? It was their home. What was I to do? Say sleep in the corridor? How were they to know David Isaakovich was dead? They had nowhere to go . . .'

'It was they who left the Soviet Union!' says Mother.

'There wasn't one to leave!'

'No,' she says thoughtfully, drawing her violet flannelette house-coat about her, hennaed hair ruffled by the draught from the open window vent. Henna was out, I should tell her, but don't because I know she has a dozen more packets of her eternal, inviolate Iranian henna in the cupboard.

'So look,' she says to bring our night conversation to an end, 'we go and see them tomorrow. They're not chucking my son into the street! Now off to bed!'

I am suddenly aware of the flat smelling different, as if my smells have been ventilated from it. The air, no longer what I breathed in the past, is now Mother's and I am expected to be out of it. 'They're not chucking my son into the street!' makes it perfectly clear: for me it's either a room in a communal flat or the street . . .

169

Kiev, December 2004

The letter from the Zurich clinic arrived at 8 a.m., just as I was leaving the flat in something of a hurry, only to find myself nose to nose with Special Delivery.

Once in the car, I slit open the envelope and took out the two word-processed sheets of German.

'Post? This early?' asked Viktor Andreyevich, registering his surprise in the driving mirror.

'Special Delivery,' I said, continuing to scan the text for recognisable words.

I got Nila to ask around for someone with a knowledge of German, and in next to no time an interpreter from Protocol came to offer his services.

'It's from the clinic,' I explained, handing him the letter.

He nodded gravely, and I watched him read.

'You need to take a written translation of this to a specialist.'

'How so?'

'There's a lot of complicated medical terminology . . . It recommends that you submit to an examination of certain organs . . .'

'Which?'

'Sergey Pavlovich, with your permission I can fax this to a colleague in Health, and have a translation in an hour or so. I don't want to mislead you.'

I took his advice and received the translation the same afternoon.

Zurich's view was of a malfunction more than likely attributable to 'the quality of father's semen'. Following a high-sounding list of possible anomalies there was a strong recommendation that I and my wife undergo thorough investigation of our reproductive organs before again attempting to start a family.

'Tea?' asked Nila, poking her head around the door.

'No, thanks.'

I was once more aware of the half-forgotten heaviness in my breast. I recalled the late-October night in the clinic on the bank of Zurich's lake. The quiet, terrible night that destroyed our family's hopes. And now this letter reminded me of our unfulfilled plans, mentioning the idea of our trying to recreate those plans.

Should I show the letter to Svetlana, who still felt she alone was to blame?

Zhanna hadn't been around for five days. Svetlana obviously knew nothing of my seeing them together, or of how it had left me floundering for three days. My hands shook and the vision of what I had seen kept coming into my mind at the most inconvenient moments.

It was me named in the letter, and I would do as recommended. Were I in the clear, the blame would be hers and we could forget children and she need not know about the letter. And if I wasn't – why speculate?

170

Carpathian Mountains, January 2016

When I came to, I was amazed at the complete and utter silence. I was clearly in a hospital ward, but one that was windowless. On a metal table in the corner left of the door, the coloured winking lights of electronic apparatus, and suspended from the ceiling, a CCTV camera aimed at me.

I tried to rise, but couldn't, my muscles were too feeble. This was alarming, though only mildly, given my utter indifference to myself and my surroundings. As if it were not me involved but a counterfeit Ukrainian President, well apprised of his own good-for-nothingness and unreality.

The door opened, and in came Svetlov, followed by another in sheepskin jacket and carrying a leather briefcase.

And suddenly I realised why I was so weak – it was the cold, a cold so severe as to inhibit my muscles totally.

'What's happened?' I asked, astonished to find myself able to speak, but hearing from afar a voice weak and trembling with cold.

While Sheepskin Jacket occupied himself with the electronic apparatus, Svetlov sat by my bed, humming and hawing until his companion signalled an OK.

'It's now clear that the plot to replace you was conceived at least a year ago, several months before your operation. The donor heart was a dodgy one. It contains an electronic device whose function we are still not entirely clear about, beyond an ability to pinpoint your position, and transmit your side of any conversation to satellite or some other receiver. There are also grounds for fearing that it may be capable of stopping your heart.'

'It's not my heart,' I responded. 'So they can switch me off whenever they like and in the meantime they can listen to what we're saying.'

'Not now they can't,' smiled Svetlov. 'We've got you completely shielded from radio waves and signals. The device is now blocked, and you've recovered, much to the amazement of your physician.

He said you were going into a classic coma, but once we got you in here, you started to recover.'

'How did you get onto all this?'

'A doctor you consulted, one Rezonenko, came to me with his suspicions.'

'And Nikolai Lvovich?' I queried, remembering Rezonenko's unease in his presence.

'Here, on the job, and OK – I've checked. I'm not sure about Mayya, though. She wasn't on the Simferopol flight.'

Logical enough. A woman who yearns for the Metropol, especially if she is an oligarch's widow, can hardly be a Ukrainian patriot.

'We've a meeting in half an hour, and the physician says you can take part.'

'Where exactly are we?'

'Carpathians, "Other Hands" prison, safe in an off-limits mountain firing range.'

'Am I the only prisoner?' I asked, remembering plans to do away with the detainees.

'Happily we've still got the Russians we meant to dispose of – representatives of Russian Federation power, who could, after all, be of use.'

171

Kiev, 21 May 1992, morning

Mira and her mother receive us with what might be called open

355

arms and a table laid with an old pink cloth clearly from the sideboard. Since David Isaakovich's death, I have touched nothing in the room and taken nothing from it, merely added a little of my own junk.

Hissing away on the table, the electric samovar within a plant-like ring of flowery teacups and saucers. Also two small bowls of biscuits and cheap sweets.

'We've got such nice tea from Israel,' says Larisa Vadimovna, rummaging in one of the stretch holdalls taking up, with cases, almost a third of my room. 'Only where did I put it? Mira, do you remember?'

'In that one, with the bag of spices and figs,' says Mira, inspecting the holdalls.

How she can tell one from another eludes me, unless by the sense that lets women tell which twin is which.

Five minutes later we are seated at table.

'I'm so grateful,' says Larisa Vadimovna. 'My neighbours have told me everything – about the wakes, and how good you were! If only I had a son like that!'

Mother looks on the point of coming out with some unpleasantness but restrains herself, and we listen on, while Larisa Vadimovna slates the filthy Arabs and equally filthy Jews.

'Well,' she grinds on, 'I knew there were water-shy Jews who smelt. There was one such here, a tailor, but there you can't move for them! And where they put us to live! Me and my cultured daughter come from a great city! A collective farm! Communal eating! Weekly meetings! What did I want with meetings? – I was never in the Party!'

I drink my tea and wait for the diatribe to end. Larisa Vadimovna is making up for years of silence.

Mother listens patiently, but her looks tell me ten more minutes will be her absolute limit.

And so it proves.

'Why don't you and Mira take a walk,' Mother suggests after a second cup of tea, 'while Larisa Vadimovna and I discuss things?'

'Where to?' I ask Mira as we leave the building. 'A café?'

'How about the Museum of Russian Art? I've so missed beautiful things.'

Apart from a slight darkening of her complexion from the sun, she has not changed at all.

'The museum it is,' I say.

172

Kiev, December 2004

'Yours is a very rare case,' says the elderly professor, removing his spectacles and concealing them in his breast pocket.

On the desk before him are the results of the tests which have caused me such indignity I still shudder to remember. Now, after all that prodding and palpating, not to mention how I extracted the specimen, the professor's matter-of-fact conclusion is like a shot in the head.

'Your spermatazoid count is 80 per cent healthy, but distinctly passive, incredibly slow, whereas the defective 20 per cent is quite the reverse.'

'You mean I'm incapable of fathering healthy children?'

'That would be to simplify.' Replacing his spectacles, the professor consults one of the sheets before him. 'One hundred per cent defective, and yes, you would be. But the outlook's not that bad in your case. It's the inactivity of the 80 per cent that's puzzling.'

'So?'

'A young specialist I know of has developed a method of sperm washing. The principle is the same as for blood washing. It would make sense, I think, for you to see him. I don't see you taking kindly to a lengthy course of treatment.'

'I'm a busy man,' I say, loosening my tie.

'I understand,' says the professor. 'You can undergo treatment later, but if you're interested in having children, you should go and see this specialist. Being young himself, he'll empathise. You want, I take it, to have a child as soon as possible.'

'Absolutely.'

'I've got his card here somewhere. He's a serious young man and becoming quite sought after. You had better take these results to show him.'

'Where now?' asks Viktor Andreyevich when I return to the Mercedes.

I pass him the card with the specialist's address.

173

Carpathian Mountains, January 2016

The problem was not my muscles, but the maximum-thickness body armour encasing me, as I discovered, when it took two of my security officers to help me to sit up.

Attending the meeting: Nikolai Lvovich, Filin, and two dark-suited civilians vouched for by Svetlov, after a cheery peep round the door by Rezonenko.

'So, for a brief word, over to you, Nikolai Lvovich,' said Svetlov.

'Sergey Pavlovich,' he began, 'Kazimir's back from Moscow again, looking happy.'

The telephoto prints he passed me showed a confident, self-assured Kazimir descending from the aircraft.

'Who he saw there we don't know, but once back, he met with the Communists, and any alliance with them would greatly reduce our chances of success.'

I got the impression that some important decisions had already been made and that Lvovich had been given the task of explaining things to me.

'Get to the point,' said Svetlov.

'So what we think you should do is resign, call an extraordinary election, immediately announcing your intention to stand, thus frustrating Kazimir and legitimising the whole process. The Communists will want to seize their chance of coming to power without Kazimir, and there'll be no alliance . . .'

'Agreed!' I declared with a feeling of relief. 'On condition that I don't in fact stand.'

Nikolai Lvovich and Svetlov exchanged glances.

'You miss the point,' Nikolai Lvovich objected. 'We've done the arithmetic, spent three whole days working on the scenario – *you* would be the winner.'

'Only to have my heart switched off, so that you need yet another election?'

'That device of yours is something we're working on,' said

Svetlov. 'Even the Americans are chipping in. Pinpoint the control signal, and we can nail the lot of them.'

'Great, only at least get me a TV in here so I can watch the news.'

'Sorry, but a TV won't work in here.'

'You're cutting me off like a bunch of conspirators . . .'

'Is whisky allowed?' asked Filin, turning to Svetlov.

'The President's allowed anything he wants,' said Svetlov. 'The country's the last thing he thinks about. It does not bother him that most of us will end up in prison if the Opposition comes to power, while the rest get stripped of everything and shoved barefoot over the frontier with wives, kids and lovers! But it's not him – it's not *you*, Mr President – it's all that we stand for that we're protecting and trying to save from those who stand for worse!'

I felt shamed. But my cold-blooded indifference remained, though Svetlov's little speech drew a slight protest against my selfishness. I could not allow myself to be totally indifferent to the fate of the nation and those serving it.

'Right,' I said, doing my best to smile approval, 'I'm with you. Keep me briefed.'

174

Kiev, 22 May 1992

What I most dislike are rows. In fact, I don't like them at all. I don't know how to row and get no pleasure from rowing. And yesterday, when we were the only visitors at the Russian Museum – so much for our being a *land of culture* – I uneasily visualised our respective

mothers 'in discussion', while Mira, on the strength of being now
something of a traveller herself, admired works of the Wanderer
Group, and I kept an eye on my watch, wondering when we should
go back.

We spent an hour touring the museum, then bought ourselves a
couple of poppy-seed ring rolls, and slowly made our way back to
the scene of the negotiations.

'Your mother's gone home, Sergey, and is expecting you to eat at
one,' announced Larisa Vadimovna. 'We're meeting again
tomorrow.'

Contemplating the protruding springs of the sofa and the four
shiny knobs of the iron bedstead, I wondered where I would be
sleeping in the meantime.

'Your mother will explain.'

I took my leave and set off to work. I had phoned Zhora, early in
the morning, and told him I was having accommodation trouble.

'Sort it, and come,' he had said calmly.

Sorted it wasn't, but I had to go to work, where I did at least have
a tiny but state-of-the-art office complete with telephone. There I
felt of consequence, a grown man, scorned only by Vera. But that
could change. Having sorted my flat, I would go to the clothes shop,
the address of which I now had.

175

Kiev, December 2004

It's strange, but for no apparent reason, undergoing treatment gives one a premonition of a better life – something I had noticed in friends, even those whose treatment proved terminal, and now I was experiencing it myself.

'Why so cheerful?' asked Svetlana on my return. 'Going out somewhere this evening?'

'No. Why?'

'I thought you must be looking forward to something . . .'

So the effects of this syndrome were that obvious. Yes, I am looking forward to something, I thought, as I hung up my coat, glancing back at Svetlana who still stood in the hallway with a quizzical expression on her face. She must have been going to the kitchen when she heard me coming in. She was wearing a tiger-patterned dressing gown and fluffy slippers.

'Are you expecting anyone today?' I asked, thinking of Zhanna. Apart from Zhanna, no one came to see us, or rather to see Svetlana, and I suppose my wife did not have to worry about what she looked like with Zhanna. I had certainly got used to the idea that Svetlana did not feel the need to visit the beauty salon just for me.

Suddenly I remembered the reason for seeing the specialist and this thought swept aside all my doubts and cynicism. I took Svetlana in my arms. I felt her go limp. She laid her head on my shoulder and wept.

'It'll soon be New Year,' I whispered.

'I don't feel like celebrating.'

'In that case we won't.'

She went to bed early, and I sat in the kitchen drinking tea and recalling my talk with the young specialist at the sperm-washing clinic, who had made more sense than the flowery-phrased old professor.

'Yours is in fact a rare form of genetic pathology,' he'd said.

'More often than not it's psychological in origin, but sometimes, as with you, it's spermal.'

Thinking at once of brother Dima, sound of sperm but sick in mind, I thought he was on to something.

'The washing process is costly, but so far as separation of sound from unsound spermatozoids is concerned, it's about 90 per cent successful. Yours is my first case of its kind. But I have successfully separated for the purpose of artificial insemination.'

Three specimens of sperm would be required for delivery within twenty-four hours of ejaculation and immediate refrigeration, in condom or other receptacle.

'And the fee?'

'Twelve thousand dollars.'

I returned home in high spirits, glad that I had not shown Svetlana the Swiss clinic report. The fault was mine, and since I was doing something about it, there was no need to confess. Our home was destined to know the happy sound of children's voices. It had been a successful day. No need to celebrate New Year. Just sit tight, and start thinking about a new life.

176

Carpathian Mountains, January 2016
Several days passed, and my condition improved, although the weight of the body armour caused me considerable discomfort.

A table had been brought, and two armchairs, and at my request, large coloured photographs of 'the view from my windows' – the two windows I should have had, but didn't, and the snowy mountains they should have looked out on.

News came to me in printout form. Following my resignation and call for an extraordinary presidential election, the situation stabilised. The collection of signatures was abandoned. Thrown off course by events, Kazimir flew again to Moscow to consult, leaving us to wonder with whom. The Communist leader renewed his declaration of war on oligarchs, appealing for a return to social justice and order. The first name on the candidate list opened by the Central Electoral Committee was a woman, one Akorytenko, of the little-known Suburbanites Party.

'Who is she?' I asked Nikolai Lvovich.

'No one special. She's been sent on ahead in case of pitfalls,' he replied with a shrug.

I seemed to have been forgotten, my resignation being taken as on a par with death. I was, I concluded sadly, not missed. Whether I was there or not was a matter of indifference. Idly, passively, the people looked on, biding their time. Indifferent to me they might be, but Kazimir they actively hate. I had not interfered. I had not applied pressure. What Kazimir would do could only be guessed at. Enforce payment for electricity for a start. By both people and the State.

Half an hour later Nikolai Lvovich came in with tea and something to eat, apologising for the simplicity of the fare.

'The prison chef doesn't know who it is he's catering for,' he said guiltily. 'Svetlov's in Kiev. Back tomorrow with the news.'

However, the chopped meat salad and gluey macaroni doused in hot tomato sauce were pretty good, and even the tea, with its aroma of autumn hay, went down well.

'Are we looking for Mayya?'

364

'Yes.'

'Found my ottoman yet?'

'That's gone a bit by the board at the moment.'

'Grand larceny springs from petty theft – one minute it's an ottoman, the next it's a whole country.'

Nikolai Lvovich only shook his head and helped himself to more salad.

177

Kiev, 22 May 1992

'She and I understand each other, having both raised children without a father,' said Mother that night in the kitchen. 'So listen to what I'm going to say.'

A pause while she heaped boiled buckwheat onto plates, topping it with curly sautéed strips of beef stroganoff over which she poured a sauce.

'They weren't intending to come back, you know,' she said, handing me a German silver fork of the set reserved for visitors. 'Tonight they'll sleep there, and tomorrow she'll go to a friend for a time . . .'

'Who will?'

'Larisa Vadimovna.'

'And what do I do?'

'You and Mira are to get married, just on paper. I'm not telling you to sleep with her. That's up to you – you're a grown man. But they've got to be registered as resident. There's no other way. Now don't interrupt! You and she register your marriage, and you register her and her mother as resident. That gets you automatically on the city waiting list for flats, and at the same time Larisa Vadimovna and I will see if we can't speed things up. Get the idea? Unless they are lawfully living somewhere, they can't find work, and they've got no money.'

'But what if I want to marry someone else?'

'That can wait. You can explain that this marriage is just a formality. As soon as you've got them registered, you can apply for a divorce and marry properly.'

I tried to fathom how Larisa Vadimovna had managed to tame my mother so completely.

'And you and Mira might take to each other,' she whispered conspiratorially. 'You never know! You can't go far wrong with Jews! They do have lovely children.'

I felt like telling her that I knew Mira as well as I knew myself, but wasn't so foolish as to quarrel.

'By the way,' Mother's face brightened, 'I promised Larisa Vadimovna that on Saturday you would take them to see David Isaakovich's headstone.'

'Right. Only it's not in a cemetery.'

'Where then?'

'The woodland setting he requested.'

'You've put a fence around it?'

'No.'

'You should have.'

'Let them do it, now they're back,' I said yawning.

178

Kiev, 26 December 2004

I began the morning by signing New Year cards. The greetings were printed, so I only had to sign in ink, and my fingers were already beginning to numb with the heavy Parker. O, for a cheap, light ballpoint. But that was out. New Year demanded a different style, a different pen.

'Your coffee, Sergey Pavlovich,' said Nila, gently setting down a cup of my drug.

A gulp or two and I was fired with new energy. My signature improved and stopped tailing off as it shouldn't.

Twenty more cards, another go at the coffee. One cup would see me through.

Now I gazed out of the window. I would have to write to Dima. It was time to face him; he had to return. I needed the remaining cash for the continuation of my own splendid stock.

'*Dear Dima —*' I wrote, immediately discarding Parker for ballpoint,

I'm sorry to say that the state of our finances is such that you will have to come home. At a rough estimate we can see you through till the end of February, so prepare for a quiet life here in Kiev.

Mother looks forward to welcoming all three of you. I'll book your tickets in the New Year, which, hopefully, you will be seeing in more happily than we shall. Svetlana is not yet over the loss of the twins, and things are not always easy. But fortunately some light has appeared at the end of the tunnel.

I'll be at the airport to meet you. Don't forget to collect full copies of your medical record from the professor.

Your loving brother

To soften the brevity I threw in a New Year card, handing the envelope to my office guardian angel to post with the rest.

179

Carpathian Mountains, January 2016

The heart can't be told what to feel.

Laying aside the news printouts, I sat at my table thinking of the last woman in my life. Thinking of Mayya, my only connection with whom was now her husband's heart.

Of the women in my life, each had been more complicated, more distant from me than her predecessor. Or had they?

All, from the outset, had been mistakes.

First had been Svetka. I had long forgotten her face and remembered only the shotgun wedding and amicable divorce.

I seemed to have learned something from that. I became more demanding of life and of women, letting them in turn become more demanding. Up to a point.

Now it was time to take stock. The dearest woman in my life had been Svetlana Vilenskaya, with whom I could have had children and a happy life.

Jolliest, liveliest, and memorable if only for that – the girl from the artificial limbs place in Podol.

Simplest, most boyishly dependable – David Isaakovich's daughter.

Coldest, most alien, apotheosis of my mistrust of women – Mayya.

This melancholy line of thought was interrupted by Svetlov, who noting my photograph windows, nodded sympathetically.

'Hang on in there, Sergey Pavlovich – everything's going according to plan. Your candidature gets registered tomorrow. Kazimir has registered his already. We'll watch the reaction.'

'And on the heart front?'

'Mayya's been found.'

'And?'

'She hasn't left the Crimea. She's living in the servants' quarters at the dacha. With the gardener. We'll deal with them later.'

'Why? Perhaps they're happy,' I said, drawing an uneasy look from Svetlov.

'All right, you can deal with her once she's chucked the gardener.'

Svetlov relaxed and, remembering something, took out his mobile phone. When he realised it would not work in my sealed room, he left without further comment.

180

Kiev, 2 June 1992, night

I am lying on my back, hands behind my head, a posture that lends added weight to the thoughts bouncing, ricocheting back from a ceiling displaying everyday banalities in which I seek to discern if not the meaning of life, then at least some explanation of what is befalling me. Tomorrow: the banality of Mira and I registering our marriage. Should I prod her into life, ask what *she* thinks and feels about it?

She is lying on her side with her back to me. Too quick, too ready to comply with our mothers' decision, on our first night together, we decided to economise on clean sheets and duvet covers. Now, two weeks later, we might have been cohabiting for a hundred years. Bed isn't love but the motions of it, Mira waiting patiently for me to tire, before turning her broad back and sleeping.

I think back to our expedition to David Isaakovich's grave on Trukhanov Island, Larisa Vadimovna was not much impressed by the headstone or the site, and with a shake of her head and a sigh, she set about planting and pressing in with her bare hands the violets she had brought with her.

Mother had been so afraid that Larisa Vadimovna and Mira would not like the sound of

CHERISHED IN MEMORY BY THE BUNINS,

that she had forgotten that the dates were also out of keeping with reality. But, as it turned out no one was bothered. David Isaakovich was dead, had a grave, a headstone, and that was that.

Too hot, Mira throws back the blanket. No beauty before emigrating, she is no better in semi-darkness. Thinking back to our first intimacy in the attic of the Opera Theatre, try as I might, I cannot recall the feelings and emotions that accompanied it.

'Never enter the same river twice,' I whisper into the darkness, but sound is enough to wake Mira and she stirs.

'What was that?'

'Just a quote.'

'Why aren't you asleep?'

'Not sleepy. Thinking.'

'About getting spliced?'

I want to say something nasty in reply, but I hold my tongue and the intended words seem to float up silently into the air and evaporate.

'Am I the river you were talking about?'

'Could be.'

'But a body's not a river. Enter a body as often as you like – there's nothing special about it.'

No, I thought, not in your case.

181

Kiev, 31 December 2004

All the same I did go in search of a New Year's present for Svetlana, and in New Hermitage on January Uprising Street found a silver double candlestick which, rather than wait for the midnight chimes, I presented on my return. Svetlana accepted the gift with a faint, sad smile.

'You go and celebrate, if you want,' she said. 'I'd rather be by myself.'

'Sitting up alone?'

'No, I'll go to bed.'

I noticed, not for the first time, how unkempt she looked.

Remembering how much she had worried about her appearance during pregnancy, it occurred to me that only another one could restore her pride in herself. But then she didn't know about the analysis results and what I was doing about them. What if she feared history repeating itself?

'Do go if you can think where,' she said wearily.

'I'll see,' I said, making for the kitchen.

It was dark outside and snowing lightly. Only the yellow, dandelion-like flowers of headlights indicated where the boulevard was, and watching them scurry, I tried to think where to go, and all I could think of was Nila's, though I had no reason to expect her to be greeting the New Year at home and alone.

I rang her on my mobile.

'Happy New Year!'

'Sergey Pavlovich! The same to you, and I wish you happiness, love and good health!'

'You celebrating with friends?'

'In an hour or two I'll pop round to my aunt's for a bit, then come home to the telly.'

'OK to pop in?'

'*Of course*! When?'

'After your aunt's. Say, about ten.'

'I'll be here.'

Ringing off, I returned to the window and the New Year's Eve bustle in the street. Svetlana wasn't bothered where I went. It was understandable. Neither of us actually needed the other at the moment. For me it was enough to know she was there, while she was sometimes glad I wasn't. It was a difficult phase. We'd just have to wait it out.

Carpathian Mountains, January 2016

With every day that passed, the more convinced I became of my team's political acumen. Not yet recovered from the lengthy period of celebrations, the people showed no surprise at my standing for re-election. Polls put the Communist candidate first, and me and Kazimir practically neck and neck. Kazimir was calling for a public debate with me on TV, threatening to produce compromising material. But as Svetlov and Nikolai Lvovich said, he just wanted to get my heart in range of his remote control.

By way of a morale raiser, Nikolai Lvovich produced an election poster headed 'NO STRANGER TO HONEST TOIL!', showing me with blistered hands, looking genuinely fatigued.

'That was when I cured myself of stress.'

'Exactly. I thought a photo of those hands would come in handy one day.'

'I don't think much of the caption.'

'I wouldn't buy it myself,' he smiled, 'but that's for the people. We have to speak to them on their level, during the election period at least.'

'You know best. But this chip in my heart, can't it be taken out? We've got the surgeons.'

'We've considered that. We've got surgeons, but not 100 per cent trustworthy surgeons. And your heart's not strong. Still, so far, all's going according to plan.'

And rolling up the poster and returning it to its tube, he left.

Kiev, 3 June 1992

The registry office ceremony took no more than twenty tedious, unceremonious minutes. Instantly taking us for a marriage of convenience, the female embodiment of the state thrust papers at us for signature in businesslike fashion, hustling our witnesses, as if anxious to see the back of us as quickly as possible. Our witnesses, a couple from the communal flat who were aware of our situation, but had nevertheless smartened up for the occasion.

Our respective mothers and the neighbours emerged from the registry office with a sigh of relief. The talk was now of a celebratory meal, and the reason for the Mother's weighty camel-skin bag dawned on me. Revolted, I said I'd catch up later. They, to my surprise, made no objection.

'Ready in an hour and a half,' warned Larisa Vadimovna.

I nodded and walked away, taking every turning that came up until I came to an unfamiliar cellar bar with a basketball sign, which made me wonder what basketball players drank.

No one there was tall enough for the game, but vodka and cognac were reasonably priced, and the sandwiches under a glass dome to protect against circling flies looked appealing. Noticing a pile with Doctor's Health Sausage, I was suddenly glad that Mother had not brought Dima today.

A little later I was sorry that she hadn't, because then I could have had my marriage stamped into his ID card. To him it wouldn't have mattered, but I hated it. Actually I have an aversion to stamps altogether.

It was after midnight when I got back to the communal flat. Apart from the drip of the kitchen tap, not a sound.

Mira was asleep in the bed, but she had made up the couch for me. Her little gesture of revenge, I thought smiling and swaying from the vodka I'd drunk. It was fine before we married, but it's not OK now, is that it? I undressed and slipped into bed with Mira.

184

Kiev, 31 December 2004

In a supermarket near Nila's I bought a bottle of sparkling red Artyomovsk and a big box of chocolates, throwing in a packet of three condoms at the checkout, only later awakening to the happier dual purpose they were capable of serving.

Nila's flat was much as last time. Nila, looking very elegant in a short, claret-coloured cocktail dress, was clearly delighted to see me.

'So much for an evening alone with TV!'

In the event, it was an evening of TV with the sound off, chatting away, drinking her wine, then mine.

At the appearance on screen of Grandfather Frost and the Snow Maiden, we turned up the sound and danced the New Year in.

Then still dancing, pressed close, we made our way to the darkness of her bedroom. But I did not forget my sperm-washing specialist's instructions. After each wave of passion, I lay for a while quietly stroking Nila's delicate skin and then got up to deposit in the fridge a knotted condom containing seriously inactive sperm. Invisible tails all dreaming of becoming people.

In the morning Nila asked me to make coffee. I obliged, but seeing she had no intention of getting up I whispered an apology for my hasty departure and, retrieving my treasures from the fridge, I left, closing the front door quietly behind me. Kiev was asleep. I found my watch in my jacket pocket. Ten thirty and no one about, only the occasional taxi or police car. I tried to remember what day it was, but only the date came into my too relaxed mind: 1st of January.

185

Carpathian Mountains, January 2016
My second week in the Carpathians proved good for my health. Long indifferent to the ceiling CCTV, I had taken, at quiet moments, to performing ten press-ups – a source of pride, given the weight of my body armour, and more like weightlifting than physical training. I could have been a boxer, working out in preparation to enter the ring and fell my opponent with a single blow. A pleasing illusion, not so far removed from the reality, with Nikolai Lvovich, Svetlov and others in the role of trainers and psychologists concerned to prepare me for the world and the world for me.

'Think of your heart!' advised Svetlov, entering as always without knocking, just as I was completing my tenth press-up.

Getting to my feet, I went and sat at my newly introduced desk.

'What is there to report?' I asked, feeling a good deal livelier than of late.

'Awkward thing to ask,' he said quietly, 'but were you ever into erotica?'

'Into what?'

'The thing is they're opening an exhibition today in Kiev, sponsored by Kazimir, of erotic photographs taken by you.'

Lost for words, I gestured helplessly.

'I'll check the Internet. The poster gives a website.'

Left to muse on the erotic and sensual and the singular dearth of both in politics, I fell prey once more to a feeling of total isolation, being only among men, eating prison food prepared by men for male prisoners. How had I not gone mad? Or had I? Long ago. In becoming a politician. From that moment, life had been as sterile and cold as my surgeon's knife; feeling nothing, deriving no pleasure or joy from anything. Whisky and cold the only colour to an existence white as a hospital sheet.

Svetlov returned with an armful of papers and an unusual warmth of expression that put me on my guard, and sitting opposite, gently spread out on the desk, a number of nude photographs.

'Know her?' he asked.

'It's Nila. My secretary.'

'Good photographs. Candid, but nothing smutty about them.'

'Damaging?'

'I've a funny feeling, but let me check the file before I say.'

'What file?'

'The dossier on you.'

'Does the President have one?'

'Everyone does. What matters is *who* compiles it, not *what about*.'

His step, as he left the room, verged on the jaunty.

I got up from my desk. I didn't want to do any more press-ups. I wanted a cold, or at least a tepid bath, tepid but with ice so that the cubes stung my skin and reassured me that I was still able to withstand hardship habitually with no ill effect. Indeed, I wanted hardship to be an essential part of my life.

186

Hurghada, Egypt, end of June 1992

'From each according to his abilities, to each according to his needs.' A good slogan, but not one that I, brought up by my mother to be modest, had made my own. Then, a couple of days ago, a pleasant surprise. I had been devoting my abilities to the tasks at hand, not expecting anything, just accepting what I was given, when Zhora burst into my mini-office, eyes bright with generosity.

'In two days' time, you're off on holiday! By air! to Egypt. Free voucher, courtesy of Eastern Express Tour Agency. We've made the owner our Vice-President.'

'What should I take?' A silly question, I knew, but I was quite overwhelmed.

'Never been to the sea?'

'Of course.'

'So seaside things. And remember it'll be hot.'

Vera brought me my holiday pay in a pink envelope.

'You got married?' she asked in a whisper.

'No, registered,' I corrected, pleased to see at least $500 in the envelope.

'What's the difference?' she whispered mockingly.

Slim, black skintight slacks, bright blouse, boyish crop, cheeky-faced, she was just lovely.

'The difference,' I answered, also in a whisper, 'is that you register to get a stamp in your ID card or establish residence, whereas marriage is a mutual declaration of sexual intent.'

'You're brighter than I thought,' whispered Vera, glancing over her shoulder at the half-open door.

'What made you think I was stupid?'

'You were when they brought you in.'

'I've grown in wisdom. Your influence.'

'Pity it wasn't me who got the voucher,' she said with a sigh.

'You and I could have gone together, but there was only one voucher going.'

'You've got the money,' she said, indicating the envelope.

At that moment someone knocked, saving me the trouble of extricating myself.

'Tea or coffee?' Vera, now all innocence, enquired of a potential of our Private Enterprise Association.

'Coffee,' he said.

'And for me,' I said, to be rewarded with a smirk.

But now, at breakfast in the hotel restaurant, amply self-served with salad, olives, mutton sausages and chicken, I am bored. At the next table a saccharine couple from Moscow are shamelessly recounting, for all to hear, the events of a steamy night. I, too, had a double room and an enormous bed. Maybe I should have brought Vera, supposing she was being serious.

Sighing, I drink my orange juice and consider my fellow holidaymakers, all having a thoroughly good time, while I have to content myself with the thought that whatever pleasure I am getting is free of charge.

187

Kiev, 1 January 2005

Since last night I've been in a state of euphoria. At first I could not get hold of my specialist doctor with the unusual surname of Knutish. But at 6 a. m. he turned on his mobile and joyfully replied to my message.

'The material's ready? That's great! Bring it to the clinic in about an hour.'

I arrived a bit early and stood waiting on the snow-laden porch for some fifteen minutes. Knutish drove up in his dark blue BMW and climbed out unhurriedly, pulling a key from the pocket of his sheepskin coat.

He turned the corridor lights on and then opened the heavy metal door of the laboratory. The rest was like a science documentary. Standing at a lab table I handed over the three little bags and he carefully decanted the contents into test tubes. Holding them up at eye level, he gave each one a gentle shake. Having labelled each tube with a number, he sealed them with rubber caps and lifted the lid of a large, chrome cylinder from which emerged a frosty mist. The doctor carefully lowered each tube into the cylinder and as he did so

I noticed the label on another test tube already in cold storage. It read *Ukrainian Gene Pool.*

'Rest assured, Sergey Pavlovich. Within a month my techniques will have your sperm perfectly refined and you'll be able to put it to good use.'

'And when should I pay?'

'Will you pay in instalments or all at once?'

'All at once.' I noticed that the specialist seemed to like my response.

'Let's say around the 15th, after the holidays,' he said glancing at a wall calendar.

188

Carpathian Mountains, February 2016
A man who knows nothing of the world can be convinced of anything. The blind can be taken to any window and told it looks onto the Eiffel Tower or the Pyramids of Cheops. The deaf, given a CD of Ruslana can be told it's Mahler's Ninth. The deaf, the blind have to take, or not take, on trust what they learn of reality.

'All going splendidly,' Nikolai Lvovich, unhealthy of complexion, bags under eyes, reports at breakfast.

'Meaning?' I ask, tackling my boiled egg with an aluminium teaspoon.

'You're up in the ratings.' Pause to sip his plastic mug of tea. 'Svetlov and I spent the night reading your dossier, and we've hit on something useful. Nila's been found. In Budapest. We've sent a man. He's seeing her this evening. We'll keep you informed.'

'Can I read my dossier?'

'It's not allowed. We haven't passed the law that would allow citizens to see their files,' he says evenly.

'We'll have to see about that.'

'Not worth it. Could bring an element of corruption into the work of the Intelligence Services. And you could do with a shower.'

'Not the only one,' I quipped, having noticed the greasy mark around his collar. 'Isn't there a bath here?'

'No hot water. The generator's packed up.'

'I don't mind cold.'

Nikolai Lvovich leaves, looking rather more tense and weary than when he came in. What has upset him is hard to say, and I don't much care. I am thinking of Nila, trying to imagine what took her to Budapest. After all, it's hardly New York or Paris.

189

Kiev, July 1992

While I'd been enjoying the Red Sea, a heat wave had drawn locals and visitors to the Dnieper like so many flies. And now I would have headed there too, but I was already sun-bronzed and relaxed and, after Egypt, the Dnieper's murky waters and beer-cap-littered strands held little appeal.

Mira was as little pleased to see me back as she was with the present of a souvenir copper vase. No sooner had I dumped my bag on the floor than she was throwing off her housecoat, tugging sky-blue Israeli jeans over podgy thighs, and making ready to go somewhere. My vase, after no more than a glance, got put on the table.

'Back this evening,' she said, and left.

Alone, I noticed a change in the atmosphere of the room. There was a cheaper, more youthful quality about it. The antique, faintly aristocratic mustiness of naphthalene and old leather (as of the sofa) had yielded, given ground. Casting around, I quickly discovered why in the shape of a lavender air freshener and a pink bottle of eau de cologne labelled in French.

A fresh marking of territory – the sort of thing that cats do!

While I was boiling potatoes in the communal kitchen, the wearer-in of David Isaakovich's shoes looked round the door.

'She had a man here while you were away,' he confided.

Fascinated by the tattoo peeping from the overshort singlet and the baggy-kneed tracksuit trousers, I was momentarily at a loss what to say.

'Young, at least, was he?'

'No, middle-aged.'

'Slept here, did he?'

''Fraid so.'

'I'll look into it,' I said.

As I ate, it occurred to me that my other neighbours would be equally concerned, and awaiting developments now that I – the lawful husband, as they saw it – was back from my holiday.

I checked the bed. The sheet was unmarked.

That evening, when Mira came back, I asked about the man the neighbours had seen.

'What's it to you?' She sounded surprised. 'We've got ourselves on the housing list, so now it's time to divorce, time to move on.'

'What you do is up to you, but try to see it as our neighbours must.'

'Men come, men go, but women are forever,' said Mira loftily. 'Get yourself a woman to go to until she's bored. And let's agree that while I've no other room, I'll have him here when you're not. Provided you tell me.'

'Tell you when I won't be here?'

'Yes.'

'Like a drink?'

'To celebrate what?' she asked, genuinely taken aback.

'Our divorce.'

'Fine.'

'The food store shuts in twenty minutes. What would you like?'

'A bottle of Cahors and frankfurters, if there are any.'

The row our communal flatmates were no doubt hoping for failed to materialise.

After a bottle of Cahors and Hungarian salami sandwiches – sausages being unavailable – we went to bed, our independence of each other now fully acknowledged. And after perfunctory sex, we fell asleep.

190

Kiev, 15 January 2005

I woke several times during the night. Leaving my office-cum-bedroom, I went into our bedroom to watch Svetlana sleeping on her back, face upwards, pillow to one side, as if she had pushed it away.

'I'll come back to you,' I said to myself, standing over her perhaps for the fourth time.

The night is almost over. The winter mornings do not begin with the dawn, but with the hum of traffic in the street below. You can't hear it if you keep the windows closed, but I can't do without the cold air. My down duvet keeps my body warm, even hot, but my head remains out in the clean, cold air full of cold, street noises.

I'm out of bed now, tying the cord of my dressing gown and going to the kitchen.

I count the dollars withdrawn from the bank yesterday. Twelve thousand: two packs of fifties and one of twenties. All crisp and new as if they'd been printed round the corner.

At eight I phone Knutish and he suggests we meet at Kampai on Saksagansky Street.

'Do you know where that is?' he asks.

'I'll find it.'

At exactly midday, Viktor Andreyevich drops me at the Japanese restaurant.

'Pick me up in half an hour,' I command, getting out of the Mercedes.

He nods, businesslike.

My micro-cleaning specialist is already inside and I join him at his table.

'The food here is great,' he says in a confidential tone.

He's wearing a tweed jacket with leather elbow patches, on top of a black polo neck.

I look at the menu and choose a soup and some sushi and Knutish orders sushi with caviar and salmon.

'How's the process going?' I ask.

'Great!' he says confidently. 'One more wash and we'll have a refined product.'

I nod. For me the word 'refined' is associated with 'sugar' and now I have to associate it with sperm, which until recently sparked no associations at all.

I pick up my briefcase, and taking out three fat envelopes, place them on the table.

Dr Knutish surveys them carefully and then looks at me. I can see he is preparing to tell me something important.

'I'll inform you as soon as the process is finished. Then we can either freeze the material, or keep it refrigerated for a short time, but really it would be best to use it immediately. Your wife will need to undergo some preliminary procedures in order to facilitate that. Not the nicest business for her.'

He spoke in a calm, businesslike manner. I was fascinated by his choice of words and his intonation.

'All right,' I say, pushing the envelopes towards him.

The doctor stuffs them into the inside pockets of his tweed jacket.

Our food is served and we eat in comfortable silence.

'They're waiting for you at the museum,' Viktor Andreyevich informs me as soon as I am seated in the car. 'The Director asked us to meet there at twelve thirty.'

'He can wait,' I reply.

We drive out onto Bolshoi Vassilkovski Road, to our left a block of flats dressed in an advert for Adidas. I've absolutely no desire to go to that museum, but the boss himself charged me with the task of finding a valuable painting, in good condition, for the Prime Minister's office, two metres by one metre sixty.

I wonder why the dimensions are so important. Is there a patch of damaged wallpaper? I wish I knew a bit more about art. I recognise beauty when I see it, but only if it coincides with my tastes. I can't differentiate between beauty in life and beauty in art, let alone evaluate a painting. What's more, the Director of the museum is a worm. He'll never part with a really valuable piece. He'll try to palm me off with some rubbish.

191

Carpathian Mountains, February 2016, Monday

Today, a marked easing of my incarceration and a boost to morale with the removal of my body armour. Lighter than air for a moment, I feel that a mere jump would set me high above the brown carpeted floor, level with my 'windows' or two-month-old snowy fir-and-pine-obstructed view.

'The room and corridor shielding is now doubly reinforced,' explains Svetlov, helping me out of my body armour, and dumping it on the table, amazed by the weight of it.

I notice a briefcase laid against the leg of my desk and am reminded of an attempt on Hitler's life that failed because of the strength of the oak desk beneath which the briefcase with a bomb inside was left.

'Is that your briefcase?' I ask.

Svetlov, at first alarmed by my question, quickly replaces a frown with a tired smile. He pulls the case up onto his lap and, opening it, takes out a bottle of Hungarian whisky. I lean forward to study the label: the indecipherable vocabulary as sharp on the eye as on the tongue.

'So it was you who went?'

'It was no great distance.'

'And?'

'All's well. They gave her €100,000 for the film and, if needed, an interview for the tabloid press about life as your lover of years gone by.'

'What's good about that?'

'The fact that she told me everything. The man who contacted her was one of our former colleagues, who had been her controller when she worked for you. He's now working for Kazimir and he knew about the film and that Nila was alone and penniless in a tiny flat.'

'How is she?'

'Much as in the photographs – facially.'

'What else?

'She's been in Budapest three years. She married one of our nouveau riche who borrowed hugely and then scarpered to Budapest where he bought the little flat in Nila's name and then disappeared. Since then she's been scraping along, nannying for Ukrainians living over there, and chambermaiding. She was glad to see me. She asked after you.'

'What exactly?'

'Had you put on weight? Were you married? How many children?'

'And you said?'

'That you were very lonely, living in a tiny room, deeply concerned for the country's future, striving to save it from the abyss ... We've found her somewhere better to live in a little place outside

Budapest, and provided her with money. She'll happily do what we tell her.'

'Good. Now give me half an hour to take all that in.'

Nodding sympathetically Svetlov left, briefcase in hand.

Alone again in my silent room I felt the pangs of self-pity. I sat down at my desk and studied the photos. I must have been blind when I took them. I had somehow failed to notice just how beautiful Nila was. I'd had eyes only for Svetlana. So happy with her that no other woman existed for me.

Now I was amazed by what I saw, especially the openness of her facial expression combined with the bold eroticism of her poses. But perhaps my being at an age where maintaining physical fitness requires ever increasing effort has sharpened my appreciation. Perhaps maturity has opened my eyes to things that youth cannot see. Our moments of freedom had not coincided, nor our moments of desire.

I poured myself a glass of the Hungarian whisky and leaned over the photos.

At least your face is still as beautiful as ever, I whispered.

192

Kiev, July 1992, Saturday

A divorce certificate has a much nicer look and feel about it than the certificate of marriage. Something I had not noticed when I divorced from Svetka. That time nothing seemed real. The gloomy restaurant wedding breakfast, Svetka's note asking for a divorce, my non-involvement in the divorce procedure. Now it's completely different. Now there's hearty rejoicing at my unthreatened freedom, with nothing worse than the flea-bite irritation of due record on my ID card.

So betaking myself to the shop kindly recommended by Vera, I spent $500 turning myself into something approaching the cover boy of a Hungarian glossy magazine, not so very far short of the French or American equivalent, gaining for my outlay the self-assurance to ring Vera at work and invite her to a bar. To my amazement she accepted.

We opted for a sympathetic place in Podol, where we drank until one, when the striptease show was about to start and Vera, having no interest in that form of entertainment, began to yawn.

A bright starry sky inspired us with vigour for the ascent of Vladimir's Descent, halting every so often to cuddle and kiss like teenagers, me, teenager-fashion, having nowhere to take Vera to stay with me till morning. There was no sense in our staggering on through the deserted streets, and so, finding a taxi outside the Dnieper Hotel, I took her home to Pechersk.

'Tightwad!' retorted the driver when I protested at being stung for $10. 'For what you paid for that jacket, you could have half my car!'

I chose not to argue and gave him $10, but a quarter of his ancient Volga would have been nearer the mark.

193

Kiev, 16 January 2005

Last night I dreamed of the Cossack with his mace and now, gazing down at the picturesque view of the snowy city over coffee in the kitchen, I realise no one told me which way the picture is to hang: horizontally or vertically. The one the Director thrust on me is vertical. I wouldn't have chosen it for my wall, but a grim, threatening, ill-tempered Cossack is just about perfect for a Premier's office. A patriotic subject, which, knowing even less about art than I do, the Prime Minister could hardly object to. Size is what matters to him, and I wonder which wall he will put it on. Best would be facing the door confronting all who enter with something in the nature of a double image!

It's still snowing. Svetlana is still asleep. Suddenly I notice the two lipstick-smudged glasses on the stainless-steel draining board, and find two empty cognac bottles in the sink cupboard waste bin.

When did they manage that? I wonder.

Then I remember. It was about midnight when I got back, after hanging on at the Chief's request, for some vital foreign phone call and dozing off until eleven thirty, when I got myself driven home. The flat was in total silence.

I peep into the bedroom, and there are Svetlana and Zhanna asleep in each other's arms again. Zhanna, lying face towards Svetlana and me, has thrown off all covering to the waist. Her shapely back and neat breasts disturb me. I feel disturbingly attracted, but I am unable to deal with that attraction now. At the moment I am thrown by the realisation that Svetlana does not need me at all, at least right now. For the moment she needs a woman who can empathise with her better than any male of the species. The shock of the twins' deaths is as much an emotional as physiological experience, and instinctive. We males are rational, rational to a fault – hence the fact that I have not told Svetlana about the test results or about how I have gone through this sperm-refining process so that we can have a healthy child.

Returning to the kitchen, I finish my coffee, dress and leave. My car is waiting at the entrance, Viktor Andreyevich more joyless than usual.

'Something up?'

He nods. 'Got your foreign-travel passport?'

'At the office? Why?'

'No idea. Just told to make sure you had it.'

'Who by?'

'Director's secretary.'

'Just that?'

'Yes.'

As we drive on in silence I try to remember any hint there'd been of a foreign trip in the offing. January isn't the time for delegations. Well, let it be anywhere but Outer Mongolia.

194

Carpathian Mountains, February 2016, Wednesday

'We need to react,' Nikolai Lvovich said agitatedly, laying a number of newspapers on the table.

'FORMER PRESIDENT INTO EROTICA' was the headline over an article reporting that a calendar of my photographs had topped sales of two millions, a record.

'We could sue,' I suggested. 'The photographs are mine and being used without my permission . . .'

'We could,' said Svetlov, 'but not now. What's called for now is a change of image. Otherwise, come the election it won't be you the voters have in mind, it will be Nila's body! It's serious decision time.'

As if I hadn't been making serious decisions every day.

'We're very close to locating the remote control, which means it will soon be safe for you to return to Kiev. But Kazimir has pushed the business of these photographs further than we expected.'

'So what do I do? Pose for *Playboy*?'

'No.' He turned to Nikolai Lvovich as if for artillery support.

'We think you should marry,' said the latter.

'Who?'

'Nila,' said Svetlov. 'Nila's a fine, beautiful woman. She'll make a splendid First Lady. I can vouch for that.'

'You can vouch for my future wife?'

'The wedding to be on March the 8th, the day of the election,' continued Nikolai Lvovich. 'Nila being presented as the love of your life, mother of your grown-up child . . .'

'And by the wedding day expecting another,' threw in Svetlov.

My reaction to this picture of my personal life so brazenly drawn by my colleagues was to bare my teeth and clench my fists. I had a strong desire to clout Nikolai Lvovich, but the old rat had seen it coming and was busying himself with the whisky bottle and glasses.

'Decision time,' he said nervously, handing me my glass. 'If you agree to this, we've won.'

'Nila's agreeable,' Svetlov said uncertainly.

'Is she? Up to me, then. You know what came of my last shotgun marriage.'

'This time it will be for Ukraine, with everything above board.'

'And Kazimir will take all this lying down, will he?'

'Kazimir's got problems of his own,' smiled Svetlov. 'We have leaked information about how he's got you held hostage somewhere in the Carpathians, and has kidnapped certain Russian government officials. That should keep him busy –'

'Busy looking! And you've told him where.'

'He won't look where he's been told. No, it's up to you, Sergey Pavlovich. For Ukraine's sake, please say yes.'

My hand shook, the shallow brown sea of whisky lapping against the glass cliffs of my tumbler.

I held the glass against my bottom lip and my favourite smell reached my nostrils. For that moment my whole mind and body were concentrated and, perhaps for the first time, I felt the weight of real responsibility.

My gaze fell on the black-and-white photo of Nila and remained there, fixed like the anchor of a large ship finally hitting the seabed.

'I agree,' I said.

We drank in silence for some minutes.

'You said something about a grown-up child of mine.'

'Your daughter Liza in America. It's time she came home, at least for a bit.'

'Liza!' Tears came to my eyes. 'But I haven't seen her for so many years.' I was sobbing.

Svetlov and Nikolai Lvovich exchanged glances.

'We'll pop back later,' said Nikolai Lvovich.

I watched two blurred figures leave the room. The door shut behind them.

Perhaps I was drunk. Perhaps my nerves weren't up to this pressure. Perhaps I was genuinely struck down by guilt for abandoning Liza, the only remaining strand of my almost extinct family line.

195

Kiev, August 1992

'Men come, men go, but women are forever,' Mira said, but now she is demonstrating the reverse. Her beau has a job as hospital boilerman, working one twenty-four-hour day followed by three days off, which are easily kept track of. The boiler room has a divan, a table and even a little fridge. Comfort, clearly, for a semblance of happy family living. Mira now works the twenty-four-hour shift with him, hopefully not proving a distraction. Though it's hard to imagine what duties there are to distract him from, in August, with an outdoor temperature of 33°C and an indoor of 25°C, apart from heating water for washing.

But whatever it is, Mira comes back happy and contented and, most surprisingly, goes straight to bed.

I decided finally to tell Mother of our divorce, thinking she'd take it well, but she didn't.

'You knew from the start it was all a fiction,' I protested.

'Half what happens in life starts as what you call fiction, only to become living truth and reality. There is such a thing as grown men accepting responsibility for what they do.'

'Maybe you should stay with Dima for a while – they would agree instantly with you there.'

That was yesterday and our exchange ended, as might be expected, in tears, reproaches and admonition along the lines of 'When you have children, you'll know what it feels like!'

I made no answer. I had no wish to. I just felt sorry for my elderly mother being stuck with absurd ideas. It could have been the onset of senility, except that I thought senility was more characteristic of men than women. So I put it all down to a sense of confusion caused by the collapse of Soviet morality. Indeed, no morality functions any more. Morality went out at about the time of the Russian rouble. Now it's dollars, and as I remembered from childhood: where there are dollars, morals and justice evaporate.

Still, my monthly envelope has grown fatter, now containing $600. I've changed too. I'm now more composed and kinder to those near to me and others. Mother doesn't know it, but I'm going to buy her a $100 microwave. I am also going to buy something for Dima. And for Vera, although we have still not progressed beyond kissing and cuddling after drinks. I don't like the idea of using Mira's spells at the boiler room to ask Vera back to the flat with its reek of the past. And strange as it seems, she is a well-brought-up young lady. At twenty plus, she has not yet prepared her parents for her bringing a boyfriend home!

196

Ukrainian Airspace, 16 January 2005
We had taken off from Borispol at 1500 hours and it was now just after five.

'Would you care to eat?' asked the flight attendant.

'No, but I'd like another whisky.'

She made for her trolley. I was her sole charge in business class. Good psychologists as they are, flight attendants know who to feel sorry for and who to be firm with, and seeing the state I was in, this one was immediately sorry for me.

Waiting at the door of my office that morning had been Colonel Svetlov with the news that my brother and his wife had jumped to their deaths. Details to follow from the embassy . . .

I felt myself sway. There was a humming in my head and my mouth went dry. I stared dumbly back at Svetlov, unable to speak, my lips were numb and there was a lump in my throat, as cold as ice. I tried to swallow but could not. Eventually I felt it slide down into my inside, still frozen, but no longer preventing speech.

'How? Why?'

'You'll have to fly there. Our embassy people will meet you. Not a word to anyone,' he advised. 'Given the implications for you, us and Ukraine. The Swiss have been accommodating, and very likely there'll be no press involvement. You fly at 1500 hours. You'll have the tickets in half an hour.'

'How about the child?'

'Safe in hospital. That's a problem to be solved in accordance with Swiss law and our interests . . .'

And before I knew it, he was gone, noiselessly as an angel, leaving me to wonder why Liza was in hospital.

I was still asking myself this question on the plane hours later.

'More ice,' I told the flight attendant, handing her my tumbler.

She looked questioningly at my empty tumbler and asked: 'More whisky with ice?'

I looked at my tumbler but was unable to answer, my head was swimming.

'Yes, more whisky with ice,' I managed at last.

197

Carpathian Mountains, February 2016, Thursday
Someone knocked and, telling them to wait, I got up and dressed, supposing it to be Filin. Recently everyone else had taken to entering regardless. It proved to be Svetlov, bearing an already opened envelope addressed to me.

'*Dear Sergey*,' I read, a familiarity the ornate signature did nothing to explain,

> I have, I realise, been playing with fire, or rather was, till the end of the year. I'm all right now and would like to remain so as long as possible. Which is why I'm buying myself out with some information which may be of assistance, may even save your life. In return for which I ask you to forget me, and to order those who serve you to do the same. I'm staying in the Crimea with the man I love. Minusenko, surgeon at the October Hospital, is the person you want. Give him a bit of a shake and he'll tell you what you need to know about your new heart. Our contract no longer exists, I've destroyed it. It was a link with a very happy past. I only needed it until I found first real love. Now that I have found it, I've decided to forget the past and everyone connected with it.

'Where did this come from?'

'Mayya Voytsekhovskaya in the Crimea.'

'As I see. But why was it opened?'

'In case it contained anthrax spores or other noxious substances,' said Svetlov.

'This Minusenko – have you found him?'

'Of course.'

'What did he have to say?'

'Nothing. He just gave us this.' He produced something very like a vehicle remote locking device. 'This is your personal remote control.'

I took the device and held it in the palm of my hand.

'And he gave it to you, just like that.'

'Not exactly,' Svetlov smirked, 'but he did tell us a funny story about how he had given a similar device to Kazimir in exchange for a huge flat on Sofia Square, only to realise afterwards that what he'd given him would only lock and unlock his ancient Audi and have no effect on your heart . . . We'll have to protect him for a while.'

'So this thing's my freedom?' I said, trying to calculate its weight.

'Your life. Now we can get cracking on our plans.'

'Good. You've served me well.'

Svetlov rose and, reaching the door, said, 'Have a good sleep. We've a long heavy day tomorrow. Could be taxing . . . Should I take that for safe keeping?' he asked, seeing me still holding the key to my heart.

I shook my head.

198

Kiev, August 1992

'I'm going to have a baby!' Mira announced as we sat over breakfast. Her bed was still unmade and my sofa not yet covered with its rug.

Trying to remember when we'd last had what passed for sex, I almost choked on my scrambled egg. I had my suspicions, but they were quickly dispelled.

'We go to the registry office in a day or two, Vitya and I.'

'Will you have a celebration?'

'A small one, just for his friends.'

'Here?'

'No, at the boiler room, when he's on there.'

'Will I be invited?'

'If he agrees.'

I nodded.

'Do you mind if we make him resident here?' she asked anxiously, after a long silence.

'Here? As well as me and your mother . . .?'

'How many's not the point.'

'With the baby that'll be five of us. They'll never wear that!'

'For fifty dollars they'll add a couple of grannies and three Jewish uncles,' she said, as if addressing an idiot child.

'Register whoever you like,' I said, with an airy wave of the hand.

Half an hour later she had gone, leaving me sitting at the table still, regretting my last remark, and seeing my living space reduced from seven to four square metres. What then? Back to Mother's? No, there must be some other way.

That evening I rang Father Basil, saying we should meet. He liked the idea and we decided on an evening swim.

My thoughts, as I headed down towards the Alexander Column that evening, were of Vera. On Saturday I must invite her to a beach. Trukhanov Island or Hydropark.

I found Father Basil waiting, and in good heart we made our way across the footbridge and swam in the Dnieper. It was no longer so scorchingly hot, but the sand still retained the solar energy of the afternoon and we lay on it rather than on towels.

I told Father Basil about Mira, her pregnancy, her wedding and residence registrations.

'Worldly vanity!' he declared with a wave of the hand. 'And that room is a nonsense! Cheaply come, cheaply go. Or put it this way – you have kept it for David Isaakovich's nearest and dearest, and have his thanks from on high.'

I shrugged. Practical advice was what I wanted, not a sermon.

'Let's pay him a visit,' Father Basil suggested, when we were dry.

We found tractor tracks, but grave mound and headstone were gone, quietly made away with just as the dugout had been – handiwork that was like a dagger to my heart. The problem of Mira and her prospective family suddenly seemed trivial and unworthy. If it was that easy to remove a man's grave and efface his memory, why worry about oneself in life? Four square metres is what each person is entitled to. The dead got less and could be robbed of that!

'I'll have to tell Mira and Larisa Vadimovna,' I said.

'Man, as you see, is a rare sort of swine, and as a species not to be saved by any kind of religion,' boomed Father Basil. 'It's people like you, kindred spirits seeking support, who must be saved. The rest can sod off the Ark!'

It was the first time I'd heard him swear, let alone with such conviction, and I didn't blame him.

Yes, sod off, sod off, the lot of them! I thought.

And then it occurred to me that what he had said applied to what I had just been pondering. We had to focus on saving our own!

I would buy Mother her microwave tomorrow and Dima some books. He was now into history, and at our last visit had told me any amount about the life of Marshal Zhukov. I would try and find him a biography of Marshal Budyonny.

199

Zurich, 16 January 2005, evening

At the airport I was met by the embassy driver, who checked me in at the Florhof. He had not much to say for himself, and neither had I. My room looked out on rain, and puddles reflecting the street lamps as drearily yellow as in autumn. If only there had been a bit of snow it would have looked pretty, but the puddle-strewn road reflecting the glint of the street lights was simply miserable. Autumn misery.

Next day I would be driven to Bern to meet one of our embassy staff who would accompany me to Leukerbad. Next day did not bear thinking about. Any more than thinking in general, or sleeping.

Availing myself of a hotel umbrella I set out to wander. Five minutes brought me to a square, all tram stops, a Museum of Modern Art, but lifeless. Life was behind the windows and glass walls of cafés.

They were both complete schizophrenics, I thought to myself. They had brought a healthy child into the world only to take themselves out of it. It was impossible for a normal person to understand.

A group of young people came surging out of a bar. I had to dodge as their umbrellas clicked open around me, but I caught a glimpse of the cosy interior of the bar they had come from.

Shown dollars and credit card, the barman, opting for dollars, threw open the choice of his well-stocked shelves.

I chose bourbon and, sitting myself at a table by a window running with Swiss winter rain, wondered how long it would take to get drunk. To be on the safe side, I left my room key with the name of my hotel on the table beside me.

200

Carpathian Mountains, February 2016, Friday

That night I didn't sleep at all, running constantly to the bog, and when not, perched on the edge of a chair gripping an aching stomach.

Clearly the fault of the prison chef. Or of the past-its-best tinned meat mixed in with the boiled potato. Anyway, supper had left a nasty taste in the mouth, and very soon I began to feel sick. A drink of tea resulted in stomach pains, and then the real trouble started. That neither Svetlov nor Lvovich had joined me for supper that evening occurred to me only later.

In the early morning, when it was still dark, I heard bursts of automatic fire, but felt no sense of alarm, my priority was to get to the lavatory in time. Heavy footfalls in the corridor followed. Hefty men, masked and wearing camouflage fatigues, came bursting in, took me under the arms, and without a word carried me off down the corridor, passing other men dragging someone. How soon could I put bum to bog, with or without seat, was all I could think of, but at no door did we stop.

A helicopter engine throbbed into life. The blades were speeding up. I was given a tablet and water to drink it down with.

There's more than one helicopter, I noted, before falling asleep.

'No questions! No questions!' I was awoken by a familiar voice shouting excitedly. I opened my eyes to TV cameras and light so bright I used a hand to shield myself from it.

Questions slowly formed in my head. What was happening to me? Where was I? Had I been kidnapped?

Given another tablet, I withdrew into the warm if somewhat still confused state of knowing that my stomach was at last settled.

'Straighten his pillow,' came a voice from above, which, bringing an unsteady gaze to bear, I saw to be that of a Svetlov red-eyed with fatigue. I tried to ask him something, but he raised a forbidding hand.

'All's well,' he said.

201

Kiev, August 1992

'A week today we fly to Poland,' Zhora announced cheerfully. 'We've a Polish-Ukrainian Enterprise Conference to organise.'

'How long will that take?'

'Three days. Why? Got something important on?'

'No.'

'What's up?' he asked, his cheerfulness turned to concern.

'Flat trouble. My ex-wife's getting married. She's expecting and her husband will have to be registered as resident in our one room . . .'

He thought, looked hard at me, then passed a hand over the bristly stubble of a renewed close crop.

'Let's deal with Poland first, then give thought to the flat problem when we get back.'

A promise that had a more cheering effect on me than Vera's coffee. He might well think of something. The Young Communists of the nineties were an enterprising lot, and hadn't forgotten the art of helping one another out.

The sound of his footsteps on the corridor parquet receded in the direction of the Chief's reception office, while I sat pondering the fact that of the six of us I was the only one without cropped hair. Vera had started the fashion, or rather had been the first with cropped hair at the time I arrived. But hers of course was more *en brosse*. My hair, though the same length as hers and regularly washed under the great bath tap at the flat, was a mess. From the Chief down, everyone but me had recently visited the hairdresser, acquiring a sporty appearance in keeping with the times. And it troubled me.

Telling Vera I was going out for an hour, I took a number 20 trolley bus to Kreshchatik Street, and looked into Salon Sorceress. Seeing no one waiting, I quickly took the chair that was free.

'How do you want it?' asked the violet-tinted woman in her fifties who appeared in the mirror.

'Crew cut.'

As I returned to the office, the Chief, busy seeing off a clearly high-ranking client, was momentarily distracted by my change of hairstyle.

'*Esprit de corps*, that's the thing!' he said with a smile.

Mindful of which, returning to my desk, I phoned Vera to pop in for a minute. Hers was the reaction that mattered to me.

202

Switzerland, 17 January 2005

An hour out of rainy Zurich saw us among snowy mountains.

My driver was now like a second secretary, of whose name I'd caught only Vladimir.

'Bad night?' he asked, stowing my bag in the boot of the silver Audi.

'Short on sleep.' No need to mention the bar and my drinking bourbon after bourbon till five. I was amazed how my constitution had stood up to it. I had even managed to talk to a prostitute who had sat down beside me chatting away in German before switching to Bulgarian. I explained that I was more interested in alcohol than sex and she left me and went to sit on a stall at the other end of the bar.

'I'll interpret and help out where I can,' Vladimir said, intent on the narrow road we had turned on to from the motorway. 'Generally they meet us halfway, and so far there's nothing in the local press. First we've to visit the police, then it's the painful part.'

It had long been in my mind that I should have to identify their shattered bodies. Death was something I fought shy of, though as constantly in contact with it as anyone else. Possibly that was the secret of life's continuance – to go on rubbing shoulders with death until the time came for someone to rub shoulders with your own.

'Something you have to decide,' said Vladimir after a while, 'is whether you want to take the bodies home for burial. It's difficult and expensive, but the embassy will help if that is what you want. The alternative is to have them cremated here, interring the ashes here or in Ukraine. You've not informed your wife, I take it.'

'No.'

'Good. The police say they have something to show you. Probably personal effects.'

It was twelve thirty when we reached Leukerbad and the local police HQ, where Vladimir introduced a pleasant little uniformed officer with a neatly trimmed moustache.

'The Herr Major will show you to an office where you can examine documents found with the deceased, and we'll take it from there,' Vladimir translated.

The tiny office was cell-like in its furnishing – desk, desk lamp, chair. The officer handed me a file of folders, and went out closing the door. The topmost folder contained my last letter to Dima:

Dear Dima, I'm sorry to say that the state of our finances is
such that you will have to come home. At a rough estimate
we can see you through till the end of February . . .

My blood ran cold. He had sworn never to return to Kiev. He had
kept his word. I had failed to take him seriously. In the next folder
was a letter addressed to me.

My dear brother,
Thank you for your best wishes for the New Year, and for
all that you have done for me. I realise that you are not able
to do any more, and must feel fate has treated you unfairly.
I agree, it has. Such misfortune was more than you
deserved. You are both good people. It is, I know, a poor
consolation, but we leave you our daughter Liza. A healthy
family should have children! Thanks to some error made on
high we and she have been lucky. In making good this
error, I wish you every happiness!
Dima.

Idiot! What sort of happiness could that be! I feel the sting of
tears and, unable to hold them back, am grateful for the solitary
confinement of this tiny office. I rest my head on the papers. My
shoulders shake and I feel horribly cold inside.

Sometime later the door opens and I see the attentive face of the
Major. I get up and he indicates that I should follow him.

'The Herr Major has explained that all papers remain here
pending the accidental death verdict, after which they will be
destroyed,' said Vladimir.

'But this was suicide.'

'Suicide in the case of the mentally ill is classed here as accidental death. Which is of importance for us also.'

I nod, relieved that the telltale letters would soon be no more.

'Would you like to visit the place from which they jumped?'

'I'd rather not. And the child Liza, where is she?'

'In a children's hospital. It was the only place for someone so young.'

'My brother has left her to me,' I said, pointing back along the corridor towards the tiny office.

'Yes. It's a very complicated situation,' said Vladimir, looking straight into my eyes with an expression which could have sent anyone packing. 'We'll discuss it later. Next port of call is the Leukerbad registrar.'

At the mention of 'registrar', I am reminded of the woman in the black cassock who helped us to decide about the funeral for little Vera and Oleg.

'A hospital here or in Zurich?'

'Bern. More convenient for the embassy. But we must be off.'

The silver Audi stood bright in the Alpine sun. Not a cloud in the sky. A beautiful winter day. As we drove back we passed one expensive car after another heading for Leukerbad with skis and snowboards on their roof racks. The winter season continued, but not for me. For me it had ended even before it had begun, back in October.

203

Kiev, February 2016, Saturday

'Run it through again,' I told Nikolai Lvovich weakly, as we sat before the wide-screen TV in my Desatinaya Street sitting room.

For some minutes, darkness, then, without commentary, headlights, torches, automatic fire, loud effing and blinding, men in camouflage fatigues. Then an unsteady, highly agitated voice announcing how, as a result of a pre-dawn special operation, the President had been freed from the location at which he had been held hostage. Entirely by chance at the same location the rescuers discovered thirteen high-ranking Russian Federation officials who had disappeared months earlier, two of whom were accidentally killed in crossfire with guards of the secret prison. Of the hostage takers killed, two had been identified as bodyguards of Kazimir, who has since flown to Moscow in his own aircraft. Our Foreign Ministry has sent Russia a note in the appropriate terms. After which, shots of my haggard, sleep-deprived face, clearly that of a man as yet unable to grasp the turn of events, and Svetlov shouting, 'No questions!'

'What the hell was it you gave me?' I asked.

'Normal army tinned meat, but we didn't expect it to work quite so well.'

'Bastards! Well done!'

He smiled. 'How about a cold bath?'

Beyond the bathroom window, the unending darkness of a winter evening.

Placed ready on the marble window ledge, a bottle of '48 Glenfiddich and a tumbler. My cold bath was already run.

I tightened the belt of my Imperial bathrobe and hearing the bathroom door open, I turned to see Lvovich carrying a champagne bucket full of ice cubes, which he tipped into the bath.

'What's become of my aide?' I asked.

'What was his name?'

I shrugged.

'We're organising a complete change of staff, and after what's happened, new people have to be carefully vetted. So patience, Mr President.'

When he'd gone, I filled the tumbler and as soon as I was in the bath, captured a couple of cubes for the whisky.

The quiet of the world about me gradually seeped into my mind. The whisky entered my bloodstream, and my thoughts, as though in harmony with the process, grew peaceful. All that had recently occurred was now history – the Ukrainian state's. Only the calm of my inner world remained.

Whisky finished, I stepped from the bath into my bathrobe and crossed to the window.

In the murk of the winter night, St Andrew's Descent looked more familiar and dearer than ever: lying motionless, as might a freezing orphan in expectation of a coin or kindness. The one lone warm, yellow light was that of a semi-basement window. There were no pedestrians or cars.

I stood gazing at the static scene for some time until at last there was movement in the shape of a woman in a long overcoat, who came out from near the church carrying a lighted candle. The trembling flame flickered, strangely distinct, in spite of the distance between us. I saw her pause, huddle against the railings, head lowered over the candle, as if attempting to shield it from the wind.

For quite a while I watched her proceed. My mouth suddenly dry.

Without altering my gaze I reached for the whisky bottle and poured, looking away for only a split second to check the level in my glass; and she was gone.

Without her the scene lost its attraction. Even the pleasant taste of the whisky could not compensate for my disappointment. It was as if I had missed the end of an interesting film.

The semi-basement window still shone forth something of the family life behind it, but the woman with the candle was no more. I went back to my bath, added a few of the now smaller cubes to my glass, and with my neck supported by a rubber cushion, closed my eyes.

204

Kiev, August 1992

In the boiler room it's even hotter than outside, and the guests come in football shorts and jerseys. Bottles, tins, bowls of salad are being laid out on a long common table composed of three strips of stout plywood. The guests are a free-and-easy-looking lot, men of my own age or a little younger, with a strange air which I can't quite put a finger on. Maybe it's because they came bringing bottles and good humour as presents, and I a $40 food processor.

'Need any help?' I ask Mira, who is looking around as if as much at a loss concerning the guests as I am. She has make-up on, and her jeans are pressed with neat creases, but that doesn't improve her look. The only clothes that would suit her figure would be those that hide it.

'Where's your mother?' I add, feeling suddenly protective as I am about to give her away in marriage.

'Not coming,' she says sadly. 'Vitya's not Jewish, he's from Moldova.'

'And that's the reason?'

'Not entirely. She doesn't frequent boiler rooms, she says.'

'There are boiler rooms and boiler rooms,' I try to reassure her.

This one is vast, and the old broken sofa, spotted in a far corner, may well have figured in the conception of the child, whose presence Mira's body as yet betrays no sign of.

The only windows are small and at ceiling level. The furnace, a confusion of iron pipes, a mountain of briquettes are well away at the other end of the room and hidden by clouds of cigarette smoke.

Mira's eyes are all for Vitya, a long-haired, lanky fellow in jeans and Hawaiian shirt not tucked in, but he is deep in conversation with two of his friends.

Thinking to distract her, I describe the fate of her father's grave.

'That was us. We reburied him,' she says calmly. 'Syrets Cemetery. Where his mother is.'

'Who paid for all that?'

'The Jewish Memorial Fund.'

So much for my agonising over whether to tell her! Running their Jewish bulldozer over David Isaakovich's past, they had resettled him in the kollektiv, where he would not stand out, denying him in death the hermit existence that he had preferred in life. Father Basil and I had known better!

Now thirty or so are milling about the groaning board. Time to sit down and get started, seating now ready in the shape of planks on stools. A signal is called for.

'Gorko!' I call in the traditional manner, only to be greeted with stares of bewilderment. I catch the gaze of a girl with red cords round her neck and wrists and realise that she is staring at my tie, as if at a cobra poised to strike. Her expression is one of horror . . .

Well, Mira, what have you got yourself into here? I ask myself, aware that it's time for me to leave.

'Right, lads,' comes a shout, 'open the champers before it explodes!'

And they all sit down to table, handing round paper plates and taking the covers from plastic bowls.

Maybe they're all from Moldova and that is why they seem foreign, I muse.

'Hi, Mira!' calls Vitya, slapping the vacant place beside him, while I stand undecided, whether to go or stay.

'Hi, open this, I can't do it,' says a girl in a T-shirt and black leather shorts, passing me a bottle of vodka.

I unscrew it and give it back.

'Don't stand there like a spare prick, take a seat!' she calls, patting the place beside her.

'Blowing my mind on this stuff,' complains a joint-smoking man on my right.

Affecting sympathy, I offer him vodka, at which he looks aghast.

'Ruinous and right stuff don't mix!'

For me, the ruinous, I thought, filling my plastic glass with vodka.

205

Swiss Airspace, 18 January 2005

Outside the Boeing it's -52°C. My inside temperature is zero. My glass contains vodka. For the first time in ages I don't feel like whisky. Something I told Vladimir that morning at the airport, while he, calm, expressionless, heard me out as a psychiatrist might a patient's tantrum.

Still, we settled the main issues, with Vladimir shouldering no few burdens and the embassy smoothing the melancholy way for me. Poor Dima and Valya would be cremated tomorrow and their ashes scattered near the Lewis Carroll Garden and the roses Vera and Oleg. Adults did not have roses named after them. And rightly so. Even briefly terminated childhood deserves its privileges.

This time it's a crew-cut steward hovering over me, aware of my low state and alert to refill my glass as often as required.

My goals of yesterday are no longer achievable and I'm full of doubts. Vladimir was right to insist on the little girl's remaining in Switzerland for the time being. One, she is less than three months old. Two, the appearance of a baby in my family would give rise to any number of questions and lead someone to unearth the tragedy. And three, in view of Svetlana's present psychological state, it is better that she should remain in ignorance of what has happened to her sister and Dima.

I wonder at Vladimir's knowing so much about my wife's psychological condition, though not with any feeling of indignation or irritation. I tried to recall our conversation of yesterday as we sat in his pleasant room at the embassy.

'We'll look into the possibility of placing Liza in a good private crèche,' he said, sipping Campari and orange juice. 'Guardianship or adoption will be time consuming and call for a mass of paperwork. When the time comes, we'll help. But for the moment make as if nothing has happened. You've simply been off on an urgent assignment. Your brother and his wife are moving to America with their daughter, having received a medical grant. If you yourself believe that, so much the better.'

So there's the basis of a cover story for Svetlana and Mother. A nod is as good as a wink.

'What has happened must remain secret. We'll find a way of keeping you informed about Liza's well-being.'

Strange, but the vodka does nothing to warm me, and not feeling like any more I order tea.

'With cognac?' asks the steward.

'Please, and don't forget the lemon.'

206

Kiev, February 2016, Monday

So excessively hot did my office seem after my long absence that I was forced to open the windows for ten minutes.

The gold-trident-embossed leather folder was bursting with decrees and laws awaiting signature, and as I sat drinking tea, wondering whether to tackle them now or later, Nikolai Lvovich came in looking his old immaculate self again.

'Let me take those to check through,' he said, eyeing the folder. 'It's last year's stuff and a great deal has changed.'

I nodded.

'In any case you'll sign them after the 8th of March, when you're re-elected. Oh, and the big news is that Moscow has arrested Kazimir and his Russian accomplice. Unsanctioned contact with Chechen militants and the abduction of Russian citizens are the charges so far.'

'Think he'll get off?'

'Not on those charges. It'll be twenty years before we see him again. The main thing's not to request extradition.'

'So we won't,' I said, smiling, but was suddenly arrested by a sharp pang of discomfort. Why was I being so nice? What had become of my presidential firmness, the arrogant boorishness proper to my position?

After only a few seconds my indignation waned. I couldn't keep it up. I was obviously still not on form. And here was Nikolai Lvovich, smiling away in front of me bold as brass. While I sat lethargic and bemused, as if I had woken up after a long sleep to find him completely changed.

'Svetlov has asked to see you. Shall I call him?' he asked.

'Do.'

After Lvovich had gone, I felt anxiously in my jacket pocket for my heart-control, and put it on the table in front of me. I scanned the desk for the leather folder. It was gone. Nikolai Lvovich had been going to take it, but I had not actually seen him pick it up or leave with it. Still, taken it he must have, or it would still be there.

I shook my head and it began to ache as if a wave were beating against the inside of my forehead.

I hid the heart-control in a drawer of my desk, then stared at where Major Melnichenko's ottoman had stood.

Svetlov entered and I stood up to greet him. Our handshake was warm and hearty.

'All's well,' he announced. 'All but the Communist candidate have withdrawn. The workers are petitioning for the election to be called off, and held in two years' time as per Constitution. But I think we should carry on with our plan. One: it will be a vote of confidence; and two: you get another two years.'

'Indeed I will,' I sighed.

'Something else, Mr President —'

'Do drop the formality.'

'Sergey Pavlovich, the other thing is a request from the Directorate of Penal Establishments. They want to hold the poll in prisons and corrective labour institutions one week in advance so as to show the people who the bottom of the pile vote for.'

'The idea being?'

'The prisoners reckon you would get 100 per cent support – genuinely, no fiddling – in gratitude for introducing educational courses.'

'Mykola is the one to thank for that.'

'Yes, but you gave him the OK.'

'So fix it with the Central Electoral Committee. And could you take charge of the search for my ottoman? Comb the whole country if need be.'

'I'll try,' he said, depositing a letter on my desk and leaving military-style, with a salute.

Again I was beset with physical weariness. Noticing that the envelope had no name of sender, I imagined it to be another communication from Mayya in the Crimea, exchanging yet more secrets for freedom and immunity. The very idea of Mayya bored me. I preferred to forget having spent nearly a year under her tattered banner. A year that had brought one unpleasantness after another to my detriment and that of the country. What was it Stolypin said to the revolutionaries? 'You want great upheavals, I a great Russia!' I wanted a great Ukraine . . .

A knock at the door and a well-groomed eighteen-year-old in dark suit and stylish shoes looked in.

'Tea, coffee, cappuccino, Mr President?'

'Tea, with lemon and honey,' I said, adding, 'You're new, aren't you?'

'My first day.'

Tempted to ask him about himself, I contented myself with a friendly nod.

The envelope contained two snapshots of a woman and a girl, both very familiar. The accompanying note in an unhurried female hand was brief and to the point,

Dear Sergey Pavlovich,

Liza and I are now friends. She's charming, though she has difficulties with Russian, having been taught by Estonian émigrés.

I'm now artificially inseminated. It went well, the professor says, with a 97 per cent promise of success. So our 'little ones' are now in a sense together, and I shall be overjoyed when they are in fact. It's all as the fortune teller said! Till the spring and our meeting,

Nila and Liza.

The photographs showed Liza to resemble both Valya and Svetlana. Another ten years would make her a self-assured beauty.

Nila was the Nila of old, except, perhaps, for an odd wrinkle beneath a mocking eye.

My new aide delivered my tray of tea in silence so as not to interrupt my thoughts.

Svetlov's a good man, I thought. He knows what to report and what to just leave on the table.

207

Kiev, September 1992

Mira's Vitya proved to be a loser. A prime example of life's unfairness, although Vitya was clearly producer-director of his own misfortunes.

The day before he had been summoned in the small hours to help resuscitate a friend suffering from a drug overdose. The friend recovered, but on his way home Vitya paid dearly for his errand of mercy. He thumbed down a Zhiguli. It stopped, three men got out and proceeded to beat Vitya up. They pulled off his jacket and went through the pockets before dropping it down a drain whose cast-iron manhole cover had been pinched by metal hunters. A case of one crime facilitating another.

Bleeding and muddy, he turned up next morning at six, and at seven Larisa Vadimovna arrived to discuss Vitya's registration at the communal flat. Happily, Larisa Vadimovna had put the registration process on hold after Vitya's failure to attend the wedding breakfast which she had laid on in the aircraft factory canteen for her friends, and since then she had been keeping a close eye on him. She had put him on a month's probation, and the month was up that very day. She came back to take stock, only to find him bruised, bloody and soaking wet.

The circus played out before me since the boiler room wedding was coming to an end. A circus, with no acrobats, no lion-tamers, just clowns – and dismal ones at that. I, too, had become something of a clown by virtue of refusing to abandon my legal entitlement to four square metres of the room and move out. I had put down a mattress by the radiator and made that my lair, leaving the young couple the sofa and the bed, which, though not of equal height, they had pulled together, and sometimes had silent, half-hearted sex on. Maybe they thought me asleep at such times, and maybe sometimes I was. But even when I wasn't, I took no interest in their personal lives.

Larisa Vadimovna had not been in the room five minutes before, declining instant coffee, she delivered her verdict.

'Registration is out!' she declared, and left, banging the door.

'In that case, *we*'ll go,' Mira called after her.

'Where?' I asked.

'Germany! They've started taking Jews. They owe us for Babi Yar.'

I said nothing, suddenly conscious of a strange, barely intelligible spiritual kinship with Mira. As if she were a sister I'd been at odds with all through childhood, and now that she was going, was missing already.

'Will they take him?' I asked, nodding towards the Moldovan asleep on the sofa, still in his filthy clothes.

'Yes. The real Jew's here,' she said softly, smoothing her stomach. 'Dad's a disaster, but still his father.'

Glancing at my watch, a present from our Mayor 'for organisation of and active participation in the first Polish-

421

Ukrainian Enterprise Conference', I saw it was eighty thirty. Central to the watch face was a golden Ukrainian trident.

'Bathe his wounds with vodka and bandage them, otherwise he won't live till Germany.'

She gave me a doleful, reproachful look even, as if I were to blame for everything.

Hang on in there, Mira, I thought, tying my red Polish eagle tie, a present from the same conference, before setting off to the office.

208

Kiev, January 2005, evening

Dumping my bag in my study-bedroom, I make my way to the kitchen, failing to take in how surprisingly quiet it is. The sink is full of washing-up – Svetlana has not yet learned how to load the dishwasher. That I can forgive her. A housewife she never was and never will be.

Feeling like tea, I settle for cognac as stronger and more warming.

Reacting at last to the silence and I check the clock. Eight thirty is too early for Svetlana to be sleeping, I look into the bedroom.

The bed is especially well made, and after gazing dully for a while at our erstwhile marital couch, I see the note on the pillow.

'*Sorry but still feel I want to be alone. I'm going to Zhanna's on 239-00-45. Tell Valya if she rings. Don't phone, except in a real emergency. Love, Svetlana.*'

Perched on a bar stool in the kitchen examining the note and

Zhanna's number, I wonder which district she lives in. Maybe that's her mobile number. It's snowing again. I don't want tea, coffee. I don't want loneliness either. My one comforting, ameliorating thought is that I won't have to lie about where I flew to and why. Svetlana has closed herself to the truth. Perhaps she had a premonition of it. More likely, though, she just doesn't need anybody now. Not even Zhanna. But she does feel responsible for her. 'We answer for those we domesticate.' And now Svetlana has a dressed, coiffured Zhanna from the Ring Road much as other rich ladies have their pedigree chow chows and similar. Pedigree Zhanna is not, but quick to learn and able to talk.

I am amazed by my own bitterness towards her, poor thing. I shake my head. Zhanna is a good person, but unfortunate because it won't be possible for her to be happy for long at Svetlana's side.

Would anyone be happy in my company? I wonder.

As I topped up with cognac the telephone rang.

'Sergey Pavlovich? Dr Knutish. All done. All's well. The microscope confirms near 100 per cent success. We can go ahead right away.'

'Go ahead?' I asked puzzled.

'It's me, Knutish, sperm-washing clinic.'

'Ah, yes. So go ahead with what?'

'Artificial insemination. I could see your wife tomorrow morning.'

'Not on. We'd better wait.'

'So which is it – refrigerate or freeze?'

'What's the difference?'

'Refrigerate for a matter of two or three days, otherwise freeze.'

'Freeze,' I said firmly.

'You sound done in,' said Knutish. 'Let me ring you again tomorrow.'

'Do that,' I said, ringing off.

209

Kiev, February 2016, Wednesday evening

Snow piles against my bathroom window as if thrown from a shovel, quickly now blocking the view of St Andrew's Descent, now dropping away to reveal my favourite landscape: the church with its railings, the snow-covered stone steps and the bronze statue of two characters from an old Soviet comedy. Comedy films have long since gone out of style. This would be a good time to produce an epic tragedy about everyday life, but we don't make any films in this country now. What was it the Minister of Culture said? 'Ukrainian cinema has no future because of the lack of creative cadres.'

What I like about my vast bathroom is the chilliness of it – the desirable effect of having, years ago, had the underfloor heating disconnected. I feel good here, even in the company of Nikolai Lvovich who always enters as if he fears he is being drawn into a trap.

Once I was as happily attached to a poky, chilly kitchen with a smoke-blackened ceiling, the ever-present smell of burnt sunflower oil and two potted aloes on a much repainted windowsill. A wonderful place of romance and freedom, close to the source of sustenance. How I loved to sit there while Mother and Dima were asleep, gazing out at the lighted windows opposite. At that hour most of them would have been kitchen windows with someone seated at the table thinking possibly of eternity.

These days I also have an opportunity to think about eternity, Nikolai Lvovich having reminded me that as Acting President until the 8th of March, I could take no firm decisions. Which, since there are none I want to take, is fine. True, there are the lists, submitted by Svetlov and Filin at my request, of those deserving a reward for upholding constitutional order, but until Women's Day and the General Presidential Election on the 8th, even rewards, great or small, are out.

'I've got one of those,' said Nikolai Lvovich, seeing the lists on my desk.

'Let's have it, then,' I say, adding jokingly, 'and why not include yourself.'

My jibe is lost on him.

'I'm in Filin's and he's in mine,' he says.

The photographs of Nila and Liza, now in silver frames, stand on the marble window ledge, drawing the eye icon-fashion and engendering a special kind of warmth. They both photographed amazingly naturally, with no hint of affectation, pose or big American smile. Helping myself to a little whisky and swirling it around in the tumbler to bring out the nose, I am reminded of the wall of death motorbike riders at the circuses of my childhood. As another mass of snow slips away from the window and before the next shovelful strikes.

I catch a glimpse of the lighted semi-basement window I noticed before, and feel drawn by the warm yellowness of it.

'Shall I call for a car?' the floor guard asks, surprised to see me in my long black overcoat at 1.30 a.m.

'No, I shan't be long . . .'

Biting wind, stinging snowflakes. Crossing the cobbles of the Descent, I very nearly fall. The window, when I reach it, is stuck over with something making it impossible to look in, but I can hear male voices in unhurried conversation. I go into the yard and find steps leading to a metal-clad door. I knock, then let myself in, immediately encountering the gaze of four men seated around a low table in a niche to the left of the door.

'May I?' I ask.

'Have a seat,' says their grey-haired senior.

Sitting gingerly on the edge of a cracked leather couch, I am given vodka in a silver cup, and pointed to a plate of brawn and a jar of horseradish.

'Your health!' says the older man, raising his own silver cup inscribed with a design and the number '6o'.

'And yours.'

'Don't I know your face?' asks a man with a moustache.

'I live around here. In Desatinaya Street.'

'Ah! That explains it . . .'

'We have a problem,' sighs the older man.

'How so?'

'They want to kick us out of here,' he says, pointing through to a room hung with paintings.

'Who wants to?'

'The authorities . . . I'm Milovzorov,' he adds, handing me his card. 'And these are two of the best artists in the country who nobody gives a damn about: Bludov and Lebedinets. And this is Sergey Ternavsky,' he gestures to the man with a moustache.

'How is it nobody cares?' I ask.

'Another time. It's a long story,' Milovzorov says wearily, then turning to Moustache and indicating my empty cup, 'Pour, Sergey.'

'I may be able to help,' I say, spearing myself some brawn with the communal aluminium fork.

'A bottle and a painting from each of us, if you can!'

'Agreed.' I smile confidently.

'Could you leave us your card?' asks Sergey.

'I don't have one, but here's my secretary's number.' And having written Nikolai Lvovich's mobile on a catalogue of prices, I take my leave.

It is still snowing heavily. Parked at the courtyard entrance, a Toyota Jeep, with several men, and at the beginning of the church railings, another, just where I saw the lady with a lighted candle.

I re-enter the gallery, standing just inside the door.

'Would you happen to know who the woman is who walks around here at night with a lighted candle?'

'Sounds like Mariya Kapnist,' says Milovzorov. 'Run over and killed thirty years ago. But she always carried a candle on church holidays.'

'Mightn't it be someone else with a candle?'

Milovzorov shakes his head.

'Do you suppose it's possible for a window to look out onto the past as well as onto the street?'

'Why not,' smiles Milovzorov. 'All my windows do . . . The young have that to come. You and me are different . . .'

Shaking hands all round, I again set off into the night snow of Kiev.

210

Kiev, October 1992

Golden autumn. An excellent time for change. Green turning yellow and red, the ripe falling, the dead strewing the ground and withering beneath an enfeebled sun.

Three days before, Mira and Vitya had left for Germany. Larisa Vadimovna and I saw them off at the station. There again, like so many émigré visiting cards, were the three identical holdalls Mira and her mother had come back with from Israel. Onto the Kiev–Warsaw–Berlin train they went, and off went the train.

Mira had signed off as resident in the communal flat. So now Larisa Vadimovna and me were the only official residents. I lived there alone. Larisa Vadimovna was living with a friend somewhere in Syrets, but she often rang complaining about her friend or life or inflation, which she could not get sufficiently accustomed to so as to make ends meet.

The Enterprise Association was bubbling over with activity. Everyone was excited and talking in whispers about various rumours, chief among which was that the Association was to become a special Governmental Enterprise Committee which all of us, Vera included, would be on.

Dear Vera, who, fresh from the hairdresser, had contrived to whisper, with a wink, that her parents were flying to Malta . . .

'You up for promotion, then?' Zhora asked cheerily, looking round the door.

'If a flat goes with it.'

'Of course. I promised.'

'So, yes.'

As I spoke, in my mind I was actually saying 'yes' to Vera's invitation, but I had nothing against promotion either.

211

Kiev, February 2005, Tuesday

Ten at night and still at the office. Apart from an empty twelfth-floor flat I have nowhere to hurry away to.

'Coming?' asks Nila looking round the door. 'You look worn out.'

'You go, Nila, I'll sit on for a bit. Get Viktor Andreyevich to drive you.'

I still have to select organisations to lobby Parliament over constitutional reform. But all, even the most loyal ones, like Crimea and Ivano-Frankovsk, have grown a bit big for their boots and invariably ask for a great deal in return. It's easier and cheaper to create a new organisation, an association of steel-foundry veterans to be exploited in the cause of state structuring until such time as it becomes monstrous. I'm beginning to think in formal, meaningless expressions. There is a simpler way – form a group of puppets, supply a bit of money and a one-room flat as legal address and entrust them with a couple of initiatives too awkward and shaming for our own politicians and legislators to present. Anything morally inconvenient has to be initiated from below.

The Chief is understandably concerned about the coming presidential election. If the President isn't re-elected, the whole bunch of us will be out. I'll miss my cosy corner in the shadow of the

Minister for the Economy whoever it is. The temperature in the presidential offices at present averages 25°C, and even the corridors are draughtproof. A special microclimate gives rise to special micro-organisms, a distinct fauna, which could not survive outside this environment. Any change would be death to them. Such are the thoughts born of a reluctance to go home to a flat less warm than my office. I could, I suppose, go to Nila's for warmth?

I phone for the duty car, and while waiting look at tomorrow's schedule. Nothing there to cheer the heart. There are 364 days to the presidential election, hence the present marathon of crazy projects aimed at keeping the President in place and all of us in his shadow. I, to be honest, like neither President Fedyuk, nor his shadow, nor the Chief, nor that shadow of a shadow of myself. Myself I dislike most of all.

I give my anonymous driver Nila's address and the Toyota Camry moves forward.

212

Kiev, 8 March 2016

March began with something of a thaw and a sun testing feeble rays on the faces of passers-by. The young were quick to leave off their fur caps, but not the old. They knew to expect tricks from all sides. This time it would be the weather that tricked them.

Waiting for the election was irksome, and I longed to be reunited with Nila and Liza. Sometimes I just sat drinking tea, while affairs of state managed themselves in my office, with Nikolai Lvovich amassing papers to dump on my desk the moment the election result was declared, and Parliament went on wearily debating the Official Language Law. A group of Deputies were pressing for recognition of Crimean Tatar as Co-Official Language. While another argued that we were not a partial state but a whole, and so Crimean Tatar should be Second Official Language. They brought me printouts of the debates. I had a laugh and a whisky, thinking that someone somewhere must already have hit on the brilliant idea of assembling all gasbags in one place and tossing them subjects to argue about.

Twice a day, without flashing lights or escort, I made a tour of the city, simply looking at life, and posters: those of my blistered hands, and those of my red-faced, long-nosed opponent whose ratings were plummeting.

This election should have been abandoned immediately after Kazimir's arrest in Moscow. But everyone was reluctant to stay the process. The army and prisons had their polling day a week ahead of the election date, as per petition, and 98 per cent voted for me, o per cent for him, but even this hardly interested me at all.

I missed Nila and Liza, whom I now looked upon as guardian angels, having no longer anyone else close to me. There was my spinning top of a country, reeling west one minute and east the next, and nothing I could do about it. There were enemies, both secret and open. And there were also those for me, again both secret and – some on my team – open. Indeed I had everything, except the warmth of those near and dear to me.

I understood that this, my greatest moment, had been reduced to the level of a national soap opera, but I could not have cared less. All that concerned me was my weary solitude and the thought that soon my lonely I was to become *we*.

213

'You pleasantly surprise me,' whispers Vera, forehead moist with perspiration, breathing more a series of satisfied sighs. The subdued bluish light of two bedside lamps create a fairy-tale atmosphere.

'Did you ever doubt me?' I ask, running a finger across her forehead and putting it to my lips.

'I did, but never again.'

Bending over me, she kisses my lips then collapses upon me, her beautiful body light as thistledown, apple breasts pressing lightly on my chest.

'My last –'

'The one who's gone?'

'The one who's gone – held that men come, men go, but women are forever. Seems she was right. I come to you, I go, I come to you again.'

'Wrong,' she laughs, moving so as to lie more comfortably. 'When you've a flat of your own, I'll come to you. I may even stay.'

'I've already got a flat on my own,' I say proudly. 'Only it's a one-roomer and a bit of a way out. Present from the Mayor.'

'Nothing wrong with that. It was the same with us once. We only had a run-down private house in Zaporozhe to begin with, then a one-roomer in Troyeshchin, a two-roomer in Darnitsa, and now this four-roomer in Pechersk. And soon they'll buy me a place of my own.'

'What do your parents do?'

'Daddy's Deputy Minister for the Economy. Mummy runs two beauty salons. And yours?'

'Much simpler folk. My father was killed on a firing range. Mother's a pensioner.'

'Poor little orphan,' she says, kissing my neck and running her slender fingers over my body. 'Still, orphans get on in life! They're out for revenge.'

'Against who?'

'Not who – against life. I've nothing to be revengeful about, so I'm not bursting to get anywhere. Boring subject. Like a drink?'

'What's on offer?'

Leaving the bed, she beautiful in her nakedness, me unashamed of my own, I follow a beckoning finger to the sitting room.

She throws open both doors of a tall, elegant glass-fronted cabinet crammed full with bottles – whisky, vodka, wine . . .

'Everything,' I murmur with a touch of sadness.

214

Kiev, February 2005, Sunday

Yesterday, a surprise visitor. True, he rang in advance, even asked permission to pop in. He arrived dead on time, at 8 p.m. It was Colonel Svetlov, who had advised me on a number of occasions and had dealt with my Swiss problems the month before. I imagined it would be to do with Switzerland. Svetlana's departure had pushed the sad events of January to the edge of my mind. At the centre was my own unhappiness.

He arrived with a bottle of eighteen-year-old Jameson. Offered a stool at the bar, he preferred the window table, being, as I should have realised, too short in the leg for bar stools.

'How's it going, Sergey Pavlovich? Not so good?'

'You could say that,' I said after sipping my whisky. 'But what could I do? Vladimir, from the embassy, made clear what was required.'

'Today's what concerns me, not your brother and his wife. You're lonely, domestically disorganised, empty, and trying to fill that emptiness.'

'With Nila, you mean?'

'Yes.'

'Which I shouldn't.'

He gestured dismissively.

'Not for me to say. I just thought you might welcome some advice. Apart from which there's something I'd like to put to you. Svetlana's not likely to come back to you. You should divorce. An old friend of yours is sniffing around.'

'Who?'

'Marat Husseinov. They've met twice. No, she's not been unfaithful. They simply dined together – Lipsky Villa and Da Vinci's in Vladimir Street. My concern in this is for your image. If you want, he could be removed. Permanently. If not, you should think about divorce.'

As he spoke his voice grew colder and colder. As I drank my whisky I did my best to picture Husseinov and Svetlana in a restaurant together, but couldn't. They had so little in common. How could they be together at all?

'You would like time to think then,' Svetlov prompted. 'Though you can't have much time to think about things like this. What with the election, there'll be even less soon.'

'Oh, let them,' I said wearily.

'What?'

'Go to restaurants.'

'Very humane of you. We'll speak to Svetlana, and do the paperwork *per pro*. OK by you?'

I was suddenly very hot and there was a strange pain in my head, as if a sea wave had found itself enclosed and was trying to push its way out through my skull. My eyes watered, perhaps because of the pain, perhaps not.

'I spent my last penny!' I moaned. But the sound of my voice alerted me to my own strange behaviour and I pulled myself together.

'You've got money trouble?'

'No. I just wanted children, I splashed out on treatment, and now I'm treated, I have to say goodbye to their mother. I mean . . .'

"You mean the sperm washing?"

'You know about that?'

'Don't worry – you told them to freeze the material. Look on the bright side – if there's a gun on the stage-set wall in Act One, it's bound to go off in Act Four.'

'You like theatre?'

'You need a good rest. Take tomorrow off at least. Another thing, Viktor Andreyevich and Nila – they're trustworthy, but taking the duty car to Nila's, well! Think! Be more careful. Your private life is now, to an extent, the state's . . .'

When he had gone, I lay in my bath thinking back over the past, and of Svetlana, Dima and Valya. Had that part of my personal life been, to an extent, the state's?

Today, in line with Svetlov's advice, I'm resting. I lie about in our big bed, readjusting to its orthopaedic mattress. I lie here and cannot get used to my loneliness, which is highlighted by the size of the bed. How could Svetlana have slept here alone? Then I remember the times I saw Zhanna with her. It was all the bed's fault. If it had been smaller, Svetlana would never have let Zhanna in under her duvet. Could that be so? It's certainly nicer to think that. I cannot believe that Svetlana preferred sleeping with Zhanna.

215

Kiev, 13 March 2016

Drizzle one minute, sun the next, a caressing breeze, and Borispol Airport, for once amazingly quiet, in expectation of a special flight from Budapest, all other incoming traffic being stacked.

An aide holds an umbrella over me, and there's another at my side holding two bouquets of yellow roses, and behind us a whole retinue. Despite the sealing off of the airport, reporters were here in their hundreds. So a brief camera call would be necessary, followed by the wedding at St Vladimir's Cathedral, a trip to the polling station, then, at long last, a respite from flashbulbs, questions, public gaze, hubbub.

The little aircraft touched down, and taxied towards us.

I heard whispering behind me and noticed that all around was sunshine, I alone was standing in shade. I glanced at my aide who understood immediately and put the umbrella down, suddenly exposing my cheeks to brilliant sunlight.

The aircraft stopped. A wheeling-out of steps. An unrolling of carpet.

I walked forward briskly. There were shallow puddles, but I was not looking at my feet. I was advancing and could hear my entourage bustling along behind.

Steps at oval door, carpet run out, I moved onto the corner nearest to me, pleased to see that it was not red, but homely with wavy blue lines and bordered with a Ukrainian embroidery-type pattern.

A scared-looking air hostess, perhaps unaware just who she had on board, emerged, and after her, Nila and Liza. Seizing the bouquets, I rushed forward, beside myself with happiness. My salvation was here! And the country's salvation, but that did not matter to me or Nila or Liza. The country was just using this happy event to its own advantage.

'Presidents,' Dogmazov once advised, 'do not run.' Remembering these words of my old colleague, I was struck by the clarity of my memory. I must be growing younger, I thought as I ran up to the steps and into the arms of my two girls. We stood there tearfully embracing, oblivious to the wretched TV cameras and onlookers. We remained there a long time, unaware that the rain had started again. Eventually I noticed my aide, hovering with an umbrella, unsure how to behave in a less than formal situation.

Nikolai Lvovich wanted us to travel in different cars, but I made clear that the three of us were travelling together.

Then, in cavalcade, swiftly along the militia- and military-lined Borispol Highway, spring sun emerging from cloud and promising the very best Sunday of my life.

The wedding was shown live on every channel, followed, I learned later, by a reminder that it was Presidential Election Day.

And the TV audience went out and voted. They voted for me in the spirit of army and prisoners before them, with only 6 per cent going to my poor Communist opponent.

The Desatinaya Street apartment became the jollier for being shared, with only the end-of-block bathroom remaining strictly my province, there being another for Nila and Liza at the other end of corridor. I sent my aide down to the service floor below with instructions to come only when called for. The guard on our floor caught on to the changes in my private life immediately and took to saluting all of us, which Nila particularly enjoyed.

A new life had begun. For me and for the country. And I resolved that, so long as I was happy, I would do all I could to make the country happy too.

EPILOGUE

Two days of distinctly disturbing news. Firstly from New York, that the Melnichenko ottoman was up for auction at Sotheby's – a fact publicised by the aged Major draping himself on it, arms extended along the back. No bids were received, so it was sold at the reserve price to Lazarenko, former Ukrainian Prime Minister, newly released from penitentiary. CNN ran the item a number of times, together with a map showing the location of Ukraine.

Nikolai Lvovich was inclined to laugh the whole thing off, but I, studying the video recording, was not. The theft of the ottoman was tantamount to a theft of national honour. Those responsible had not been found.

The other item, the Moscow Patriarchy's announcement of its intention to bestow on Ukraine a gift in celebration of its twenty-five years of independence, was, as I saw at once, likely to have more serious consequences for the country. The gift, which was to be given to the Caves Monastery, was in the shape of the relics of the Great and Holy Martyr Vladimir Ulyanov. Russian TV channels showed the route whereby those relics were to be borne on the shoulders of true Orthodox believers from Moscow to Kiev, taking in the great cities of east and south Ukraine. A holy march ending in one could only imagine what.

But I would leave Svetlov and the presidency's specialists to worry about that. The important thing for me was Nila's pregnancy. I wanted it to go smoothly, as the early check-ups suggested it would.

I thought too of my own future. My heart remote control I gave into the safe keeping of Svetlov. And as soon as my child was born, I saw myself quietly retiring. It would be so much easier to love my own tiny child than a whole country. Easier and pleasanter. Children usually return love. Countries usually do not.